# A Very British Ending

**EDWARD WILSON** is a native of Baltimore where he attended the same high school as Dashiell Hammett. He went on to study International Relations on a US Army scholarship and served as a Special Forces officer in Vietnam. He received the Army Commendation Medal with 'V' for his part in rescuing wounded Vietnamese soldiers from a minefield. His other decorations include the Bronze Star and the Combat Infantryman's Badge. After leaving the Army, Wilson became an expatriate and gave up US nationality to become a British citizen. He has also lived and worked in Germany and France. He is the author of five previous novels, *A River in May*, *The Envoy*, *The Darkling Spy*, *The Midnight Swimmer* and *The Whitehall Mandarin* all published by Arcadia Books. The author has lived in Suffolk since 1976. He was a lecturer at Lowestoft College for twenty-one years and continued to teach in Suffolk schools while becoming a full-time writer.

# A Very British Ending

EDWARD WILSON

A

Arcadia Books Ltd
139 Highlever Road
London W10 6PH

*www.arcadiabooks.co.uk*

First published in the United Kingdom 2015

A catalogue record for this book is available from the British Library.

ISBN 978-1-910050-50-7

Typeset in Minion by MacGuru Ltd
Printed and bound by CPI Group (UK) Ltd, Croydon CRO 4YY

Arcadia Books supports English PEN *www.englishpen.org* and
The Book Trade Charity *www.btbs.org*

ARCADIA BOOKS DISTRIBUTORS ARE AS FOLLOWS:

*in the UK and elsewhere in Europe:*
Macmillan Distribution Ltd
Brunel Road
Houndmills
Basingstoke
Hants RG21 6XS

*in the USA and Canada:*
Dufour Editions
PO Box 7
Chester Springs
PA, 19425

*in Australia/New Zealand:*
NewSouth Books
University of New South Wales
Sydney NSW 2052

For David and Nancy

## Author's Statement

Although a number of real historic events are referred in this book, it is a work of fiction. A few real names are used, but no real people are portrayed. All of the characters in this book are fictional. When I have used official titles and positions, I do not suggest that the persons who held those positions in the past are the same persons portrayed in the novel or that they have spoken, thought or behaved in the way I have imagined.

## Prologue

It was a very British ending. The soldiers stayed in their barracks, the Prime Minister resigned and the detention camps in the Shetlands remained empty except for puffins and gulls. Life went on. An hour's average wage still bought five pints of bitter. Liverpool won the league, but Southampton upset Manchester United in the FA Cup Final. The Two Ronnies made you laugh and Abba made you dance. An oblivion of unknowing stretched across the land. The record-breaking temperatures of the following summer lulled the country into a dozy complacency. Most had no idea what happened – and no one was going to tell them. The tarmac at Heathrow baked in the sun, but the ring of tanks and armoured vehicles had gone. No heads were chopped off, but a government had changed. No one talked and the Secret State kept its secrets.

William Catesby had to brake hard. Otherwise, he and his bicycle would have gone over the cliff. But the press would have loved it: **Body of Top Spy Found on Remote Suffolk Beach**. *The MI6 officer, reported to be under investigation for serious misconduct, had been summoned to answer questions before a secret Whitehall Committee...*

Catesby was surprised how much of Covehithe had fallen into the sea during the winter gales. It was the worst erosion he had seen for years. The road now ended abruptly with broken black tarmac hanging over the cliff edge – the warning sign and barrier had been claimed by the last storm. Just as Catesby had seen no warning of the lethal cliff edge, there had been no warning of his summons to appear before the Cabinet Secretary. On the other hand, it wasn't unexpected either. Catesby wasn't good at burying bodies so they stayed buried. He knew that his own fall was just as inevitable as Covehithe tumbling into the sea.

What, he thought, did they want? A full and frank confession in exchange for immunity from prosecution? Not likely. They wanted his pension and his freedom. Catesby knew he was going to lose everything. Maybe he shouldn't have braked before the cliff edge.

The north-east wind was biting and cold, but Catesby was oddly happy squinting against the salt spray out to sea. He had been born a few miles up the coast. Catesby's job had sent him around the world, but the Suffolk coast was the only place he felt complete. He looked north towards Benacre where the cliffs ended and the dark woods began. When the tide was high, acorns and chestnuts fell directly into the sea. During the long summers of childhood, it had been a place for secret dens and midnight swims. Suffolk was a private hinterland that no one could ever take from him. They could put him in prison, but they couldn't erase the place from his brain.

What had Catesby got to hide? A lot. It wasn't just murder – and there were more than one – and it wasn't trampling over the

Official Secrets Act. What mattered was that he had betrayed himself and those he loved. Catesby looked out over the cold sea. How many of his family's bones lay rolling there? Tossed and ground by the sea into smooth pale lumps. Crawled over by crabs and nosed by what was left of the cod. Catesby, the spawn of a Lowestoft sailor and an Antwerp barmaid, belonged to the North Sea – and felt as empty as that salty waste. He had grown up fluent in three languages, but couldn't say what he had become in any of them.

Catesby had served the state for thirty-three long turbulent years. First in the Army and then as an officer in the Secret Intelligence Service. He was tired and battered. His stepchildren used to have a running joke that he was ten years older than his real age. When he was forty, they gave him a birthday card wishing him a 'Happy 50th' – and so on every year until he actually did turn fifty. The step-kids, now grown-ups, suddenly realised his premature ageing was no longer funny.

His jobs had left him with few physical injuries – bullets seemed to curve around him – but very deep emotional scars. The worst was what had happened to him in the war. In fact, it wasn't a scar, but a deep open wound that would never heal. The puss of mental pain and self-recrimination was still coming out nearly thirty-two years later. Could he have prevented what happened?

Thirty years in SIS had left a different set of emotional wounds: the inability to trust anyone; the hard-faced rationality of inflicting pain; the guilt of complicity with the merciless machinery of the state. Three decades as a spy had earned Catesby a pension, but ruined his marriage and his closest friendships. And now that pension was in doubt too. But they were not just out to get him, they were out to get the Prime Minister too.

## The Board of Trade, Milbank, London: March, 1947

It had been the coldest winter on record. Ice flows off the Suffolk coast had disrupted shipping and pack ice had suspended the ferry service between Dover and Ostend. Drifting snow had blocked railways and roads. Many power stations had been forced to shut owing to lack of coal deliveries. German PoWs and British troops worked side by side shovelling snow by hand to clear essential rail lines.

Britain wasn't just cold; it was hungry too. Straw-covered potato clamps were no match for the severe frosts and 75,000 tons of potatoes were destroyed. Meanwhile, many winter root vegetables remained un-harvested because they were frozen hard in the ground. Cattle fodder was in short supply and there were fears for the survival of British herds. There was a real danger that food supplies would run out and rationing measures, more severe than during the war, were introduced.

The Board of Trade canteen had just been refurbished and was considered the best in Whitehall. The mood in the canteen was egalitarian as suited the time. Mandarins from on high sat at the same long tables with secretaries and the most junior clerks. The civil servants who dined there came from all government departments – including the Secret Intelligence Service, whose basement club only served senior officers and didn't do lunch. Eating in works canteens was also popular because the food was 'out of ration', which meant your ration card coupons weren't cancelled. A lot of people were scraping the butter off their buns to take it home for the family. But when Catesby tried to do the same, his new boss and mentor, Henry Bone, advised him: 'Don't do that, Catesby. They're plebs and you're supposed to be an officer.'

The BOT works canteen was not Henry Bone's natural habitat. He described lunch there as 'feeding time at the zoo', but also a good place to observe 'the mood of the Whitehall fauna'. Henry Bone looked like his name: tall, gaunt and sepulchre. His manner was patrician and his eyebrows arched as he spoke. But beneath Bone's droll hauteur, there was a very complex person that Catesby never completely unravelled. Bone's personal life was only a secret to the naive and unsophisticated, but his deeper loyalties were far more complicated. Spies spy on each other and Catesby had done the requisite snooping on his boss. Bone's most famous ancestor was an eighteenth-century artist of the same name who enjoyed royal patronage. Bone himself was a devotee of the arts and a talented musician. He had also helmed a yacht in the 1936 Olympics.

3

'Do you know him?' said Bone staring at his food, but giving a barely perceptible nod.

'Who?' said Catesby.

'The young minister with the moustache sitting next to Stafford Cripps.'

'It's Harold Wilson. I briefly met him at the Labour Party conference in 1945.' Catesby had campaigned for a parliamentary seat while still in uniform, but had been soundly beaten by a Tory landowner.

'By the way,' said Bone, 'are you still a member of the People's Party?'

'No, I followed the rules and terminated my membership – as instructed.' Catesby frowned. 'Terribly unfair.'

'Not at all. SIS officers cannot be seen as politically partisan. Why are you smiling?'

'Because many of our colleagues are the most political beasts in the Whitehall jungle.'

'My exact words, Catesby, were *cannot be seen* as politically partisan. In any case, what do you think of Wilson?'

'Very intelligent and sharp.' Catesby glanced at the minister under discussion. 'That's odd.'

'Don't turn your head when you look at someone. Swivel your eyes. What's odd?'

'Stafford Cripps just pushed his chicken leg on to Wilson's plate. Is he trying to fatten him up for higher office?'

'Cripps is a vegetarian – he's also a completely teetotal Christian. But higher office for Wilson is on the cards.'

Catesby smiled. 'You seem, Mr Bone, well informed about the People's Party.'

'While remaining non-partisan, it is our job to be politically astute. It is almost certain that Stafford Cripps is going to become Chancellor in the next reshuffle and that Wilson will replace him as President of the Board of Trade.'

'He's a rising star.'

'Wilson will become the youngest cabinet minister since Pitt the Younger. Look at him again, Catesby, but swivel your eyes this time.'

Catesby gave a furtive glance.

'You're looking at a future prime minister. But first,' Bone smiled, 'he will have to shave off that ridiculous moustache.'

'But otherwise, you seem impressed by him.'

Bone nodded. 'I had to give Wilson a security briefing about his planned trip to Moscow next month. We were together for over an hour and discussed the wider context.'

'Why's he going to Moscow?'

'I'm disappointed in you, Catesby. You don't seem very well informed at all. Do you even know what Wilson's job is at present?'

'He's secretary for something.'

'He's Secretary for Overseas Trade – a very important position for a junior minister. You need, Catesby, to keep your ear to the ground in Whitehall too. There's more to this job than spying on the Sovs.'

Catesby nodded. Bone was head of USSR P Section, which was responsible for meeting R Section demands for intelligence about the Soviet Union. Although Catesby was assigned to the intelligence branch of the Control Commission for Germany, his own post came under Bone's expanding jurisdiction.

'Have you heard,' said Bone, 'anything about the Rolls-Royce jet engines deal with Moscow?'

'I've heard it was still under discussion and that Tedder was busy twisting arms at MoD.'

'Much better, Catesby. We were involved too – under pressure from Downing Street. We had to convince the Air Ministry that selling those jet engines to Russia would not give the Sovs a long-term strategic advantage.'

'Is that true?'

'Not very. We lied through our teeth – which is part of our job. Spies are professional liars.' Bone sipped his tea and made a face. 'Ghastly. Not only over-brewed, but cold. In any case, the deal with Moscow is almost certain. The MoD has now agreed to the Board of Trade granting an export license for fifty-five Rolls-Royce jet engines.'

'What did you lie about?'

'We lied about the Soviet Union's industrial capacity to turn those jet engines into a power source for jet fighters and bombers. They are, by the way, an utterly marvellous example of British technology: centrifugal flow turbojet engines that are five years ahead of the rest of the world.'

'But we're only flogging fifty-five of them.'

'Don't be naive, Catesby. As soon as the Russians get their hands on them, they will strip down those beautiful Rolls-Royce engines and reverse engineer their construction to make their own copies – the fifty-five jet engines will soon become 500.'

Catesby already knew the answer, but he asked the question anyway. 'Why are we doing it?'

'Look around you. Look at that lean clerk scraping the butter off his bun and wrapping a chicken leg in a piece of paper. His poor, freezing family have probably used up their ration coupons. Not good management, but hungry people don't always make wise choices.'

'What are we getting back from the Russians?'

'That's for Wilson to negotiate. We need 800 tons of grain, cattle fodder and timber.'

Almost on cue, the Minister for Overseas Trade and his boss got up to leave. Wilson nodded a greeting at Bone as he passed by – and gave Catesby an odd look.

'I think,' said Bone, 'your former comrade was surprised to see you supping with the devil.'

'He has an excellent memory for faces and names.'

'The rest of his memory is just as formidable. During our most interesting discussion he rattled off figures and facts with uncanny accuracy.'

'A bit like the classroom swot showing off?'

'No, Catesby, not at all. He's passionate and sincere about his job. There is, however, something of the insecure little boy about him. Wilson wants to win approval by doing a good job.' Bone paused. 'He needs hardening up. I don't think he fully realises how malicious and dangerous this world, the world of power, actually is.'

'Will he be all right in Moscow?'

'I should think so. I explained to him about Moscow Rules and how to avoid honey-trap compromises. But I was a bit concerned when I warned him about the dangers of marathon vodka sessions; he said that as a Yorkshire man he could drink any Russian under the table.'

'Bravado.'

'I hope so. He won't have any problems because the Sovs are desperate to get those jet engines.' Bone paused. 'But there is a problem, a big problem. The Americans are not going to like this. They're going to be furious.'

'Why don't the Americans buy the engines instead?'

'Because they think we should give them the technology for free. The Yanks say it's part of a wartime agreement to share expertise and intelligence. They're impossible. I think Wilson is going to find the Americans far more difficult than the Russians. We talked at some length about this.'

'Did you convince him?'

'To some extent. He confided that Stafford Cripps had warned him that negotiating the jet engines deal could turn out to be "a poison chalice". Ironically, Wilson had nothing to do at all with the original decision to sell those engines to Moscow. It was made before he was appointed. But the deal will always have his name on it. That is how ministerial responsibility devolves.'

'Not very fair.'

'Nothing is fair in our game. Mark my words, the Americans will never forgive Harold Wilson for selling those jet engines to Moscow. It will come back to haunt him over and over again.'

Catesby had chosen the ruins of the U-boot bunker as the best place to carry out the execution – remote and off-limits. It was the first time that Catesby had killed a man face to face. Killing in the war had been different, impersonal. Afterwards, Catesby was surprised – and shocked – by how little he had felt.

Catesby didn't regard what he had done as murder. It wasn't revenge either. He didn't know a single person who had been killed in the massacre. But the images were still haunting him seven years later. Catesby thought that by killing a war criminal, one who had operated in the region, he could get rid of the ghost that haunted him. It was a form of exorcism. Catesby wanted to remove the phantom of Oradour-sur-Glane so he could sleep at night and stop the recurring images. He didn't know that you can't kill a ghost – you had to find a way of living with it.

Catesby had been parachuted into France in 1943 along with a radio operator and a courier who doubled as an explosives expert. Their principle job was to send intelligence back to London about the enemy. The resistance group they worked with, the Maquis du Limousin, was the largest in France and numbered more than 10,000. The resistance fighters were busiest in the days following the D-Day landings as German units streamed north to join the fight in Normandy. The Maquisards sabotaged rail lines, blew up bridges and attacked troop movements. The Germans responded with reprisals against the civilian population. Owing to a stroke of luck, Catesby's resistance group captured a high-ranking German officer, SS-Sturmbannführer Helmut Kämpfe. What to do with the captured SS officer became a problem and a matter of contention. One of the resistance leaders wanted to execute him; others wanted to use him to negotiate a prisoner exchange.

Catesby never found out exactly what happened, but never forgave himself either. He wished that he had stood up to the Maquis leader who wanted to execute Kämpfe. Catesby couldn't see the point of risking reprisals for the satisfaction of killing an SS officer. But what happened? No one seemed to know – or wanted to admit knowing. Was Oradour-sur-Glane a reprisal for the killing of Helmut Kämpfe? Or was the execution of Kämpfe a reprisal for Oradour-sur-Glane?

Catesby had been warned not to go to Oradour because the Germans were still in the area. But he needed to verify whether or not the rumours were true. It was a long cycle ride through the dark forests of Limousin warmed and scented by the summer sun. His fake identity papers were in order and his French was so fluent that he was sure he could talk his way out of confrontation with the *Milice*, the French paramilitary police who collaborated with the Gestapo. In any case, the *Miliciens* were pretty thin on the ground in a sparsely populated countryside dominated by increasingly well-armed resistance fighters. Just north of Limoges, Catesby rendezvoused with a Maquisard who accompanied him the rest of the way to Oradour. When Catesby asked him what had happened, the resistance fighter simply shook his head and remained silent. The news was unspeakable.

It was the day after the massacre and the ruins of the village were still smouldering. The first thing that Catesby noticed was the overpowering stench of burned flesh. It was inescapable – and most of it seemed to be coming from the church. The second thing that he noticed was the large number of lost-looking dogs. The animals were prowling around sniffing with their tails down – probably, thought Catesby, looking for their owners. Other dogs were howling and whining in a chorus of despair. The sound made his flesh crawl.

The people, on the other hand, were silent. There were fifty or so wraith-like figures poking through the ruins looking for loved ones. When people did speak it was in hushed whispers. Everyone seemed numb. Catesby heard one person whisper that the Germans had left only a few hours before and weren't far away. Another said they were on their way back. But no one seemed afraid – and neither was Catesby. The enormity in front of them blanked out all other emotions. If a tank appeared in the village square and started firing, no one would have dived for cover.

Catesby was drawn to the church whose ancient stone walls

had survived the flames within. He couldn't resist its dark pull. He didn't want to look inside, but he had to. The whispers he had heard were still echoing in his head: *all the women, all the children; burned alive.* He was later told that the church contained the bodies of 247 women and 205 children, but on the day he was unable to count – or even to recognise the charred corpses as women or girls or boys. In many cases, the only remains were blackened carcasses with thigh and upper-arm bones sticking out. The only thing that differentiated the bodies was their size. The smallest blackened bundles were obviously infants. There were other charred body parts that could have belonged to children or adults. It was a confusion of dead burned flesh that defied description. The smell in the church must have been terrible, although Catesby couldn't remember it. It was as if some of his senses had been abruptly shut down. But the visual image stuck in his brain forever.

Catesby had wanted to explore further into the church, only it was impossible to move forward without stepping on the bodies. The floor of the church was a singed carpet of women and children. He couldn't member how long he stared at the horror. But it wasn't a horror then; it was just dead bodies. The images on his brain were like a film that hadn't yet been fully developed. Eventually, he felt someone touching his elbow. It was the Maquisard he had cycled with. He gestured for Catesby to follow him.

There were more bodies to see: a bedridden elderly man burned alive in his bed and a baby baked alive in a bread oven in the village *boulangerie*. But most of the bodies, nearly 200 in number, were those of men who had been machine-gunned or shot in various barns and outbuildings – and then covered with straw, wood and petrol and set on fire while they were dead or dying. Once again, there were few bodies that were identifiable – just trunks of carcasses with bones sticking out, a grotesque reminder of Sunday roasts. Catesby felt more and more numb. It was too much to take in.

At the time, it was impossible to find out exactly what had happened. Some said there were only two survivors; others said there were twenty. It seemed certain that a few boys had escaped by running into the woods – and a woman had jumped from a church window and hidden in a patch of garden peas. But she was badly injured and had been taken to a hospital in Limoges. Confusion in the wake of chaos.

Catesby knew it was important to identify the troops who had carried out the atrocity. A boy of about eight, probably one of those who ran away, said the soldiers were dressed in greenish-brown camouflage smocks. Another survivor turned up – a male of about nineteen. He said that he and five others had fled a burning barn after hiding under dead bodies, but one of his companions had been shot and killed. There were rumours that many of the soldiers spoke good French, but with strong Alsatian accents. It turned out to be true. The revelation that former French citizens, from German annexed Alsace-Lorraine, had taken part in the massacre rocked France for years afterwards. There was always a twist.

The people were more talkative now and Catesby took notes with a shaking hand. The entire population had been ordered into the marketplace to have their identity papers checked. But once they were there, the Germans didn't bother to check their papers at all. Following a brief conversation – oddly polite – between the commanding officer and the mayor, the men of the village were led into outlying barns to be questioned. The women and children were ordered into the church and the doors locked behind them. The executions soon followed. The village was then looted – someone showed Catesby a few dozen empty champagne bottles – and set on fire.

Catesby later found out that the atrocity had been carried out by a battalion of the 2nd SS Panzer Division, also known as *Das Reich*, under the command of Otto Diekmann. The battalion had been involved in other war crimes – in Russia as well as France. Diekmann was killed in Normandy two weeks later.

The ruins of the U-boot bunker weren't the ideal place for a clandestine rendezvous. The bunker was dark, massive and echoed every footstep. And Catesby didn't like being dressed as a Roman Catholic priest either. It brought back too many childhood memories. His Belgian mother had brought him and his sister up as Catholics in an East Anglia where Catholics were an oddity and minority. Children don't like feeling different. It wasn't so bad speaking Flemish and French in the home, because that was hidden and private – and when school friends came around they always reverted to English. But being marched down Lowestoft High Street to Our Lady Star of the Sea on Sundays and holy days of obligation was public and humiliating. By the age of fourteen Catesby was a sceptic; by the age of sixteen, he was a militant atheist. As he used to explain to his smart new friends at Cambridge: 'I lost my faith as soon as I found my brain.' During visits home he used to humour his mother by going to Mass, but it soon became apparent that she didn't care what he did – and he stopped going all together. He began to realise that his mother didn't do things out of faith, but out of habit. But perhaps habits, however empty, give people a moral centre. Maybe, thought Catesby, if I hadn't lost the habit of Mass and confession I wouldn't be waiting in the ruins of a submarine pen with a greasy pistol in my pocket. But the priest disguise was, for a lad who had grown up among East Anglian fishermen, amusing and ironic. The wooden club that Lowestoft fishermen used to knock out cod thrashing about on the deck was called 'a priest'.

The U-boot bunker was a dark and spooky place. A few weeks before the end of the war two eleven-ton Grand Slam bombs had finally managed to penetrate the fifteen-foot-thick roof rendering the submarine pen useless. Steel reinforcing rods now hung down from the blasted concrete roof like the venomous snakes dangling from Medusa's head. Catesby didn't like being alone there in the middle of the night. It was a place of monsters where hidden eyes seemed to be tracing his every movement. Catesby touched the Webley MK IV revolver, a dead dank weight that stretched his trench-coat pocket. He liked the Webley. It was big and awkward – two and a half pounds and ten inches long – but simple and reliable, like a friendly black Labrador. The Webley could vanquish a gunman who was a poor shot or an assassin coming at him with a garrotte or a knife. But it couldn't silence the ghosts.

How many ghosts were squeaking and gibbering against

those massive concrete walls? Catesby didn't know. No one ever would. The deaths of the Polish and Russian slave labourers who built the U-boot bunker were too numerous and insignificant for the construction company to keep a record. Not long after the war Catesby had been assigned to the intelligence branch of the Control Commission for Germany. His real job was spying, but his cover job had been compiling a report on the activities of Organisation Todt, the construction company that had used *Zwangsarbeiter* – forced labour – in Bremen. One of his sources of information had been a mild-mannered bespectacled man who had been an accountant for Todt during the construction of the Weser submarine pens. The accountant was very apologetic about his role – and desperate to avoid a trip to Nuremberg – but he was safe. There were far bigger fish to hang. The accountant estimated that the project had used 10,000 slave labourers, of whom 1,700 were registered as dead, however he admitted – sighing and wringing his hands – that the actual number of deaths may have been 6,000 owing largely to *Unterernährungoder physischer Erschöpfung* – malnutrition and physical exhaustion.

Catesby looked through the huge hole in the ceiling. The clouds had parted and starlight poured into the bunker illuminating the rubble like ancient ruins. He knew that he was alone and safe from anyone other than himself. He touched the revolver again and wondered if the American was going to turn up. Kit Fournier wasn't always reliable. Catesby knew that Fournier had his own demons. He had bribed Fournier's *Putzfrau* to do some snooping. The *Putzfrauen*, the cleaning women of post-war Germany, were Catesby's most reliable agents. Fournier's *Putz* didn't even require training; she had used a Minox spy camera before. The snaps of Fournier's private diaries, letters and sketches revealed a private passion that had tortured the American since adolescence, if not before. The blackmail card would always be ready if Fournier didn't do what was asked.

The ruined bunker wasn't a quiet place. There were drips of water and the scuffling of rats – and the grinding tectonic shifts of loose rubble. But a footstep was distinct and human. Catesby froze and gripped the handle of his revolver. He was good at making enemies – and his extracurricular vendetta against Nazis had singled him out as a troublemaker. The problem – and a constant source of friction with his American intelligence colleagues – was the Gehlen Organisation. Reinhard Gehlen, the *Wehrmacht*'s former Chief of Intelligence for the Eastern Front, had cut a deal with the CIA. In return for generous funding and immunity from prosecution for their agents, the Gehlen Org provided intelligence to the Americans about what was supposedly going on in the East Bloc.

Catesby knew that Gehlen Org intelligence was useless. Nazis were terrible spies. The real purpose of the Org, thought Catesby, was to save war criminals and mass murderers from the Nuremberg hangman. One Org operative had been in charge of the Drancy concentration camp in the bleak northern suburbs of Paris and was responsible for the deaths of 140,000 Jews. But it was too late to get him – he had escaped to the Middle East. Others had winged their way to South America – a place that cynical US intelligence officers called the Fourth Reich. Catesby and a French colleague were still on the trail of Klaus Barbie, the Butcher of Lyon. When the French found out that Barbie was in American hands they demanded that he be handed over for execution, but the US High Commissioner for Germany, John McCloy, refused. Catesby had since heard that Barbie had been 'ratlined' to Bolivia with the help of a Croatian Catholic priest. That's why Catesby was wearing a Roman collar – Nazis on the run always expected priests to help them. Catesby was sure there were good priests – and tried hard to think of one.

Another footstep echoed in the bunker. Catesby checked that he wasn't silhouetted by the starlight pouring in from the broken roof and took out his revolver. Someone coughed. Catesby called out: '*Ich sehe dich; Hände haut.*' Catesby was bluffing. He couldn't see the other person in the darkness and would have had no idea whether or not their hands were up.

A disembodied voice answered, '*Wer sind Sie, bitte?*' The 'who are you, please' was unmistakeably American and disarmingly polite. It was Kit Fournier.

'It's me – Catesby.'

'Golly,' said Fournier, 'you had me worried. You sounded just like a genuine kraut. Where are you? The sound in this place bounces all over the place.'

'Are you alone?'

'Yes. I left your present in the car.'

'Have you got a torch?'

'No, but I've got a flashlight.'

'Same thing. Shine it in your face so I can see where you are.'

A light flashed on and Fournier's boyish smile appeared – a cheerful out-of-place Disney-esque cartoon in a tomb where thousands of slave labourers had sweated out their lives. But there was something fragile and false about Kit's smile – he only pretended to be the American naïf. It was part of his act. Spies shouldn't only be taught to stalk and use secret codes – they should go to drama school too.

Catesby removed his hand from the revolver and crunched across the rubble to the American. 'Why didn't you bring your friend?' said Catesby.

'He isn't my friend.'

'Is he alone in the car?'

'Yes, he is.'

'How do you know he won't run away?'

'He thinks I'm his friend – and he knows this is his last chance.'

Catesby looked at Fournier. His face was shiny with sweat and beads were forming under the brim of his trilby. 'You don't look well, Kit.'

'Kraut food gives me wind.'

'And too much schnapps?'

'Maybe.'

Catesby was afraid that Fournier was going to blow it. 'Do you want to practice your lines again before you hand him over? It could be awkward if he smells a rat.'

'Maybe I'm not going to hand him over.'

'What's the problem?'

'You haven't done your part of the deal.'

'I have,' said Catesby. 'I've told you everything I know and answered all your questions.' Catesby was lying, but they all lied.

'My boss in Washington keeps pestering me for more. He wants stuff that he can pass on to the state to put pressure on London. You guys aren't doing enough – and you owe us a big favour after selling those jet engines to the Sovs.'

Catesby knew that the Labour government was under a lot of pressure from Washington to increase military spending and send more troops to Korea. The Chancellor, Hugh Gaitskell, had scrapped free NHS prescriptions and specs in order to spend more on defence. A handful of ministers on the Labour Left had resigned in protest – and the CIA man in London had ringed their names.

Fournier continued, 'Last month was bad, real bad. The worst day was called "Black Thursday". Did you know, Catesby, that most pilots shit themselves when they get shot down?'

'So I've heard.'

'And their last words are seldom a prayer, but almost always "shit" or "fuck".'

Catesby knew that the Americans were taking a kicking in Korea on both the ground and in the air – and London's biggest fear was that Truman might give into his generals and use atom bombs. It could spiral into another world war that would destroy Britain.

'A lot of our guys,' said Fournier, 'are calling for blood, British blood. They think there are people in your government who betrayed the alliance and are siding with the Russians.'

Catesby sighed and shook his head.

'Why did you sell Moscow those jet engines?'

'We made a mistake,' said Catesby.

'I'm glad you admit that.'

'We made a mistake because if we had known the Russians were going to use our jet engines in their MiG-15s, we would have made them display the Union Jack on one side of the fuselage red star and the Rolls-Royce trademark on the other.'

'That's not funny, Catesby.'

'Then why are you laughing?'

'Because I like your dark sense of humour. But, Catesby, don't ever try making that joke in front of my American colleagues or they will have your guts for garters.'

'Then maybe I'd remind them that Britain fought in the war twice as long as America and took five times as many casualties per head of population – and now you're squeezing us dry over the war loans.' Catesby smiled. 'If you didn't want Moscow to get those engines, why didn't you outbid the Sovs?'

Fournier shook his head. 'It doesn't excuse trading with the enemy.'

'What about Wall Street financing Hitler?'

'We were neutral then – but we're not now. We're fighting to stop the spread of Communism.'

Catesby yawned.

'Sorry if you find me tedious.'

'Because we've had this conversation so many times before. Listen, Kit, you said I hadn't done my part of the deal. What part of the deal?'

'My boss wants dirt to throw.'

'Which boss?'

Fournier smiled bleakly. 'I can't tell you that – but I think you can figure it out yourself.'

'He thinks he's a genius, but he isn't.'

'Regardless, my boss thinks there's a Communist conspiracy at the heart of the British government. Why are you laughing?'

Catesby answered in Russian.

'I don't know the language. What did you say?'

'It's a Russian proverb: it's about people who believe you can milk chickens and use cows to hatch eggs.'

'Pigs might fly.'

'That's right; you got it.'

'You're being glib, Catesby. Americans don't like smart asses – especially when they're British.'

'Washington has gone mad about Reds-under-beds. Your leaders need psychiatric help as much as they do lessons in foreign policy.'

'No more lectures. Tell me more about the guy who sold the jet engines to the Commies.'

'Look up the newspaper files. It's all public. The decision was made by Stafford Cripps, the President of the Board of Trade, with the approval of the Prime Minister.'

'We need dirt, Catesby.' Fournier smiled. 'The sort of dirt that only a London insider like yourself can provide. Tell me straight, is Cripps a Communist?'

'No, he's a vegetarian.'

'Your so-called English sense of humour is getting on my nerves.'

'I wasn't being funny. Stafford Cripps is not just a vegetarian; he's also a puritanical non-drinking evangelical Christian. Let me tell you, Kit, something about Britain that you might not know. We may be a complex people with many contradictions, but there are *no* British Communists who are teetotal vegetarian Christians – not a single one.'

'You know something, Catesby?' Fournier smiled. 'You might be right. I understand Mr Cripps isn't very well – too much tea and not enough meat. I believe he suffers from colitis which is aggravated by stress – and has been on sick leave.'

Catesby knew that Fournier was showing off. The CIA and FBI had a reputation for 'black bag ops' – burglaries – and getting medical records was one of their favourite pastimes. But sex smears were even better.

'Nah,' said Fournier, 'the guy we're really looking at is the real Commie who succeeded Cripps – the one who actually went to Moscow to seal the jet engines deal with his comrades over generous libations of vodka. You know who I mean – Harold Wilson.'

Catesby laughed. 'If your boss thinks that Wilson is a spy, he is absolutely barking.' Catesby could see that Fournier didn't know English slang. 'Barking – it also means mad, crazy.'

The American smiled. 'Why are you assuming that it was my boss who told me that Wilson was a Communist? Maybe you should look closer to home?'

Catesby felt a frisson of doubt run down his spine. Fournier wasn't the American naïf he seemed.

'I'm surprised, William, that they haven't shown you the file.'

Catesby felt a twinge. A drop of sweat had begun to form on his spine. He had just remembered that in a short time he would be carrying out an execution, but there was also something in Fournier's voice that was sinister and worrying.

The American was smiling. 'Would you like to know more about this file?'

Catesby didn't answer.

'I'm not,' said Fournier, 'going to copy it down for you. It's not the sort of thing I want in my own handwriting. But I'm sure you can remember it. There's a report dated 26 March 1947 entitled East-West Trade. And it's a purely British file – parallel red stripes and all. It's classified top secret and was compiled by MI5. Maybe if you ask in a nice way and say please, they'll let you have a peek.'

Catesby put his right hand in the pocket of his trench coat and touched the cold steel of the Webley.

'I know,' said the American, 'you're just dying to ask me how I know about it. But you don't have to ask, I'll tell you. One of your colleagues showed it to me last time I was in London. If you think I'm full of bullshit, Catesby, ask some questions next time you're home in Limey Land.'

'You're playing games, Kit.'

'If they let you have a look – and I don't think they will – you ought to read MI5's comments about the Russian Wood Agency. It's a cover story for getting Soviet intelligence officers into Britain posing as timber merchants – and you need wood to build houses.' Fournier paused. 'Why don't you tell me more about Harold Wilson? We know that you were a socialist candidate in the 1945 election – you must have been close comrades.'

'We were Labour candidates.' Catesby smiled bleakly. 'And I got beaten. By the way, no Labour Party insider would ever describe Wilson as a socialist, much less a Communist. He's being smeared. Mark that top secret and put it in your files.'

Fournier kicked a piece of rubble, which set rats scurrying. He could see that he wasn't getting anywhere. 'In any case, Wilson ought to be arrested for trading with the enemy.'

Catesby smiled. 'I'll pass your suggestion on to London.'

'Thanks.'

'Are you going to turn him over?' said Catesby. He was getting pretty close to playing the blackmail card.

'Who?'

'Your German friend.'

'Christ, I almost forgot. Stay here. I'll fetch him.' Fournier paused. 'But before I get him, isn't there anything else you can tell me?'

Catesby shook his head.

'Fine. You're like squeezing water out of a rock.' The American turned to leave.

There was, however, one piece of intelligence that Catesby had withheld and would never let Fournier anywhere near. It was a toxic intelligence pill that would have sent the Pentagon into paroxysms of mass rage and carpet chewing. The MiGs over Korea were largely flown by elite Russian pilots. Catesby had first heard the rumour via a bribed and honey-trapped Soviet cipher clerk in East Berlin – and later had the information confirmed by a piece of used toilet paper. Soviet troops on exercise in East Germany were not provided toilet rolls and had to use whatever paper was available – training manuals, code books and unit rosters. The beshitten paper was an intelligence treasure trove and Catesby employed a small army of scavengers to collect them up under cover of foraging for mushrooms. At first, Catesby had been sceptical about the cipher clerk's info, but an excrement-covered page from a Soviet flying manual resolved his doubts. The page contained a list of Korean-language flying terms spelled out phonetically in Cyrillic characters – just the sort of thing a Russian pilot pretending to be a Korean pilot needed. Catesby reported his find to London who quickly decided not to share it with Washington. They didn't want to give an excuse to trigger-happy US generals. World War III was not in Britain's national interest.

Catesby listened to the American's footsteps echoing around the U-boot bunker. He suspected that Fournier was an actor playing a role he didn't much like – and working for people he secretly despised. Fournier's diaries had revealed more than his secret sex fantasies for a member of his own family. At one point, probably after a late-night drinking session, Fournier had written a comment about the PAPERCLIP war criminals that he was supposed to be helping escape – *Hang them all!* Perhaps Kit wasn't as reluctant about handing one over as he pretended.

The sound of muffled voices and footsteps jolted Catesby back to the business at hand. He was now in a cold sweat. For the first time he was sorry that he had got involved – but it had to be done. The silhouettes of the two men appeared like one-dimensional cut-outs against the light from the hole in the roof. Fournier was speaking to the war criminal in bad German explaining that Père Roux was going to take him away in a boat to a ship that was embarking for Cartagena. Catesby touched his Roman collar and tried to put on a priestly air as the two stumbled across the rubble towards him.

The German spoke first in French, 'Good evening, Father.'

Catesby answered in German. 'Have you got your passport?'

As the German reached into his pocket, Catesby addressed Fournier in English: 'You can leave us now. Everything is taken care of.'

Catesby listened to the echo of Fournier's receding footsteps as he left the bunker. He turned to the German. If the German had been perturbed by hearing Père Roux speak English, he didn't show it. He held up a passport. It carried his own photograph, but the name and details were false.

'I'll need that,' said Catesby. 'It is best that you have as little contact with the crew as possible – and important that none of them see your passport. It will be safe with me.'

The German handed over the document. Catesby would have a close look at it afterwards. He wanted to see how good the Americans were at forgeries.

'Are you coming with me?' said the German.

'No.'

It took the German a second to realise that a revolver was pointing in his face. 'What are you doing?'

'I'm taking you to the boat. I've heard you are a dangerous man.'

'This is nonsense.'

'Turn around and keep walking until I tell you to stop.' Catesby didn't want to have to drag the body through the bunker. 'It isn't far.'

The German stumbled through the rubble for thirty paces. There was a sound of flowing water.

'Don't fall in,' said Catesby.

They had come to a massive man-made channel that diverted water from the Weser into the bunker. It was where they had intended to launch and hide the completed submarines. The German had reached the edge and was staring into the abyss at the fast ebbing dark water.

'Kneel down,' said Catesby.

'There isn't a boat and you're going to kill me.' The German's voice was strangely devoid of emotion.

Catesby was trying to hold the revolver steady, but his hand was shaking.

'Are you really a priest?'

'Yes,' Catesby lied.

'Will you hear my confession before you kill me?'

'I can't give you absolution unless you tell me everything.'

'I know that.'

'I'm listening.'

'Bless me, Father, for have I sinned. It has been ten years since my last confession. I have frequently failed to go to Mass on Sundays and other holy days of obligation...'

'Tell me about your other sins.'

'I was unfaithful to my wife on three occasions...'

'They are sins of the flesh. Tell me about what you did in Russia and France.'

'I carried out my duties as a soldier.'

Catesby was sick inside and boiling with rage. 'At Tulle. What happened at Tulle? You were there – you were in command.' Catesby knew that every man between the age of sixteen and sixty had been arrested. Ninety-nine had then been chosen at random for torture and hanging. Another 150 were sent to the death camp at Dachau. The terror reprisals spread throughout the Limousin.

'I carried out General Lammerding's orders.'

Catesby knew it was pointless to explain that what he had done was murder and a crime against humanity. He was pointing his gun at a clockwork military puppet. But one more try. 'And Oradour – tell me about Oradour.'

'The action at Oradour-sur-Glane was an act of passion.'

Catesby blinked – language had lost all meaning. 'Does passion mean evil?'

'I believe, Father, that you are from that part of France and that is why you are doing this to me.'

At last, a glimmer of understanding. 'Yes, I was there.'

'You know then that the officer who commanded the troops at Oradour was Otto Diekmann?'

'Yes.'

'Otto Diekmann was in love with Helmut Kämpfe.'

Catesby felt he was drowning in a pool of sick and excrement with Wagner's *Tristan und Isolde* blasting away in the background.

The German's voice turned wistful. 'Helmut was a beautiful man and such a brave soldier. When Otto heard that Helmut had been executed by the resistance he carried out an act of revenge.'

'Against innocent women and children; burning them alive.'

The German shrugged. 'Otto wasn't following anyone's orders. He was killed two weeks later in Normandy – you could say that his death was suicide.'

Catesby had heard enough. Understanding did not mean forgiving. And this wasn't genuine understanding – it was an attempt to sentimentalise and romanticise evil.

'Helmut was married and had three children.'

Catesby frowned. The mystery of what happened to Helmut Kämpfe had finally been resolved. Or had it? Some said Kämpfe had been shot trying to escape, others said that he had been executed. But was the German's story true? Was the Oradour atrocity a reprisal for Kämpfe's execution? Catesby knew it would still keep him awake in the dark watches of the night. What could he have done? Could he have persuaded the Maquis to keep Kämpfe alive as a hostage for bargaining? Would that have prevented the massacre at Oradour-sur-Glane? Or not made any difference at all? Nothing had been resolved.

The German was muttering an Act of Contrition.

'Stop that,' said Catesby.

'Are you going to give me absolution, Father?'

Catesby smiled. He still remembered the words from his

childhood: *Ego te absolvo* – and, hey presto, your soul is as fresh and clean as a new pin.

'Have I time to do penance?'

'No,' said Catesby. He pointed his pistol at the base of the Nazi's skull and pulled the trigger.

'How much of this slum do your parents actually own?' Catesby was well into the bottle of sparkling Portuguese rosé that he had bought in an off-licence on the way to his wife's flat.

'They own the whole house.'

'Well, they must be breathing a sigh of relief.'

'Why?'

'Now that the Tories are back in power, there's no longer any danger of it being confiscated and turned into council flats.'

'That's not fair, William, you know my parents are Labour supporters – and, in fact, wouldn't mind having this house off their hands.'

'What a shambles.'

'You mean the house?'

'No, I mean the election.' Labour had won the popular vote, but had taken fewer seats owing to boundary changes, which benefited the Tories and returned an elderly Churchill to power.

Catesby's wife got up and straightened her skirt. 'I think the lamb is nearly done.'

'I'm sorry, Frances, I really apologise.'

'For what?'

'For being a shit husband, a shit step-dad – and I was also a shit Army officer and now I'm a shit intelligence officer. *Je suis simplement une grosse merde.*'

'I think we need to flush you down the toilet. But I'll serve the food first.'

As Frances padded off to the kitchen, Catesby surveyed the flat. It badly needed redecorating and repairing. There were botched repairs from wartime bombing that still needed putting right. The Regency ceiling was water damaged from burst pipes and loose-hanging plaster was concealed with wallpaper. The house was a five-storey terrace divided into flats overlooking Stanhope Gardens. Catesby knew that his parents-in-law hadn't the money to put things right. They were shabby genteel idealists.

As his wife came back into the dining room bearing a steaming casserole, Catesby lifted his glass of semi-sweet sparkling rosé, 'Votes for women!'

'You're out of date, William. Women now have the vote.'

'But if wasn't for your brave cousin, you wouldn't have the vote.'

'She was my father's cousin – and I'm not sure that throwing herself under the King's horse made much of a difference.'

'I was also being ironic, not about your cousin, but about you doing all the work. What can I do to help?'

'You can pour me a glass of wine.'

'It's ghastly – I apologise.'

'Stop apologising, William. Once again, your Roman Catholic guilt is driving me mad.'

'And once again, Frances, I am not a Roman Catholic – I am an atheist and a socialist. I lost my… Why are you yawning?'

'Because I've heard that line so many times before: "I lost my faith when I found my brain".'

'Don't you think it's clever?'

'I did the first time you said it. But, in any case, I don't think it's true: once a Catesby always a Catesby.'

'The Catesby jibe is as tiresome as my repetitions – my name is just a coincidence.'

'You get teased a lot about it in SIS, don't you?'

Catesby sighed and nodded. The fact that he bore the surname of the fanatical recusant Roman Catholic who led the Gunpowder Plot wasn't lost on his colleagues. Catesby, like most British working class, couldn't trace his family tree back further than his grandparents, but the name came to haunt him. Catesby had never heard of his alleged ancestors until he studied Shakespeare's *Richard III* at the grammar and discovered that a William Catesby had been one of the hunchback king's henchmen:

> *The Cat, the Rat and Lovell the Dog,*
> *Rule all England under a Hog.*

A few weeks later a history master, using an embarrassed Catesby as a cue card, recounted the story of Robert Catesby, a direct descendant of William 'The Cat'. Catesby had masterminded the plot to blow up Parliament, but Guy Fawkes was more famous because he had been so publicly hung, drawn and quartered for high treason. Catesby, on the other hand, had escaped to Holbeche House in Staffordshire where he had been shot in a last-ditch stand and died clutching an image of the Virgin Mary. But had, dreamed Catesby, that really happened? Could the man killed have been another? And had the real Robert Catesby escaped to the Suffolk coast where he had waited in vain for a rescue ship from the Spanish Netherlands? Then, finally realising that no ship was going to appear and aided by undercover Jesuits, Catesby had disappeared forever into the Suffolk countryside. For a year or two, Catesby relished the romanticism of a famous rebel as an ancestor, but then came to realise that Catesby-the-recusant-Catholic was even more reactionary than those he had plotted against. He became ashamed of his adolescent fantasy.

'This lamb,' said Frances, 'comes from a flock that grazes on the marshes near Aldeburgh. Dad knows the farmer.'

Catesby put his fork down. 'If your father didn't buy it with his ration book I'm not going to eat it. I won't eat black market meat.'

'William, meat rationing ended in 1945.'

'I was joking. You never laugh at my jokes.'

'I do when they're funny.'

'This is delicious – you can taste the samphire from the marshes where they were grazing.'

'Would you like some Algerian red? I found a case left over from the war.'

'Don't you like the rosé?'

'It is a bit sweet, maybe we should save it for the pud.'

'As I said, I never get anything right.'

'Would you like this casserole poured over your head?'

'Then I hope you would lick it off.'

'Don't be rude.'

'You look very fetching tonight.' Catesby had felt pangs of desire ever since he walked in the door. It had been so long.

'How's your mother?'

Catesby stared at his wife; then laughed aloud.

'What is so funny, William?'

'You are a master of the passion-killing reply. Sorry, ignore that. My mother is a mystery. I don't even know how old she is.'

Catesby knew that his sailor father had met his mother in an Antwerp bar the very day that the Great War had broken out. The Bastins weren't a particularly poor family, his Belgian grandparents apparently owned the bar, but he had never met them – or any Bastins other than an uncle. The uncle had turned up one day in the 1930s with his Russian émigré wife. They helped the Catesbys find a larger house in north Lowestoft and moved in with them. It was bliss compared to the cramped house on Roman Hill – it even had indoor loos. The aunt by marriage was extremely glamorous and taught Catesby and his sister basic Russian. Ten years later, at the end of the Second World War, the aunt and uncle disappeared as mysteriously as they had appeared. It was a story that caused a lot of frowns and head shaking whenever he had a security vetting – but Catesby and his sister had grown up as skilled linguists. His sister went on to study Slavonic languages at the London School of Economics.

'I'm going to get some red,' said Frances getting up.

'By the way, Freddie sends her love.'

Frances smiled bleakly. 'Send her my love too.'

Catesby didn't know how to make things better. Relations between his sister Freddie and his wife had never been good and were getting worse. Maybe Frances knew things about Freddie that she had never shared. Spying was the family business. Frances worked for MI5 and Freddie was a translator at GCHQ.

Frances got up and came back blowing the dust off a litre bottle of Algerian red. 'I hope this hasn't turned into vinegar.' She poured the wine into Catesby's glass.

He sipped. 'It's quite good, actually. Was it liberated by your father?'

'I'm not sure.'

'I think it came from Admiral Darlan's private cellars.'

'We don't talk about that.'

The assassination of the pro-Vichy Darlan in Algiers was hush-hush – and Frances's father had been involved. His father-in-law would never even hint at what had happened. But Catesby suspected that the British had done the dirty work as a favour to de Gaulle? Spying was her family's business too.

'It's a pity,' said Catesby, 'that the children aren't here.'

'I think they need some time to get used to you again.'

'Does that mean…'

'I don't know what it means.'

Catesby looked at his plate; then continued to eat in silence. Their marriage seemed permanently on hold. He didn't know what she wanted – and he wasn't sure what he wanted. Frances had been wild during the war. It was a frightful time, but a glamorous time. She celebrated VE day by giving birth to twins. She was seventeen – and the Royal Canadian Air Force officer who had fathered them had already slimed off back to Saskatchewan where he had a wife and three kids.

At times, Catesby and Frances had been incredibly close. But there were problems that neither of them talked about. Their jobs kept them apart too. Frances certainly needed to work for the money, but also for her self-esteem. She came from a family who, when they weren't throwing themselves under horses at the Epsom Derby, were devoting themselves to making the world a better and fairer place. They were anarchists, socialists, Fabians, feminists, humanist aesthetes and members of the Bloomsbury group. You could find them at literary salons and in the Houses of Parliament. Some were conscientious objectors, while others commanded infantry regiments. Frances felt she had to do her part, but didn't know what that part was. She juggled child care with a secretarial course – and then, through the inevitable network that encased women of her class, drifted into MI5.

'Your collar's frayed and you need a haircut. Sometimes, William, you look like you've been dragged backwards through a blackthorn hedge. You need looking after.'

Catesby smiled. 'I'm practising the Fitzrovia look. I'm going to quit SIS and go to art school. You've never seen my creative side.'

'You're not serious?'

'I suppose not. But my new cover story is as a very junior dip, a tenth secretary or something, in the cultural attaché's office – so I'm trying to look the part.'

'Oh no, William, that's not the part at all!'

'I knew you were going to say that.'

'You've got to be very polished, suave and elegant.'

And not, Catesby thought, carry a greasy gun in a stained mackintosh and execute Nazi war criminals in the ruins of a rat-infested U-boot bunker surrounded by the ghosts of slave workers. She didn't understand. It was one of the things that separated them – but he immediately felt a pang of guilt. She was a loving person who understood pain and loss: both her brothers died in the war. Maybe he was the one who didn't understand, who was too self-pitying.

'I've got a pair of jade cufflinks that I can lend you.'

'The Canadian's?'

'No, someone else's.'

Catesby didn't bother to enquire further.

Frances saw the pained look on her husband's face and gave him a warm smile. 'They're my dad's. He wanted you to have them.'

Catesby gave a bleak smile, his only smile. Was she telling the truth – or quickly making up a story? MI5 trained their staff well.

'You look a million miles away, William. What's wrong?'

'I was thinking of something.'

'What is it?'

'I don't know.'

'You do know. Why don't you ever talk?'

'Don't be cross.'

'I have every reason to be cross.'

Catesby reached out a hand and put it on her wrist. 'I do care about you.'

'Then why don't you spend more time with me?'

'It's difficult when I'm in Germany saving Britain from the Russians and the Americans.'

'Which ones are more dangerous?'

'The Americans because they've got more money and think they speak our language.'

'You know, William, those views don't make you very popular at Leconfield House.' Frances was referring to the not-so-secret headquarters of MI5 in the heart of Mayfair.

Catesby laughed. 'On the other hand, the Russians are more likely to blow us up with atom bombs – which, I suppose, is an even worse fate than being inundated with chewing gum and Hollywood films.'

'I don't think that you're going to be assigned to Washington anytime in the near future.'

'What a pity? I was hoping that I was going to replace Guy Burgess.'

Frances frowned and looked away.

'Sore point, isn't it?' Catesby gave Frances a sly look. 'Why don't you admit it?'

'Admit what?'

'You were ordered to let Guy and Maclean do a quiet fade.'

Frances pursed her mouth and looked away.

'You look as if someone just made an indecent suggestion,' said Catesby.

'I don't think you understand our limitations – and the pressure we're under.'

'I do. We've both got shit jobs.'

Catesby knew that Frances was part of A4, the MI5 section responsible for surveillance. A4 was composed of three women and nineteen men. A total of twenty-two MI5 officers were responsible for keeping an eye on all Britain's enemies the width and length of the entire UK twenty-four hours a day – except they didn't work evenings or weekends. Consequently, there were no trench-coated, trilby-wearing shadows on the Southampton docks when Burgess and Maclean hopped on board the *Falaise* for a trip to St Malo – it was late on a Friday and A4 had clocked off for the weekend.

'You would have thought,' said Catesby, 'that you could have altered the duty rotas to put a tail on them.'

Frances smiled. 'I volunteered to work overtime that evening, but couldn't get a childminder.'

'Being a good parent is more important than catching spies – but you could have taken the kids with you; no one would have ever guessed you were a watcher.'

Frances shook her head. 'No, William, no.'

Catesby did, in fact, advise his agents to take children with them when picking up dead drops or making rendezvous. It was a perfect cover.

Frances lowered her voice, 'But they didn't need me. There was someone on their tail.'

'Who?'

'Don't ever tell anyone. It was the DG himself.'

'Good lord.'

'But…' Frances had a fit of giggles, '…he couldn't follow them to France because he'd forgotten his passport.'

Catesby shook his head. 'He didn't forget his passport and he wasn't on their tail. The DG went to Southampton to see them off and wish them *bon voyage*.'

'By the way,' said Frances, 'I've got something else for you.'

'Let me guess.'

'Don't you remember, you asked me?'

'I shouldn't have – it was too risky for you.'

'I didn't get it. Hortense got it for me.'

'Does she still live downstairs?'

Frances nodded. 'She'll do anything for you.'

Hortense had been parachuted into France at the same time as Catesby. She had fallen in love with a member of the resistance who was captured and shot by the Germans. Catesby was certain that the relationship had never been consummated. Hortense was one of a small army of genteel spinsters that managed the Registry. The Registry was a vast catacomb of vaults and shelves that contained all the files and archives of MI5. The women were the only ones who could decode the arcane index cards and navigate the labyrinth.

Frances got up and unlocked an oak roll-top desk. 'She even copied it for you. Here it is.'

Just as Fournier had said, the document was dated 26 March 1947, titled East-West Trade and classified top secret. Catesby smiled and looked up. 'I owe Hortense a bottle of Harvey's Bristol Cream. Have you read this?'

'Yes.'

'What do you think?'

'I'm suspicious of why it was classified top secret. It simply reiterates the objections of the Chiefs of Staff about the proposed sale of Rolls-Royce jet engines to the Soviet Union. Not a big surprise – and it was even referred to in *The Times*.'

Catesby read the document again. Fournier had lied. There was absolutely no reference to Harold Wilson – the only politicians mentioned were Cripps and Attlee. The decision to sell the engines had been made months before Wilson became President of the Board of Trade. Catesby looked up. 'Do you know why they've classified this top secret?'

'It is strange.'

'It's an old trick. By denying access to a file you create suspicion about what it contains. You make people think there is fire when there isn't even a whiff of smoke.'

'Don't patronise me, William. I know more than you think.'

'Sorry. What do you know?'

'They're trying to smear Harold Wilson – and they're doing it to curry favour with Washington. They want the Americans to think that Wilson is the sole villain involved – a sort of evil genius – and entirely responsible for selling those jet engines to Moscow.' Frances sipped her wine. 'I keep my ears open, William – they think I'm just a compliant girlie, part of the wallpaper – and I hear things that chill my blood.'

'Usually after lunch.'

'Lunch is a big tongue-loosener at Leconfield House. They've mastered the art of the high volume whisper that you can hear through two walls and a ceiling.' Frances paused and smiled. 'When the indiscretions end, the postprandial snoring begins. By three o'clock the place sounds like the sea lion enclosure at Regents Park zoo.'

'May I have some more wine?'

'Not if you're going to snore.'

'I didn't know I was staying.'

Frances filled his glass.

Catesby stared blankly and tried to separate the professional from the personal. He wanted to concentrate on seducing his wife, but Kit Fournier's words about Harold Wilson kept getting in the way. 'Are they passing on these rumours about Wilson to the Americans?'

'Of course.'

'To the CIA?'

'Even worse, directly to Republican congressmen and to the right-wing Hearst press.'

'Have you got proof?'

'Of course not, but it wouldn't make any difference. They're not passing on state secrets; they're passing on disinformation, lies.'

'If they're not guilty of treason, they're guilty of libel and slander. It reeks.'

'But there's nothing we can do about it. They cover themselves. Nothing is in writing or ever said in front of witnesses – and they pass rumours on to Members of Parliament too, usually Conservatives. Keep your eye on Hansard for the latest.'

Catesby leaned forward and whispered. 'You're winding me up, aren't you? None of this has ever happened.'

'It would be better for me if you think so.'

Catesby knew it was all true, but didn't want to know more. Power was a blood sport in which there were no rules.

'But William, there are good people in MI5. Most of them are good and honourable people – Sir Percy, for example – but there is also a nest of vipers who can't be controlled.'

'Name them.'

She did.

Once again, Catesby had no regrets about his choice of career. *Quis custodiet ipsos custodes?* Who guards the guardians? It was Catesby's biggest secret. He would never say it because it sounded so sentimental, so embarrassing. But Catesby loved his country.

Frances pushed her chair back and stood up.

'Let me help,' said Catesby.

'I'm just getting the pudding.'

Catesby was already up standing next to her. Their mouths met and he felt her arms entwining his neck like a spinning spider. It had been so long. She felt warm, sleek and silky. He brushed her hair aside and kissed her neck. Her breath was hot on his neck and they were so close. The telephone rang.

'I'll get it,' said Frances.

'Leave it.'

'I can't. It could be about the children.'

'You'd better answer it then.'

Frances disappeared into the bedroom to pick up the phone, but didn't close the door behind her. Catesby listened as her voice turned from concerned to annoyed: 'Knightsbridge 1803 … Yes, he is here … Would you like to speak to him? … Of course, I will get him.'

She came back into the room. 'It's your sister. She said it's urgent.'

'Fuck.'

'Don't swear.'

'I suppose I'd better speak to her.'

'Why does she always disturb us?'

'She doesn't always disturb us.'

Catesby went into the bedroom. He knew the evening was ruined. His heart sank when he saw that Frances had laid out for him a neatly ironed pair of pyjamas. He picked up the phone. 'Hello, is that you, Freddie?'

'Thank god you're there, Will.'

He shifted into Flemish. 'What's happened? Has *Moeder* died?'

'That's not funny, Will.'

He went back to English. He knew that Frances was listening and didn't want to hide anything from her. 'I suppose, then, she hasn't. Why are you ringing?'

'It's about Tomasz. This is really serious. I'm frightened of him.'

Catesby sighed. They had been there before. Tomasz was Freddie's mad Polish live-in lover. He had been an RAF fighter pilot during the Battle of Britain. During one encounter Tomasz had run out of ammunition so he rammed the German bomber with his Hurricane instead. Both planes had been destroyed, but Tomasz had somehow managed to parachute out of his mangled fighter. He had stayed in Britain after the war because he had no desire to return to a Poland under Soviet occupation: 'They will execute me because I am member of *szlachta*.' Whether or not Tomasz was really an aristocrat, one of the *szlachta*, was something that

Catesby had never determined. But he did have the arrogance to be one – and loads of charm too when he chose to turn it on. Tomasz worked irregular hours for the Polish Service of the BBC.

'What's happened?'

'He's having an affair – and now he's accusing me of having a lover to justify himself. When he comes home drunk I think he might kill me.'

'Have you got a lover?'

'Of course not, but he's suspicious about the move to Cheltenham.'

'Sure.' GCHQ's move from Hillingdon, outer London, to Gloucestershire was creating a lot of problems for staff – and lots of opportunities for affairs. The security services were not well known for marital faithfulness. Spies were professional liars and deceivers.

'Will?'

'What?'

'I don't want to be here alone when Tomasz comes back.'

Catesby sighed and rolled his eyes at Frances who had come into the room. Then spoke into the phone: 'Why don't you come here?'

Frances shook her head, but then raised her hands and nodded yes.

'No,' said Freddie.

'Why not?'

'I don't want to.'

'Where's Tomasz now?' said Catesby.

'I don't know. I think he's with her – and then he'll go out to drinking clubs with his Polish Service friends. They're lethal.'

'I know. Why doesn't he stay with her?'

'She's married.'

'That's good.'

'Don't be flippant, Will. He's going to come back drunk and angry. I'm frightened. Please come here.'

Catesby looked at Frances. She was nodding yes and whispering, 'You've got to go.' She had either heard or surmised what Freddie had said.

'Okay, I'm on my way. See you soon.' Catesby put the phone down and looked at his wife. 'I don't want to go. She's crying wolf.'

Frances didn't reply.

'I'm going to call her back and say I'm not coming.'

'No, William, your sister needs you – or she might. You can't take the risk.'

'You're very generous.'

Catesby left the house into a mild autumn night. At least, he thought, it wasn't raining. There were even stars above the plane trees in Stanhope Gardens. The residents had keys to the private green space – and some had turned part of it into a Victory Garden during the war. But now all that idealism was draining out of Britain like a bucket with numerous holes.

Catesby looked at his watch. It was too late for the underground and it was an hour's walk to the flat in Pimlico. He turned north to Cromwell Road where he was going to have to splash out for a taxi. He hadn't walked far when he saw them. They were sitting in a stately four-door Austin 8. It was one of the clumsiest sur-veillance stakeouts that he'd ever seen: two men wearing trilbies sitting smoking in a parked car. Why, Catesby thought, didn't they just hoist a sign saying MI5 Surveillance Team? But maybe they wanted to be seen. Was it a form of intimidation aimed at him or Frances? Or a warning? Catesby was pretty certain that some of his wife's bosses wouldn't be happy about a marital rec-onciliation. In any case, he wasn't playing the game and the wine made him bold. Catesby strode over to the car. It was a bit odd, he thought, that they were staked out in an Austin instead of a Humber from the Security Service garage pool in Kennington. Catesby stood next to the passenger side window, which was too fogged up for him to recognise who was inside. He didn't know what he should say. A brisk 'fuck off' seemed most in character. On the other hand, he could turn it into a joke and ask them for a lift to Pimlico to save them the trouble of trailing him. Catesby smiled and tapped on the window.

As soon as the window began to crack open Catesby knew that something was wrong. It smelled wrong. MI5 'watchers' don't smoke Gauloises. The driver spoke first, but it wasn't in English or French – and the words weren't addressed to Catesby. He was giving an instruction to the man in the passenger seat. Catesby was already sprinting at full stride before the first shot was fired. He heard the car door open. He didn't look behind, but heard two more shots. Catesby now was weaving and twisting like a hare trying to outwit a lurcher. He heard the driver shout another order. Catesby recognised the language, but didn't understand it. The car door shut and the engine started.

Catesby was now on Cromwell Road where there were people and a fair amount of late night traffic. He ducked into the shadows of a passageway next to the Gloucester Road tube station and kept an eye out for the Austin 8. He reckoned they might have given up the chase. He waited until he saw a taxi before stepping into the light. He quickly hailed it looking both ways.

'You sound like you've been running,' said the driver.

'I'm being chased by a jealous husband waving a meat cleaver.'

'Happens to all of us.'

'Listen, I hope you won't mind, but I'd like to take evasive action to make sure we're not being followed.'

Catesby then put the driver through a series of manoeuvres and feints, which he had been trained to do as 'counter-surveillance' craft. When they finally arrived in Pimlico, Catesby was almost certain that they hadn't 'grown a tail', but he still asked the driver to drop him off a couple of hundred yards from the flat in Tachbrook Street. He would make his way there via a series of back alleys and 'choke points' to make sure he wasn't being followed – he didn't want to put Freddie in danger.

The driver looked at Catesby with suspicious admiration as he accepted the tip and fare. 'You seem to know your stuff, guv.'

'You have to when you play around.'

'Thank you for coming, Will,' said Freddie taking Catesby's jacket. 'You look like you've been dragged through a hedge backwards.'

'A blackthorn hedge.'

'It doesn't matter what sort.'

'Aren't you going to lock and bolt the door behind us?'

'I have to leave it open. Tomasz forgot his key ring.'

'Then at least he won't lose it while he's out shagging and getting pissed with his mates.' Catesby knew that Freddie had made up the story about Tomasz as a pretext for getting him away from his wife. For some reason his sister despised Frances and wanted to keep them apart.

'Would you like a cup of tea?'

'You lied to me. Didn't you, Freddie?'

'Would you like something stronger? We've got some Spanish brandy.'

'Republican or Fascist?'

'We've also got Slivovitz, plum brandy from Czechoslovakia – you might find that more ideologically sound.'

'Not necessarily. You know, for an anti-Communist member of the *szlachta*, Tomasz has quite a store of East Bloc spirits.'

Freddie shrugged.

'I think,' said Catesby, 'I'll take my chances with General Franco's brandy.'

Freddie smiled. 'I always suspected you were a class traitor. I'll get you a glass.'

Catesby sat down to a creaking of springs. 'We need a new sofa.' The Tachbrook flat was also Catesby's home when he was in London. It was located in the basement of yet another building owned by Frances's family. The top floors were lived in by eccentric aunts with artistic and musical connections – a whiff of Bloomsbury in Pimlico. You often heard musical instruments being played through the ceiling.

Freddie came back with the drinks. 'I take it for granted that you lied to me,' said Catesby, 'so I can rest assured that Tomasz isn't going to burst through the door wielding an axe.'

Freddie nodded.

'Good. I've already had someone try to kill me this evening.'

'Was it Frances?'

Catesby smiled. 'You said that with a real gleam of hope in your eye. No, we were having a loving evening until you telephoned. Don't pout.'

'Don't patronise me and treat me like a child.'

Catesby sipped his brandy. His sister was two years younger than him. They had both experienced the grinding poverty of 1930s Lowestoft – and their politics had been formed by it. There was no one closer to him, but no one that he understood less.

'I'm sorry that I snapped at you.' Freddie smiled. 'Did someone really try to kill you?'

The exhilaration of his brush with death was now wearing off and Catesby had begun to feel numb and empty. It was always like that. Being in battle was always better than the depression that came afterwards. Catesby nodded, 'Yes.'

'Who? Why?'

'I don't know. I'm still trying to put the pieces together.' Catesby looked at his sister. 'You're a better linguist than I am.'

'That's not true – but I studied harder.'

'Who do you know who speaks Elsässerditsch?'

'No one, but I've heard it spoken during a visit to Strasbourg.'

'And it's only spoken in Alsace?'

'As far as I know – and maybe a tiny corner of Lorraine.'

Catesby didn't need further convincing. He was sure the two men in the Austin had been speaking the low German dialect of Alsace. He had heard it before. It was a distinct dialect that couldn't be mistaken for Swabian or Swiss German.

'Their "no",' said Freddie, 'is something like *naan*.'

Catesby nodded.

'Is this something to do with Oradour-sur-Glane?' asked Freddie.

'They tried to shoot me.'

'What?'

Catesby briefly explained what had happened, then stared blankly into space. He hadn't told her everything about Oradour-sur-Glane, but he had confided in his sister more than anyone else. Oradour was a war crime that was tearing France apart. At least a third of the soldiers who had carried out the massacre were not Germans, but Alsatians who had been French citizens before 1940 and became French citizens again after 1945. It was an unhealed wound and the trial of the Alsatians who had been part of the SS battalion at Oradour kept getting delayed. Although

Catesby had only seen the aftermath, the French prosecutor had summoned him to be a witness if the trial ever took place. The request had caused consternation at SIS and the British government were trying to assure Catesby's anonymity.

'They want to shut you up, don't they, Will?'

'I don't know.' Catesby did know that a lot of people wanted him dead, but he didn't think it had anything to do with a French war crimes trial. The art of getting rid of someone was to make it look like someone else did it for a completely different reason. Catesby wanted to change the subject. 'Where's Tomasz?'

'He's on the nightshift at Bush House.'

'Nothing more dramatic?'

'Sorry, Will.'

'What have you got against Frances?'

Freddie drank her brandy and tossed her hair back. Her eyes were sparkling. 'What has Frances got against Tomasz?'

'Can we start answering questions instead of asking them?'

'You first.'

'You're jealous of Frances. You didn't want me to get married – you wanted to keep me as a big brother to lean on and to deal with *Moeder*.'

'What a stupid, silly and egotistical answer.'

Catesby smiled. 'But it was an answer. Your turn. Tell me about Frances and Tomasz.'

'She's spying on him.'

'Personally or professionally?'

'Both. Tomasz is sure that Frances has put him under surveillance – that she opens his mail and that our phone is tapped.'

'Do you want me to check the phone for a bug? I can show you how.'

Freddie smiled knowingly. 'Of course you can, Will. But no one can check if a phone is tapped at the GPO exchange.'

'Good point.' Catesby kept a straight face. If a UK phone itself was tapped, it was a sign that the person listening in was a foreign spy, a criminal or a jealous lover or spouse. The UK Security Services worked with GPO telephone engineers.

'Frances,' continued Freddie, 'is trying to destroy Tomasz and our relationship by putting him under suspicion as a spy – and that is utter nonsense.'

'Why does she want to do this? What's her motive?'

Freddie smiled slyly. 'I think it's jealousy. Frances has always fancied Tomasz – and can't bear the thought that someone as lowborn and mousy as myself could have landed him. I'm sure she made a play for him and Tomasz rejected her – and now she wants revenge.'

Catesby smiled. 'So my wife doesn't love me.'

'You've just realised that, Will?'

'You're being especially poisonous this evening.'

'You have every reason to be jealous, Will. Tomasz is far more interesting and attractive than you.'

'Thanks.'

'I am winding you up a bit.'

'How,' said Catesby, 'has Tomasz discovered that he's under surveillance and suspicion?'

'He says that people have told him that people are asking questions about him?'

Catesby kept a straight face and hid his annoyance. Bad security. Someone was spying on Tomasz, but it wasn't Frances.

**Bonn:** November, 1951

Normally, Catesby had two clerical assistants in his office at the British embassy, but Miss Greenwood was off on maternity leave. She was no longer, of course, a Miss. She was now married to a major general who had divorced his wife to start a new family. The former Miss Greenwood, now Lady Laetitia, celebrated her fortieth birthday by having a baby.

Catesby's sole remaining office help was Gerald, an ex-RAF engineer who was invaluable. There were fewer hands, but the office atmosphere was a lot lighter. The proudly proletarian Gerald and the posh and prim Miss Greenwood used to circle each other like opposing warships about to do battle. One of Gerald's duties was accompanying the British Liaison Team tasked with observing Soviet military exercises in East Germany. In the wake of those exercises, Gerald and others surreptitiously collected the fragments of letters, manuals and even codebooks that the Red Army soldiers used as toilet paper. Gerald always proudly bore his intelligence trove back to the office in Bonn. It was, of course, invaluable stuff. He tried, once too often, to show it off to Miss Greenwood.

Her piercing 'Fuck off!' was the loudest noise Catesby had ever heard in the embassy. He later found out that even the Ambassador had heard it.

There was a long awkward silence before Miss Greenwood began typing again. Catesby looked at Gerald and shook his head. Catesby waited a moment; then said, 'Miss Greenwood.'

'Yes, Captain Catesby.' She was the only person in the world who addressed him by his former rank. She stopped typing.

'I apologise. We shouldn't bring such material into the office.' Catesby furtively winked at Gerald. He wanted to keep him onside as well, but fully understood Miss Greenwood's just anger. 'In future, Gerald, could you photograph and file intelligence of that nature?'

'Yes, sir.'

'Then send the originals on to the Americans. We owe the cousins a favour – they do so much for us.'

After Miss Greenwood went on leave, Catesby was surprised how flawlessly Gerald had taken over her clerical duties. He dealt with routine correspondence efficiently and typed replies in Catesby's own style for signature – and sometimes forged that too.

'Sir.'

'I wish you wouldn't call me that.'

'How should I address you?'

'Just say what you want to say.'

'You have an invitation to dinner.' Gerald smiled. 'And it's addressed to "Your Excellency" – so maybe my calling you "sir" is too modest.'

'Is it to some arty thing?' Catesby's dip cover, third secretary in the cultural attaché's section, meant he had to go to a lot of concerts and exhibitions.

'I don't know. The address appears to be a Rhineland *Schloss*.'

'From a baron, I hope?'

'Indeed it is. Baron Roman Nikolai Maximilian von Ungern-Sternberg. Oddly, he signs his name in Russian. Look.'

Catesby took the letter and smiled. 'Have you never heard of Baron Roman von Ungern-Sternberg?'

'No. Is he famous?'

'Infamous, I should say – and very dead.' Catesby went over to a bookcase and found a history of the civil war that tore Russia apart after the Bolshevik Revolution. He turned to the appropriate page and handed the book to Gerald.

'It sounds,' said Gerald, 'that he was a bad guy.'

Catesby shrugged. 'We shouldn't make moral judgements in our business.'

'But you always do.'

Catesby smiled. 'That's top secret.'

Catesby decided it wouldn't be a good idea to drive a British Humber emblazoned with *Corps Diplomatique* number plates to the castle. His section had access to a few German cars with ordinary plates. Catesby chose a rather grand Opel Kapitän six-cylinder saloon – the sort of car a bloated black market profiteer would have wrangled for calling on an ex-SS general who wanted to fence a looted work of art. A lot of the reborn Germany stank. At times, Catesby thought the gallows at Nuremberg and Hamelin hadn't been busy enough. On one occasion, just after the Hamburg Ravensbrück trial, he had met Albert Pierrepoint in the Officers' Mess at Celle. Pierrepoint went on to swing 202 German war criminals – and that day had just executed three women; the oldest sixty-one, the youngest twenty-seven. The hangman sipped his whisky and looked at Catesby. 'It doesn't make any difference, you know?'

'What doesn't?'

'Hanging them. It doesn't deter people.'

'But it punishes them.'

'It certainly does that.'

The road to the castle was winding and when it turned east there were stunning views of the Rhine reflecting the full moon. It was deliciously spooky and a bit corny. The builders of Rhineland castles didn't aim at subtlety and understatement. It was, Catesby thought, the very opposite of his native East Anglia. When the castle finally silhouetted itself against the darker night sky, Catesby counted five turrets. There was also a wall with battlements.

The final approach was across a drawbridge that spanned a deep gully. There was a gatehouse that guarded entry to the outer bailey. A cast-iron gate with spikes had been winched up and Catesby tried not to imagine it crashing through the roof of the Opel Kapitän and impaling him like a kebab. As he drove into the bailey he spotted a Rolls-Royce and decided to park next to it.

As soon as he got out of the car, Catesby heard muffled footsteps approaching – a swishing sound, as if the person were wearing velvet boots. A slight figure appeared out of the shadows wearing a calf-length leather tunic with a high collar and wide cup-shaped sleeves. The dress, thought Catesby, seemed somehow Asian – and the face, when illuminated by the moon, was that of a young East Asian woman. Catesby greeted her in English, 'Good evening.'

The woman answered in German. Her accent, in total contradiction to her appearance, was very upper-class East Prussian. She shook hands, bowed and silently clicked her soft boots.

'Do you live here?' said Catesby.

'I am staying here for the moment, but I don't know for how long.'

'Was it you who invited me here this evening?'

'No, it was my uncle. I must tell you about him before you go up.' She stirred nervously and reached into a deep hidden pocket. 'But you will be safe.' She extended her palm. It bore a dark flat needle-shaped object about two inches long. 'I took the precaution of removing the firing pin from his pistol. But I don't think he would have used it in any case.'

'How very kind.'

'My uncle is mad, but doesn't always seem so. Follow me closely – it's easy to get lost here. A visitor recently died when he stepped on to a staircase that wasn't there.'

The dining room was high Gothic with add-ons. The fireplace was marble with a carved lintel depicting a primal battle between beasts, demons and naked men. The panelling and chairs were carved oak – with more laughing demons. It reminded Catesby of the pew ends at Blythburgh Church that had escaped being vandalised by Cromwell's soldiers. The room was dominated by two life-size oil paintings. One was of Baron Roman Nikolai Maximilian von Ungern-Sternberg wearing the imperial Russian St George's Cross for Bravery. He had won the medal for leading Cossack cavalry charges against German troops in 1915–1916. The Tsar had personally presented him the medal. The other oil painting depicted Nicholas II, the Empress Alexandra and their son, Alexei Nikolaevich, translated to heaven and wearing the hallows of sainted martyrs. Catesby rightly surmised that he was the only atheist socialist in the room – but he still deplored what the Bolsheviks had done to the Tsar and his family. And yet, Catesby realised, he was a murderer too. He was beginning to wish that he hadn't done it.

The host, despite having an Asian niece, had blue eyes and greying blond hair. He greeted Catesby with formality and showed him to a low table where they seated themselves on richly brocaded cushions.

'Do you like fermented mare's milk?'

'I think I could acquire a taste for it.' Catesby held out a silver goblet and studied his host while his eyes were averted pouring.

'The Mongolians call it *airag* – it's their national drink.' The host lifted the lid of a silver tray. 'These dumplings are called *buuz* – they are filled with minced mutton, but any meat can be used.'

'Thank you. Is your niece Mongolian?'

'She is a Manchurian princess, but she also has the blood of my own ancestors. We are Baltic German aristocracy, but related to the royal families of Finland and Russia.'

'Have you a name?'

'Quite a long list of names, but I'm not going to tell them to you.'

Catesby smiled and nodded to the portrait of Baron Roman von Ungern-Sternberg. 'But you obviously are not him?'

'No, but he is a close kinsman.'

Catesby looked at the painting and then at his host. They both had the same mad – completely insane – eyes. One of the baron's eyes was so demented and glaring that Catesby had thought it magnified by a monocle, but there was none. 'There is a resemblance.'

'Thank you for saying so.' The nameless host raised his goblet and drank. '*Airag* has a calming influence. They say you should drink it if you suffer from a nervous condition.'

Catesby laughed.

'You find that amusing?'

'I was thinking of Genghis Khan – did *airag* calm him down?'

'It might have made his strategic planning more thorough. Genghis Khan was a great and visionary conqueror.'

For the first time Catesby noticed a number of strange objects hanging from a bright yellow cord affixed to the oak panelling next to the baron's portrait. 'Are those things Mongolian?'

'What things?'

Catesby pointed.

'They're sacred,' said the man. 'But I'll let you see them and touch them – it is a great honour.' The man got up with difficulty; he seemed to have a gamey leg. He limped across the room, unhooked the yellow cord and brought the objects to the table.'

Catesby guessed they were talismans of some sort. The largest was a round copper disc with an outer ring inscribed with symbols. There were also leather pouches, tiny mirrors with blue strings attached, painted pieces of wood and various chains and charms. The most sinister was a silver plaque embossed with skeletons.

'They're not all Mongolian,' said the host touching the copper. 'This is a Tibetan zodiac disc. The yellow cord, by the way, was blessed by Gautama Buddha. But these are my favourite toys.' The man picked up a pouch with a leather drawstring. He loosened the string and emptied four yellow-white objects on to the table. 'They are Mongolian dice. We use them for divining the future.'

Catesby was tempted to ask how Ipswich Town were going to finish the season, but bit his tongue.

The man picked up the objects and rolled them.

'Good news?' said Catesby.

The man stared for a second. 'Outside force will influence you.'

'They look like bones,' said Catesby.

The man smiled and picked up the first die: 'This one is from a horse.' He then pointed to the other bone dice: 'Cow, goat, man.'

Catesby gave a cold smile. 'May I roll them?'

'Please, you are my honoured guest.'

Catesby gathered the bones. They were dry and smooth. He momentarily pressed the human one between his thumb and forefinger. Then shook them in his fist and rolled them.

The man looked at them from two angles and frowned.

'What's the verdict?' said Catesby.

'Others might try to harm you, better be careful.'

'How do you know they refer to me?'

'You were the one who rolled them.' His host smiled. 'Would you like to try again?'

'No, thank you. I'll leave fate alone.'

'Sometimes that is wise. Meanwhile, we must eat.' The man lifted another silver lid. 'The next course is *khorkhog*. It is a popular dish from the countryside that you eat with your fingers.'

As Catesby ate he felt the mad eyes of the baron burning into the side of his head. And when he looked across the table he saw the same demented eyes staring at him. 'You like *khorkhog*?' said his host.

'It's lovely.'

'It was a staple of the great Khan's warriors as they pillaged the lands of the Jin Dynasty. As you know, they conquered Zhongdu in 1215.'

'Modern Peking,' said Catesby wiping his lips.

'And it will happen again.' The nameless host paused and glared. 'You are a strange person, Herr Catesby.'

'In what way?'

'You have not asked why I invited you.'

'I assumed you would eventually tell me.'

'You assumed correctly. First of all, I owe you an apology – even though I did not personally arrange your attempted murder.'

Catesby struggled to keep his composure. It wasn't what he had expected to hear. He assumed that his host was just another right-wing monarchist nutcase. Catesby reckoned that one in five of his agents claimed blood ties with the Romanovs. He calmed himself. Perhaps the 'attempted murder' was just another of his host's fantasies and had nothing to do with what had actually happened that night in Kensington. Catesby smiled blandly. 'Which particular attempted murder?'

'You mean there have been others?'

'Yes, but I can't give you the details.'

'I didn't realise that being a very junior cultural attaché was such a dangerous job.'

'Artists are very sensitive – and sometimes explosive creatures.'

'The people who tried to kill you were not artists – they were low-level criminals of the most common sort. I was utterly appalled when I found out.'

'Are they likely to strike again?'

'I very much doubt it. They are legionnaires and both have been sent to Indochina.'

'Alsatians?'

'Naturally, that's why they were chosen.'

Catesby nodded. His host wasn't a complete fantasist.

'Your would-be assassins are now part of a Foreign Legion unit composed largely of ex-SS. They have been tasked with fighting behind Viet Minh lines and few are expected to return.'

Catesby glanced up at Baron von Ungern-Sternberg. He was wearing his St George's Cross on his Mongol caftan. How, Catesby thought, the mad baron would have loved the war in Vietnam. And yet, his hands were small and delicate, his right gently holding his left as if to stop it from shaking.

'We had the painting commissioned from a photograph that was taken the evening before he was executed by firing squad. At least the Bolsheviks gave him that honour.'

Catesby smiled. He doubted that the Bolsheviks had regarded von Ungern-Sternberg's execution as an 'honour' – more likely as a warning to others.

His host suddenly looked sly and suspicious. 'How much do you know about my kinsman?'

Catesby had done his homework on von Ungern-Sternberg, but he preferred to hear his host's own account. 'I only know the barest details.'

'My noble kinsman was a great warrior. He fought for the Tsar in East Prussia in 1915 and 1916. Following the Bolshevik revolution, he pledged his allegiance to the Romanovs and fought against the Bolsheviks in Siberia during the civil war. After the White Guards were defeated by the Reds, my kinsman led the remnants of his division thousands of miles into Outer Mongolia. He added Tibetans and Mongol tribesmen to what was left of his White Army Cossacks. Against all odds, he succeeded in driving the Chinese out of the capital Urga.' The host nodded at the portrait of Baron Roman. 'It was a stunning feat of arms – worthy of a Teutonic knight. The Chinese outnumbered my kinsman's tiny army by five to one.'

Catesby knew that his host's version of his kinsman was a glorified one that left out ugly details. He had said nothing about von Ungern-Sternberg's rabid anti-Semitism, his use of unspeakable forms of torture, his execution of anyone with physical defects, his drug addiction – his dinner party set piece of roasting the hearts of his victims and serving them in their own skulls.

'In the end, he was betrayed.'

'By whom?' said Catesby.

His host got up and limped over to the baron's photo. If, thought Catesby, von Ungern-Sternberg should suddenly step alive out of the painting, his host had better hide that physical imperfection or he was for the chop. Catesby smiled bleakly and drank his fermented mare's milk. It was, surprisingly, not unlike a mild, malty ale.

'Who betrayed him? It might have been his Mongol translator, who subsequently disappeared with two thousand kilos of gold – or a Bolshevik agent hidden in the ranks.'

'Was it,' ventured Catesby, 'a good idea to invade Siberia?'

'The peasants of Siberia were ready to rise up against Bolshevism. My kinsman proclaimed Siberia a sovereign Russian land under Emperor Mikhail Alexandrovich.'

Catesby thought it pointless to add that Grand Duke Mikhail Alexandrovich had been executed well before von Ungern-Sternberg's invasion of Siberia.

His host shrugged. 'Perhaps his actions were ill timed. The Siberian uprising never took place. He was betrayed and handed over to the Red Army on 22 August 1921. He was executed by the Cheka on the fifteenth of September. He was ambushed while riding at the head of a column of his most loyal followers and it happened too suddenly to fight back. They were starving; for weeks their only food had been grass and the flesh of lame horses. They say he was gaunt and naked at the end.' The host picked up the yellow Buddhist cord bearing the amulets and talismans. 'This was all he was wearing when they captured him.'

Catesby stared at his host for a long second. When the explanation didn't come, he said, 'Is it not odd?'

'What?'

Catesby nodded at the talismans. 'That the Cheka returned those to you. I didn't realise that they were in the habit of returning personal belongings to the next of kin.'

His host gave a sly smile. 'I have my connections. The Soviet Union is one of the world's most corrupt regimes – and that is why it is about to fall.'

'And what will replace it?'

'Monarchy, of course. Not the feeble sort you have in England, but absolute monarchy. It is the world's most natural and civilised form of government. All our great monuments have been built under kings and queens – the pyramids, the cathedrals, the Potala Palace in Tibet. And all our great works of art too – Shakespeare didn't write his plays in a socialist republic.'

Catesby wasn't going to alienate his host with counter-arguments. He regarded him as an agent, however mad, to be humoured and milked.

'My kinsman was right. It must begin with the restoration of the great Khan's empire – a movement spreading from Mongolia and Tibet. Let me get a map and I will show you the plan.'

The man returned with an ancient atlas where Leningrad was still Petrograd and where the North Sea was the German Ocean. He described a pincer movement of new Mongol hordes heading west while Baltic, Ukrainian and Polish monarchists pressed eastwards. Pointing to Warsaw, he said, 'The *szlachta* are fear-some horsemen, almost the equal of the Cossacks.'

Never, thought Catesby, write off an agent as mad and useless. 'How well do you know the Polish aristocracy?'

'Very well, but many of them are mad and unreliable.'

That seemed to describe his sister's boyfriend, thought Catesby. It was worth a try. 'Does the name Tomasz Król ring a bell?'

The host gave a hearty laugh.

'You do know him.'

'Tomasz Król is a pretender. His claim to be a member of the *szlachta* is exaggerated. He cannot be trusted.'

'Can you tell me more?'

'I don't think so – not yet.'

Catesby racked his brain for another German equivalent, but *Der Elefant im Zimmer* was the only one he could recollect. He looked directly at his host. The blue eyes were growing madder. 'What,' said Catesby, 'did you do in the war?'

'I fought.'

'For whom?'

'For European civilisation and against barbarism.'

Catesby struggled to hide his disgust and revulsion. His host belonged to a cult that glorified violence. You couldn't defeat them with words, but only with violence. London's finest hour was when the heroes of Cable Street drove Mosley and the Blackshirts out of the East End with fists and bricks. But at the moment, Catesby's job was spying. The fighting might come later.

'How did you find out about the attempt to murder me?'

His host picked up the last piece of *khorkhog* and slowly macerated the meat as if the food of the Mongolian nomads was helping him think. He finally wiped his mouth and spoke. 'I heard rumours that you were considered troublesome in some quarters. One has to occasionally make tactical alliances. Among those who wanted you removed were staunch and fierce anti-Communists – who had, in their own way, been fierce warriors in their lost cause.'

Catesby detected echoes of the Gehlen Org.

'I now regret that I did not intervene to prevent the attempt on your life.'

'Why?'

His host smiled. 'You are a Catesby – a descendant of England's most noble family.'

Catesby felt his stomach churn. He ought to have changed his name by deed poll.

'Your ancestor tried to overthrow a regime that began England's degeneration into a nation of shopkeepers and sly merchants. Your country's break with Rome threw away a thousand years of civilisation. Catesby, Fawkes, Percy, Wintour, Keyes and the others were noble knights fighting to restore England to its proper place in the Holy Roman Catholic Empire. Had they succeeded, England and Spain together would have conquered the new worlds for monarchy and not profit.'

Catesby wished there were something stronger than fermented mare's milk. His host's interpretation of history wasn't easy to take in with a clear head. But he didn't want to express scepticism and lose him.

His host smiled. 'A lot of your fellow Englishmen, Protestant shopkeepers too busy counting every last penny in their tills, would not understand what I'm talking about, but you do.'

Catesby smiled back. 'Have you any brandy?'

'I believe I have a Frapin Grand Cru cognac. Please wait a moment while I fetch it.'

Catesby didn't like being left alone in the room with von Ungern-Sternberg. There was something hypnotic as well as demented about his eyes. Catesby knew he would never fall under the spell of such monsters, but he understood why many did. It flattered the ego to be part of an elite secret order. Indeed, it was even part of the allure that attracted many to the Secret Intelligence Service. Catesby's own boss in SIS, Henry Bone, had once given him a priceless piece of advice: 'You must never forget, William, that most of our colleagues are mad.'

His host came back clanking two enormous tulip-shaped glasses and a dusty bottle. As he poured, the night was shattered by the steam-horn of a Rhine barge. Catesby refrained from quoting Heine. The poet's humane liberal politics would have been out of place.

'There are a few things,' said his host in a tone that was low and conspiratorial, 'that I must tell you.'

Catesby waited and watched as his host sipped his brandy. His eyes remained alert, fixed and unblinking above the huge glass.

'Your country is heavily infiltrated by Soviet agents at the very highest level.' The piercing whistle of a train both mocked and underlined his words.

'I have,' said Catesby offering encouragement, 'always suspected that.'

'Would you like to copy their names down?'

Catesby shook his head. 'I've got a good memory.'

The host started with a list of Labour politicians, the usual suspects routinely bandied about by right-wing disinfo, but he also added a Conservative and a Liberal. The host then spat out the name of a novelist, whom he described as 'a Communist pretending to be a Catholic.' He then launched into an attack on a Scottish poet who had indeed been a member of the Communist Party – but then was thrown out of the Communist Party for being a Scottish nationalist and thrown out of the Scottish Nationalist Party for being a Communist. If anyone, thought Catesby, would fight tooth and nail against a Soviet takeover of Britain, it would be that awkward squad poet, Hugh MacDiarmid. Every significant trade union leader was, of course, name-checked. The most disturbing list contained Catesby's own SIS colleagues – one of which he also suspected. Catesby was especially concerned that his host knew the names of some very secret people. The fires of paranoia were easy to light. The list of Communist subversives ended with a Church of England bishop.

'How,' said Catesby, 'did you find out this information?'

'As I said before, the Soviet hierarchy is corrupt even unto itself. The Soviet Union is a rotten tree ready to be pushed over. The Caucasus, the Ukraine, the Baltic and the Islamic south are ready to revolt and the Red Army will not be able to stop them.'

'But an autocratic Tsar would?'

'Of course – and, by the way, Stalin will be dead in less than eighteen months.'

Catesby took the last bit with a great pinch of salt. He was ready to leave and stood up. For the first time he addressed his host in English, 'Thank you for a most enjoyable and informative evening.'

'And thank you for coming.'

Catesby continued the formalities and small talk in English. His host was far from fluent, but Catesby detected what he was looking for – a slight American accent.

Catesby declined the help of his host in finding his way out. He was careful not to step on to a 'staircase that wasn't there' and was relieved when he found himself in the cold night air. He felt that he had spent two hours swimming in a cesspit. As he opened the car door, she loomed out of the shadows. Catesby wondered where 'the niece' had been while they were dining. Had she been waiting there the whole time? She suddenly extended her right arm in a clenched fist salute and shouted something in Chinese – a language Catesby didn't know. She remained rigid like a soldier on parade and then shouted again in English: 'The East is Red! Long live Chairman Mao!'

Catesby gave an ideologically non-committal wave and got

in his car. The drive back to Bonn was going to be long and thoughtful.

Catesby looked at Gerald who had just entered the office carrying a folder bearing the parallel red stripes that denoted top secret. 'Have you signed the card for Miss Greenwood?' asked Catesby.

'Yes.'

'And I wouldn't mind a bob or two as your contribution to the flowers and bath stuff.'

'Not D marks?'

'No, I got the stuff from the NAAFI.'

Gerald searched his pocket and put a half crown on Catesby's desk.

'Thanks.'

'Cheers.

'What else have you got for me, Gerald?'

'Can I ask a question first?'

Catesby yawned.

'Why did you wait until after your visit to give the baron a butcher's?'

'I don't want to frighten him off. If he knew that someone like you was poking around in the undergrowth he might have cancelled the invite.'

'You thought the *Schloss* was a dodgy one, didn't you?'

Catesby nodded. 'Not the castle, but him being in it.'

Gerald opened the file. 'This wasn't easy. The owners of the castle no longer live in Germany – and the person representing them refused to provide a forwarding address. In fact, they refused to talk to me at all until I went back with a frightening *Polizei* type from the BfV.'

Catesby doodled BfV on his notepad and drew an arrow from it pointing east. The BfV – *Bundesamt für Verfassungsschutz* – was the Federal Office for the Protection of the Constitution, the West German equivalent of MI5. 'I wish,' said Catesby, 'you hadn't done that without asking me.'

Gerald gave a sly smile. 'I think I know why.'

'I bet you do. Why?'

'The BfV have been heavily infiltrated by the HVA.' Gerald was referring to the *Hauptverwaltung Aufklärung*, the foreign intelligence branch of the East German Security Service.

'And you thought you were being really clever?'

'Yes, and that's why I used Fritz the Violin.'

'Fucking hell.' Catesby winced. Fritz the Violin, a BfV officer who played and made his own violins, was under high suspicion of being a double agent, but they didn't arrest him because they hoped leaving him free would lead to others.

'And it paid off.' Gerald handed Catesby a piece of paper with a typed name and an address in Paraguay.

'If they're not careful, they're going to blow Fritz's cover.' Catesby closed his eyes and tried to piece together the chess moves involved. The East German intelligence service was not being helpful and idealistic by exposing a Nazi on the run. They wanted to smear the West Germans for protecting war criminals – and the smears were not completely untrue. The HVA also wanted to cause friction and suspicion between the Western intelligence services.

'Have you got it now?' said Gerald.

'This is dangerous. We can't be suspected of cooperating with any East Bloc intelligence service, even if we have mutual interests – like stopping the earth being destroyed by a giant meteor.'

'Why?'

'Because the Americans will use it against us and start shouting about Reds under the bed.'

'Or in the bed.'

'That too. Okay, let's go back to the beginning.' Catesby waved the piece of paper with the Paraguay address. 'How did you get this?'

Gerald smiled. 'No dead letter box, no brush pass or clandestine RV – it arrived in the post.'

'Where from?'

'It had a Bremen postmark.'

Another piece of paranoia bait, thought Catesby. But probably just a coincidence. 'Destroy the envelope, but file the letter.'

'Sure, boss.'

'Tell me about the castle.'

'The agent responsible for letting the *Schloss* finally started spilling the beans after some ungentle persuasion from Violin Fritzie. The person who rented it was a woman...'

'Did she look Asian?'

'No,' Gerald looked at his notes, 'she was about fifty and very glamorous – tall, blue-eyed. She spoke fluent German, but with a slight accent – probably American or Canadian. She said they – the people she represented – wanted to rent the castle as a film set.'

'For a remake of *Frankenstein* or *Dracula*?'

'She didn't say, but the let was for two months.'

'How did she pay? In American dollars?'

Gerald smiled and shook his head.

'You're really full of yourself, aren't you?'

'It is, Mr Catesby, totally delicious. She paid the rent in gold.'

'In bullion?'

'No, in gold Tsarist roubles.' Gerald paused. 'You don't look as surprised as you should be.'

'Don't assume you know what I'm thinking or feeling – you're not my wife.'

'Sorry.'

'Anything else?'

'Yes, I managed to get some info out of a *Putzfrau*.'

Catesby smiled. 'Go on.'

'You weren't the only visitor to the castle.'

'I'm not surprised.'

'The *Putzfrau* wasn't there, of course, when the dinner parties took place, but she knew that they were frequent – two to three a week.'

'Any idea who the visitors were?'

Gerald shook his head.

Catesby closed his eyes and reflected.

**Near Walberswick, Suffolk:** 1 January 1952

The weather was windy and mild; light rain and patches of

sunlight. Frances and Catesby were dressed in jumpers and unbuttoned waterproofs as they crunched along the beach. They were at the head of a dispersed and untidy line of family. The twins and grandparents were closest behind and then a scattering of cousins and in-laws. But none of Catesby's family.

'Next year,' said Frances, 'why don't you ask your mother and Freddie to stay with us for Christmas? There's plenty of room.'

'And there's Tomasz too.'

'Fine – and it doesn't matter if they share a bed. My parents are open-minded.'

'My mother likes to do things her way – and she isn't open-minded.'

'Sometimes,' said Frances, 'I think you want to keep us apart – that you don't want Freddie and me to compare notes.'

Catesby looked out to sea. There were no ships. The docks were shut down for the holidays.

'Why haven't you answered me?'

'I didn't know you had asked a question.'

'You're being beastly, William. I'm going to push you into the sea where you belong.'

'Please don't.'

Frances was the same height as Catesby. She gave him a strong shove down the shingle bank. He finally dug his feet in, but still got one foot wet.

'Children,' shouted her father, 'early to bed and no supper.'

Catesby climbed back up the bank and turned around. He smiled a thank-you to his father-in-law

'That,' said Frances, 'is the first time you've smiled all day.'

'Let's have a race.'

They ran through the loose shingle for a hundred yards and then slowed to walking pace again.

'I don't want the others to hear,' said Catesby.

'Hear what?'

'I can't tell you everything, but the last few weeks have been difficult.'

'What's wrong, William?'

'I think I'm losing my mind.'

'Would you like to talk about it?'

'No.' Catesby stared at the shingle.

Christmas was an awful time of year for him. It was supposed to be a time of joy and family warmth. But when he played games with his stepchildren or read stories to them, the memories flooded back. He turned cold and uncommunicative. He no longer saw happy and live children next to him, but the burned corpses of Oradour-sur-Glane. It was ruining his marriage – his life. But he couldn't talk about it. And he couldn't talk about killing a Nazi war criminal in a ruined U-boot bunker. Catesby's worst fear was that he might become the person he had killed. He often imagined the body floating face down in the Weser back and forth on the tides. The body was found three days later. Catesby was certain that the *Polizei* knew the corpse's identity, but weren't admitting it. The investigation was ongoing, but Catesby was not going to expose himself by taking an interest in it. He didn't feel guilt, but he was guilty – of murder. Worrying about it made Catesby feel selfish and squalid. If the crime was traced back to him, he doubted that diplomatic immunity would protect him from prosecution. In retrospect, murdering the Nazi war criminal had been as pointless as it was illegal. No one had told him to do it. And killing the German hadn't wiped the images of Oradour from Catesby's mind. He still had nightmares and sleepless anxiety.

Frances put her arm through Catesby's. He felt dragged back to a reality that wasn't real.

'Have you found out who took a shot at you?'

'Three shots. I wish I hadn't told you about it – and I hope you haven't told anyone else.'

'Why?'

'I don't want your colleagues at Five to know. They'll find a way to use it against me.'

'You seem very nervous – nervous all the time.'

'I can't settle. I find it difficult to concentrate – I can't sleep at night.'

'It's the war, isn't it? But no one will admit it or talk about it.'

'Like we can't talk about your brothers?' One of them had been killed in an air crash; the other had been burnt to death in a tank in Normandy. But Catesby had known neither of them.

'Maybe we should – but not to Mum and Dad.'

'But one mustn't complain.'

'That's part of the problem.'

Catesby pulled her to him. He hated talking about the war. 'I want to run away.'

'With me?'

'With anyone.'

Frances laughed. 'You are *so* romantic!'

'Okay, with you then.'

'Thanks. Where will go?'

'To the South of France – and we'll breed snails to sell to restaurants.'

'God, you are romantic.' Frances brushed her hair aside and looked closely at Catesby. 'Actually, it might not be a bad idea – and maybe the best way to stay together.'

'I'm glad you agree.' Catesby gave his wife a suspicious look. 'Why did you say going to France might be the best way for us to stay together?'

'Because I've been told that my being with you would not be useful to my career.'

'Who told you?'

'I can't tell you.'

'Why? Are you having an affair with him?'

Frances withdrew her arm from him. 'You are awful. Maybe I shouldn't be with you.'

'Sorry. I'm paranoid – about everything.'

'Then I shouldn't tell you about the anti-Catesby whispering campaign at Leconfield House.'

'I'll be less paranoid if you do tell me.'

'The chief whisperers are…' Frances gave their names.

'No surprises there.' Catesby paused. 'How did you respond to being warned that getting back with me would be bad for your career?

'I became very angry and told him that my personal life was none of MI5's business.'

Catesby smiled. 'But it is.'

'Yes, my response was a bit naive – but there is another issue.'

'He fancies you.'

'Yes, but I assure you I find him utterly repulsive.'

'I'm not really jealous you know.'

'The problem, William, is that your job trained you to be a professional liar.'

'And what about yours?'

Frances shook her head. 'No, absolutely not. My job isn't like yours. I don't recruit agents with lies and spread false rumours. I'm just a watcher, a mere surveillance operative.'

'And you listen and eavesdrop too.'

'Of course.'

'So what have they been saying about me?'

'They say you're too close to our enemies?'

'Which ones? The Russians or the Americans?'

Frances smiled. 'I think, William, your response says it all.'

Catesby smiled back. 'What's the latest from A1A?' He was referring to the top secret MI5 subsection that burgled and bugged.

'I wouldn't know, I'm in A4.'

'I think I've touched a rough nerve.'

'A1A is a sensitive subject – I shouldn't even talk to you about it.'

'There shouldn't be any secrets between us; we're still husband and wife.'

'Some of us are going on to the pub at Dunwich.'

'Please, don't be evasive.'

'I'm worried about you, William. I don't know who you are.'

Catesby looked out to sea. That's where he belonged – somewhere in that dank wet wilderness between Suffolk and his mother's Europe. 'I don't know who I am either.' He bent down and scooped up a handful of gritty shingle. 'But this is my home and I love it.'

'Oh dear, you are a drama queen. And speaking of queens – how's Henry Bone?'

'You shouldn't be judgemental.' Catesby smiled. 'A minute ago you were bragging about being open-minded.'

'I meant it affectionately.' Frances gave him a lopsided look. 'If we don't keep secrets from each other, tell me the latest about the mysterious Bone.'

'Your bosses want to know, don't they?' Catesby shook his head. The relationship between MI5 and SIS, never good, was turning venomous. And his boss, Henry Bone, was one of the reasons.

Frances shrugged.

'Actually,' said Catesby, 'Henry is an enigma to us as well.'

'But he confides in you?'

'Obliquely. I don't think, by the way, you should make assumptions about his love life. He is the heart of discretion – a very prim and refined bachelor. And a very talented pianist.'

'With an impressive art collection?'

Catesby frowned. 'Why don't you just ask the question directly? Is he shagging Anthony Blunt?'

'Is he?'

'No. And they haven't been lovers for decades.'

'But they're still friends?'

'Yes, they socialise occasionally.' Catesby paused and looked at his wife. 'He asked you to interrogate me.'

'Yes.'

'I thought you found him repulsive?'

'Yes, but if you only discussed things with nice attractive people you wouldn't find out a lot in our business.' She looked at Catesby without blinking. 'Don't you realise, William, that I'm more your spy than his?'

There were shouts along the beach. The children were running towards them.

'Tell me quickly,' said Catesby.

'There is a secret cabal, a sect within a sect, who are out of control.'

'What are they doing?'

She told him.

Catesby turned and looked out to sea. His face was etched with pain and fear.

**Washington:** January, 1952

The DDP, Deputy Director for Plans, began each day by reading the Director's Log, a top secret summary of intelligence and operations from around the world. Allen Dulles had been DPP for exactly one year. He was in charge of CIA covert activities, but Dulles knew that after the next election – which General Eisenhower, barring a cardiac event or a flare-up of the Kay Summersby rumours, was sure to win – he would see himself promoted to the top job, DCI, Director of Central Intelligence. Things were looking up for both Dulles brothers. Foster was pencilled in to be Secretary of State.

Allen Dulles took out his pipe and tamped it down with Dobie's Four Square Mature. His man in London bought him tins of Dobie from a tobacconist in Pall Mall and dispatched them to Washington via the diplomatic bag – thus avoiding import duties. It was, thought Dulles, a good way to test diplo bag and courier security. That, at least, was his justification.

As soon as his pipe was drawing well and filling his office with an aromatic haze, Dulles opened up the Director's Log. Sometimes the pleasure of first reading was pre-coital, like the first sight of a young woman disrobing and the thought of what would ensue, or post-coital, the warm after-glow of a successful black op. For the DPP, intelligence operations and extra-marital sex were closely linked. Both were about the pleasure of exploring the unknown.

Dulles's man in London provided far more than pipe tobacco. He seemed to have penetrated the British Security Service to its very heart.

Major General John Alexander Sinclair has won approval of the Joint Chiefs of Staff and the Joint Intelligence Committee to replace Major General Sir Stewart Graham Menzies as Chief of the British Secret Service.

The DPP sucked his pipe and frowned. He would miss Menzies

whom he regarded as a wily coot. Menzies was a thorn in the side of the Labour Party, which from Washington's perspective was a good thing. Dulles also suspected that Menzies had more to do than he ever admitted with the Zinoviev letter. The letter was a forgery, allegedly signed by Grigori Zinoviev, head of the Communist International, addressed to the Communist Party of Great Britain calling for a workers' uprising. Copies of the forged letter were sent to the press four days before the 1924 general election scuppering Labour's chances. Allen Dulles knew Sinclair only slightly, but he had heard that Sinclair was a man of 'great personal integrity'. It was a quality that might be admirable in a husband, at least from the wife's point of view, but Dulles wasn't certain that 'great personal integrity' was the best character trait for the head of a secret intelligence service. The right-hand side of the Director's Log was for 'actions and comments'. Dulles uncapped his fountain pen and wrote a note for OSO (Office of Special Operations) London: *Please send a frank assessment of Major General Sinclair. Opinions, please, from your contacts in MI5 and your man in SIS – and we need more contacts in the latter. AD.* He went on the next item, which seemed indeed from SM/HOUND, OSO's sole informant in SIS.

Conservative sensitivity to Labor charges of 'warmongering' is becoming a worrying political factor in British politics. It has led Foreign Secretary Eden to recently redefine British foreign policy objective towards

(a) a reduction of the temperature of international debate and
(b) a resolution of certain areas of conflict with the Soviet Union by building a mosaic of lasting peace.

SM/HOUND indicated his personal concern lest this policy curtail or preclude more aggressive Secret Service operations, such as air dispatch of agents behind the Iron Curtain. Eden's fear is that such operations would involve too great a risk of adverse publicity in the British press if uncovered. Such publicity would be capitalized on by Labor who would then accuse the government of risking war with the USSR. Such British timidity could seriously jeopardize our operations behind the Iron Curtain.

Dulles frowned and closed his eyes. He tried to obliterate the annoying news from London with a sex fantasy about a liaison scheduled for lunchtime. She was a young journalist – journalists were almost too easy. The DPP opened his eyes and focused on business instead of fellatio and spanking – apparently, she liked that. His intelligence network covered many spheres. The problem in the British sphere was the Labour Party – they even weakened the resolve of the Conservatives. There were two solutions to Labour: either destroy it or reform it. The latter was probably the better idea. There was a pro-American faction within the Labour Party that needed to be cultivated – and plans for that were already in progress. Dulles glanced back at the log. The next item was good news from OSO London.

Our man, SM/REVEAL, from the London *Daily Express* called on me this morning for a background fill-in for an article he is preparing for publication about Communist infiltration in the UK. I provided him with those materials we have available explaining that he must disguise the source. SM/REVEAL is a master of conjuring innuendo out of partial facts and half-truths. SM/REVEAL has enemies in all the right places, especially left-wing academia and the Labor Party. I suggested that we check his article for 'accuracy' when he completes it.

Dulles drew on his pipe and sat back. The British journalist was a gem – and he was sure there were more like him. Dulles leaned forward to pen a note in the 'actions' column. *I would like to have a private meeting with SM/REVEAL if he comes to Washington. Please use him also as conduit for DISINFO, but make sure that the planted stories are plausible. Please advise DPP which Labour politicians could be most usefully targeted by SM/REVEAL.*

Dulles walked over to the window. The view from 2430 E Street was bleak and unimpressive. Through the bare winter trees he could see the severe modern lines of the State Department, the ugliest public building in the capital. *Deo volonte*, his older brother would soon be installed on the hallowed 'seventh floor' as the 52nd United States Secretary of State – following in the footsteps of his grandfather, John Watson Foster (32nd US Secretary of State) and his uncle, Robert Lansing (42nd). Allen Dulles found his office accommodation cramped and undignified. The E Street site had formerly been the US Navy Bureau of Medicine and Surgery. Dulles sometimes imagined that he could detect a lingering whiff of formaldehyde. He had been assured that the CIA HQ was temporary, but plans for relocation were still undecided. The DPP went back to his desk.

The next item in the log was a piece of what Dulles called 'oriental exotica', but still something to be taken seriously in the fight against the Communist menace.

> Gayalo Thondup, another brother of the Dalai Lama, has arrived in the U.S. accompanied by his Chinese wife and child. At present, the three are guests in Virginia of the Dalai Lama's brother Tak-teer, supported by the CIA-controlled Committee For A Free Asia.
>
> The Dalai Lama of Tibet has responded to the State Department message conveyed to him in July by his elder brother, offering covert US assistance to maintain the autonomy of Tibet. The response expressed deep regret that the Dalai Lama was unable to take immediate advantage of the US offer. The Dalai Lama said that he was forced by circumstances and the needs of his people to return to Lhasa but hoped that the US would not lose confidence in him and would continue to be friendly.

Dulles emptied the ash from his pipe and folded his arms. The expansion of Red China was an enormous strategic problem. The surprise intervention of Chinese land forces in the Korean War had been a disaster for the Americans. The Chinese vastly outnumbered the US Marines and soldiers, who had reached Korea's northern border and been poised on the brink of victory, and hurled the Americans back down the Korean peninsula. And there was now a personal factor for Dulles. His only son, Allen Macy Dulles, was serving as a Marine lieutenant in Korea.

The first problem was China. What America needs, thought Dulles, is a Mongolian ally – a new Genghis Khan. And are not the Mongolians faithful adherents to the Dalai Lama's form of Buddhism? Things were linking up in the DPP's mind. Never dismiss an op or an agent as too bizarre, too strange. The world was full of screwballs who worshipped other screwballs. Dulles was pleased that he had never dropped ST/ATARS. He wasn't expensive to run; he was dripping with Romanov gold. But he did want funding and weapons for guerrilla operations along the Soviet Union's southern borders from Turkmenistan to Mongolia. ST/ATARS argued a good case in favour of monarchy – and so, remembered Dulles thinking back to his student days at Princeton, did Thomas Hobbes in *Leviathan*. Dulles picked up his pen and wrote an action note: *Can we arrange a clandestine meeting between Gayalo Thondup and ST/ATARS? DPP would also like to know more about ST/ATARS fishing trip along the Rhine.* He knew it would be difficult for ST/ATARS seldom stirred from his fake Mongolian palace in Paraguay.

The DPP went to the next page of the log. It was London again.

OSO Update: SM/OATSHEAF is now a director of import company Montague Meyer who specialize in timber imports from the Soviet Union. OATSHEAF is obviously using high-level Soviet contacts that he made during his frequent visits to Moscow while President of BOT (Board of Trade). His new position will give him reason, 'cover?', to make frequent visits to USSR.

Allen Dulles picked up his unlit pipe and aimed it eastwards: 'Get him!' OATSHEAF was a very sore point in the Pentagon as well as CIA. While President of the BOT, OATSHEAF had negotiated the deal that sent Rolls-Royce jet engines to the Soviet Union in return for cattle feed. The Sovs, of course, broke their contractual agreement on patent and reverse engineered the Rolls-Royce engines to produce jet engines for the MiG-15s that wreaked havoc in the skies above Korea.

There were many in Washington who wanted SM/OATSHEAF prosecuted for 'trading with the enemy'. Dulles, however, was not one of them. During the 1930s, he and his brother had worked for Sullivan and Cromwell, a law firm that had been brokering deals between Wall Street and Nazi Germany. In 1935, Allen Dulles visited Germany and returned very disturbed about Hitler's regime. He recommended that the firm close its Berlin office. His brother objected strongly, but the partners finally voted to close the Berlin office. Unfortunately, Foster later backdated documents to falsely record that the Berlin office had been closed in 1934. It was a sleeping dog that the Dulles brothers did not want to disturb.

Dulles re-tamped his pipe and lit it. He wanted to calm himself and think clearly and contextually. The Rolls-Royce engines to Russia fiasco was a symptom of a wider-ranging British disease. Socialism and cuts in military expenditure were bigger problems. The island of Great Britain was the USA's most important offshore base. If the rest of Europe fell to the Red Army, Britain would remain as an unsinkable – not matter how bombed and battered – American aircraft carrier. The USA still did not have missiles with sufficient range to hurl themselves across the polar icecap at Russia. Britain, whether the British people liked it or not, was a bastion of last resort and must not be allowed to wobble or sell out. Dulles began writing. *DPP to OSO London: Everything possible must be done to destabilize and neutralize…*

## Broadway Buildings, London: January, 1952

Henry Bone was staring out the window and cradling his long fine fingers around a saucer and cup from an eighteenth-century Sèvres tea service. The hand-painted roses on the cup were blushing. Catesby wondered if the original owners had been guillotined in The Terror. Bone had been silent for several minutes, but finally spoke in quiet even tones – more to himself than Catesby. 'The VE celebrations were a lie. We lost the war – to the Americans.'

Catesby wasn't paying attention. He was preoccupied with another matter. The cat had been lying in ambush waiting for him. The first stage of the seduction had been brushing against his legs and purring with tail up. Catesby replied with 'tsik, tsik, tsik' bird noises and held an index finger tauntingly above the cat, who finally stood up on his hind legs with a throaty purr and rubbed a nose and ear against Catesby's finger.

'Did you say something?' said Bone.

'Sorry, I was talking to the cat.'

'Hmm, he's hungry; that's why he's playing the harlot.' Bone sighed and left his window-gazing. He put his cup and saucer on a sideboard and went back to his desk. 'Please sit down, Catesby, you're making me nervous.'

As soon as Catesby lowered himself into the leather armchair, the cat plopped onto his lap.

'Don't think he likes you,' said Bone sliding behind his desk, 'he knows you're an easy touch.'

'What's his name?' said Catesby stroking.

Bone frowned. 'Zadok. I know, it's dreadful. I didn't name him. In fact, he's not even my cat.'

Catesby smiled.

'Zadok belongs to a neighbour – who, as you ought to have guessed, is a musician.'

'And you're looking after Zadok while your neighbour is – on holiday? But surely, not this time of year. Is your neighbour visiting friends?'

'I don't think he has any friends in Wormwood Scrubs, but he may have made a few since he began his sentence.'

'What interesting neighbours you have.'

'He isn't a common criminal. He was, however, indiscreet and was sentenced under a barbaric law.'

'I see.'

'In any case, he should be out in less than two months.' Bone smiled. 'My neighbour used to summon Zadok by putting "Zadok the Priest" on his gramophone, but I haven't got the record.'

'So you play a piano version and he comes running?'

'You are clever, Catesby.' Bone lifted a folder on his desk. 'And thank you for writing this report.'

Catesby stirred nervously. He wasn't sure he should have put it in writing. 'What are you going to do with it?'

'I'm going to put it in the burn bag.'

'Thank you.'

'I'm not even going to take notes – I'll rely on your memory for anything I forget.'

Catesby looked at Zadok. 'Shhh.'

'If cats could talk, our friends at Five and Scotland Yard would run out of notepads.'

Catesby began to stroke the cat who purred blissfully.

'You have a rapport with animals, don't you, Catesby?'

'As you said, they know I'm a soft touch.'

'Have you still got Schwarzer Hermann?'

'Yes, he's a noisy bugger.' Black Hermann was a mynah bird that Catesby had inherited from his SIS predecessor in Germany. The predecessor had been sold the bird in 1945 by a very worn middle-aged woman who wanted nothing to do with it. There was a sad history attached to the bird. The woman's son had been a waiter in a café frequented by an underground youth group called the *Edelweisspiraten*. The Edelweiss Pirates hid deserters, tried to avoid military conscription and often stalked Hitler Youth groups and beat them up. Black Hermann was the café's mascot and had mastered a German vocabulary of three words: *Deutschland kaputt* and *Scheisse*. In the closing days of the war,

71

the café was raided by the Gestapo looking for Edelweiss Pirates, but only found the woman's son and Black Hermann – who kept screeching *Deutschland kaputt*. The Gestapo arrested the teenage waiter for spreading defeatism and summarily executed him. Neither Catesby nor his predecessor had ever worked out why the Gestapo hadn't executed the mynah bird as well – nor why the bird eventually stopped shouting *Deutschland kaputt*.

Bone perched his half-moon reading glasses on the end of his nose and picked up a sheet from Catesby's report. 'Your host at the Rhineland castle may not be as mad as you think – and it could be useful that you linked him to an address in Paraguay.' Bone paused. 'But maybe not directly in an intelligence sense.'

'In what sense then?'

'I have a friend who is an art dealer – in fact, he used to work with us. You must meet him. It would go with your dip cover as a cultural attaché.'

Catesby sensed that Bone was scheming. The best way to deal with him when he was like that was not to ask questions – for then Bone simply shut up – and just let him scheme.

'His name is Tommy.'

'Who?'

'The art dealer. Next time he has a party, I will get you an invitation.'

'Thank you.'

'The important thing,' continued Bone, 'about Russia's aristocratic diaspora is that they are everywhere – and know everyone. There are, I believe, rather a lot of them in Hollywood.'

Catesby detected a note of snobbery in Bone's voice, but didn't comment.

Bone was now re-reading the rest of the report and looking concerned. He finally looked up. 'What your wife has told you is very disturbing.'

'Do you think she is being alarmist?'

Bone shook his head. 'No.'

'It's not a conspiracy,' said Catesby, 'they're too stupid to run a conspiracy.'

'How little you know about conspiracies, Catesby. They don't appeal to geniuses.' Bone smiled. 'No disrespect intended for your famous ancestor.'

'He's not my ancestor. I wish people would stop harping on about it – the name's a coincidence.'

'If you go back far enough most of us share the same forebears – that's what makes noble ancestry such nonsense.'

Catesby raised an eyebrow.

'Do I surprise you?'

'I didn't expect, Henry, to hear you express such egalitarian sentiments.'

'How little you know about me.'

Catesby looked at his boss. Bone's face bore the half-smile of inscrutability that alternatively charmed and infuriated.

'Back to the conspiracy,' said Bone. 'It may not be fully fledged yet, but there are people in the Security Service who are already starting to weave half-truths into poisonous lies. The Rolls-Royce jet engines were traded to the Soviet Union with the full knowledge and approval of the Air Ministry and MI5. They are now trying to change their tune – and we can see why. The first part of the conspiracy will be a smear campaign. Has your wife managed to see the original documents?'

'I don't believe so.'

'And it's unlikely that she will, for they must be very well buried.' Bone regarded Catesby with hooded eyes. 'Does your wife know that you are passing on this information?'

'I assume that's why she told me.'

'So you don't think you're betraying her trust?'

Catesby shrugged.

Bone looked at the standard civil service clock on his office wall. The clock had a large brown Bakelite surround. The second hand gave a monitory click every time it jerked forward. 'No clock,' said Bone, 'should be pretty – which is why I haven't replaced that Kafkaesque monster. Time is a relentless, ugly process and we should be reminded of the fact.'

Catesby was tempted to tease Bone about his philosophising, but held his tongue. He wondered if his boss had been drinking and the tea was a cover ploy. It had been rather late for tea-drinking.

'Have you, Catesby, ever been to the underworld?'

'Metaphorically?'

'No, in reality. Surely, you've heard of Q-Whitehall?'

'But I've never achieved the status necessary to be privy to its secrets.'

'Your luck, if not your status, has changed.' Bone nodded at the clock. 'It's past closing time. Most of our colleagues are now well on their way back to the ghastly suburbs where they will silently swear about the pram blocking the hallway before walking the dog.'

Catesby gave a wistful smile. Part of him wished that he was one of them.

Bone got up and went to a light-oak wall unit – an oddly tasteful example of civil service issue furniture. He slid open a door and took out two canvas holdalls. 'I keep one,' he said, 'for VIP visitors. I hope it's not too big for you.'

Catesby took the bag and followed Bone out of the office.

'We'll take the service stairs.'

The stairs, lit by low-voltage bare light bulbs, continued below the ground floor. On one level there was the hum of boilers and the gurgle of plumbing, then an unlocked steel door to another level. They were descending into total silence. When they reached the bottom of the staircase they seemed to have come to a cul-de-sac. Bone unzipped his holdall. 'It can be a bit messy in the tunnels.'

Catesby took a pair of blue overalls out of his holdall and slipped them on. They were a bit big and he had to roll up the legs and cinch in the waist. There was also a yellow miner's helmet with a head torch.

'Right,' said Bone, 'you might need to help me with the hatch.' He pointed to a steel ring that was embedded in the concrete floor.

Catesby gave it a heave. It was heavy, but not impossible.

Bone switched on his head torch and disappeared into a vertical unlit shaft. Catesby followed him down a steel ladder.

As they reached the bottom, Bone said, 'I hope they haven't changed the combination.' There was a heavy, round iron door that looked like the door to a bank vault. Bone began to turn the combination wheel. 'If Charon is on duty you might have to put an obolus in your mouth to gain entry. If you haven't got one, I'm sure a sixpence would do.'

'Woof,' said Catesby.

'Who's that?'

'Cerebrus.'

'You should have said, "woof, woof, woof" – Cerebrus has three heads.'

Catesby smiled bleakly at Bone's compulsive one-upmanship as the door swung open smoothly with a hiss. The other side of the door was a brightly lit tunnel about twenty feet wide. Each side of the tunnel had layered racks laden with heavy cables.

'This,' said Bone, 'is the main tunnel of Q-Whitehall – and they don't call it the Styx, but simply Tunnel L. A lot of people know about this one. It requires so much engineering and maintenance that it's impossible to keep its existence totally secret. Most of the cables were laid during the last war by the GPO and Signal Corps so that communications could be maintained during heavy bombing or an invasion.'

'A lot of people at the MoD still complain about the drilling and noise.'

'They shouldn't. The bunkers and tunnels under the Admiralty and Horse Guards are being deepened and reinforced to provide protection against an atom bomb attack. Follow me. I'm going to show you some things you shouldn't know about.' Bone lowered his voice. 'But may have to know someday.'

It was a short walk, only about five minutes, before Bone suddenly stopped and turned to Catesby. 'How many side tunnels have we passed?'

'One on the left and two on the right.'

'Good. I'm glad you were counting.' Bone turned right from the main tunnel into one that was dimly lit and about eight feet wide. After a hundred yards or so, Bone pointed to a steel door on the left, 'That's number 20, originally the Tithe Commission, now part of the Treasury.'

'Should I be taking notes?'

'Mentally, yes.'

They walked fifty more yards and came to an impressively heavy steel door that looked blast reinforced. That part of the tunnel was also better lit.

'And that's where they keep the gold bullion,' said Catesby.

'No, that's where they keep the Prime Minister, Number 10.'

Catesby smiled. 'There's a doorbell.'

'Yes, but I wouldn't advise pressing it. This tunnel is an escape route, but it is frequently used when the PM wants to avoid press cameras and have a quiet chat with someone in Whitehall.'

'He could pop over to Broadway Buildings for a cup of lapsang souchong.'

'I think a strong brandy would be more likely – and he has visited.' Bone paused. 'Did you hear something?'

'Movement behind the door – you shouldn't have mentioned brandy.'

'Let's go. Our tour isn't finished.'

Catesby and Bone retraced their steps to the lower bowels of Broadway Buildings. The air was warm and dry.

'There are twelve miles of tunnel under Whitehall alone,' said Bone.

'Can we get under the Houses of Parliament?'

Bone smiled. 'Absolutely not. Completely forbidden – for historical reasons. And, if there was a tunnel under the Palace of Westminster, I wouldn't want to be found in it with a Catesby. Do you know, by the way, that Fawkes had stored twice as much gunpowder as was needed? If it had gone off the king's head would have landed in the Oval cricket ground.'

'So, in one way, not having a tunnel makes the Houses of Parliament more secure. But, in another way, it makes it more difficult for Members of Parliament to escape. If, say, there was a full sitting and … something awful happened. And having the river blocking one side makes it even more difficult.'

'I am sure, Catesby, that there are people less loyal than yourself who have had the same thoughts – which is worrying. But if, say, there was a whiff of serious danger in the air, any MP with half a brain wouldn't go near the Palace of Westminster.'

'I suppose,' said Catesby, 'that the MPs not attending could be of two sorts: those who were part of a conspiracy and those who had very good intelligence antennae.'

'Or those who were simply seriously paranoid. What's wrong, you look pale?'

'Are you sure we should be having this conversation?'

'I wish we weren't,' said Bone, 'but power is a poison – and even more deadly when it exists in confined spaces and among a group as small as...'

'Our ruling class?'

Bone shook his head. 'That's the usual answer – and the ruling class may well decide the budget and how we conduct international relations. But who are the people on our beautiful island who could – in a fabricated emergency – actually take over?'

'The military, the police, those in control of communications and transport, the press and the Security Service.'

'Not bad, Catesby, not bad.'

'Is there a tunnel that leads to Leconfield House?'

'Would you like to break into the Registry?'

Catesby smiled. 'Of course not.'

'In fact, there is no tunnel to Leconfield House – and MI5 have always regarded it as a slight. They feel that not having direct access to Q-Whitehall somehow devalues them. But they do have machine-gun loops on the top floors. Most of the gun positions face north – as if the real threats would emanate from Islington, Hackney and Tottenham.' They reached a tunnel junction. Bone pointed down a tunnel that was even more dimly lit and mysterious. 'Which direction is that?'

'To the west, towards Buckingham Palace.'

'Well done. Who knows, Catesby? You may one day get a gong – and how impressive it would be if you, as a member of Her Majesty's Secret Intelligence Service, turned up for your investiture through a trapdoor in the ballroom floor.'

One question that bothered Catesby was why Henry Bone had never been 'gonged'. Most officers of his rank had been given, at the very least, OBEs.

'We're coming up to an important tunnel, Catesby. One of the most important.'

'The Ritz Hotel – I've been there, you know.'

'Who hasn't? But the Ritz is too far north – as well as gauche and ostentatious. By the way, keep your voice down, it's here.'

The tunnel branching off was wider and less obstructed than the other side tunnels. There was a slope with wooden slats that had a sprinkling of fine sand.

'Look at that,' said Catesby pointing with his head torch.

Bone frowned staring at the manure.

'Have they got pit ponies down here?'

'No, the cavalry have been exercising.'

They continued for another fifty yards until they came to a large steel door emblazoned with regimental colours. 'That,' said Bone, 'leads to the Wellington Barracks.'

'Ideally positioned, I suppose, to protect Her Majesty from subterranean attack.'

'You ought, Catesby, to be running their press office.'

'You think it could be something more sinister?'

Bone remained silent.

Catesby found himself breaking into a cold sweat.

'How,' said Bone, 'would you block that door and this tunnel?'

It was Catesby's turn to be silent.

'We have, William, to think the unthinkable – it's our job. What do you do if an army turns against its lawfully elected government? It happened in Spain.'

'It's not going to happen.'

'You're more optimistic than I am. We'd best be getting back.'

'Aren't you going to show me the underground entrance into Buck House?'

'Actually, I've never seen it. But I've heard there's an escape tunnel under Green Park and on to Heathrow.' Bone gave a bleak smile. 'Sorry to disappoint you, Catesby, but I don't know every secret.' Bone gave a sideways look. 'There is, however, one more thing I have to show you.'

Bone led Catesby back to the main tunnel where they retraced their steps back towards Broadway Buildings. They came to a set of steps that led over the cables to a door. 'Executive loo,' said Bone taking out a key.

It was, indeed, an ordinary gents with urinals, cubicles and sinks. They both had pees and, while Catesby was washing his hands, Bone opened a door to a closet full of extra loo rolls and mops. 'Look closely, Catesby, what do you see on the ceiling?'

'Absolutely nothing.'

'It's well hidden. What you need to do is press the end of a mop handle onto a spot two inches from the corner at thirty degrees. Just like this.' Bone picked up a mop and demonstrated. At the precise point, the ceiling slightly gave way and there was a distinct click. 'The opening button is covered by a circle of rubber which blends perfectly with the surrounding plaster. Then you push on this shelf with the bleach bottles and, hey presto.' The back wall of the cleaning closet swung open. Bone reached in and flicked a light switch. Bare light bulbs revealed an austere dormitory of bunk beds in tiers of four. 'It's pretty basic,' said Bone, 'but this *is* the bunker of last resort.'

Catesby walked in and noted the thin grey blankets folded, Army barracks-style, on each thin mattress.

'Sheets and pillow cases will be issued,' said Bone. 'There's accommodation here for eighty-four of us. I'll show you the rest of the complex.'

There was a large kitchen well supplied with tinned food, sterilised water and dried food in rat-proof containers. There were toilets and sinks, but no showers – and a small medical room with dressings, splints and morphine. The centrepiece was a 'command and control room' with maps, desks, telephones and radios. 'We have wireless communication,' said Bone, 'provided no one discovers our ground-level antennas, which are connected to road signs for better reception and transmission – not that the signs would survive an attack with atom bombs.'

'So this is a command centre for World War III?'

'Of course it is. Otherwise we would never have got the funding – but we've adapted it for other contingencies. Come into the costume section.'

The room was long and narrow and packed with racks of clothes on hangers. There were military and police uniforms – and kit for firemen, posties and even bus drivers. There were also wigs and women's frocks. 'Our disguise specialist,' said Bone picking a maternity dress from a rail, 'thinks that SIS officers impersonating pregnant women are a sure way to deceive sinister forces.'

'But we employ real pregnant women as well.'

'We'll have to disguise those as police constables with moustaches.' Bone put the dress back. 'This is all utterly absurd – but the next room isn't.'

The room was seriously locked and bolted, but Bone had the key and knew the lock combination too. 'This, Catesby, is where power ultimately resides.'

The room smelt of gun oil, but there were few standard rifles.

'As you can see,' said Bone, 'the emphasis is on street fighting.'

Catesby noticed a predominance of compact submachine guns including Stens, Thompsons and Swedish Kpist 45s. There were also light machine guns and boxes of hand grenades. The most impressive arms, however, were the anti-tank weapons. 'I've seen enough,' said Catesby, 'the whole thing makes me sick.'

'You've had enough war?'

Catesby nodded.

'There are some, however, who like it and can never get enough.'

'I know, I've met them – but the worst war, the most soul-destroying, is civil war. Can we leave this place?'

Bone nodded towards the entrance and shut the armoury door behind Catesby. 'I'm not surprised at your anti-war views, William, but you're not a pacifist – you've killed people.'

Catesby stiffened. He wondered how much Bone knew about Bremen.

Bone continued, 'And how do you square your views with the ruthless things we have to do as members of SIS?'

'The people we use and betray are not innocent civilians. In this game, we are all players and know the rules. What we do in the shadows is far less violent than war.'

'But how far would you go if things escalated beyond covert dirty tricks?'

Catesby didn't answer.

Bone smiled, but his eyes turned to blue steel. Bone was a mysterious man with a mysterious past. He looked hard at Catesby and finally raised a clenched fist in salute. *'¡No pasarán!'*

For a second Catesby thought it was a joke. But the smile faded from Bone's face and he remained with his clenched fist against his temple. Finally, Catesby realised what was expected of him. He raised his own clenched fist. *'¡No pasarán!'*

## Washington: February, 1953

Eisenhower had been elected President the previous November. As a result, Allen Dulles and his brother Foster were appointed to two of the highest offices in the new administration. But in the end, Allen Dulles's promotion to Director of Central Intelligence had left him with a mouth full of ashes. His only son, Allen Macy Dulles, had been seriously wounded by a mortar fragment ten days after the Eisenhower landslide. The shell fragment had penetrated the right side of his son's head and it seemed likely that Allen Macy would be permanently brain damaged.

Dulles had just returned from visiting his son at Bethesda Naval Hospital. When he looked into the young man's eyes he could see that his former son was no longer there. Life had played a dirty trick on him – and, as often happens to people, grief made the new DCI harder and more ruthless than before.

The top item on the agenda was Guatemala – followed, as always, by keeping Britain under Washington's thumb. The code name of the operation to overthrow Guatemala's Jacobo Árbenz was PB/SUCCESS. Dulles had chosen the code name himself and it was going to be nothing less than that. No quibble about Árbenz being elected by a landslide even larger than Eisenhower's, he had to go. Dulles opened the Director's Log to see the latest horror from Central America.

OSO Nueva Guatemala de la Asunción to DCI. Árbenz (ST/ ANDEL) is determined to carry out his program of land reform. He refers to the peasants as 'victims of debt-slavery' – obviously parroting the language of Marxism. Árbenz's latest policy is to expropriate large tracts of un-farmed private land and redistribute it to landless laborers. Just to

show you how stupid he is, Árbenz himself has given up a
large portion of his own land-holdings! This proposed land
redistribution policy is greatly resented by UFCO (United
Fruit Company), who had benefited greatly from Árbenz's
predecessor. UFCO has lobbied us to topple Árbenz – and
pointed out that their investment in the entire region might
be in danger if we do not act.

Dulles lit his pipe to calm his nerves, then picked up his pen: *Is this the beginning of Soviet expansion in the Americas? One battalion of US Marines should be enough.* The DCI went on to the next item in the log.

OSO London to DCI. The annoying thing about the Brits is
that they always want to do things their own way – even
when they're on our side. The British equivalent of Operation
Mockingbird is the IRD, Information Research Department,
which is run by the FO. Do we need both? We could end up
leaking information and payments to the same journalists.

But in the film industry, we certainly outsmarted the
Brits in their own backyard. George Orwell's *Animal Farm*
is set for release next year. There is not a single fingerprint
pointing at CIA funding. We've used go-betweens all the way
and it looks like an authentic all-British production. Orwell,
of course, was a socialist who was damning capitalism as
well as Stalinism, so we've had to alter the script accordingly
– and great credit to OSO operative E. Howard Hunt for
masterminding the scripting. It's going to be an outstanding
example of anti-Communist PSYOP.

More good news: SM/REVEAL of the *Daily Express*
remains firmly in our camp.

The new DCI had mixed feelings about the situation in Britain. British newspapers and British politicians could prove fickle. Dulles hoped that the US would never have to launch a PB/SUCCESS in the United Kingdom – and the best way of avoiding that was influencing the press, the politicians and even the trade union movement. Dulles went to the next log entry. It was from HICOG, High Commission Germany, and highlighted more Brit awkwardness.

OPC Pullach (POB) reports that WILLIAM CATESBY, the British rep at the BND negotiations, continues to be a 'pain in the ass'. CATESBY has always been a ZIPPER (Gehlen Org) skeptic and opposes ZIPPER officially becoming the BND (Bundesnachrichtendienst, Federal Intelligence Agency.) CATESBY maintains that ZIPPER intelligence on Fremde Herr Ost (Foreign Armies East) is often out-of-date, easily acquired from open sources and sometimes wildly inaccurate. CATESBY'S own intelligence assessments are, we must reluctantly admit, often accurate and detailed (perhaps suspiciously so). When asked to share the personality data on his agents, CATESBY always replies that the files are held in London and he does not have access to them. When we request them through our London station, there are always delays and non-compliance.

On occasion CATESBY has had hot-headed arguments with members of Gehlen Org and General Gehlen himself in which CATESBY has insinuated that they have falsified their personal histories and war records.

Dulles put the log down and rubbed his forehead. There were skeletons to rattle in his own cupboard – few people at his level didn't have them. And OPERATION PAPERCLIP was the biggest set of bones. After the war, Dulles had served as station chief in Berlin. In retrospect, he was given too much latitude on which Nazi scientists and intelligence officers should be helped to escape to the West. The biggest PAPERCLIP star was the rocket scientist Dr Wernher von Braun. Dulles knew that slave labour had been used in the rocket factories where von Braun had developed the V-2 rocket – and that as many as 20,000 of the slave labourers may have died from illness, harsh working conditions and executions. In an ideal world, von Braun should have been tried at Nuremberg. But they didn't live in an ideal world and America needed rocket scientists. What concerned Dulles was that President Truman's instructions about Nazi war criminals had been ignored by PAPERCLIP. And a lot of the Brits hadn't been happy either. One British officer, normally a staunch US ally, had been furious because his wife and daughter had been killed by one of von Braun's V-2 rockets. Dulles smiled grimly when he remembered the Scott quote that his father had so loved:

*Oh, what a tangled web we weave*
*When first we practise to deceive*

Allen Dulles wrote an action note in the right column. *ZIPPER will become the BND. The Catesby situation suggests that the Burgess and Maclean defections may just be the tip of the iceberg. We all know that Philby is a Soviet spy, but for some asinine reason the Brits won't do anything about it. It's the 'old boy' network.* Dulles paused and gave a wry smile. He wasn't unaware of the irony of a Dulles complaining about an 'old boy' network.

Dulles continued to the next log entry. It bore an OD/ACID cryptonym, which indicated it was from the State Department and not CIA. OD/SONOF, the new labor attaché in London was hot stuff. The McCarthyite witch-hunters wrongly regarded him with suspicion because he had been a Marxist in his youth, but this background gave him the cover he needed to infiltrate the British trade union movement and the Labour Party. OD/SONOF was a gem.

OD/SONOF London to DCI. The continued rise of the Bevanite socialist wing of the Labor Party should be a source of serious concern for Washington. We should do everything possible to support Hugh Gaitskell as next leader of the Labor Party. Gaitskell is NOT a socialist and would be a reliable US ally. It was Gaitskell as Chancellor who introduced prescription charges to divert money to UK defense spending. The key dangers of the Bevanites to US interests are:

1  Nuclear disarmament.
2  The possibility of Britain's future withdrawal from NATO.
3  A British foreign policy that would be at best skeptical of
   Washington; at worst, hostile.
4  Decolonisation despite the threat of Communist
   encroachment.
5  The Bevanites believe in state control of what they call
   'the commanding heights of the economy' including
   nationalization of steel.

If Hugh Gaitskell becomes leader of the Labour Party
all this will be avoided. In many ways, a right-wing Labour
prime minister would be preferable to a Conservative one.

The most likely Bevanite challenger to Gaitskell is
SM/OATSHEAF. Everything must be done to undermine
OATSHEAF – and elements of the UK Security Service may be
complicit in this.

Dulles wasn't surprised about the dangers of Britain stepping out
of line with US policy, but thought that OD/SONOF might be
advised to lower his profile. He had been sent a clipping from the
*Daily Mirror* describing OD/SONOF's Kensington flat as a 'salon
for Gaitskellites'. He picked up his pen. *Excellent work, but beware
of being regarded as a spy from the US embassy. Try to keep a more
low-key and covert profile. But, by all means, liaise with members
of the British Security Service who are sympathetic to undermining
SM/OATSHEAF and British socialism in general. We must keep
US fingerprints off the weapons involved. The trick is to influence
British behavior in ways in which that influence cannot be linked
to the USA.*

Would, thought Dulles sitting back and pulling on his pipe, a
PB/SUCCESS operation ever have to be mounted in Britain?

Catesby was proud of what he had done. Getting an agent to whistle another tune wasn't easy – and it had taken months of repetition and hard work. Some sceptics might say that the agent concerned neither believed nor understood the words he was parroting, but when Catesby looked into one of his eyes – it wasn't possible to look into both at the same time – he was certain that the agent concerned had true conviction and was a true fan. Catesby had finally worked out why Black Hermann had stopped croaking *Deutschland Kaputt*. It was because, after 1945, the bird no longer heard his owner – now long dead – muttering those words as he washed glasses behind the bar while artillery shells detonated in the near distance. But Hermann still squawked *Scheisse,* because he still heard people in the office – both Brits and Germans – using the word every time they mistyped a word or misplaced a file.

It isn't easy to teach a mynah bird to say *Ipswich Town*. The *psw* is difficult for a bird, but *ich* – a bit Germanic in any case – and *Town* were easy. It took a long time, but Hermann finally started gurgling 'Ipswich Town' and then shouting it. The problem was it often came out followed by the only other word that Hermann could squawk – and 'Ipswich Town *Scheisse*' wasn't what Catesby wanted to hear. He was certain there was a saboteur in the office, but he wasn't going accuse Gerald directly. Catesby soon realised that a mynah bird's brain doesn't differentiate between words. As far as the bird was concerned, the three words were just a single sound – and it was sabotage. The trick was to say all the words you wanted at once and eventually the bird would repeat them. It took a few weeks, but soon Hermann was regularly squawking 'Ipswich Town *Wunderbar*'. Catesby soon learned that he only had to whisper the phrase to get Hermann going – and Town needed a lot of cheering as they had just lost their fourth match in a row, a humiliating 1–6 defeat to Millwall at home. Catesby was musing how to smuggle Hermann into the North Stand at Portman Road, when he saw Gerald looming above his desk with a loop of key tape from a 5-UCO cipher machine hanging from his forearm.

'That looks important,' said Catesby. The ponderous 5-UCOs, which consumed lorry loads of key tape, were only used for secret communication.

'I don't know, sir, I haven't read it.'

'Thanks.' Catesby unhooked the tape from Gerald's arm. It was from DIR/W.EUR/SOVBLOC, but as was the protocol never mentioned the holder's name. The message was brief for the amount of tape consumed. RETURN TO LONDON IMMEDIATELY FOR CONSULTATIONS. Catesby balled up the key tape and stuffed it in the burn bag. Henry Bone never wasted a word or let on to anything even when using the most secure communications. He knew there were eyes everywhere.

'I bet,' said Gerald, 'it's about Stalin's death and the Sov succession.'

Catesby nodded. 'I'm sure you're right.'

The Soviet ruler had died a fortnight before, but nothing was coming out of Moscow. Catesby's intuition told him that Bone wanted to talk about something else and that Stalin's death was convenient cover for his recall.

**Green Park, London:** 26 March 1953

The earliest daffodils had already started to shrivel into yellow parchment – and Ipswich had just lost their fifth match in a row. Things weren't going well with Catesby's love life either. Frances was polite and friendly, but she wouldn't let him stay the night. 'I don't want to confuse the twins,' she said. 'But what about me?' said Catesby. 'It doesn't matter,' she replied, 'you're always confused.'

It didn't look like it was a going to be a good spring for Catesby. The daffodils, he thought, said it all: so bright, so early, so full of promise and the first to fade – like a seventeen-year-old turning ninety overnight.

'I wanted fresh air,' said Bone. 'And I love spring in London.'

Catesby nodded and stared at the Georgian terraces that over-looked the park from the east. There were so many windows, so many prying eyes. He wondered why Bone always brought him to Green Park for confidential talks. They must look so conspicuous. Two bowler-hatted civil servants strolling along with perfectly rolled umbrellas, so obviously having a chat about the budget or foreign policy – or espionage – certainly something they couldn't talk about in front of colleagues in Whitehall. 'Have you brought me here,' said Catesby thinking aloud, 'because you think your office is bugged?'

'My office is not bugged – and no one would dare.'

'How can you be sure?'

'I don't share my anti-surveillance procedures – and nor should you yours.' Bone sighed. 'You have a way, Catesby, of ruining a beautiful spring day with your tedious concerns.'

'It isn't nice. It's turning windy and wet – look at those clouds.'

Bone smiled. 'You've made my point. Let's sit down.'

Catesby turned to a bench facing the Georgian terrace.

'That's a bit foolish, isn't it,' said Bone nodding towards the tall houses overlooking the park. 'You know who lives there, don't you?'

'No.'

'Sit there.' Bone pointed his brolly at a bench with its back towards a townhouse of four storeys that loomed behind them about a hundred yards away.

'Who lives there?'

'A press baron with a grudge against the Secret Intelligence Service. Imagine a minion with a pair of binoculars who can read lips.'

'Is he one of those who think we're the London branch of Moscow Central?'

'Very likely. But the reason for his grudge is more personal. One of our former officers went off with the baron's wife – really was a case of musical beds. She had his baby last year – and he's just published a novel about an SIS spy.'

'Based on you, Henry?'

Bone laughed. 'Our surnames are similar, but the resemblance ends there. I was asked to read parts of it to make sure it didn't contravene the Official Secrets Act – and it didn't come close.'

'Was the novel any good?'

'It's what the Italians would call *divertente* – but the prose style has the silkiness of an ironic mandarin. The wife, by the way, is a fascinating woman.' Bone gestured behind him with his thumb at the large Georgian house overlooking the park. 'She used to live there when she was married to the press baron – husband number two – number one bought it in the war.'

'Did she like it?'

'The house? Absolutely not, it's ghastly – and she knew it. We laughed about it. The exterior, as you probably noticed, reprises the bogus French Renaissance style of the late nineteenth century. The interior isn't much better. Nothing is symmetrical and sedate. Among the most hideous excesses are the pulvino architraves and a frieze with husk festoons and overly ornate paterae.'

'Phew, I can see why you don't want that press baron to read your lips. He'd be furious.'

'You're wrong, Catesby. People like that don't care about aesthetics – or the opinions of those who do. In fact, they despise people like me and Anthony as effete. The divide – and it isn't a class divide, but a divide within the class itself – begins at boarding school and continues in later life. Far from being ashamed of their bad taste, they like to flaunt it. It's the rich bully shouting "fuck you" to the world.' Bone smiled. 'But, William, I'm not telling you anything that you don't already know.'

Catesby smiled bleakly.

'As a Marxist, William, your understanding of class division and conflict has always been perceptive.'

Catesby frowned. When a senior officer of the Secret Intelligence Service refers to you as a Marxist, one might detect the beginnings of an interrogation. For a second, Catesby wondered if Bone might be wired up for recording. He decided to play safe. 'I am not a Communist and have never been a member of the Communist Party. I have been a member of the Labour Party, but had to give up my membership because it is deemed incompatible with my role as an SIS officer – a rule, by the way, that I consider unfair as well as our being banned from trade union membership.'

'But you deny being a Marxist?' There was something sly in Bone's voice.

Catesby wondered if there was a pile of his undergraduate essays that someone from personnel was sifting through with a prying eye. 'No one can completely ignore the influence that Marx has had on contemporary thinking. In that context, most people who have been to university – or have ever used the words proletariat, bourgeoisie or class – are to some degree Marxists.'

'And what about yourself?'

Catesby shrugged. 'I see Marx as a nineteenth-century proponent of scientific theory. Marx tried to analyse human society using the same scientific method that Darwin applied to natural history. But Marx failed to grasp some of the nuances of class in Britain – subtle nuances of humour and interaction that stop us from ripping each others' throats out.' Catesby smiled. 'But maybe that's just me being naive and optimistic.'

'Or you being patriotic?'

'I don't like the word.'

'But I do,' said Bone. 'I love this country with a passion – and, if you haven't noticed that, you realise nothing about me.'

Catesby stared across the park towards Buckingham Palace.

Bone gave a slight head bow and touched the brim of his bowler. 'And I am a royalist too.'

Catesby bit his tongue. There were many things he could say – especially about Bone's palace-ensconced friend – but would not. He had once received a report from one of his East German honey-traps transcribing a conversation with a Soviet MGB agent about a certain Entoni Frederik Blant. The MGB agent – spouting vodka-fuelled indiscretion – had angrily referred to 'Entoni Blant' as a 'two-faced shit'. Catesby had passed on the report to Bone who had received it with a satisfied smile. Spying was a far more complex game than chess. It was a game where a red bishop could suddenly change into a white knight – while the pawns, like Catesby, looked on in confusion.

'We must,' said Bone, 'stay two steps ahead of them.'

Catesby didn't need to ask who 'them' were. On one level, 'them' were those who posed a danger to Bone and his friends. On a more idealistic level, 'them' were the forces who wanted to turn Britain – a country that Bone genuinely loved – into something ugly and unrefined. Despite their deep personal differences, at some point the ideal Britains of Catesby and Bone overlapped. There was friction between them, but they were allies – in what was probably a lost cause.

Bone looked closely at Catesby. 'The funeral, by the way, is next Tuesday at Windsor and I've been asked to represent SIS.'

The Queen's grandmother had just died. Catesby had only known Queen Mary from news photos and cinema clips. She had struck him as austere. 'Will the coronation be postponed?'

'No, it's going ahead as planned on the second of June – but that's still top secret.'

'Are you going to be invited?'

'I would think so.'

'I bet the Sovs will be there too.'

'Only the Ambassador – it's diplomatic protocol.'

'But none of the Romanovs?'

'Your attempts at droll humour, Catesby, always fall flat.'

'But I think the Sov Ambassador would rather talk about them than Stalin's successor.'

Bone smiled. 'Now that, Catesby, was funny. But we've got sidetracked.'

'You haven't brought me here to talk about funerals and coronations.'

Bone shook his head and stared at the ground. 'Things appear calmer than they are, but the pot is slowly boiling. We always think that Britain is different – more stable – than other countries. But we might be wrong.' Bone paused. 'Treason usually, but not always, comes from the right wing. It happened in Italy in 1922. We saw what began in Germany with the Beer Hall Putsch in 1923; it happened in Lisbon in 1926; in Spain in 1936. Perhaps I'm talking drivel and nonsense.'

Catesby nodded.

'Humour me, William. If you were staging a *coup d'état* in our green and pleasant land, how would you do it?'

Catesby smiled. 'The first thing I would do would be to put a bullet in your head – and then in my own.'

'That's very flattering – and then what?'

Catesby tilted his head towards the press baron's mansion. 'And then I'd get him and others like him on the side of the coup plotters. I wouldn't do it through force or threats; I'd do it through flattery and persuasion – and also their self-interest in terms of money and gongs. I'd make the press barons feel that they were medieval barons – real players carving up and controlling Britain.'

'And what would you, Catesby, a mid-ranking intelligence officer on £1,500 per annum, have to offer someone as grand and rich as a press baron?'

'Something that money can't buy – or shouldn't be able to buy – Her Majesty's most closely guarded State Secrets.'

'Precisely. Secrets are gold bullion – and intelligence officers are, relatively speaking, paupers compared to the press barons. It's an institutional weakness, a fatal weakness. Which is why any officer who violates the Official Secrets Act should be hung, drawn and quartered. Don't you agree?'

Catesby nodded.

'The Security Service is out of control – and so are we.' Bone smiled. 'At least, we don't have to worry about budget cuts – any minister who dares make such a suggestion will be covertly briefed against and smeared.' Bone looked at Catesby and laughed. 'And you think we need a trade union?'

Catesby shrugged.

'Secrets are currency, William – and we control the exchange rate. Why are you laughing?'

'Thank you for destroying my naive illusions.'

'You've never had any illusions. Back to the coup – what next, William?'

'The Americans. The plotters would need Yank money and Yank glamour to support the coup.'

'What about US Marines?'

'Absolutely unnecessary and it would be a mistake. British people would never accept foreign troops patrolling our towns. The plotters would need our military on their side.'

Bone stared into the distance. 'We have to take risks. If others ignore the Official Secrets Act, so do we.' Bone paused. 'Don't you think it's time to tell him?'

Catesby hadn't a clue who Bone was talking about, but nodded agreement.

Bone reached into his coat pocket and handed Catesby a thick envelope fastened by string. 'Don't look now. But when you do, you will find documents and photos that neither of us should have.'

'What should I do with them?'

'Show them to him – but don't let him keep them. Bring them back to me.'

**Hampstead Garden Suburb:** Saturday, 28 March 1953

A well-polished Oxford Morris saloon was parked outside the house gleaming in the cold late-morning sun. It was a quiet tree-lined street. Catesby looked at the house. It was just as perfect and pristine as the car. He couldn't take it all in and decided to keep walking. He had never been to this part of London before – and it seemed wrong to call it London. It was something else.

Never before had Catesby felt such a complete alien. He knew city; he knew countryside. He had been in posh houses and squalid houses – but this was something completely different. It was every clerk's and skilled worker's dream of an English heaven. It was a garden suburb. Catesby continued walking until he came to a park with playing fields, tennis courts and a cricket pavilion. A football game was in progress and two couples were playing doubles. This, Catesby knew, was what the people wanted and deserved. But very few of them were going to get it. The place was indeed seductive – and a different Catesby in a different century might have been happy there. But today Catesby felt like a cuckoo invading a perfect English nest. He knew, of course, that the parent birds of the garden suburb were too polite and friendly to attack him with sharp beaks. Instead, they would invite him in for tea and engage him in witty conversation – a much more lethal way of dealing with him than sharp beaks. Catesby turned around and retraced his steps to the house with the Oxford Morris saloon. He had a job to do.

The woman who answered the door was very pretty and tidy looking. The thing that most impressed Catesby was the warmth of her smile. She didn't ask who he was or why he was there, just 'Good morning.' He could hear two children in the background.

Catesby took off his trilby and tried a warm smile, but it was a facial expression that didn't come natural to him. He fingered the brim of his trilby and looked down. He wished that he was a million miles away. 'I'm so sorry to disturb you on a Saturday morning, but … I'm from the Foreign Office.' It was technically true. SIS was under the jurisdiction of the FO, just as MI5 was under the Home Office.

'Please come in. Let me take your coat – and hat.' She quickly had both. 'Would you like tea – or coffee?'

'No, thank you. I'll…' Catesby had already been led into a lounge with lace antimacassars on the armchairs and an ormolu clock on the mantelpiece.

'Please take a seat, I'll tell my husband you're here.'

As Catesby sat down, a shy boy of about four put his head around the door. He was wearing a Russian fur cap that was too big for him. An older boy's voice summoned him, 'Giles, come back here.'

A minute later there were quick footsteps and the ex-minister appeared in the door. 'Nice to see you again.' The voice was just as Yorkshire in private as it was in public.

Catesby looked up. They had met before, but Catesby was surprised that Wilson remembered.

'We met at conference in 1945. You were still in uniform and had been given an unwinnable seat to contest.'

Catesby smiled. The ex-minister was renowned for his remarkable memory. 'And it was even more unwinnable after I took it on.'

'Mary tells me you're now with Foreign Office.'

'Yes, but in a rather specialist branch.'

Wilson gave Catesby a knowing look. It was obvious he knew who he was – and probably remembered seeing him with Bone in the BOT staff canteen. 'Why don't you come into my study so we can have a talk?'

The ex-minister's study was lined with shelves full of documents and books on economics. The window overlooked rear gardens with hedges. The neighbourhood ethos seemed very communal. There were no fences or tall light-blocking hedges. Everything was open and non-threatening. Mary and their two sons came in and out of the study at will. When Catesby heard footsteps on the stairs, he simply covered up the documents he had brought with him and talked about something else. The thing that most impressed Catesby about Wilson was his calmness. Nothing he said shocked him. The machinations of the Security Service and CIA against him seemed no more threatening than a foot-ball bounding over the garden hedge. In fact, Catesby was the far more nervous of the two. He looked on as Wilson once again picked up a photograph of himself and a woman near a bridge over the Moscow River.

'I can't remember her name. In fact, I was never told her name – but I believe that she was an interpreter.'

Catesby smiled. 'It is ridiculous. When the Sovs do blackmail photos, the snaps are naked bed scenes in full *flagrante*. And I'm also sure this photo has been cropped.'

'It certainly has. I remember the walk well. We numbered about a dozen and four of us – including Mikoyan – lined up for a photo at the Bolshoy Moskvoretsky Bridge. You can't see the others.'

Catesby could see that any attempt to compromise the ex-minister in a honey-trap situation was doomed to fail. There was something very straight and puritanical about him. Catesby real-ised there was no smoking gun, but lots of innuendo. He was sur-prised that someone as ambitious and pragmatic as Wilson could also be so naive about his connections in Moscow – and how they could be used against him.

'It is extraordinary,' said Wilson picking up a document, 'how facts are completely ignored. I had absolutely nothing to do with the decision to sell Rolls-Royce jet engines to the Soviet Union. The decision had already been made by Cripps and Attlee before I became President of the Board of Trade.'

'But Cripps is dead and Attlee will stand down as leader before the next election – they need fresh meat to get their teeth into. And it's you, Mr Wilson.'

'But the actual date of my appointment to BOT is an easily verifiable fact.'

'When you're mounting a smear campaign, facts don't matter.'

'Surely there are people in MI5 who could be prosecuted for violating the Official Secrets Act.'

'It would fail,' said Catesby. 'There are no fingerprints linking those documents to any MI5 officer who could be identified. They are experts at covering their traces – and so are we.'

'How did you get them?'

'I can't tell you.'

'So you're withholding information from me.'

'I'm protecting a colleague who doesn't want to be identified.'

Wilson looked at Catesby. His blue eyes had turned cold and shrewd. 'How do I know that you haven't come here to frighten me, to threaten me – to warn me not to go to Moscow next month?'

It was a reaction that Catesby had anticipated – and he had an answer ready. 'I didn't come here anonymously and undercover. You know my name and who I am. If you made a complaint about this visit, I would lose my job and probably go to prison – and, by the way, I didn't know you were planning a trip to Moscow.'

'I might call your bluff.'

Catesby pointed at the black Bakelite phone on Wilson's desk. 'I recommend you ring Scotland Yard, the Cabinet Secretary and your best lawyer friend. But you don't need to ring MI5 – they'll be listening in already. That phone is tapped and so is your office line at Montague Meyer – where I believe you are a consultant.'

The ex-minister gave a slight nod.

'It would, by the way, be useless to get in an engineer to find a bug. Your lines are tapped at the exchange. Our mutual friends have an excellent relationship with the GPO.'

Wilson continued to stare. His face showed no emotion. He finally broke a silence that had become more and more uneasy. 'Why have you told me these things? What do you – or whoever you represent – hope to gain?'

Catesby was a little shocked by the question, but then he remembered that politicians were pragmatists – and had to be. 'I have ideals; I know that sounds stupid and naive.'

Wilson's face softened and his voice was a whisper. 'And so do I.'

The passion and sincerity of the words surprised Catesby. He realised for the first time that Wilson was utterly different from anyone he had met in East Anglia, at Cambridge or in the Secret Intelligence Service. The Wilsons were Northerners from a Non-conformist religious background that encouraged hard work, plain living and personal propriety. There was also a tendency towards pacifism – but not an absolute one. When Congregation-alists marched to war they did so with reservations. Catesby real-ised that the ex-minister was a more reliable and more rational man than himself, a sane person who hadn't been poisoned by the horror of battle. Catesby could see that Wilson was capable of ruthlessness, but not violence. And there was a big difference between the two.

'It's nearly lunchtime,' said Wilson. 'Barbara and Ted Castle are coming to lunch – you're very welcome to join us.'

'It's very kind of you, but I think it best I slink back into the shadows where I belong.'

'But please have a drink?'

'Thank you.'

'Whisky?'

'That will be fine.'

Wilson opened a cabinet and took out a bottle of very fine single malt. The strictures of Northern Nonconformity had at some point been loosened. The measures were generous too.

'I am surprised that you didn't know about the Moscow trip. I briefed the Prime Minister about it and he was very enthusias-tic. In fact, he bought me a drink in the Members' Bar. I've also promised to give him a full briefing when we return. I must say that Churchill is much more enthusiastic about East-West trade than his party colleagues.' Wilson lifted his glass. 'Cheers.'

Catesby drank and looked through the window at the garden. It was all beginning – cherry blossom, prune and blackthorn. The suburb was turning into a fresh riot of unfolding green leaf and colour. He gave a weary smile. 'Isn't it odd?'

'Isn't what odd?' said Wilson.

'That we're not using you. The company you work for, Mon-tague Meyer, specialises, I believe, in importing timber from the Soviet Union.'

'That's correct.'

'We should be making use of your visits to find out what's hap-pening in Moscow – especially while Stalin is still marinating in the embalming fluid. And, apparently, no one has asked you to keep your eyes and ears open, other than Churchill?'

'No one at all. I do find the lack of interest from the intelligence services extraordinary.'

'It looks like they're more interested in spying on you than having you spy for them.'

'Why do you think that?'

Catesby sipped his whisky.

'I think you need a top-up.'

'Thanks.'

Catesby watched Wilson pour the fine whisky and wished that he had never come. He knew that he had dropped himself into a whirlpool that might drown him. He had already trampled all over the Official Secrets Act – and was now making accusations that he couldn't support.

The ex-minister looked concerned. 'Are you okay?'

'What I am expressing, Mr Wilson, are personal thoughts – but there are facts too. MI5 doesn't like East-West trade – and you can find minutes of meetings that bear this out. One practical and understandable reason is that it makes the job of the Security Service much more difficult. They only have a couple of dozen operatives to carry out surveillance. And if London and Birmingham and Manchester are going to be swarming with trade delegations from Moscow and the East Bloc, MI5 are going to be stretched beyond their resources.'

'This assumes that trade representatives from the East will be engaged in espionage.'

'Mr Wilson, everyone is a spy. Spend a weekend in an East Anglian village and see how many of your personal details remain personal.'

'Lace curtains twitch in Huddersfield too.'

'But there are issues other than surveillance problems. Basically, the intelligence and security services are not politically neutral.'

'And neither are you,' said Wilson.

'That's a fair point, but I would think that I'm a needed counterbalance to a predominantly right-wing bias.'

'But what about Burgess and Maclean?'

'They were public schoolboys playing at being Reds.' Catesby lifted his whisky. 'And usually totally pissed.'

'Are there others like them?'

Catesby had his views, but he wasn't going to express them. Instead he made a joke. At least, he hoped Wilson took it as a joke. 'Sometimes I think that I'm the only person spying for Britain, in a service where everyone else is either spying for Moscow or Washington.'

'You know that you have friends in high places.'

Catesby laughed.

'How,' said Wilson, 'do you think you ended up in the Secret Intelligence Service?'

Catesby stared blankly. It was a question that had always baffled him. 'Who is this person?'

'The former Chancellor of the Exchequer, Hugh Dalton.'

Catesby nodded. It made sense. Dalton had been Minister for Economic Warfare during the war and responsible for setting up SOE, the Special Operations Executive. Churchill's instructions to Dalton had been to 'set Europe ablaze'.

Wilson continued. 'When Dalton was setting up SOE, your name, as a working-class grammar-school lad, stood out. You have, by the way, lost your accent.'

Catesby gave an uncomfortable smile. He could see that the broad Yorkshire Wilson didn't approve.

'It was obvious to Dalton,' said Wilson, 'that most of those who had the language skills necessary for SOE came from posh public school backgrounds. That wasn't a problem during the war – all of you were gallant – but, afterwards, it was. When we came to power in 1945, Dalton passed on your name.'

'I find it remarkable that you remember – or even know – such details.'

'I have a good memory – but I was also warned that you were coming.'

Catesby smiled bleakly

'By the way,' said Wilson, 'I am an enthusiastic supporter of East-West trade. It is a far better way of avoiding another war than doubling our defence spending – as the Americans want us to do. Trade relationships foster peace. No one wants to go to war with a trading partner.'

Catesby remembered Wilson's sensational resignation from the cabinet over Gaitskell's introduction of prescription charges in order to finance more defence spending. Beneath the calm surface Britain was a country at war with itself – and the division within the Labour Party was particularly bitter and lethal. The convention of international law that forbids states to interfere in the domestic politics of other states is laughable. The British values that Catesby held most dear were values that America wanted to crush. He looked across at Wilson and remembered what he had told Kit Fournier in the U-boot bunker: the ex-minister wasn't a Communist; he wasn't even a socialist. He was a plain-living Northern Nonconformist who had views on war, international friendship and social welfare that the Americans didn't like.

Wilson picked up the documents that Catesby had brought and put them back in the envelope. 'I suppose you'll be wanting these.'

Catesby nodded.

'It is illogical,' said Wilson handing the papers back, 'that they are trying to smear us as Communists. I once heard a trade union official accuse our government of having rescued capitalism from revolution. He then said, and I'm not sure he was joking, that he always voted Tory because Tory governments were the best way to get the workers angry enough to revolt. It is, of course, in the disease spots of uncontrolled capitalism where Communism is most likely to breed and spread. I want social reform through peaceful change.'

Catesby felt a frisson of fear run down his spine. Not everyone shared Wilson's peaceful vision. He sensed it was time to leave.

As Catesby got up to go, he looked closely at the ex-minister. 'There's one thing,' said Catesby, 'that you should never forget. The Americans will never forgive you for selling those Rolls-Royce jet engines to the Soviet Union.'

'But as I said before, it wasn't my decision.'

'That's true, but the Americans always need someone to blame – and, as far as they're concerned, the deal is stamped with your name.'

Catesby never forgot his meeting with Wilson. He had just turned thirty and his encounter with a future prime minister became a benchmark by which to measure his own life. In most ways, Wilson seemed to be doing better. As Catesby got older, his own hopes began to extinguish like candles slowly blown out on a birthday cake. There was a brief expectation of a new family, but Frances had a miscarriage. After that his marriage was permanently on hold. He tried to be a good stepfather, but was useless at discipline or giving the twins a sense of direction. In fact, he made a point of never correcting or criticising the children at all. It sometimes infuriated Frances, but at other times she agreed. 'You're not, after all, their real father. If you tried to show authority over them, they would resent it.' Catesby succeeded in keeping the relationship calm and relaxed. The kids called him by his first name and regarded him with bemusement. Catesby wasn't so much a husband or father, as a stray dog that occasionally turned up and got fed.

Meanwhile, his mother continued to rattle around in the cold draughty house in north Lowestoft. She occasionally made some extra cash by bookkeeping or doing translations. She was a mystery – and so was Catesby's sister. Her relationship with Tomasz lurched from crisis to crisis. Catesby knew there was something fishy about the Polish lover – and even had some evidence – but he didn't do anything about it. More ammunition for the Security Service if they ever decided to pounce on Catesby. The scales were finely balanced – and, after much soul-searching, tilted in favour of his sister's happiness.

Catesby's own happiness was something he seldom considered. He didn't always hate his job. At times he liked the excitement – and, although he was ashamed to admit it, the power and the influence too. But he also loved literature, art and intellectual discussion. He would rather have been a university don than a spy. But what Catesby wanted most was the security of family and love – with endless summers in Suffolk and France. Gardens, boats and rivers.

## 18 Frognal Gardens, Hampstead, London: January, 1956

It was a short walk from the Hampstead tube station to the party – and it was going to be an extremely smart party. Catesby had used Frances to wrangle an invitation. He wasn't going to the party to socialise. He was going there to spy on the new leader of the Labour Party and his new American pals. Both he and Henry Bone were particularly concerned about the US 'labor' attaché who doubled as a CIA spy.

It was a clear frosty evening and Frances looked beautiful, elegant – and desirable. But, as usual, it was hands off. He was resigned to that, but Catesby was also trying to prepare himself to be pleasant and sociable – his most difficult undercover disguise.

'Please, William, you will behave yourself.'

'I'll do what ever's required – and, if being rude and outrageous is required, I will do that too.'

'Oh, please don't. Listen, you'll love Dora – she is so warm.'

'And long suffering.'

'They have an understanding and the marriage works – and the daughters are lovely and happy.'

'I'm going to vomit.'

'Stop it.'

'Don't think for one second, Frances, that I'm being judgemental about where Gaiters… do the smart set really call him that?'

'Apparently.'

'Where Gaiters puts his plonker is not relevant – even though that's what everyone gossips about. What does matter is what he's doing to the Labour Party – and to our country. He's a shit; he's what my French comrades used to call a *collabo* – and there's no worse insult than that.'

'The comparison is totally unfair – the Americans are not the Germans. Shhh. Listen.'

'What?'

'Music.' Frances looked at Catesby; she was swaying in sync. 'Don't you recognise it? Isn't your dip cover cultural attaché?'

Catesby smiled. 'It's Miles Davis playing "Solar" – but I think it's only a gramophone.'

'It's coming from their house – maybe Miles Davis is there.'

The jazz musician wasn't there, but it was a glittering party. The first person Catesby recognised was Isaiah Berlin who, not surprisingly, was talking to a group who were hanging on his every word – as well they should. They had just been greeted by the Gaitskells' eldest daughter, a perfectly mannered teenager, who relieved them of their coats and gestured to a huge sitting room where her mother was talking to a man in his forties – the gramophone playing Miles Davis was beside them. Dora Gaitskell smiled warmly at Frances and greeted her with open arms and a double kiss. She shook hands with Catesby who was impressed by her solidity and warmth. Dora seemed ten times more genuine than her errant husband.

'I'd like you to meet Joe,' said Dora.

'Pleased to meet you,' said Joe. He had an American accent with a hint of Eastern Europe.

Catesby knew who he was, but was going to pretend he didn't.

'Joe,' said Dora, 'has just brought us this new release of Miles Davis – hot off the presses. And I couldn't wait to hear it.'

'I love Davis – and Charlie Parker too,' said Catesby. His words were true – he did admire the jazz musicians – but the polite tone was false. Catesby imagined that the record had recently arrived via diplomatic bag. It was round one of the Culture War. The Soviet Union launched the Bolshoi Ballet and America retaliated with jazz – played by black musical geniuses who couldn't ride in the front of an Alabama bus. Rosa Parks had just been arrested the previous month for so doing.

'Don't worry,' said Joe winking and pointing his glass of champagne at two men on the opposite side of the room, 'you guys have got some culture too.'

Catesby turned and looked. Lucian Freud was having an intense conversation with Francis Bacon. They were oblivious of the social whirl around them. Catesby and Frances slightly knew Freud. His family had a house in Walberswick and they sometimes met him walking on the Dingle marshes.

Frances gave Lucian a little wave and the painter winked back.

Catesby nudged his wife. 'Get your clothes off, Frances, and see if he wants to paint you.'

Frances frowned and kicked Catesby, but Dora and Joe laughed. It was the sort of remark you could make at a 'smart' Frognalite party. But Catesby immediately wished he hadn't said it.

Hugh Gaitskell was now making the rounds and pouring champagne. He looked directly at Catesby with a winning smile. 'Nice seeing you again, so glad you could come.'

Catesby smiled back. It was the first time he had ever met Gaitskell. 'Warmest congratulations,' said Catesby lifting his champagne flute. He didn't need to say congratulations for what. Everyone knew – it was what the party was all about. Gaitskell had seen off the left wing of the Labour Party and been elected leader the previous month.

Gaitskell gave Catesby a wink and a nod and moved on.

Catesby sensed Joe staring at him and trying to place him. It was the sort of party where you didn't tell people who you were. They either knew who you were to begin with – or they found out by other means.

'Hugh is a wonderful host,' said Joe.

Catesby could see that Joe was fishing; trying to get Catesby to recollect former parties that might explain who he was.

'He's also a wonderful dancer,' said Catesby launching into a smokescreen lie. 'I was with him in New York in 1951 just after he was named Chancellor. He took us all to a jazz nightclub to celebrate. We were exhausted, but Hugh was still dancing at half-past four in the morning. And, you know, I can't remember the name of that club – I was a bit blotto.'

'It sounds like it might have been Birdland on West 44th Street.'

'I think you might be right.' Catesby felt Frances tugging on his sleeve. 'Excuse me, Joe. I think my wife has urgent business. Maybe I forgot to take my tablets.'

'Sure.'

Catesby found himself being dragged towards the front door. 'What's wrong?'

'I've got to leave.'

They found the eldest daughter who offered to get their coats, but Frances insisted they get the coats themselves. All the coats were hanging from racks or piled on beds in a spare room. Frances closed the door behind them.

'Have you seen someone you're trying to avoid?'

Frances nodded. 'I'm supposed to be a French au pair.'

'Your surveillance cover?'

'A bit more than that.'

Catesby frowned. 'You're a honey-trap?'

'I don't know. Nothing's happened yet. He's arrived early. We didn't expect him to take up post so soon.'

'Who's the target?'

'The new CIA Head of Station. He's operating under dip cover as a senior political officer.'

'Fucking great.'

'Help me find my coat.'

'Shit.'

'You're annoyed?'

'Why shouldn't I be? My wife's being dangled as a honey-trap whore – and, on a lesser professional note, MI5 can't be fucking bothered to tell us about such an important change of personnel.'

'Stop swearing – and I'm not a whore.'

'Here's your coat.'

Frances began to put it on. 'You don't have to leave.'

'I'm not going to. It's a great party – maybe I'll pull.'

'I hope you do.'

'Now you're turning bitter.'

'Sorry.' Catesby thought of Hampstead Garden Suburb, which now seemed so much healthier than Frognal Gardens. 'I just wish that we could have had a more normal life.'

'Look at yourself.'

'You're blaming. Sorry, let's stop squabbling.'

'Stop apologising.'

'Okay,' Catesby forced a smile. 'Who is the new Head of Station?'

'Kit Fournier.'

Catesby laughed. 'I'm definitely staying.'

'Don't do anything foolish.'

'It is very odd.'

'What is?'

'Your gang trying to do the dirty on Fournier. I thought MI5 and CIA were best pals.'

Frances looked away.

'You're being furtive.'

'No one at Five knows about the surveillance except the DG and myself.'

The DG, Dick White, was the one person in MI5 for whom Catesby had complete respect. He was a professional with complete integrity trying to control a service that was poisoned by rogue elements with political agendas.

'What,' said Catesby, 'is White up to?'

'I think he realises that some of our officers are making unauthorised contacts with the CIA and he wants to know who they are.'

'Why didn't you just tell him?'

'I haven't proof – but there's something…'

'Go on.'

'I shouldn't tell you.'

'Let me guess. Henry Bone?'

'You guessed right. He was at the meeting with the DG – and said that you passed on a Fournier file to him from Germany.'

Catesby smiled. Blaming Bone for being a duplicitous bastard was like blaming the sun for rising.

'Don't think, William, that Henry betrayed you. He didn't want you to know because he didn't want to hurt your feelings.'

'What feelings?'

'Jealousy.'

Catesby looked at Frances.

'There's hurt in your eyes.'

'So your plan for getting Fournier isn't just a flirtation, but a full honey-trap with cameras whirring away.'

'I hope not, but I will if I have to. Don't look so despondent.'

'For fuck's sake, how am I supposed to look?

'But it probably won't be a honey-trap – how could it be?

Fournier is a single man, there's no blackmail potential. It's a question of surveillance.'

'Close surveillance?'

'Perhaps.'

'Just like the war, isn't it?'

'What do you mean?'

'The women of Britain were issued with utility knickers – one yank and they're off.'

'Or in my case, a Canadian.'

'Thanks for reminding me.'

'But, Will, I'll just be keeping an eye on him.'

'But if it goes further than that, ask Bone to show you the Fournier file in its entirety. It might be an idea to dress up as a Roman Catholic nun and tell him that you're his long-lost twin sister. A full psycho-sexual portrait of Kit Fournier makes an interesting canvas.'

Frances smiled. 'We'll have to ask Lucian to paint it.'

'I'd love to see him paint you.'

'Why?'

'I'm sure that he'd reveal complexities that I've missed.'

'I had better go.' Frances turned up her collar. 'I hope he doesn't see me.' Catesby accompanied his wife to the door and saw her into the cold night. He blew her a kiss, but she didn't turn to see it.

Catesby went back into the house. He wanted a drink and found his way to the kitchen where he swapped his champagne flute for a glass of white wine. As he began to drink, he felt someone at his elbow. A silky familiar voice said, 'Hello, William.'

It was Stuart. They had trained together as Army officers. Although Stuart had a first in Literae Humaniores from Balliol College, he proved totally incapable of disassembling and assembling a Sten gun and was transferred to military intelligence. They had worked on intelligence matters after the war before Stuart returned to academia.

'Shh,' said Catesby, 'I'm undercover.'

'How interesting. But you can tell me, what are you doing here?'

'I'm here to get drunk, meet glamorous people – and, if possible, get laid. What about you, Stuart?'

'My heart is palpitating over Sonia.'

'Sonia who?'

'Peter Quennell's wife.'

'Good luck.'

'My luck won't be good. She even turned down Lucian Freud.'

'I'm sure he only wanted to paint her. Where are you now?'

'I'm disappointed that you don't know. Am I not important enough to be under surveillance?'

'Last I heard you were tap dancing in a top hat and spats in front of semi-naked ladies at a club in Paris?'

'No, no, you're confusing me with Guy Burgess. No, I'm back at All Souls where I'm a resident fellow. Have you read my book on Spinoza?'

'Not yet, but I will.'

'I remember that you were fond of Spinoza – we used to talk about him in France.'

'You thought he was a logical positivist.'

'But tonight I'm more interested in women. Aren't they glam? What do you think of her?'

'Which one?'

'The vamp wearing the off-the-shoulder number.'

'Does she like Spinoza?'

'I don't think she's read him, but I'll tell you what she likes.'

'Go on.'

'The important thing is not to judge her, but to understand her – and to understand why she likes the things she likes. Do you know who she is?'

'Very flinty eyes,' said Catesby, 'and I'm sure the pearl necklace is priceless. I bet she's the real hostess and half the people here are from her address book.'

'Well done. Gaiters didn't collect her; she collected him. She wants a prime minister for her trophy room. And now she's looking at you.'

'What does she like?'

'In the state of nature, wrong-doing is impossible – and nothing is forbidden by the law of nature, except what is beyond one's power.'

'Spinoza?'

'Well done again. You ought to apply for a fellowship – and here's the question I set: "Does the moral character of an orgy change when the participants wear Nazi uniforms?"'

'Yes.'

'Is that all?'

Catesby shrugged. 'Nothing more to say.'

'Congratulations and welcome to All Souls. I'm going to circulate, see you later.'

As soon as Stuart was gone, the woman looked at Catesby and picked up a bottle of champagne. She came over to him. 'You need a top-up.'

'I'm drinking white Sauvignon.'

'Finish it and I'll fill you up.'

Catesby did as he was told.

'Stuart's an old friend of mine, horribly clever. Where do you know him from?'

'The Army.'

'He often talks about some beastly prisoner you had to execute.'

'It wasn't his decision – and it wasn't mine either.'

'Stuart treats it as a philosophical dilemma.'

'The prisoner refused to talk unless we promised him that he wouldn't be executed. So we lied and he talked. The Maquisards shot him the next morning. Stuart thought the lie was an ethical dilemma.'

'Why didn't you just torture him? He would have talked then.'

'Telling the lie seemed more humane.'

'Stuart does have some funny ideas. He's a bit of a Lefty you know.

'So I gather.'

'My husband and I used to have him around for dinner to explode his pathetic belief in equality – and now we have the same problem with Hugh.'

'Have you succeeded?'

'More with Hugh than Stuart. Hugh's political life is pretty dire and boring. He needs pleasure and intellectual stimulation.'

'Don't we all?'

'Hmm.'

Catesby was leaning back against a kitchen unit with his hand on the corner of the unit. The woman also leaned back against the unit – with her bottom firmly resting on Catesby's hand.

'Have you ever been to the West Indies?' she said.

'No.'

'My husband spends a lot of time there – we have a place on a bay with a private beach.' The woman paused. 'Why don't you squeeze my buttock?'

Catesby turned his hand palm upwards. There was a lot of rucked-up dress material, but he managed to grab a handful of flesh through the fabric.

'Squeeze hard. Squeeze as hard as you can – I want you to hurt me.'

Catesby squeezed, but not as hard as he could. He didn't want to leave bruises for Gaiters to ask questions about.

'You ought,' she said, 'to grow your fingernails longer. You can stop now.'

'But you don't want me to.'

'You are perceptive, but this isn't the place.'

Catesby removed his hand when he was sure no one was watching.

'Where do you live?' she said.

'I'm a dip stationed in Bonn.'

'Where do you stay in London?'

'Pimlico.'

'When I visit, make sure there are lots of towels and ice. Hugh doesn't hurt me enough. Why are you smiling?'

'I'm thinking about what I'm going to do to you.' Catesby lied. He was really thinking how much fun it would be to pass their conversation on to the left wing of the Labour Party. But he wasn't going to play politics. It was one thing to expose intelligence officers who did, but it wasn't a game that he was going to play.

'I've heard, by the way, that being a diplomat isn't your real job.'

Catesby smiled and nodded towards a guest who had just entered the kitchen. 'Ask him.'

Kit Fournier was waving an empty glass and exuding American

boyishness. The woman filled his glass with the remains of the champagne. Then she pointed to Catesby. 'Do you know this gentleman. He's being very mysterious.'

'He has every reason to be mysterious,' said Fournier, 'he's the Third Man. Kim Philby is completely innocent.'

Catesby smiled bleakly. Kit had obviously been drinking.

'Sorry, William, how rude of me to expose you in such an uncouth manner.' He turned to the woman. '*Excusez-moi, madame, je suis un américain sauvage et grossier – absolument sans manières et culture.*' Fournier was dangerously swaying with his wine glass.

'I think,' said the woman, 'I'd better help Dora with the canapés.'

As she disappeared, Fournier winked at Catesby. The American wasn't drunk at all. 'Talking French always gets rid of Englishwomen like that. I was afraid I might have to tell her about the anaconda *caché dans mon pantalon* – or pour my drink down her cleavage. I hope, by the way, I haven't spoiled anything for you.' Fournier lowered his voice to a whisper. 'By the way, do you know who she is?'

'I was hoping you were going to tell me?'

'She's Ann Fleming, Gaitskell's mistress. And I must say, Catesby, it is rather bad manners to get invited to a party like this and then try to screw your host's girlfriend.'

'Thanks for your advice on etiquette.'

'Sure.'

'And congratulations on your promotion.'

Fournier shrugged. 'I didn't really want to come here. I wanted to go back to France.'

'But the French aren't an unsinkable aircraft carrier.'

'They certainly weren't in 1940, but I prefer them to you guys – they don't bother with hypocrisy and duplicity. Or maybe they're just lousy at doing them.'

'You can't make generalisations about people.'

'You can if you're an American.' Fournier looked closely at Catesby. 'Why have you been telling fibs?'

'Because it's part of my job.'

'Yeah, but telling fibs is pretty damn stupid when you know you're going to get found out. And now you're doing the supercilious smile.'

'Actually, Kit, I don't know what the fuck you are talking about.'

'It was an insult to Joe.'

'Joe who?'

'Joe You-goddamn-well-know-who: Joe, the labor, without a 'u', attaché. You told him you were an old friend of Gaitskell's and went dancing with him at a jazz club in Manhattan after he became Secretary of the Treasury.'

'Chancellor.'

'Or whatever. Anyway, Joe thought you were a Member of Parliament – and maybe even part of the shadow cabinet – and felt he made a damn fool of himself when he asked Gaitskell about you. You owe Joe an apology.'

'Okay. Let's find Joe. I'll apologise – and also give him a lesson on the English sense of humour.'

'Which isn't meant to be funny.'

'Not always, but sometimes.'

'In any case, let's forget about Joe, he can take it. He's a tough guy and a great labor attaché.'

Catesby knew more about Joe than he was going to let on. The problem with the CIA is that they occasionally let people with consciences slip through their recruitment net. One such was Paul, a CIA man who had been acting undercover as US labor attaché in Paris when Catesby met him. After a few Pernods, Paul confided that Washington was 'paranoid as hell' about European trade unions coming under Communist influence. He explained that any trade union that wanted CIA money simply needed to smear their rivals as being Communist-controlled. The 'Commie' smear tactic worked a treat in Marseilles and turned over the docks to unions with criminal connections who swapped socialism for drug trafficking. Paul also warned him that Joe was a rising star and on his way to England.

'I bet,' said Catesby fishing, 'that Joe is finding the British Trade Union movement a bit difficult. If he goes up North, he might even need an interpreter-translator.'

'He's already been – and made a great friend of a Durham miner leader named Sam Watson. We're not as naive about Britain as you think.'

Catesby smiled inwardly. Watson's name was on two lists. One had been passed to him by Paul and contained 'CIA agents of influence' in the UK. The other was a list of attendees – along with Joe, Gaitskell and Fournier's predecessor as CIA London Head of Station – at a series of secret meetings at the Russell Hotel. The purpose of the meetings was to discuss ways of expelling the left wing – including Wilson – from the Labour Party. At what point, thought Catesby, does scheming with spies from a foreign country to influence domestic politics become treason?

'What we're trying to do,' said Fournier, 'is help Britain. We love your country and we want to help make you strong and secure.'

Catesby nodded and hoped that his smile wasn't supercilious again. The only British thing that Washington cared about was the British defence budget – and, if spending less on health and welfare was the best way to spend more on guns and bombs, so be it.

'I need another drink,' said Catesby, 'I'll see you later.'

Catesby wandered out of the kitchen into a maelstrom of sumptuous sociability. The house was bursting with refined British voices and urbane British elegance, but the strings were being pulled by American puppeteers. The power strategists in Washington weren't always as stupid as they seemed. They were grooming the non-socialist pro-American wing of the Labour Party for power – an Oxbridge-led elite that felt comfortable within the traditional ruling circles of Britain. There was no way that Washington was going to let its unsinkable aircraft carrier be taken over by mutineers who wanted to rid its decks of US planes and nuclear weapons.

A woman in a strapless cocktail dress was walking around with canapés on a tray. Catesby helped himself to a caviar blini – and then made his way to a sideboard where there were pink cocktails with sticks of fruit. Upon closer inspection, he decided to look for wine. Meanwhile someone nibbling an olive on a stick smiled at Catesby and gestured to a bottle of wine in an ice bucket.

Catesby nodded a thank you to the man and refilled his glass. The man, who looked to be in his late forties, was bald and solidly muscled. He looked a lot rougher and harder than the other guests. He came over to Catesby and started speaking French. His French was fluent, but with a strong hint of Central Europe. After sociable small talk about the party, the man's voice dropped to a whisper. 'May I shake your hand?'

Catesby smiled and shook his hand.

The man continued in a throaty whisper. 'I want to thank you for what you did – and my people want to thank you too.'

'Are you sure you're not mistaking me for someone else?'

'No. We know who you are, Monsieur Catesby.'

Catesby replied in a guarded tone. 'What exactly are you thanking me for?'

'What you did in Bremen.'

Catesby felt his bowels turn with dread. It was a ghost that wouldn't stay buried.

'If,' said the man, 'you ever want to do something like that again, let us know and we will help you.'

'What if I'm not in a position to do so?'

'Then tell us what you know – and we will do it ourselves.'

'If I ever need your help, how would I contact you?'

'Go to the grave of Charles Baudelaire in the Montparnasse Cemetery. You will see a likeness of the poet recumbent on his grave. Put a tiny chalk mark on his left big toe – then return to the cemetery at noon on the first Friday of the month. Someone will be there to meet you and will say, "*Venge-moi*". You will identify yourself by replying, "*Demain, après-demain et toujours!*" Then tell them what you want.'

'Thank you.'

'You are our friend.' The man saluted with his wine glass and drifted off.

Catesby had a good idea who the man worked for, but wasn't going to make enquiries. Meanwhile, Stuart had turned up again.

'Who,' said Stuart, 'do you see when you look in the mirror?'

'Sometimes I see a murderer; other times, I see a traitor.'

'Do you tell them that when you go for positive vetting?'

'I lie. Everyone lies. The only ones who get caught are the ones who aren't very good liars.'

'Is Kim Philby a good liar?'

'I'm not going to answer that question. What do you think? You knew him at Bletchley.'

'I used to always say, "There's something wrong with Philby." But no one paid any attention – and they still don't.' Stuart paused. 'And I don't think Philby is a good liar. He doesn't even try to be convincing. He's almost bragging about being a liar – like at that press conference last year. It was as if he were saying, "I am lying, so what? What are you going to do about it?"'

Catesby kept a straight face. He wasn't going to be drawn. Being an SIS officer was walking a tightrope between friends of Philby and friends of Washington. Catesby was neither – and it made him a very lonely man.

'What do you think of this party?' asked Catesby.

'I'm enjoying the food, the drink, the people and the sparkling conversation. But I don't like it. It's a bit like that dinner party where the Goths cut the last emperor in half. Where's your girlfriend?'

'One of the Goths chased her away.'

'She has an interesting history – used to be married to a press baron and still has powerful connections in the industry.'

'Who do you see, Stuart, when you look in the mirror?'

'I would love to see Spinoza, but I see the *collabo* the Maquisards executed after I interrogated him. He was, like me, a young intellectual who wanted to be an academic or writer – and moviestar handsome. We'd read the same authors – except he became a Fascist. Who knows?'

'When we look into a mirror, Stuart, we've got to start seeing ourselves – we're not bad people.'

'Wouldn't it,' said Stuart, 'be nice if that were true?'

The plot had succeeded. Catesby realised that as soon as he left the Gaitskell's party in the early hours of the chill morning. The CIA and their British collaborators had won. They had vanquished the socialist wing of the Labour Party and installed their own poodle, Hugh Gaitskell. Washington's unsinkable aircraft carrier bristling with US nuclear weapons was more safely afloat than ever – a change of government wouldn't make any difference.

During the years that followed, Catesby remembered Henry Bone's advice that it was part of an intelligence officer's job to be 'politically astute'. He followed the power games of Westminster as closely as he followed those in the Kremlin. Catesby knew that Gaitskell's becoming Labour leader hadn't come without a price. He had to appoint Harold Wilson as Shadow Chancellor of the Exchequer in order to buy peace with the Left of the party. But being Shadow Chancellor didn't mean that Wilson got invited to the smart cocktail parties at Frognal Gardens. The Gaitskellites snubbed him and even made snide remarks about the Wilsons having flying ducks on the sitting room wall. There were no ducks, flying or otherwise. Catesby knew there weren't any, because he occasionally visited the family home to fill in Wilson on the latest dirty tricks his enemies in the Security Service were getting up to. The house was warm and tasteful – and totally without pretension. The visits were dangerous for Catesby. His briefing the Shadow Chancellor could be construed as gross misconduct. Not enough to go to jail, but sufficient to get sacked.

The anti-Wilson plot hadn't been abandoned, but was slowly simmering on the back burner in case he ever came to power – which now seemed increasingly unlikely. But Wilson continued to make enemies who stored up grudges. The Americans were suspicious of his conciliatory line towards the Soviet Union – and suspected the worst. Wilson carried on working for the export-import firm Montague Meyer and made frequent trips to Russia and Eastern Europe. Catesby warned him to watch his back and not to trust the telephones at the company's office in the Strand. Meanwhile, Wilson had begun to make serious enemies in the City. As Shadow Chancellor, he condemned insider trading and cartels. Big money, as Catesby came to realise, was the worst enemy of all. It could do anything it pleased.

As Catesby got to know Wilson better, he realised they had much in common. Both were grammar school outsiders who had clawed their way up via Oxbridge and government service. But

Catesby was in serious trouble and his estranged wife was furious. When he went around to Stanhope Gardens to talk about it, Frances dragged him into the small courtyard garden so the children wouldn't overhear what she had to say.

'I'm freezing,' he said, 'can't we go back inside?'

'No, you stand there and listen. You have no idea how difficult it is bringing up teenagers as a single parent with a full-time job.'

'No problem, I'll move in and help.'

'No way are you moving in after what you've just done. My son is going through a difficult phase and you've made things worse.'

Catesby smiled to smooth things over, but he quickly realised the smile was a mistake.

'It's not funny and you shouldn't have given him the idea that it was. He needs boundaries and guidance. I'm trying to instil some responsibility and sense of discipline – and then you go and undermine it.'

'How long is the suspension?'

'A week.'

'That's outrageous.'

'No, it isn't. We're lucky he didn't get excluded – and it is a good school.'

'I'm glad you sent him to a comprehensive.'

'But, Will, why did you laugh when he told you the story?'

'Because it was funny.'

Catesby thought the chemistry teacher had handled the situation badly. Okay, his stepson had been messing around in the lab, but that was no reason for the teacher to have reacted the way he did. The teacher had prodded Catesby's stepson with a ruler and shouted, 'There's an idiot on the end of this ruler!' And the stepson had replied, 'Which end?' When he told his stepdad what had happened, Catesby had laughed out loud. Which, he now realised, was probably not the right response. Catesby then made things worse by praising his stepson for being witty and standing up to authority.

'Sometimes,' said Frances, 'I think the rumours about you might be true.'

'Which rumours, that I'm a Soviet spy?'

'No, William, I don't think the Russians would have you – they would find you too immature.'

'Why are you smiling?'

'Because it's impossible to take you seriously. No, you're not a Sov mole; you're an adolescent revolutionary. You shouldn't be at Broadway Buildings, you should be marching up and down Oxford Street handing out "Ban the Bomb" leaflets.'

'I think we should ban the bomb, don't you?'

Frances shrugged.

'Sorry, do you want me to have a word with your son?'

'No, he likes you the way you are.'

The last three years had been a difficult time for Catesby personally. He and Frances had continued to drift apart, but they were still friends and sometimes lovers – even though they had both been unfaithful. During an operation aimed at penetrating East German intelligence and getting rid of a double agent, Catesby had an affair with an East German artist. He had almost fallen in love with the woman, but she was killed in the operation – and guilt replaced love.

Another personal tragedy involved the fate of Catesby's sister, Freddie. She had been sacked from her job as a translator at GCHQ, but Freddie was lucky not to get a long prison sentence. Catesby had long suspected Tomasz, Freddie's lover, of being an East Bloc Romeo agent. Tomasz was too good to be true – and too handsome and charming for his sister. It was heartbreaking, but Freddie's mad passion for Tomasz had led her to pass on secret information. When Catesby found evidence of what she had been doing, he destroyed it. In the end it didn't matter because Freddie was arrested in any case – and then released because a trial would 'not be in the public interest'. Even though Catesby had risked his career and freedom to protect his sister, she never forgave him for betraying Tomasz.

In the end, Catesby realised that Bone had been manipulating all the players – like a cat tossing a mouse from paw to paw. Tomasz's death was convenient and cleared the air for all concerned.

Whether or not Bone had killed Tomasz to protect British interests or to protect his own interests was a question still to be answered. But Bone knew where all the bodies were buried – and Catesby could point to a few fresh graves as well. Bone's unwavering belief in Kim Philby as a 'triple agent' remained a sore point between them. It might have been a genuine belief – or an alibi. Catesby had a view, but kept quiet about it. Bone's secrets were safe with Catesby – as were Catesby's with Bone. The terms of the insurance policy were simple: 'If you grass me, I'll grass you'.

Meanwhile, despite setbacks in his personal life, Catesby's career prospered and the promotions came as regular as spring blossom. One of Catesby's most successful operations had been a sting that busted a nuclear spy ring. The op also trapped Kit Fournier and turned him into a British agent and prisoner. Catesby had always known of Fournier's dark incestuous secret – and used it to entrap him. The Americans were glad to see the back of Fournier – and accepted the myth that he was missing and probably dead. Fournier's imprisonment on a remote South Atlantic Island became an SIS legend, but also its most closely held secret.

## 1 January 1963

It was brutally cold and the roads blocked with snow. Catesby had bought a cottage in a Suffolk village, which was his rural hideaway. It wasn't too far from where his mother lived in Lowestoft – but not too near either. He needed a bolthole in the countryside he knew and loved – and now he was stuck in that bolthole. Catesby had spent Christmas with his sister and mother and Boxing Day with his estranged wife's family. Then it happened. It was already cold, but the Arctic finally said, 'Fuck you, Suffolk'. It was Thursday afternoon, 27 December.

Catesby saw it coming as he was walking back from the Rumburgh Buck. He liked going to a pub full of people who did useful things – like ploughing, looking after livestock, nursing, repairing tractors, cooking school meals and building houses. If you wanted someone to repair your electricity line or unblock your drains, the Rumburgh Buck would be a better place to find them than the common room at All Souls College Oxford – or anywhere in Whitehall. The people in the pub knew that Catesby was a Suffolk person, but they still treated him with suspicion – which is why he left after a single pint of bitter. Billy-No-Mates, he thought, as he set off down the lane with bleak frozen fields on either side. Hunched against the cold east wind, Catesby watched the sky turn a dirty yellow. It was an odd colour for a Suffolk sky. Then it began to snow, not the usual big wet flakes that melted as soon as they hit the ground, but small steely ones – and it didn't stop.

It was three o'clock in the morning on New Year's Day and Catesby was alone in his draughty rambling house. He had gone to bed at 10 p.m. on New Year's Eve and slept through the fireworks at a nearby farm. Midnight on New Year's was, of course, the ideal time to shoot someone if you didn't have a silencer for your gun. Catesby ran his fingers over his temples and forehead – there weren't any holes. Otherwise, it would have been easier to sleep. He put on a dressing gown. It was absolutely freezing. When he went for a pee, he had to break the ice in the toilet bowl. Catesby went back to bed and crept under heaps of blankets. But he still couldn't sleep – and it wasn't just the cold. He got up again and went downstairs. A fire was still smouldering in the inglenook. Catesby picked up an old copy of the *East Anglia Daily Times*. He glanced again at the two leading news items. Harold Macmillan had agreed to buy Polaris missiles from the United States and the Beatles had become the first British band to reach Number One on the American charts. Catesby smiled. It was a trade-off – and, as usual, the Americans had got the better end of the deal. He crunched up the newspaper, piled on kindling and poked the fire back into life.

The early hours of New Year's Day were always a time for personal reflection. Even though Catesby had moved up the career ladder and was in line for an OBE, his position was precarious. The hoof-beats of the dark knights of comeuppance always echoed in the distance. The OBE was in recognition of the role he had played in helping resolve the Cuban Missile Crisis. Catesby had ping-ponged back and forth between London, Havana and Washington more as a back channel diplomat than as a spy. No one, thought Catesby, would ever know how close the world had come to nuclear war. And he realised that most of the credit for averting the nuclear apocalypse belonged to a KGB general who sacrificed his life and to a submarine officer called Vasili Arkhipov. Unlike war, peace required heroes on both sides.

In the course of his career, Catesby had made a lot of enemies with scores to settle. It probably wasn't a brilliant idea being alone in a remote rural cottage – especially at night. At first, Catesby had taken precautions. During times of particular paranoia, he set warning devices along the path to his house. The devices varied from tins with stones in them to loud electronic alarms. When the neighbours began to gossip about jealous husbands and London villains that had it in for him, Catesby decided to abandon the warning alarms. Instead he kept his Browning 9mm close at hand, but he wished that he still had his old Webley revolver – they never jammed. The Webley, of course, had blood on it – and Catesby had made sure that it had been melted down.

He didn't want a forensic team to have a look at it at the eleventh hour.

In a way, the dark knight of death was the one Catesby feared least – and there were times when he would have greeted him with a welcome. But the other dark knights stalking him were the ugly ones, the ones who preferred torture and humiliation to a clean kill. The knights were prison, dismissal, exposure and shame. Catesby had never been a traitor, even though he had covered up for those who were. When shapes changed so often in the mists of bluff and double bluff that Catesby wasn't always certain what he had done. But he had protected his sister and would never regret that.

Catesby was less of an outsider than he had been in the early years – and the OBE would prove it. Maybe, he thought, a gong went with the house. Catesby had bought the property from a retired colonel who also had an OBE. And now money was no problem either. Catesby, as an SEO, made twice the average male wage – and had little to spend it on. But most important, and satisfying to his vanity, was having influence. He was often co-opted to JIC, Joint Intelligence Committee, and sometimes asked to write reports for the committee, which were thoughtfully discussed. Catesby's intelligence analyses maintained that the Soviet threat to Britain and Western Europe was greatly exaggerated. His views playing down the Russian threat didn't make him popular with the barking anti-Commie brigade. But Catesby fastidiously supported his analyses with statistics, facts and constantly updated intelligence. He eventually won over a general and a Tory MP. There were, however, still those who regarded Catesby as a closet Lefty – and probably worse.

He got up and drew the curtains. Catesby reckoned the retired colonel from whom he bought the house might have known more about him than he let on. The colonel, after showing Catesby around the property prior to the sale, winked and touched his nose. He made sure that no one was looking before he unveiled it. The safe was brilliantly hidden. The only gems that Catesby kept in it were documents that he shouldn't have – and it was time for a New Year's inventory. It was a serious disciplinary offence to keep them in his home, but many of the docs were there for Catesby's own protection – to prove that he hadn't been acting without authority. Copies of documents like that had a funny way of going missing when there was an enquiry. The important thing about the JIC document was the list of signatures affirming that Catesby's views had been openly presented.

JOINT INTELLIGENCE COMMITTEE REVIEW OF SOVIET MILITARY CAPABILILITIES AND INTENTIONS AGAINST UK AND WESTERN EUROPE

**UK EYES BRAVO: STRAP 2 CAN/AUS/US EYES ONLY**

LEDGER DISTRIBUTION:
FO – PUSD
CABINET OFFICE
ODA US EMBASSY
CANADIAN HIGH COMMISSION
AUSTRALIAN HIGH COMMISSION

1 DECEMBER 1962

**FROM: WILLIAM CATESBY, HEAD OF PRODUCTION SECTION EASTERN EUROPE AND WEST GERMANY, SECRET INTELLIGENCE SERVICE**

This estimate reaffirms previous judgements that the USSR does not at present intend to initiate military action against Western Europe and the United Kingdom and is not now preparing for a general war at any particular future date.

During the last ten years there has been a substantial decrease in Soviet troop levels from a high of 5.4 million in 1953 to a middle estimate of 3.8 million today. Khrushchev's claim of 4.8 million troops is clearly false and in line with previous exaggerations about ICBM capabilities. The infantry and tank divisions deployed in Eastern Europe and the Democratic Republic of Germany are, in most cases, severely under strength. Many of the formations are divisions in name only. The intention seems to be to deceive the West as to actual troop numbers.

There are sixty operational airfields in the Baltic/East German region capable of serving heavy and light bombers. The number of heavy bombers deployed in the region has halved since 1959 and the light bombers are down by a third.

Although there has been a decrease in Soviet conventional forces, there has been an increase in nuclear forces in the region. This development, in the context of fewer tanks and troops, suggests a strategy focused on deterrence and defence. Although there is little or no danger of a deliberate offensive strike from Soviet forces, there is a high danger of accidental war as the result of the USSR misreading Western intentions. The Kremlin is clearly bluffing about Soviet military capabilities. The more astute Soviet and East Bloc intelligence officers are aware that Western intelligence officers know that the Soviet leaders are bluffing. The great fear among Soviet commanders is that the West, having perceived Soviet military weakness, will launch a pre-emptive strike. A Soviet response to a real or falsely perceived imminent attack by the West would completely devastate Britain and Western Europe. It is essential that Western military commanders make absolutely certain that military exercises – or surveillance over-flights of Soviet territory – are not construed as preludes to an attack.

Intelligence reports also suggest that there are tensions between Khrushchev and the Soviet high command. Khrushchev's economic reforms are aimed at cutting military expenditure in order to meet the pressing needs and rising expectations of the civilian economy. Sabre-rattling on the part of Western leaders would strengthen the hand of the Soviet military.

In summary, Soviet military strategy has two objectives: deterring a Western attack and preserving its East European buffer zone. It is important that the West does not confuse traditional Russian geo-political interests – hegemony over the Baltic and Eastern Europe – with an ideological campaign to spread Communism. In fact, the Kremlin is just as hostile to Communist rivals – such as China and Yugoslavia – as it is to Western Capitalism.

**This paper was discussed by JIC and approved on date.**

Catesby smiled and put the paper back in its folder. The Americans couldn't complain. In fact, he had cribbed the first paragraph from a CIA report. Dealing with the Americans, Catesby had come to realise, was like working with someone who had schizophrenia or some sort of multiple personality disorder. He was convinced that every American intelligence agency had a Team A and a Team B. Team A were, generally, rational and sane. They were willing to consider détente and nuclear test ban treaties. They were pleasant to know socially – and even had a sense of humour. Team A types often had an interest in the arts and could speak a language or two. In the aftermath of the Cuban Missile Crisis, Kennedy had begun to lean towards Team A. Team B, on the other hand, thought that Kennedy 'chickened out' over Cuba and should have let the missiles fly. While Team A were in favour of containing the Soviet Union, Team B wanted to roll it back. Catesby dipped back into the safe to find a CIA Team B document that had been circulated prior to a JIC. It had the rather bizarre name of 'The Soviet Strategic Military Posture'. *Posture?* Catesby wondered if the CIA imagined that Soviet soldiers adopted various poses before they struck: *the malevolent lean-forward; the deceptive slouch; the coiled crouching spring.* It was a document that revealed more about the Americans than it did the Russians.

> The aim of the Soviet Union is world domination and they will pay any price to achieve this. That it was a Communist rocket that first ventured into space proves to them that they are marching in the vanguard of history. They think they see a response to their doctrines and influence in the revolutionary struggles of Asia, Africa and Latin America. The Soviet leaders expect to associate the peoples emerging from colonialism and backwardness with their own cause, mobilizing them against a more constricted world position of the Western states. The relative stability of Britain and Western Europe at present they see only as a transient phrase.

Catesby stared into the fire. The Team B Americans seemed unaware that Trotsky's scheme for world revolution had been rejected long before Trotsky had been murdered with an ice axe. Since then, the Soviet Union had turned into a paranoid and inward-looking state. Catesby reflected – and not for the first time – what would have happened if Trotsky had come to power instead of Stalin. And what role, thought Catesby, would he himself have played in such an alternative universe? Despite the cold, he felt a tingle of sweat rolling down his spine. Catesby got up. It was after all New Year's. He went to the drinks cabinet and poured himself a brandy.

Catesby had never been a big fan of JFK, but hoped that Kennedy would rein in the Team B faction. They were already spoiling for a fight in Laos and Vietnam – which, Catesby was certain, would end badly for the Americans. Team B were touting something called 'The Domino Theory'. The problem, as Catesby well knew, was that the British intelligence services were also divided into Team A and Team B. The big danger – and it was already happening – was that the British Team B would link up with the American Team B.

The battles between allies and friends are always more vicious than battles between enemies. It's painfully evident at National Day receptions when embassies roll out booze and food to celebrate. The NATO dips always get on better with the Warsaw Pact dips than they do with their own side. Embassy receptions are also notorious for recruiting double agents or defectors. Catesby remembered a St Patrick's Day bash when a Sov dip swayed up to him reeking of Jameson and said, 'Are you thinking of defecting?'

Catesby shrugged and said, 'No, I can't be bothered.'

'Good choice,' said the Sov, 'my country is shit.' He then headed back to the bar for a refill.

At first, Catesby had assumed that the diplomat was pretending to be drunk and playing a double game. Perhaps, the Sov wanted Catesby to think he was disaffected and ripe for recruiting – and when they met again, the fake double would pass on disinformation. It happened all the time. But on reflection, Catesby could see that the Russian really was drunk and meant what he said. On the other hand, the world of spying was a maze of mirrors where gut instincts, warmth and sincerity could be just as false as a string of fake pearls. The problem is: you have to cut the pearl in half to see if it's genuine.

In an odd sort of way, the sanest people in the international power game were the arms dealers. They weren't interested in ideology, even if they mouthed the slogans, they were interested in profit.

Catesby's rise in status inevitably meant more Christmas cards. He turned to the mantelpiece above the fire and looked again at the one from the Wilsons. He loved it because it was so splendidly non-Christmassy. It was a family photo that had been taken the previous summer on the Isles of Scilly. It included Harold and Mary, their two sons – who had grown very tall. Catesby loved the solid ordinariness of the card – absolutely no pretentiousness.

Catesby counted the cards. There were forty-one altogether, not bad for an estranged husband living alone. He wondered if he got more Christmas cards than Henry Bone. He would ask when he got back to London. Bone had, in fact, shown him one of his cards – after warning Catesby that the card was more hush-hush than the most secret document. It was from Kim Philby in Beirut. It featured the Three Wise Men on camels in a starlit desert. Philby had drawn an arrow pointing to the third wise man and written, 'That's me!' A very dangerous joke, but typical of Philby's arrogance. The fire was now warming the room. Catesby poured himself another drink and was soon dozing on the sofa.

Catesby didn't know how long he had been asleep when he heard a tapping at the window. He wished it was the ghost of a woman he had loved and betrayed so he could say sorry, but he reached for his pistol in case it wasn't. The wisteria needed pruning. It was probably a loose branch in the wind – but there wasn't any wind. Catesby turned out the light and went into the boot room. He silently slipped on a pair of wellies. The tapping was there again – it was a very persistent wisteria branch. Catesby put on a heavy coat and slipped the Browning automatic into one pocket and a torch into another. He wrapped a scarf around his face as camouflage and made his way to a back door.

The cold was piercing and the snow was crisp. The utter silence was broken by the long woo of a male tawny owl – a few seconds later the shrill shriek of a female tawny answered. Catesby paused and said to himself, 'What the fuck?' The owl noises were mating calls – and tawny owls don't mate until March. He stood still and reached for the Browning in his pocket. On cue, the male owl hooted and a second later the female gave a long response – and they both seemed to be calling from the same place. Catesby didn't know how to creep silently in crisp snow. Instead, he drew his automatic and ran quickly around to the front of the house. There was a dark figure standing next to the window. Catesby knew it would be rash to pull the trigger, so he flicked on the torch instead.

She was smiling and had something that looked like a recorder in her hand. She put it to her mouth and the night was pierced again by the mating call of the female tawny owl. She reached out with her other hand, which was holding a second recorder-like thing. 'Here,' she said, 'this one does the male tawny. Why don't you blow it?'

'Happy New Year, Frances.'

'And Happy New Year to you, William.'

'How did you get here?'

'I walked over from Dunwich – it was beautiful when the moon was out.'

Catesby took the male tawny whistle from Frances and blew a good long woo. His estranged wife replied with hers.

'They were stocking fillers,' she said. 'Aren't they clever?'

'But we've hopelessly confused the local owl population.'

'I think they've ignored it – as they do must human eccentricity.'

'Speaking of human eccentricity, why are you here?'

'Because I wanted a walk in the cold beautiful night – and because I thought you might be lonely on New Year's morning.'

'I'm never lonely.'

'I don't believe that.'

'You've never seen the ghosts.'

'Which ghosts, William?'

'Don't ask.'

'Nothing has changed, but I was so hoping it had.'

'Sorry, I shouldn't have said that. I'm glad that you're here. Please come in.'

'I don't want to impose on you, William. Maybe I should turn around and leave you in peace. I am exhausted, but I will walk back and most likely collapse in a heap on the footpath – and then freeze to death orphaning my children.'

'That wouldn't be fair. Let's go in.'

They sat in silence for a few minutes basking in the glow of the inglenook fire. Catesby spoke first. 'I'll make up a spare bed for you.'

'That won't be necessary – I might just lie here, in front of your glorious fire.' Frances stretched out on the sofa. Catesby sat on a cushion on the floor.

'When are you due back in London?'

'On Thursday, but it doesn't look like I'm going to make it. Do you know the sea is frozen off Kent?'

'Is that another gem from an A4 Watcher?'

'No, it's from *The Times*. What have you got to tell me?'

'I hear that Nick Elliot's off to Beirut to have a chat with Kim.' As soon as he said it, Catesby wished that he hadn't. The brandy must have loosened his tongue. On the other hand, it was important to swap intelligence with Frances. Her keeping him up-to-date with what was going on in MI5 was invaluable in the struggle between the two services. If her bosses knew, she would lose her job. Passing on information to SIS was worse than passing it on to the KGB – or, in the view of the cynics at Five, pretty much the same thing.

'Everyone likes Nick,' said Frances, 'and I find him very kind.'

'I don't like him – and he's also a complete idiot.'

In Catesby's view, Nick was responsible for the debacle that cost Lionel Crabb his life in Portsmouth Harbour – and also for bugging Khrushchev's suite at Claridge's during the Soviet leader's 1956 visit. Both ops had been expressly forbidden in writing by the Prime Minister – and both had failed miserably. The worst fallout was the resulting breakdown in Anglo-Soviet relations, which destroyed the possibility of détente between the two countries. But maybe, thought Catesby, that was why his SIS colleagues had disobeyed the Prime Minister's instructions. And were the Americans involved?

'Why is Nick off to meet Philby?' said Frances.

'I honestly don't know,' lied Catesby with a smile. 'What have you got to tell me?' He wanted to keep the conversation focused on their jobs. It was less dangerous than the personal. But there were places where the two overlapped.

'I recently met someone who knows you,' said Frances.

'That sounds ominous. Who is he?'

'It's a she.'

'That sounds even more ominous.'

'I met her through Susan.'

'Who's Susan?'

'Susan the journalist-author.'

Catesby smiled. They were playing a parlour game called 'Whitehall Insiders' Bluff'. The object was to trump the other person with superior insiders' knowledge.

'Point to you,' said Catesby. 'I still don't know who you're talking about.'

'And you call yourself an intelligence officer? Tsk, tsk. Susan is Tony's wife.'

'I'm getting warmer.'

'Go on then.'

'Susan is the wife of Tony Crosland,' said Catesby, 'a Labour Member of Parliament. Tony, by the way, had an affair with Roy when they were at Oxford.'

'You are clever. I didn't know about the Roy business.'

'It's pronounced "Woy".'

'You mean Roy Jenkins,' said Frances triumphantly. 'But can you guess then, the name of the woman who knows you?'

'Ann Fleming. She's Hugh Gaitskell's mistress.'

'Well done,' said Frances. 'But how did you work it out?'

'Her and Gaiters,' said Catesby, 'meet at Tony's place to have sex.'

'How do you know? Have you got the house under surveillance?'

'Of course not.' Catesby smiled. 'As you know, we're not allowed to do surveillance in the UK. No, she told me.'

'Did you have an affair with her?'

'No. I would describe it as a cross between a dalliance and a fact-finding mission.'

'What facts did you find?'

'That her husband, the one who writes the books, is a sadist – and she, although not completely masochist, liked the spanking a lot. But they no longer have sex – haven't for years.'

'What does she see in Gaitskell?'

'Power, but she likes his brains too. She also wants to wield political influence behind the scenes. She thinks she has weaned Gaitskell from what she calls his "pathetic belief in equality" – not that he required much weaning.' Catesby smiled. 'She also fancies Tony, who she regards as "sleek and debonair". In fact, she fantasises about Tony when she's having sex with Gaiters.'

Frances had gone steely-eyed. 'Who does she fantasise about when she's in bed with you?'

'Who do you fantasise about when you're in bed with Kit Fournier?'

'You have no right to say that – you know nothing.'

'You're supposed to be his agent handler, not his agent fondler.'

'You've been misinformed, William. I was supposed to be his new agent handler, but I've been transferred to D Branch.' Frances frowned. 'Someone's been winding you up.'

Catesby nodded. Spies are professional liars and they practice on their colleagues. 'What actually happened?'

'I wasn't part of the honey-trap. I surveilled Fournier disguised as a French au pair – and we did have a cuddle on the train to Portsmouth. Susan Crosland, by the way, knew Fournier – they're both old money from Baltimore.'

'Not common Baltimore riff-raff like the Duchess of Windsor.'

'Absolutely not.'

'Sadly, the Americans have infiltrated us at every level.'

'We are allowed to marry them. In any case, we certainly nailed Fournier.'

'Would you like a drink?'

'What have you got?'

'Brandy, absinthe, wine or beer.'

'A small glass of red, please.'

After Catesby poured the drinks, he raised his glass. 'To the Fournier op – our finest moment.'

'Cheers. But,' added Frances, 'it made the Americans distrust us even more.'

'They haven't a clue what happened.'

'Don't be so sure.'

The Fournier op, masterminded by Henry Bone, had been brilliant. SIS had looked on as Kit Fournier, CIA's London Head of Station, had become ensnared in a Soviet honey-trap centred on a spy ring stealing UK nuclear secrets. The two principals were shot on a remote Suffolk beach – and Kit Fournier was later kidnapped by SIS en route, or so he thought, to join his lover in Moscow. The op was clinical perfection – a totally hermetically sealed secret. Fournier was now completely broken and stashed away on a remote South Atlantic island. All the secrets that Washington had for years kept from London were spilling out of Kit Fournier.

'And what, Frances, do you think is CIA's most successful op in Britain?'

'You're about to go off on one, Catesby.'

'It's the creation of the bleeding right wing of the Labour Party. If you pull down Hugh Gaitskell's trousers, you'll find "Made in the USA" stamped on each buttock.'

Frances laughed. 'Did his mistress tell you that?'

'She's even photographed them for me.'

'You're making that up.'

Catesby smiled. 'Yes, I am.'

Frances looked closely at Catesby. 'Have you proof that Hugh Gaitskell is a CIA asset?'

'No, I was hoping that you might.'

Frances shrugged. 'There is CIA money behind *Encounter* magazine, but you'll never trace it to source.'

'Try.'

'The money is laundered through a philanthropist in Ohio who made a fortune selling gin. But, William, there's a big gap between CIA funding an arts and politics magazine and Gaitskell being their stooge.'

'It's not explicit. The CIA has created a mood among the British intelligentsia, the smart set around Gaitskell, where American ideology and foreign policy are never criticised – and where Socialism and unilateral nuclear disarmament are rubbished.' Catesby looked at his wife. 'What's wrong, you're frowning disapproval?'

'Sometimes, William, your anti-Americanism becomes obsessive. Why are you laughing?'

'Tell me more about your transfer to D Branch. I'm intrigued.'

'I knew that you were waiting to pounce.'

'D Branch is very secretive,' said Catesby, 'but last I heard D is now responsible for all of Five's counter-espionage. You're working under D1 – aren't you?'

Frances shifted uncomfortably.

'One minute ago, you accused me of being "obsessive". How ironic, that anyone from D1 – Five's home for demented swivel-eyed paranoiacs – should call anyone else obsessive.'

'You've had too much to drink, Catesby.'

'I'm not drunk; I'm tired.' Catesby closed his eyes. D1 was Five's section responsible for Soviet counter-espionage. Catesby frequently clashed with a D1 officer who had wormed his way into the section from Scientific Intelligence. He called the officer Ferret because he resembled the animal in looks and behaviour.

'I know what you mean, William. There are people in my section who give me cause for concern.'

'They're obsessed with Reds under the bed. They think every trade union official has pockets full of Moscow gold – as well as any Labour MP who doesn't like Gaitskell.' Catesby walked over to the mantelpiece and picked up the card from the Wilsons. 'Look, I got a Christmas card from one of them.'

Frances smiled. 'I'll have to report that to D1.'

Catesby thought it best not to mention Bone's card from Philby.

'Peter,' said Frances using Ferret's real name, 'is particularly insidious when he brings back dangerous paranoia from Washington.'

Catesby shrugged. 'Maybe we're all mad.'

'The intelligence services are not, William, a healthy world. Do you still think of leaving?'

'I don't want a job teaching modern languages to rightfully bored school kids.'

'What about politics – your first love?'

'It isn't my first love, you are.'

'I don't believe that.'

'Why should you? Spies are professional liars.' Catesby paused and stared at his wife.

'What's wrong?'

'I was hoping you would look hurt.'

'Back to politics. You would be a fantastic Member of Parliament.'

'There's no place for me in Gaitskell's Labour Party. Did you hear about that outrageous speech he gave at Stalybridge?'

Frances shook her head.

'Gaitskell actually said that Communists had infiltrated the Labour Party – smears and lies about his *own* party. No wonder Washington loves him.'

Frances yawned. 'Sorry, I'm sleepy. Maybe Gaitskell will fall under a bus.'

'I wish someone would push him under a bus.'

It was a tired late-night conversation. But it wasn't long before Catesby deeply wished he had never said those words.

## Broadway Buildings, London: 18 January 1963

Catesby first heard the news from Henry Bone, but had been told to keep quiet about it until it was officially announced. The second time he heard the news was during a meeting about NATO in the DG's office.

Catesby was exhausted. He had finally managed to train down to London a week after the worst blizzard since British weather records were begun – and then was sent to Moscow via Heathrow to meet a double agent who didn't turn up. When he got back to London the snow was still lying in heaps on the frozen ground. The weather was playing havoc with the football season. There were dozens of cancelled fixtures and it didn't look like the FA Cup final was going to be played until June.

But the NATO situation was even more alarming than the weather or the botched Moscow trip. The thing that concerned

Catesby most was the way Canada was being bullied by the USA. The NATO commander was an American general named Lauris Norstad. Norstad, despite having a name that sounded like a character from a science fiction film, had Hollywood good looks and a smooth manner. The general was awfully good at press conferences. In a recent interview with a Canadian newspaper, Norstad had bluntly stated that Canada's refusal to accept nuclear weapons meant that 'she is not actually fulfilling her NATO commitments'. The general's statement had set off a chain of events that was threatening to bring down the government of Canadian Prime Minister John Diefenbaker. Kennedy clearly wanted to get rid of Diefenbaker too. He ridiculed the Prime Minister by intentionally mispronouncing his name at public events – and by referring to the Canadian PM as 'a boring son of a bitch' in a 'non-attributable' chat with a coterie of journalists.

The meeting at Broadway Buildings had also been attended by representatives from the Foreign Office. The aim was to make sure that every spy as well as every diplomat had a clear and unambiguous understanding of Britain's NATO commitments. It also stressed that senior Americans be handled with kid gloves. In the aftermath of the Cuban Missile Crisis back-down and a series of bloody noses in Vietnam, the mood music from Washington was to get tough again. An FO mandarin, who had been silent and droll for most of the meeting, finally drawled, 'And never, ever, be boring.'

The meeting was a late-night one and it was well after 10 p.m. when there was a loud knock on the DG's door.

'Ah, that must be the drinks trolley,' said another voice from the FO.

The DG said, 'Come in.'

It was the NDO, the Night Duty Officer. He nodded at Catesby, who he regarded as an old pal, and handed a note to the DG. The DG raised his eyebrows as he read the note, but didn't look overly surprised or shocked.

'Anything else, sir?' said the NDO.

'No,' said the DG.

The NDO turned and left.

The DG looked first at his own staff and then at the visitors from the FO. The DG's bearing was calm, but solemn. There was a hushed silence.

He finally spoke. 'Hugh Gaitskell has just died. Many of us knew that he was ill, but this comes as a complete shock.'

'I thought it was just a bad case of winter flu,' said one of the FO people.

Catesby kept a straight face. He knew there was trouble on the horizon.

Despite the news, the meeting continued for another half an hour. The death of a leader of the opposition and a future prime minister was not enough to halt the business of the Secret Intelligence Service and the Foreign Office.

Catesby picked up a late-edition newspaper on his way back to the flat, but didn't read it until he was comfortably ensconced in an armchair in front of a spitting gas fire with a glass of brandy close at hand.

## Labour Leader Hugh Gaitskell Is Dead

Hugh Gaitskell died today after a sudden deterioration in his heart condition. Mr Gaitskell, who was 56, had been in hospital since the fourth of January suffering from a virus infection.

A statement issued by Middlesex Hospital in Marylebone said: 'Mr Gaitskell's heart condition deteriorated suddenly and he died peacefully'.

Mr Gaitskell had suffered a bout of flu in mid-December, but appeared well over Christmas. A medical check-up declared him fit to travel to Moscow on the first of January for talks with the Soviet leader Nikita Khrushchev. The trip was, however, postponed when Mr Gaitskell became ill with another virus infection and was admitted to hospital.

Two days ago Mr Gaitskell's condition began to deteriorate rapidly. It became clear his kidneys had been affected. A team of nine doctors and 30 medical staff succeeded in linking Mr Gaitskell to a kidney dialysis machine. The strain on his heart, however, proved too severe and he was taken off the machine.

Hugh Gaitskell had led the Labour Party for seven years. During that time he initiated reforms aimed at making the party 'relevant' to modern Britain. He died at a time when Labour seemed poised for victory at the next election.

Catesby put the newspaper down and stared into the gas fire. He could hear alarm bells ringing. Too many things were happening at the same time. A scandal involving Jack Profumo, the Secretary of State for War, was about to break. Profumo had been having an affair with a young woman who aspired to be a model. In normal circumstances, such an affair would be brushed under the carpet. But these weren't normal circumstances. The young woman was also rumoured to be having an affair with Yevgeny Ivanov, the Soviet naval attaché – thereby posing the question of a security risk. Espionage sprinkled with sex was a sure-fire way to sell newspapers – and so was murder and conspiracy. Catesby looked again at the Gaitskell article. The key words were 'sudden', 'died' and 'trip to Moscow'. Catesby knew that Gaitskell's death was not murder. He couldn't think of any poison that would have caused the symptoms described – and still gone undetected. Although Gaitskell was only fifty-six, he hadn't been that healthy. Catesby often got detailed reports from his mistress. Gaitskell was prone to colds and flu and was often overworked and tired. She also suspected that he suffered from high blood pressure – and sometimes during their love-making, his face got so red that she feared he would burst a blood vessel.

But who, thought Catesby, would have benefited from Gaitskell's death? At first glance, it would be the left wing of the Labour Party. But now that Gaitskell was gone, his most likely successor would be George Brown, who was in some ways even more right-wing than Gaitskell. Brown, of course, had a drink problem and was prone to gaffes. The Tories would probably find him easier to defeat than a smoothie like Gaiters. On the other hand, thought Catesby, if Harold Wilson defied the odds and became the next Labour leader, the rumour mills would churn.

What next, thought Catesby? The worst thing, the straw that

might break the British unicorn's back, would be the uncovering of The Third Man.

## Washington DC: 20 January 1963

James Jesus Angleton hated his middle name. Pronounced in the Hispanic way, beginning with a 'y' sound and ending with a silent 's', the Jesus betrayed the Mexican origins of his mother. In many ways, Angleton preferred the code name, FURIOSO, that British secret intelligence had given him. In fact, he sometimes called himself FURIOSO. It wasn't very good as a code name, for code names are supposed to contain no clue as to whom they identify. FURIOSO was, in fact, the name of the literary magazine that Angleton had edited while an undergraduate at Yale. The magazine's name derived from the eponymous hero of Ludovico Ariosto's epic poem, *Orlando Furioso*. Furioso is a Christian knight fighting in the war between Charlemagne's Christian Europe and the Saracen hordes. The war against the Saracens takes Furioso to the four corners of the world – and even includes a trip to the moon where Furioso finds his lost marbles and recovers his sanity. Angleton took it as a compliment that the British referred to him as FURIOSO. Little did he know that Henry Bone was thinking more of Angleton's lost marbles than his chivalry when he chose the code name.

Angleton preferred having lunch at Harvey's Restaurant on Connecticut Avenue rather than the cafeteria at the Langley HQ. Despite a love of French poetry, he preferred American food and drink. He hoped his lunch companion, the CIA's star Soviet Bloc defector, wasn't having trouble with a menu that featured canvasback duck, terrapin soup, Louisiana possum with yams and scalloped oysters.

The defector looked up and asked in heavily accented English, 'Is the duck cooked in canvas?'

'No, that's the name of the species of duck. Large numbers of them overwinter on the Chesapeake Bay.'

'And the possum?'

'It's correct name is *opossum*. It's a small marsupial that is native to the American South. T.S. Eliot sometimes uses "Old Possum" as a nickname, as in *Old Possum's Book of Practical Cats.*'

'You are, I believe, a friend of famous poet.'

'I have known Tom for years.'

The waiter had left an ice bucket and a full bottle of Jack Daniels on the table. Angleton topped up their glasses.

'I think I have oysters and roast pig.'

'A good choice.'

'And I'm developing a taste for Mr Daniel's bourbon.'

Angleton lit a cigarette from the stub of his previous one. He gazed at his lunch companion through a haze of smoke. Angleton thought the defector looked like an Impressionist painting. He was a mysterious man who drip-fed his secrets. The slowly unfurling secrets became part of an allusive pattern of thin brush strokes and subtle changes of light that less trained eyes failed to perceive. But Angleton, temporarily morphing into FURIOSO, could see it all and how it fitted into a larger and complete whole.

'Is it not strange,' said Angleton, 'that Hugh Gaitskell never made it to Moscow?'

The star defector shrugged. 'Not at all. That would have been too obvious. The operations are called *mokrie dela.*' He smiled. 'It's what you call "wet affairs" – splendid name. As you know, they are controlled by Line F of Thirteenth Department. There is Line F officer assigned to each Soviet embassy.'

'Including the one in London?'

'Of course.'

'By the way,' said Angleton, 'our London colleagues have code-named you EMPUSA. I am sure you know its Greek origins and I believe it shows a lack of respect.'

'What have you code-named me?'

'TANGO. It's a vital dance full of energy and *duende.*'

'Thank you. I much prefer it.'

Angleton stared at the newly christened TANGO. 'Which assassination methods do the Thirteenth Department prefer?'

'Poison.'

'What sort of poison?'

'All sorts. Prescribed drugs like barbiturates and warfarin are useful because it looks like victim has died of accidental overdose. But number one favourite is radioactive thallium because you can deliver poison with small spray gun that looks like asthma inhaler.'

Angleton peered at his companion through the smoke haze. As soon as he began to perceive an emerging pattern, it disappeared back into the haze. He didn't want to rush the drip-feed, lest it dry up, but he felt the high-ranking intelligence officer turned defector was holding back.

'Most of the methods you have described,' said Angleton, 'have been used against Soviet Bloc émigrés and dissidents whom the Kremlin wanted silenced.'

'That is true: anti-Soviet activists have been usual targets.'

'But how would the Thirteenth Department arrange the assassination of a Westerner?'

'Plane crashes are useful – there are so many possible causes. And guns – especially in America where anyone can buy good sniper rifle.'

'But you said the Thirteenth prefers poison.'

TANGO/EMPUSA gave a sly smile. 'There is nothing more secret in the Soviet Union than *Spets Byuro #1*. They say it was shut down in 1954 after Lavrenty Beria's execution – before that it was solely under control of Beria and his closest comrades. But *Spets Byuro #1* was never shut down. The *Byuro* is experimental laboratory that specialise in development and testing of poisons in form of powders, liquids, pills and injections. The experiments are carried out on prisoners awaiting execution. No one is allowed to visit – except for staff and tiny select cadre – and no one even knows where it is.'

'Have you been there?'

TANGO continued to smile slyly. 'I can speak frankly to you. You realise that information I possess is priceless.'

Angleton nodded agreement. Some of his colleagues thought TANGO was expensive, but Angleton knew he was worth every penny the US taxpayers paid him. On the other hand, thought the American, it was only fair that the British should also pay for the priceless intelligence that was forthcoming. The Brits were always pleading poverty, but much of TANGO's insider information was utterly vital to the UK. Britain was riddled with Communist subversives and TANGO knew who they were.

'Any news,' said Angleton, 'about our friend in the Lebanon?'

'How ironic that British government continue to pay salary of KGB spy – even though First Chief Directorate has virtually unlimited funds.' TANGO laughed. 'If I were British taxpayer I would be very annoyed.'

Angleton was annoyed too, but for different reasons. Kim Philby had been his good friend and his mentor during his London days. When Philby was assigned to Washington in 1949, the friendship resumed and became deeper. When suspicion fell on Philby, one of the first things Angleton had to do was destroy nearly two years of appointment diaries that recorded more than a hundred lunches and meetings with Philby. Many of the lunches were very boozy ones and Angleton feared he had given away too much. The so-called FURIOSO had been duped by Philby. It was his biggest humiliation and one that he would never forgive.

**Beirut:** 23 January 1963

It was a filthy night. The sea was pounding the esplanades and ripping up cobblestones. The rain was relentless and the streets had turned into rivers bearing flotsam rubbish. The man scurrying from rue Kantari towards the harbour was in too much of a hurry to take counter-surveillance measures. The game was up and there wasn't any time. In any case, the surveillance teams that should have been on duty had deserted their observation points for the warm and dry. Their excuse was that no one in their right mind – particularly someone who so loved his creature comforts – would be out on such a night. There was only one watcher still on duty. He reproved himself as a 'silly muggins' as he reached for the comfort of his hipflask. He was about to pack it in when someone in a hurry brushed past and nearly knocked him over. The surveillance operative instantly knew it was him, not by his face which was covered, but by the pink and blue of his Westminster School scarf.

The watcher followed his target towards the harbour. He wished that he had backup. Despite the awful wind and rain, a lone cargo ship was loading. The watcher took a pair of miniature binoculars from his coat pocket to have a closer look at the vessel. The hammer and sickle flag snapped and fluttered from the ship's stern. Her name was the *Dolmatova*. The watcher hurried into the nearest café to telephone his boss at the British embassy, but owing to the storm the phone lines were down. He quickly went back into a maelstrom of gale and horizontal rain. It took a long time to find a taxi – and a longer time for the taxi to make its way to the embassy. By the time the watcher had filed his report, the *Dolmatova* had cast off and was pitching and plunging across the Mediterranean towards the Black Sea and her eventual destination of Odessa.

On reflection, the watcher wasn't sure that his report would have made any difference – even if the phone line had been working and there had been plenty of backup. The people at the embassy – at least, those in the know – didn't seem particularly bothered. In fact, they seemed relieved. Had the target been allowed to do a quiet 'fade'? In any case, thought the watcher, it's not something for a muggins on my pay grade to be concerned about.

### Broadway Buildings, London: 25 January 1963

'There is something in that report, William, that you obviously find amusing. And, by the way, you sound very East Anglian when you laugh.' Bone paused. 'Would you like to share the joke?'

'We need to put out an urgent warning to all surveillance teams.'

'Which is?'

'Anyone wearing an old school scarf, especially if it's Eton or Westminster, is about to do a shuffle fade to Moscow.'

'Hmm, may I have the report back?'

Catesby handed it over.

'Have you still got your Christmas card from Kim, the one where he drew an arrow to the third wise man and wrote "this is me"?'

'Funny you mention that.' Bone picked up something from his desk. 'Here it is.'

'I think you keep it as an heirloom.'

'I would, if he hadn't written my name in it along with a personal message.'

'May I see the message?'

'No. But could you empty that wastepaper bin into the burn bag, please?'

Catesby picked up the green metal bin and emptied its contents into a canvas sack with parallel red stripes and a chain and lock that sealed it.

Bone put the now empty bin on his desk, struck a match and set the Christmas card alight. The burning fragments fell into the bin.

'Why didn't you just put it in the burn bag?'

'Because, Catesby, some things are so sensitive that you don't want to let them out of your sight – even for the short trip between here and the incinerator.'

'Were you surprised by Kim's fade?'

'Nothing surprises me.'

'It's going to put us under a lot of scrutiny.'

Bone nodded.

'We can't go on hiding the fact that Philby's disappeared. The hacks and spies of Beirut will soon notice a gap at their local bar. How are we going to explain it? What's the cover story?'

'It's best to let the rumours come naturally, un-orchestrated by us. The latest rumours are true to character: Kim's off on a drinking spree; he's bedding a new mistress; he's on a secret assignment covering the war in the Congo.'

'How long before people sniff the truth?'

'Not long. Three weeks at most.'

'What do we do in the meantime?'

Bone stared at Catesby; then smiled bleakly. 'We prepare ourselves to be shocked, to be absolutely appalled and utterly stunned. Learn, Catesby, to look utterly stunned and baffled – and don't forget complete sadness and dismay.'

'How do you feel about it, Henry?'

'I'm not going to answer that question.'

'Fine.'

'But,' said Bone, 'they are going to use it against us.'

'Who are *they* and who are *us*?'

'I think, Catesby, you can work that one out yourself. On a purely bureaucratic level, we've got to protect the service from undeserved humiliation and recrimination.'

'Why did Nick go to Beirut?'

'Because he's Kim's closest friend and was the best one for the job.'

'What was the job?'

Bone stared at Catesby as if weighing him up. Bone finally made a steeple of his long fine fingers and looked over his half-moon reading spectacles. 'His job was to offer Kim a deal: immunity from prosecution in exchange for a full confession. We wanted to keep it all in-house.'

'But Philby did a runner.'

'Maybe he didn't have anything to confess – and didn't think we would believe him.'

'You're being provocative, Henry.'

'I'll be even more provocative – perhaps Kim was sent to Moscow as a fake defector, a planted double brimming with disinformation to destabilise Moscow Central by spreading distrust and paranoia.'

'Perhaps, Henry, we should replace our training manual with *Through the Looking Glass*: "Why, sometimes I've believed as many as six impossible things before breakfast."'

'You don't know the truth, William, and perhaps none of us ever will. In any case, too many things are happening at the same time. Ivanov has just been recalled to Moscow.'

'Why?'

'It concerns the rumour that he's been sharing a woman with Jack Profumo. I expect Moscow Central want to hold Ivanov's feet to the fire to find out what's really happened.'

'And what did happen?'

Bone smiled. 'As I said before, I don't know. In any case, I expect that poor Ivanov is going to get roasted for either having slept with the girl without authorisation – or for having slept with her, but having failed to recruit her as a honey-trap for Profumo.'

'It's a rough old trade.'

'In any case, we're standing astride two volcanoes about to erupt – Kim Philby and Jack Profumo. The newspapers will love it: sex, spies and scandal. And meanwhile, Hugh Gaitskell couldn't have chosen a more awkward time to die. I've already heard some odd rumours and might want you to investigate.'

'Sure.'

'The problem is that certain people will see links between these events.' Bone took off his glasses and gestured to the horizon. 'Communist conspiracy will be their rallying call. The diabolical brilliance of that hysteria is that the accusers do not have to prove there is a conspiracy, but the accused do have to prove there isn't one. It's impossible to prove a negative. How do you prove that Satan doesn't exist?'

'But FURIOSO and EMPUSA do exist.'

Henry Bone didn't reply. He simply stared into the distance.

The top storey of Broadway Buildings was Catesby's favourite place in an ugly building that anyone with any aesthetic sense hated. It was an early twentieth-century office block that completely lacked grace or character. They were scheduled to relocate to a modern glass tower in Lambeth in a year or two, which, unbelievably, was even uglier. It was obvious to Catesby that SIS was not a rising star in the Whitehall firmament.

Catesby liked the top storey of Broadway Buildings because the only other spies were carrier pigeons. It was the SIS pigeon loft. No one else ever went there except for Ralph, the caretaker who looked after the birds. Catesby didn't know whether or not the pigeons had been used operationally since the end of the war. If they had, it was a secret to which he wasn't privy. But the winged heroes had served bravely in the war and one of them had been decorated with the PDSA Dickin Medal. The framed citation was attached to one of the cages: *To Kenley Lass for successfully delivering secret communications from an agent in enemy-occupied France while serving with the NPS in June, 1944.*

**147**

Sadly, Kenley Lass was no longer there. Catesby hoped it was old age and not a cat or a sparrowhawk. In any case, he found the cooing of the pigeons more comforting than the clipped tones of his human colleagues. It made the loft a good place to think and reflect.

FURIOSO was the SIS code name for the most powerful person in the CIA. His official title was Associate Deputy Director of Operations for Counter-intelligence, usually acronymed to ADDOCI. The problem with FURIOSO was his self-belief in his intellectual superiority. Catesby knew that the American was bright and refined. FURIOSO spoke several languages and had written poetry in French while still a teenager. Catesby had once asked to see some of the poetry, FURIOSO responded with disdain: 'I don't think you would understand it.' The American had also been a friend of Ezra Pound. Catesby wondered if their friendship had survived Pound's trial for treason as the result of his propaganda broadcasts for Mussolini.

Catesby regarded FURIOSO as a dangerous chemical. The American became an even more deadly poison when mixed with others who shared his obsessions. FURIOSO's alliance with Ferret was a marriage made in hell – and the arrival of EMPUSA on the scene created a *ménage à trois* blessed by the leaping imps of Pandemonium. EMPUSA wasn't a fake defector; he was a self-promoting charlatan looking for patrons and audiences – and he found the ultimate patron in FURIOSO.

Catesby wasn't certain who had chosen the defector's SIS code name, but it was perfect. In Greek mythology, Empusa was a spectre sent to guard roads, but who preferred eating travellers. In modern Greece, Empusa is a shape-shifting troll who pesters Greek shepherds in the form of a dog. But the Eastern European EMPUSA was a more modern version. He wanted to be a Western celebrity who hobnobbed with presidents and royalty.

Catesby cooed back at the nearest pigeon, 'Wouldn't you like to eat some yum-yum cake at the Queen's garden party?' The one thing that 'walk-ins' from the East Bloc always wanted in exchange for secret intelligence was to meet the Queen. 'Your Majesty, may I introduce you to Sergei. He was a cipher clerk at the Soviet embassy in Prague and would like to tell you what General Zhukov had for breakfast.' Their exaggerated sense of self-importance was tedious. In fact, it wasn't easy to defect and most would-be defectors who turned up at embassies were turned away. The answer they usually got was: 'Listen, you can help us more if you stay in place as a double agent and pass on new information.' But oh no, they didn't want to do that. Staying in place was dangerous. They wanted Western glitter and they wanted it now. Catesby turned to the pigeon, 'No Sasha, you're not going to Buck House. We don't want you to shit on the tablecloth – fly back to Warsaw. And the fact that you are the last of the Romanovs doesn't matter. Who isn't?'

EMPUSA, however, had managed to push his way past the gatekeepers and was now listened to at the highest levels. An SIS colleague, who had met him briefly, described EMPUSA as 'unpleasant and egotistical' – characteristics that would prove far less of a disadvantage in Washington than London. Maybe, thought Catesby, we should pay less attention to manners. Catesby put his finger through the cage and the bird gave it a slight nibble, almost a kiss. He wondered what would happen to the pigeons when they moved to Lambeth – and whether Gerald was still looking after Hermann.

Catesby admired birds and other animals. They just built their nests and got on with their lives. They didn't worry about dying or anything else.

**Agency News London:** 14 February 1963

## Harold Wilson is new Labour leader

The Parliamentary Labour Party has elected Harold Wilson by a vote of 144 to 103 to succeed Hugh Gaitskell who died suddenly last month.

Wilson defeated deputy leader George Brown, who was also temporary leader following Gaitskell's death. Brown stood for a continuation of Gaitskell's policies. In the first round of voting, the Gaitskellite vote was split by the candidacy of James Callaghan, who is also on the right wing of the party.

A former Bevanite, Harold Wilson resigned from the cabinet of Clement Attlee in 1951 on the issue of prescription charges in the National Health Service. Wilson, as the most credible alternative leader for the Left, stood for the party leadership in a 1960 challenge to Hugh Gaitskell. In that election he received 81 votes (35.37%).

Wilson was the only one of the three leadership candidates with cabinet experience.

**Pimlico, London:** 14 February 1963

Catesby was pleased with the leadership election result. Politics was about the art of the possible and Wilson was the only candidate from the so-called left of the Labour Party who had a chance of unifying the party and winning a general election. But he also knew that Wilson's election was going to cause disruption and trouble. The Americans hated him and the British establishment regarded him as an outsider. Catesby knew there had been anti-Wilson plots in the past – the CIA men in London, and they were all men, had conspired against him and in favour of Gaitskell. But now that Wilson was Labour leader and odds-on-favourite for next prime minister, the plots were going to turn ugly and malicious.

As a grammar school boy who had been to Oxbridge, Catesby

knew what Wilson had been through – and knew it was probably much worse than he had experienced. Catesby had the advantage of being a native East Anglian at Cambridge – and his fluency in French and *Nederlands* had made him stand out against the toffs who were lesser linguists. Catesby defied the grammar school stereotypes, but Harold Wilson fulfilled them all. He was unabashedly Yorkshire and ended up in Jesus, the most unfashionable of all Oxford colleges. Wilson was exactly the sort of bookish Northern grammar school lad that the Bullingdon Club toffs delighted in mocking and throwing in fountains. And Catesby knew that Wilson in response would have built up a defensive carapace of cocky, but brittle, self-assurance. Wilson's problem was that he represented the people of Britain, regional and unfashionable, rather than the smart ruling elite. Even though Wilson was seven years younger, Catesby felt he was an older brother who wanted to protect him from bullies.

**Washington:** 20 February 1963

As Chief of Counter-intelligence, Angleton was the only officer, other than the DCI himself, who had access to the Director's Log. Angleton had been added to the Director's Log distribution list by Allen Dulles who was very impressed by his 'astute intelligence and perceptivity'. Unfortunately for Angleton, Dulles had been sacked following the Bay of Pigs fiasco – for which Dulles was largely responsible – and replaced by a shrewd businessman. The new DCI wasn't particularly pleased with Angleton's special status, but realised he was dealing with a dark prince who ruled a powerful fiefdom – and, as a shrewd businessman, the DCI thought the best tactic was to give Angleton enough rope to hang himself. It eventually happened, but long after the shrewd businessman had departed. FURIOSO was as mad and tenacious as his code name persona.

FROM OSO LONDON (ATTN: ADDOCI)
SM/DOGGED is now our most valuable asset in the British
Security Service. DOGGED is very concerned about the

recent death of Hugh Gaitskell and his replacement as Labor
leader by Harold Wilson, who represents the far left socialist
wing of the party. SM/DOGGED also reminds us that Wilson
made several trips to Moscow as Minister of Trade in the
late 1940s and was responsible for selling the Rolls-Royce jet
engines to the Soviet Union which later powered the MiG-15.
After resigning from the Labor government in 1951 –
following a bitter and personal argument with Gaitskell over
Britain's socialist health service – Wilson became director
of an import/export company that bases all its business
on trade with the Soviet Union. During his many trips to
Moscow, Wilson has formed close friendships with Anastas
Mikoyan, Vyacheslav Molotov and Andrei Gromyko.

Angleton leaned back and lit another cigarette. He remembered
what he used to tell Allen Dulles: 'If you don't always – *always*
– fear the worst, you shouldn't be a counter-intelligence officer.'
The problem was that too many of his colleagues didn't always
fear the worst. And not all of them were big fans of AE/TANGO's
dire warnings. TANGO had, in fact, predicted the current scenario when they had lunch at Harvey's. Angleton went back to
the Director's Log.

SM/DOGGED has signalled further concerns about the
nature of Hugh Gaitskell's sudden death. Not long after his
patient's death, Gaitskell's doctor contacted the Security
Service. The doctor was very concerned about the cause of
death. Systemic lupus erythematosus is an autoimmune
disease that is extremely rare in Northern Europe. The
occurrence of the disease is mostly confined to women of
child-bearing age in tropical Africa. The doctor estimates the
total number of cases in Europe as less than ten.

Angleton smiled. *Always* fear the worst. He felt a glowing sense
of pride as he stared through the haze of smoke at the Manet, on
loan from a banker friend, framed on his office wall. Counter-
espionage was like appreciating Impressionist art. On one hand,

the painting captures the image as a rapid passing glimpse. On the other hand, the pictures can be blindingly bright and vibrant. The situation in England was both: subtle and glaring. He went back to the log.

> SM/DOGGED confirms that Gaitskell has not recently, and perhaps never, made a trip to tropical Africa. Gaitskell had, however, been planning a trip to Moscow at the end of January to meet Khrushchev. One month before he died, Gaitskell had visited the Soviet consulate in London to obtain a visa for the trip. Despite his status, Gaitskell was kept waiting a long time at the consulate while his visa was processed. During that time Gaitskell was served tea and biscuits. SM/DOGGED is now making enquiries at Porton Down, the British Defense Department's biological warfare center, to see how it would be possible to poison someone with a fatal dose of lupus.

Angleton made a note in his diary: *Arrange urgent meeting with AE/TANGO about Line F's bio-chemical capabilities for assassination.* He had found out from TANGO how a KGB hit man had used radioactive thallium to murder the anti-Communist Ukrainian writer Lev Rebet in Munich in 1957. A lethal dose had been sprayed in his face with the type of atomiser commonly used by asthma sufferers. A pellet to induce lupus might be more sophisticated, but always assume the worst.

Angleton looked at the clock. It was past eleven o'clock and time for a pre-prandial drink. He went to the hospitality cabinet and poured himself a JD without ice or water. Philby's defection to Moscow – now certain – was another brush stroke that began as faint, almost invisible, and then burst into colour and brightness like a Monet sunrise. Angleton now regretted not having ordered a 'wet op' on his former friend, one false-flagged as a KGB assassination. Philby's treachery was a personal blow and slap in the face – and proved that no one could be trusted. But how did it fit in with Wilson and Gaitskell's murder? Philby must have known that he had been finally and positively identified as a Soviet agent. Could it be that Moscow feared that Philby would crack under interrogation and tell the truth about the conspiracy to put Wilson in power? And who in SIS had been responsible for letting Philby escape? What a pity that SM/HOUND had retired from SIS – or had he been forced out? HOUND had been CIA's only eye and ear in SIS. Angleton went to the safe and got the file for SM/HOUND. The tribute from a powerful friend of America's was glowing: *X is a noble warrior in the fight against Communism. When there is a crisis, he acts decisively and takes risks. He is willing to stand alone for a friend when everyone else has deserted that friend. X is not afraid of making enemies in the fight for freedom.* Angleton made an action note in the Director's Log: *To OSO London from ADDOCI: Make immediate clandestine contact with SM/HOUND and tell him that we offer full support.*

## Hampstead Garden Suburb, London: 28 February 1963

Catesby thought it was ironic, but totally coincidental, that Hugh Gaitskell's former GP lived two streets away from Harold Wilson. The first news that rumours were circulating about Gaitskell's death came from Frances. Ferret didn't know how to keep his mouth shut – a big problem for a rogue agent in a security service. It also didn't take long for the Gaitskell assassination rumours to reach the ear of Henry Bone who immediately summoned Catesby and gave him the assignment.

'Tell him,' said Bone, 'that you're a journalist – or at least give him that impression.'

'Should I talk "Sarf Lunnon"?'

'Perhaps, but don't overdo it.'

'Actually,' said Catesby, 'this door-stepping stuff under journo cover might be a bit below my dignity. Aren't I supposed to be getting an OBE in a month or two?'

Bone nodded. 'And, please Catesby, don't do your "Sarf Lunnon" routine with the Queen – or be chewing gum when you go to the podium.'

'I never chew gum. It pulls out my NHS fillings.'

'Good.'

The doctor's house was similar to Wilson's, but not as large. Catesby was wearing a trilby and looking Fleet Street scruffy in a stained mac. The doctor didn't invite him into the house or seem very happy to see him.

'I cannot answer any questions regarding patient confidentiality.'

'I fully appreciate that, but Mr Gaitskell was a very famous patient.'

'Fame does not make an exception to patient confidentiality.'

'But listen, doctor, I know what us lot are like. Have any other newspaper types been sniffing around?' Catesby smiled. 'We like to know who else is on the case so we can throw a spanner between their legs.'

The GP gave a weary sigh. 'I have been pestered – and, I assure you, I sent them away with fleas in their ears.'

Catesby looked at the doctor and dropped his wide-boy manner and voice. 'Were they journalists?'

The doctor looked thoughtful and seemed less hostile. 'I don't know.'

'Okay, I'll tell you what I know. I know that Hugh Gaitskell died of an autoimmune disease called systemic lupus erythematosus – and that is a very rare illness in the UK. I'm not going to ask you any questions about Mr Gaitskell, but can you tell me anything about that form of lupus?'

'I'm a GP, not a specialist.'

'Well, I suppose I'd better find one then.'

The doctor paused. 'Maybe I can help you.'

She was the most stunning and beautiful woman Catesby had ever seen. She was black, stately and tall – and one of the most respected consultants at the London School of Hygiene and Tropical Medicine. She towered over Catesby – and not just physically. Unlike him and his slithering ilk, she was someone who had devoted her life to relieving human misery. Spies, on the other hand, were the Anopheles mosquitoes of human society.

'The answer to your first question is no.' She was sitting in her office chair leaning forward slightly with her hands folded.

Catesby nodded as if he knew more than he did. She had the demeanour, he thought, of a kindly university professor dealing with a clueless undergraduate.

'SLE is not a rare disease...'

Catesby had twigged that 'SLE' was medical shorthand for 'systemic lupus erythematosus'.

'...and,' she continued, 'I cannot understand why anyone would think it is. SLE is, in fact, quite common.'

'Even in Europe?'

'In Northern Europe the rate is about forty per 100,000 people, but much higher among those of African descent. The rate among us is four times the average, 160 per 100,000.' The consultant paused. 'Statistically, the person most likely to be diagnosed with

SLE is an African woman of child-bearing age – and the condition is exacerbated by poverty.'

Catesby noticed the woman's eyes had flashed a hint of anger. She was aware of social inequality.

'The factors that cause SLE are not just genetic, but also environmental.'

'But women are much more likely to contract SLE than men?'

The consultant nodded. 'That is true. Women are eight times more likely to be diagnosed with SLE than men. An SLE prognosis is, however, much worse for a man than a woman.'

'So men, although less likely to contract SLE, are more likely to die from it when they do?'

'Correct.'

Catesby was warming to the subject. He began to wish that he had done Medicine rather than Modern Languages with postgrad qualifications in Espionage and Dirty Tricks.

'One final question,' he said, 'how many white men are likely to die of SLE in Britain in a typical year?'

'That's a difficult question. SLE is very good at disguising itself as other diseases – and, therefore, it is often not diagnosed as the actual cause of death.' The consultant paused and looked thoughtful. 'I would estimate, however, that between 500 and 1,000 white British males die of SLE per annum.'

'So, it is not a rare cause of death for a white middle-aged male?'

'Unusual, but not rare.' She gave Catesby a searching look. 'Why did you want to know?'

'Because I...' Catesby wanted to tell her everything – not just about Gaitskell, but about justice, equality, peace and friendship; about Pasteur, Curie, and Lister; about art and love – but couldn't find the words.

'You don't need to tell me.'

'Thank you.'

Angleton wasn't happy with the President. Kennedy was dismissive of the serious situation developing in Britain – and he also had scant regard for TANGO's warnings. In fact, Kennedy seemed to be sidelining the CIA altogether in preference to advice from his brother and the Harvard coterie. Angleton was a Yale graduate and the rivalry between the two universities went beyond the sports field and into the dark areas of secret loyalties. The most secret part of Angleton's counter-intelligence empire was SIG, the Special Investigations Group – and the most secret of SIG's file were the 201s. The 201 files were secret histories of Americans who were either a serious potential danger to the country's security – or, alternatively, of individuals who could be helpful to SIG. In some cases, the 201 subjects fitted into both categories.

The 201 file that Angleton had on his desk related to a former Marine who had defected to the Soviet Union – and come back again. The ex-Marine had had a troubled childhood and as a young teenager, owing to threatening behaviour at home and in the classroom, had been sent to a child psychiatrist. The psychiatrist's report intrigued Angleton: *The subject has a vivid fantasy life turning around the topics of omnipotence and power; through which he tries to compensate for his shortcomings and tendencies.* Angleton was not without self-knowledge and not without knowledge of what others thought of him. He realised that his detractors would say that the psychiatrist's report could equally have described himself. But they were wrong – otherwise he would have felt 'the rage of Caliban at seeing his own face in a mirror'.

The 201 file on the ex-Marine was dynamite. It contained records of the subject's military training. As an ex-radar operator in the Far East, the former Marine had knowledge of the CIA's top secret U-2 programme. And yet, upon his return to the United States, the CIA had not interrogated him about whether or not he had passed on intelligence to the Soviet Union. And it would have been the responsibility of Angleton's section to have done so. But in some cases it is more important to groom someone and watch them than to harass and frighten them. Angleton thought the ex-Marine could be useful and he opted for the light touch. Part of SIG was a team under the command of a retired US Army officer code-named LN/RIFLE. Their job was to deal with security threats that could not be prosecuted in open legal proceedings owing to the risk of exposing other clandestine operations and issues of high sensitivity. Sometimes the secret intelligence arm of a government has to override that government. Angleton picked up the ex-Marine's 201 file. It was time to pass it on to LN/RIFLE.

Angleton, morphing once again into mad FURIOSO, sat back, lit a cigarette and poured another JD. The smoke patterns were sinister. Was the President himself a security risk? *Always* fear the worst.


**Pimlico, London:** 3 March 1963

Catesby hadn't expected a visit. Particularly on a Sunday morning and from someone who had never been to the flat before. The visitor, wearing a black roll-neck jumper and a leather coat, was perfect Fitzrovia bohemian, just as his city-suited and bowler-hatted weekday self was perfect Whitehall mandarin. He even looked a bit grubby: unshaven and hung-over.

'Good morning, Henry,' said Catesby, 'what a pleasant surprise.'

'I was on my way to a Duncan Grant exhibition at the Tate – and, as you live so near, I thought you might like to come.'

'I'd love to.'

The Tate was a quick seven-minute walk from Catesby's flat. Bone seemed more relaxed and less guarded then he did during the week. But that didn't mean he was off-duty.

'Do you know Duncan Grant?' said Catesby.

'Slightly.' There was something in Bone's voice that was reserved and sly again.

'He used to live near me in Suffolk,' continued Catesby. 'During the Great War he worked on a nearby farm as a conscientious objector.'

'I know.'

It wasn't a big exhibition. Most of the paintings were works that hadn't been shown before. Many were nudes.

'As you know,' said Bone as they walked through the gallery, 'Grant was influenced by the Post-Impressionists, but couldn't be described as one. He was, and remains, far more radical than most critics realise.'

There was one nude of Vanessa Bell, but most were of men – often beautiful young men. Catesby stopped in front of a male nude that was only a torso – the head and lower legs were not visible.

'I bet,' said Catesby, 'that one is a self-portrait. That's why you can't identify the sitter.'

'I don't think so.' There was a faint smile on Bone's face, a smile of nostalgia. He would never admit that he was looking at the body of his younger self. 'I think your being in the Tate, Henry, is just as much of an honour as your great-great grandfather hanging in the National Portrait Gallery.'

'Let's move on,' said Bone, 'there are far more interesting paintings.'

After an hour they emerged from the gallery on to the Embankment. The weather was clear, but still bitterly cold. The Thames was in full ebb and a stiff easterly breeze whipped up the river into white horses.

'The Fournier debriefings,' said Bone turning up his collar, 'continue to reveal gems – although in some cases, jewels that we would rather had never existed.'

Catesby sensed an ominous note in Bone's voice, but, as usual, he knew that Bone wouldn't unveil the reason for the dark note until he was ready. Bone was a master at keeping people twisting on tenterhooks.

'Now,' said Bone, 'let's look again at the bright shining gems from Chez Fournier.'

'The identity of the SIS mole is absolutely priceless.'

'Do you mean,' said Bone with a bleak smile, 'that there is only one mole *chez nous*?'

'I mean only one mole who was spying for Washington.'

Bone gave another bleak smile. 'And, by the way, Catesby,

please don't agree with the Americans when they accuse SIS of being the London branch of Moscow Central. They don't understand irony – particularly your irony.'

'I wasn't being ironic.'

'Touché. Let's get back to SM/HOUND.'

'Totally barking and fanatically right-wing. I'm not surprised that Fournier revealed him as the CIA mole. Was he pushed out?'

'No, he left of his own volition. He thought Macmillan was dangerously left-wing.'

'God knows what he would think of a Wilson government.'

'He will be a problem. JJ,' said Bone using the initials by which HOUND was generally known in SIS, 'has already linked up with a few very right-wing groups.'

'What's he doing for money?'

'He's topping up his pension as a consultant to a merchant bank.'

'Passing on secrets that could be useful for insider trading?'

'I'd rather not comment.'

Catesby remembered a vile and embarrassing rant that JJ had delivered in the senior officers' canteen in the bowels of Broadway Buildings the year before he retired. JJ later printed it off as a pamphlet, a sort of farewell letter. Catesby had kept a copy. At the centre of JJ's rant were accusations of 'moral degeneracy'. JJ had somehow linked homosexuality with non-white immigration and Communist infiltration to explain Britain's decline into lawlessness and corruption. It was, according to JJ, the role of the spy to put things right by covert action to override the failures of parliament, diplomats and priests. An old hand from the Middle East and Africa P section had leaned over to Catesby and whispered, 'We all need a jolly good spanking. Your place or mine?'

'Another of Fournier's jewels,' continued Bone, 'is the identity of SM/DOGGED.'

'But we always knew it was him.' Catesby had long suspected that Ferret was leaking information to the CIA and selected members of the press.

'But we now know there is also a close bond between DOGGED and FURIOSO.'

'Angleton.'

'I prefer calling him FURIOSO. It also turns out that FURIOSO suspected Fournier long before we did – but then again, he suspects everyone. I am sure that FURIOSO's bosses realise there are mental problems, but they seem powerless to do anything about it. He is dangerous.'

Catesby suspected that there was a transatlantic battle going on between Bone and Angleton, but he wasn't going to mention it.

Bone stared across the river towards Vauxhall. 'I used to scull and row past here. The school used to keep the boats at Putney – and, I believe, still do. There's nothing like a vigorous row on a cold clear spring morning. Do you know the difference, Catesby, between sculling and rowing?'

'You scull with two oars, one in each hand. You row with both hands on one oar.'

'Good. You love boats, don't you?'

Catesby nodded.

'The problem with spying,' said Bone, 'is that we're almost always rowing and not sculling. We're not in control of the boat. We hope the other oars are pulling in the same direction, but we can never be sure. And if something – or someone – goes wrong, we all sink.'

Catesby reminded silent. He pretended to be entranced by the river, but he was really thinking about Bone. Could he be the rogue oarsman?

'The wretched EMPUSA,' continued Bone, 'appeared on the scene long after Fournier was out of the loop. Sadly, he can't give us any background – but one can deduce that EMPUSA's theatrical ravings have found an appreciative audience in paranoid FURIOSO.'

Catesby detected a defensive note in Bone's voice and manner.

'Do you know,' said Bone, 'that EMPUSA is coming to London for a debriefing?'

'I had heard rumours.'

'The situation has to be handled with delicacy – politeness and not even a hint of a wry smile.'

'On the other hand,' said Catesby, 'provoking him could bring forth even more bizarre accusations.'

'But that would make us look as if we had something to hide – and we were trying to cover up by provoking him to get him angry and irrational.'

'We'll play it your way, Henry.'

'But we might not even get invited to the debrief.' Bone stopped walking and looked at Catesby. 'But there is one more thing – and it concerns you directly.'

Catesby braced himself against the cold wind.

'I don't understand,' said Bone, 'why Fournier didn't mention this sooner. Perhaps, he thought no one would believe him – and it does seem bizarre.'

'I can't imagine,' lied Catesby, 'what he was talking about.'

Bone took a deep breath. 'Fournier claims that you murdered a Nazi war criminal in Bremen in May 1951. The victim was a PAPERCLIP German the Americans wanted to ratline to South America. Fournier said his plan was to swap the war criminal for information about Harold Wilson and his sending Rolls-Royce jet engines to the Soviet Union. The Americans, as Fournier now realises, got the wrong end of the stick about Wilson and the engines.'

'But that doesn't make any difference if you want to smear someone.'

'That's another matter. Let's get back to you, William. Fournier says that you refused to give him any insider information about Wilson, presumably because you didn't have any?'

Catesby nodded.

'In any case, Fournier decided to let you have the PAPERCLIP war criminal after all.'

'Why?'

'For two reasons. Fournier was disillusioned with the PAPER-CLIP op and thought the war criminal deserved it. But less ideal-istically, Fournier wanted to get back at you. He thought you had burgled his flat – but couldn't be sure. In retrospect,' smiled Bone, 'he thinks you're innocent.'

'I am. I paid a *Putzfrau* to do it.'

'Fournier says he now regrets doing it, but…'

'But what?'

'He passed on the details of you murdering the war criminal to his boss. Of course, Fournier sanitised his version of the story so that he had nothing at all to do with you getting hold of the PAPERCLIP German.'

Catesby smiled. 'Typically Kit.'

'Fournier told his boss that your murder of the German could be used as a blackmail lever against you at sometime in the future.' Bone paused and looked hard at Catesby. 'What I can't understand is why Fournier would concoct such an absurd story. What does he have to gain by telling lies in his situation?'

Catesby looked down the river.

'Is he lying, William?'

Catesby shook his head.

'Why did you do it?'

'I wanted to put the ghosts of Oradour-sur-Glane to rest.'

'Did it work?'

'No.'

'There is, William, one disturbing new development.'

'Go on.'

'JJ knows about it. Not all of his new friends are as mad and right-wing as he is. One of them, whom I know slightly – from rowing actually – says that JJ refers to you as "Killer Catesby". JJ is passing around a rumour that you killed the PAPERCLIP Nazi because he had information linking you – and myself – to Maclean and Burgess. Apparently, we're part of the same ring.'

'And Harold Wilson?'

'Of course, and one prominent Tory politician is also on the list. JJ hates Edward Heath.'

'I think we know why.'

'It's madness, William – almost a form of rabies.'

'How do you suppose JJ found out?'

'I'm sure that FURIOSO has Fournier's file on the incident stowed away in his safe. He might have leaked it to DOGGED who passed it on to JJ. FURIOSO's grand plan is to turn Five into the CIA's London branch and to do away with us altogether.'

'By the way, Henry, there is no evidence linking me to the murder. The forensic files are now at the bottom of the River

Weser. I blackmailed the *Kriminalpolizist* in charge of the case to deep-six them. He was involved in the black market and also lied about his Nazi past on his denazification questionnaire.' Catesby gave a bleak smile. 'Maybe I should have shot him too.'

'You still might have to – *oh what a web we weave*.'

'So where do we go from here?'

'We make our enemies look like completely mad idiots.'

'Even when they're not?'

Bone smiled. 'Especially when they're not.'

## Leconfield House, London: July, 1963

The meeting was over and Hollis and Bone were the only ones left in the conference room at the Security Service HQ. Roger Hollis had been head of the service since 1956 and was feeling battered. Bone had been at the meeting to deputise for the head of SIS – so it wasn't strange that the pair should have lingered behind for a chat. And yet, there had been a few knowing glances exchanged as the others filed out of the room.

'He's costing us a lot of money,' said Hollis rubbing his eyes, 'ten thousand pounds into his Swiss bank account every month he's in England – and taking up our best safe house. They say if you pay peanuts you get monkeys; well we're paying gold bullion and getting nothing but unsubstantiated rumours.'

The purpose of the meeting had been to give EMPUSA a stage from which to address the heads of SIS and MI5 as well as members of JIC and the Privy Council.

'And,' said Hollis, 'I'm sure you've heard that he also wants to interview the Prime Minister and the cabinet – all of them.'

'And the Queen.'

'He couldn't understand why she wasn't here.' Hollis looked at his notes. 'If I may, Henry, let me summarise EMPUSA's version of Moscow Central's cunning plan for taking over the United Kingdom. Please let me know if I leave anything out.'

'Of course, Roger.'

'Stage one was the assassination of Hugh Gaitskell, a friend of Washington and an enemy of the undercover Communists posing as members of the Labour Party. Thank you, by the way, for sending me Catesby's report on systemic lupus erythematosus. How revealing that it isn't a rare disease and not one that would generate concern as a cause of death. But, Henry, I've gone one up on you. I've now obtained a copy of Gaitskell's post-mortem – and no lupus cells were found in his body. He died of a condition called 'immune complex deficiency' – an even more common condition, but one that resembles lupus.' Hollis smiled. 'But before I had the autopsy report, I contacted an imminent virus specialist who said it was completely impossible to devise a lupus poison pill or spray.' Hollis paused. 'Are you still with me?'

Bone nodded.

'So let me summarise EMPUSA's allegation. The KGB bumped off Gaitskell using a pill that is impossible to fabricate in order to induce a rare disease – which isn't rare in any case – and a disease which, it turns out, Gaitskell didn't have in the first place.'

'I couldn't put it better myself.'

'I bet you could, Henry. But where are we now?'

'With Harold Wilson.'

'Now that Gaitskell is out of the way, the KGB had to manoeuvre their long-term sleeper-agent into becoming leader of the Labour Party. Not easy, because the person most likely to succeed Gaitskell was the deputy leader George Brown, a right-winger and fervent anti-Communist. I am sure you noticed that EMPUSA didn't explain how the KGB got James Callaghan to stand in the first round and split the Gaitskellite vote.'

'But he did say there was widespread concern among Labour MPs about Brown's drinking.'

'Fair enough. But the KGB still have to get Wilson into 10 Downing Street – and this is where it gets dirty.' Hollis paused and stared at Bone. 'And affects me personally. What do you know, Henry?'

'I know that you're being blamed for warning Kim that it was time to do a fade. But I'm being blamed for that too – and so is most of SIS.'

Hollis laughed. 'It's almost as if we were part of a pantomime audience: *They're behind you, Kim!*'

Bone smiled bleakly. There might be some truth in Hollis's words.

'Did you know,' said Hollis, 'that my own staff have put me under surveillance?'

'I have heard rumours.'

'And I can't do anything about it, because if I ordered the surveillance to be stopped, it would prove that I had something to hide, that I was a Sov agent.'

Bone gave a sympathetic smile. As far as he knew, Hollis had nothing to hide, other than the fact that he was having a long-term affair with his secretary. If, thought Bone, Hollis had a fault, it was not being ruthless enough.

Hollis seemed to have read Bone's thoughts. 'I have one officer in particular, and a few others, who ought to be disciplined – or even dismissed. But once again, if I do so, it will cast suspicion on me, that I got rid of them to protect myself.' Hollis smiled apologetically. 'Sorry, Henry, I digress. The next stage in Moscow's grand plan is…?

'Profumo.'

'Totally agree. EMPUSA maintains that the KGB is choreographing the so-called Profumo scandal in order to discredit the Conservatives and get Labour elected next year. The Ivanov angle suggests that Tory ministers cannot be trusted with government secrets because they will pass the secrets on to their girlfriends who will then share them with their Russian boyfriends. How utterly absurd.' Hollis paused. 'And now I'm being accused of not having warned Profumo.'

'A bit unfair.'

'They're out to get me, Henry. I'm going to retire as soon as I get to sixty – I've had enough. And, by the way, Macmillan has had enough too – the Profumo affair has worn him out. He's going to step down in the autumn.' Hollis smiled. 'Macmillan was never a big fan of the intelligence services. He once told me that the government could save a lot of money by simply sending cabinet minutes and other secrets directly to Moscow and cutting out the middlemen.'

'Dour.'

'I suppose, Henry, that you are already aware that EMPUSA has a big supporter in FURIOSO. It was love at first sight and they are now walking hand in hand into a sunset of shared paranoia.'

'And power.'

Hollis nodded and looked at his notes. 'It's easy to be Nostradamus when you're vague. Here's what EMPUSA predicted when he first defected: *An unknown political leader in an unknown country will be assassinated by the KGB.*'

## Rock Spring, Arlington, Virginia: 22 November 1963

It was a large detached house with a huge garden. The people who lived in the neighbourhood were the Washington elite: high-ranking government officials, members of Congress, lobbyists, consultants and the press corps. Despite the news, it was still a beautiful late autumn day and the air smelt of bonfire smoke. Angleton was a keen gardener and had a greenhouse full of rare and prize orchids. Orchids were the undercover agents of the natural world disguising themselves as bees and other insects in order to honey-trap unwitting pollinators.

Most of the neighbours were glued to the rolling television news about Kennedy's assassination, but James Angleton was tidying up his garden. It was unusual for him to be home so early and before dark. He often stayed at the office until 10 p.m. or later – and the couple living nearest him did think it odd that he would be home so early on such a traumatic day. 'Perhaps,' said the wife, 'he just needs time to himself, to get away from it all. It's so awful.'

Any other neighbour watching Angleton would assume he was burning leaves and cuttings. But, amid the garden detritus, there was also a top secret 201 file turning into ash and smoke. Angleton's file on Lee Harvey Oswald was completely toxic and had to go.

## London: 24 November 1963

It was only the second time Catesby had seen someone shot at close range – and the first time he hadn't been the person pulling the trigger.

It was a Sunday and Catesby had gone to Frances's flat for supper and to see the twins who were home from university. After supper, they turned on the television to see the news. As a family they didn't normally watch television, but recent events had made viewing compelling. The world was still reeling from the Kennedy assassination and the news was full of it to the exclusion of almost everything else. Aldous Huxley, the author of *Brave New World* and a writer Catesby much admired for his pacifism and human- ism, had also died on 22 November, but Huxley's death had been scarcely reported. A lesson to be learned, thought Catesby. If you want a good obituary, don't die on the same day that a glamorous American President gets his brains blown out.

As soon as the news came on, it was obvious that some- thing dramatic had happened in Dallas. The presenter immedi- ately introduced the television news clip of Jack Ruby shooting Lee Harvey Oswald as he was led through the basement of the Dallas Police Station. At first, Catesby couldn't believe it was actual live footage. It looked as staged as a crime film: the shooter crouched and wearing a trilby and the person shot crumpling in pain. Catesby could almost hear Ruby shouting: 'Take that, you bastard!' – even though the words had never been uttered.

When the news was over and they turned the television off, the son spoke first, 'Who do you think did it, Will?'

'It wasn't us,' said Catesby. 'But I don't know about your moth- er's gang. You'll have to ask her.'

Frances shook her head. 'Not us either.'

The children had reached an age when it was pointless to hide their professions from them. It was a myth that the close families of spies didn't know what their jobs were. But it was important that families be discreet.

'Didn't you see what really happened?' said the daughter.

'Pray tell us,' said her brother.

'Oswald's killing was faked. The bullet Ruby fired was a blank. It's a conspiracy to spring Oswald out of custody and smuggle him to another country.'

Catesby was impressed. 'Who ordered Kennedy's assassination?'

The daughter sighed. 'Lyndon Johnson, obviously. He's now

President and it happened in Texas. Any fool can see that.'

'I don't think so,' said the son. 'Johnson arranging it would be *too* obvious.'

'I don't think you should be so light-hearted about it,' said Frances. 'It's a great tragedy and could have an awful effect on our own country.'

'Like what?' said the daughter.

'Like Britain being destroyed in a nuclear war,' said Catesby. 'If the Americans think that Moscow ordered the assassination it could lead to a nuclear exchange in which we get obliterated.'

'As gloomy as that,' said the son.

His sister looked at Frances and Catesby. 'I'm surprised you two aren't better informed.'

Catesby knew that the family banter was a form of whistling in the dark. The situation was serious and dangerous. His biggest fear was that the conspiratorial madness of America would leap across the Atlantic and infect Britain too.

**Pimlico, London:** 16 October 1964

Catesby had stayed up late listening to the election results, but fell asleep before the final results were in. When he woke up in the morning, the radio was still on and Harold Wilson was prime minister. He listened to the commentary as he brewed his tea and slipped two slices of Mother's Pride under the gas grill.

> *Harold Wilson has led the Labour Party to a narrow election victory with a majority of four. Labour will replace the Tory government of Sir Alec Douglas-Home. The Conservative Party's hold on power has now ended after thirteen years. During that time there were four different Tory leaders.*

Catesby took a bottle of milk out of the fridge and sniffed it. It had gone off, but at least the Tories were out.

> *Sir Alec Douglas-Home served as prime minister for only one year following Harold Macmillan's resignation owing to ill health. Macmillan's government had been increasingly unpopular in mid-term following a series of scandals involving sex and spying. Douglas-Home had faced the difficult task of rebuilding his party's*

He turned over the bread and wondered if he should get a toaster.

> *Wilson has tried to tie the Labour Party to what he sees as 'the growing confidence of Britain'. Wilson maintains that the 'white heat of technology'…*

He definitely would get a toaster.

> *…sweep away 'restrictive practices… on both sides of industry'.*

Catesby set out the margarine and jam, but knew there was trouble ahead.

*The Liberal Party doubled its share of the vote, mainly at the expense of the Conservatives. Labour did not increase its vote share significantly, but the fall in support for the Tories was enough for Wilson to secure an overall majority of four seats.*

## London: 21 October 1964

It was one of London's oldest and most exclusive gentlemen's clubs. Dark oak panelling, leather sofas and armchairs, eighteenth-century paintings – some of which were mildly erotic – and hushed tones. But on one occasion, a crusty Scottish laird had broken the hush by throwing a servant through a bow window. When the club steward had strongly remonstrated, the laird replied: 'Put him on my bill.' Conversation is usually about sport, drink and other safe topics. Discussion of trade or business is not allowed. The members and guests who had reserved the billiard room were, however, not obeying the rule. The group consisted of a hereditary peer, a banker, a retired colonel, one serving general and JJ, the retired SIS officer. If someone had accused the five of being a combination of robber baron and imperialist they would not have been offended.

'Actually,' said the peer, 'I'm not worried about Wilson at all. It won't be long before he fucks up and there's another election.'

'The problem,' said the general, 'is that Wilson has already put in place plans for withdrawing British forces from all over the world. We're also going to end up with no aircraft carriers and no Polaris.'

The retired colonel, who had just got back from the civil war in Yemen, was the only one interested in the billiard table. He circled the baize potting reds. 'You know,' he said, 'I'm not sure we really need official UK forces. We're seeing off the Egyptians and the Sovs pretty much on our own. I always think that Housman got it spot on with that poem of his, "Epitaph on an Army of Mercenaries":

*Their shoulders held the sky suspended;*
*They stood, and earth's foundations stay;*

*What God abandoned, these defended,*
*And saved the sum of things for pay.'*

The colonel paused to pot another red. 'Lovely piece, isn't it? Makes me want to cry. I'll always put my trust in mercs and private armies.'

The general shook his head. 'Mercenaries do not come equipped with battle tanks, aircraft carriers and nuclear missiles.'

The retired colonel turned to the banker. 'Tell them, Mungo, how much we're getting from the Saudis.'

Mungo told them.

'A fine sum indeed. But,' said the general, 'I do not want to see UK defence and foreign policy dependent upon the whims of the House of Saud – or anyone else with deep pockets.'

'Or the Kremlin,' said JJ.

'Yes,' droned the colonel lining up another red, 'that is a worry. But if push comes to shove we'll get rid of him.'

'I think,' said the banker, 'that what we will be seeing in the future – without a socialist Labour government getting in the way – is the privatisation of British foreign and military policy. We had it in the nineteenth century with the British East-India Company and Cecil Rhodes' British South Africa Company. Governments are useless.'

'Governments are not useless,' said JJ, 'they are dangerous. We now have a situation where the Prime Minister of the United Kingdom is a Soviet agent who is placing other Soviet agents into positions of power.'

'Don't worry,' said the colonel, 'we'll get rid of him.'

The colonel was the most complex and, despite his ready laugh and wit, the most embittered of the five. He was a descendant of Ireland's Protestant Ascendancy. Both his family's stately homes had been burnt down during the 1919–1923 Troubles – and his father and an uncle had been assassinated. He feared that such chaos might one day come to Britain. And he was willing to do anything – no matter how ruthless – to stop it from happening.

**Washington:** Midnight, 10 February 1965

The President was not in a good mood to begin with – and the telephone call from the British Prime Minister made that mood considerably worse. A particularly vicious Viet Cong attack in the Saigon area had just killed or wounded over a hundred US servicemen. There were two other men in the Oval Office. The President glared at his National Security Adviser.

'He won't send troops,' said the President, 'he made some piss-ant excuse last December. I said, "Come on, Harold, just a single fucking Black Watch bagpiper playing in front of the Saigon British embassy." And he comes up with some feeble bullshit about Britain being co-chairman of the Geneva peace conference.'

'There are methods,' said the NS Adviser, 'to prod him into compliance.'

'But I'm not having him come over here so he can play the great statesman to the gallery back home. We've got enough pollution in Washington already without Harold Wilson coming over with his pecker hanging out and peeing all over me. We need British soldiers, not British advice. I told him, "Why don't you run what piss little is left of your empire, Harold, and let me run Vietnam?"'

'May I intervene, Mr President?'

Johnson looked at the NS Adviser. He was a dapper and smooth man, the epitome of Ivy League education and old money East Coast finesse – not normally the sort of person LBJ liked to be around. But this was a WASP who agreed with his policy on Vietnam and could be diamond hard. The President nodded.

'The British need our help to sustain an overvalued pound. Their economy has suffered for years from outdated industrial practices and militant trade unions. The British are financing their health service and welfare system by cutting military spending and withdrawing from their overseas responsibilities. They can't have it both ways. They can't expect the US Treasury to bailout sterling when there is no British flag in Vietnam.'

Johnson shook his head. 'I know what you're suggesting, but we're not going to do it. I'd love to stand on Wilson's balls, but if it ever came out in public that we used financial blackmail to force Britain to send soldiers to Vietnam that would make our position even worse.'

'I can see your point,' said the NS Advisor, even though he strongly disagreed with it.

Angleton looked on in silence and doodled an impressionistic ink sketch of the Palace of Westminster. Johnson had turned out to be an even weaker President than he had anticipated. America's hope lay beyond his term in office. Angleton had decided, at least for the time being, not to share his London files – especially, the fact that he had a mole in the Wilson cabinet. Angleton smiled at the other two as the meeting ended. He trusted neither of them – and neither of them understood the dark secrets of Britain.

**Mayfair, London:** 27 July 1965

One of the reasons JJ had left the Secret Intelligence Service was because he despised Macmillan and his soft policies – especially the casual way he was presiding over the rapid dissolution of the British Empire. Macmillan's 'Wind of Change' speech had left JJ spluttering with rage – especially Macmillan's condemnation of apartheid and white rule in South Africa. But now, in JJ's view, the Tory Party had sunk even lower. He picked up the newspaper, crisply ironed by a servant, and read again the latest outrage.

### Edward Heath Elected New Tory Leader

Shadow Chancellor Edward Heath has defeated two rivals to win the Conservative leadership contest. The leadership vote was triggered by last week's unexpected resignation of Sir Alec Douglas-Home.

Mr Heath won 150 votes to defeat Shadow Foreign Secretary Reginald Maudling on 133. A third challenger, maverick Enoch Powell, won only 15 votes, but Mr Powell's challenge left Mr Heath with a slim overall majority.

Mr Heath's unexpected victory came as a surprise. Reginald Maudling had been widely tipped to win.

JJ shook his head and shoved the newspaper aside with disgust. He turned to the general who was gazing sphinx-like into the distance. The two of them were sitting in a quiet corner of the club drinking whisky and soda.

'What has this country come to?' said JJ. 'Two of our main political parties are now led by sodomites and the third by a Communist.'

'I'm not in the Navy,' said the general, 'so I'm not up to scratch on sodomy. Can you tell me which ones are the sodomites?'

'Heath and Thorpe.'

'Oh, indeed, but not I assume...'

'Not with each other, at least not as far as I know.'

'Disgraceful.'

'There was,' said JJ, 'a very strong whiff of corruption from the Macmillan government as well.'

'I know Macmillan had a limp handshake,' said the general, 'but that was because of a shrapnel wound. You can't really blame him for that.'

'Macmillan's wife had – is probably still having – a long-term affair with Bob Boothby who is also a sodomite. Boothby likes villains: his lovers include Ronnie Kray and a cat burglar called Leslie Holt.'

The peer joined them. 'I won't hear a word against Bob Boothby,' said the peer, 'he's always the life and soul of any party. Great chap.'

JJ remained silent. He realised that not everyone shared his views. There was a decadent corruption at the heart of modern Britain that needed to be purged.

'Cheer up,' said the peer, 'it takes all types.'

## Balmoral Castle: August, 1965

The Wilsons were nervous about their first weekend as the Queen's guests at Balmoral. The Prime Minister got on well with her during their weekly audiences, but Wilson soon learned that she read the daily despatch boxes with meticulous care – and would often test him with questions about committee papers that he hadn't yet read himself. Wilson respected the Queen as a valuable confidante. She, in turn, found Harold and Mary a refreshing change. They were her first prime-ministerial couple to have been born in the twentieth century.

The driver who had picked up the Wilsons from the airport saw the Queen standing next to a Land Rover in front of the castle. She made a gesture for the driver to stop. The driver rolled down his window.

'I'll take the Prime Minister and Mrs Wilson the rest of the way. Help me put their luggage in the Land Rover.'

The PM got out and gave the Queen a head bow. His wife followed him with a slight curtsy.

'Have you not brought Robin and Giles?'

'No, Your Majesty, they're staying with my father and sister on the Scilly Isles.'

'I hope you bring them next year.'

'We will, ma'am.'

'We're putting you up at Craigowan Lodge – a bit rustic, but much nicer than the castle. There will be a couple looking after you, but they won't get in your way. Hop in and I'll give you a lift.'

The Prime Minister got in the front passenger side, but there was a box on the seat. The Queen picked it up and handed it to Mrs Wilson. 'It's only a Dundee cake. I hope you like it. My mother made it.'

When they got to the Lodge, which was a mile away over a rough track, they were greeted by two servants who unpacked the Land Rover.

'We need a cup of tea,' said the Queen. 'Don't forget the Dundee cake.'

The Queen led the way into a large farmhouse kitchen. She put the kettle on and opened a cabinet. 'Assam, Darjeeling, Ceylon, lapsang souchong, pouchong?'

There was a consensus for Darjeeling. As she waited for the kettle to boil, the Queen took off her headscarf. She shook out her hair running her fingers through it and showing her ears. The Prime Minister looked on in amazement as his wife sliced the Dundee cake. The Queen was wearing two gold earrings. One of the earrings was in the shape of a hammer; the other in the shape of a sickle.

'I am sure you have heard, Prime Minister, that there are those in the Security Service who believe that an undercover Soviet agent has penetrated the British government at the highest level.' The Queen paused and stared at Wilson. 'Who would ever have guessed?'

The kettle boiled and the Queen began to laugh.

'Apologies for teasing you.' She removed the kettle from the hob and began to undo her earrings. 'I'd better take these off before someone else sees them. They were a joke Christmas present from my brother-in-law – very naughty of him. He signed the gift tag, "Best wishes, from Anthony B.", which was even more naughty.'

That evening there were party games after dinner at the castle. One game had a guest crawling around under the table pretending to be drunk. Wilson mentioned that he had one cabinet minister in particular who could have done such with 'extraordinary verisimilitude'.

Another game required everyone to write the name of a famous person on a piece of sticky-backed paper and put it into a hat. Each guest then had to draw a name out of the hat with their eyes closed and stick it on their forehead. Each guest in turn then had to ask questions of the others to find out who they were. As soon as Wilson guessed that he was Ringo Starr, he began asking the questions in a Liverpool accent.

At the end of the evening as everyone was heading off to bed, the Queen took the Prime Minister aside. 'Thank you for coming,' she said, 'and, as regards my teasing earlier today, I want you to know that I trust you completely.'

'Thank you, ma'am.'

'And if you ever need my help, please ask for it.'

## Labour Win with Increased Majority

Harold Wilson's decision to call a snap election has paid off. The Labour government has been returned with a much larger majority of 96. With the exception of 1945, the result was Labour's best win ever.

The decision to call the election was based on the fact that a lost by-election had cut the Labour majority to just two. Mr Wilson went into the election with a manifesto entitled, 'Time for a Decision'. His purpose was clear: he wanted a mandate to govern. Now that Mr Wilson has a sound majority in the House of Commons, much of the pressure on his government will be relieved.

The Conservatives had not had sufficient time to prepare for the election. There had been little time for Edward Heath to become well known among the public.

**Pimlico, London:** 1 April 1966

Catesby wanted out. Britain was changing, but SIS and the rest of Whitehall were not changing with it. Harold Wilson, in a careful deliberate way, was part of that change and the old guard hated him for it. Catesby was fed up with being part of an organisation that was not only at war with the Security Service, but at war with itself. He respected and looked up to the DG, Sir Dick White, but knew that White would be retiring in a year or two and that SIS might quickly degenerate into a jungle of backstabbing and recrimination. Catesby's old joke, that SIS was an organisation where half the staff were spying for Moscow and the other half spying for Washington, was an exaggeration but highlighted the problem.

If Catesby's bosses discovered that he was anonymously contributing to journals dealing with politics and foreign policy, he might find himself out even sooner than he wanted. Catesby was passionately opposed to the Vietnam War and it was one of the things he wrote about. The war was not only inhumane, but was stupid and counter-productive even in terms of the coldest *realpolitik*. A reunited Vietnam would be a counterbalance to the regional power of China.

Catesby's covert journalism started when he began to hang around with Ralph Miliband and the North London intelligentsia – many of whom he knew through Frances. Catesby was more interested in intellectual stimulation than spying, but there was scope for both. The London bureau of the Russian news agency, *Tass*, was located on the same road as a friend of Frances. The flat opposite *Tass* was rented by MI5 who used it to record the comings and goings from the news agency. 'The couple' in the flat were colleagues of Frances. She and Catesby used to wave when they passed them in the street.

Like the Milibands, many of the intelligentsia were refugees who had fled the rise of the Nazis. Catesby didn't spy on them, but their networks were very impressive. In fact, they often had a better grasp of what was going on than SIS or the FO. Nonetheless, many in the intelligence services regarded North London with suspicion – and Catesby too for having friends there. When confronted by colleagues about his connections with the intelligentsia, Catesby responded with the excuse that he was 'keeping an eye on them'. He felt two-faced about having to play this game. Many of the intelligentsia were certainly left-wing, but none of them were Soviet spies or traitors. Their being largely foreign, intellectual and bohemian was, however, more than enough to smear them as such.

**London:** 1 April 1966

The exclusive Mayfair gentlemen's club was not a happy place. The five had again gathered in the billiard room, but this time the colonel had left his cue in the rack. There was an ice bucket, a soda siphon and two bottles of whisky, which were rapidly diminishing.

'Well Richard,' said JJ pointing his whisky glass at the

hereditary peer, 'your prediction that Wilson would soon "fuck up" doesn't seem to have come to pass.'

'Bad call, total disaster. I hope my racing tips are better.'

'I don't know where we go from here,' said the general. 'Heath's another bloody socialist.'

'And a bender,' said JJ.

'So you said,' said the retired colonel.

'And the blighter wants to take us into the Common Market,' said the banker.

'Getting rid of Heath,' said JJ, 'will be even easier than getting rid of Wilson. He's more brittle – and doesn't have the power of the Soviet Union behind him.'

'By the way,' said the banker, 'I've heard there was a lot of Moscow gold financing this election.'

'And the trade unions,' added the colonel. 'Those Bolsheviks are awash with Sov money. Speaking of which, I've got a plan.'

'Go on,' said the general.

'We pop a few of them off. I could easily arrange it. Chap riding pillion on a motorbike takes out one or two of them close range on a London street or someone with a sniper rifle while they're on holiday or pruning their roses. Easy peasy. I could arrange it.'

'Sounds a bit dodgy,' said the banker. 'What do you hope to achieve?'

'First of all, we get our friend in the Security Service to leak disinfo to the press saying the killings were the result of feuds within the unions – or corruption, missing membership fees...'

'Or Moscow gold going into the wrong pockets?'

'That sort of thing. In any case, the comrades in the unions are going to go berserk: strikes, general strikes, complete disruption of public services. See where we're going? No gas, electricity or telephones. Transport breakdown, food shortages – and, of course, rioting. At this point, the Communist cell in Downing Street is no longer in control or in the equation.' The retired colonel nodded to the general. 'It is now the Army's patriotic duty – and its humanitarian duty as well – to step in and restore order. And, of course, by then, no one is going to give a toss who knocked off a union leader or two. Totally forgotten.'

'I am not sure I could go along with that,' said the general.

'Would you prefer direct rule from Moscow?' said JJ. 'Because that's where we're heading.'

'Well,' said the general, 'it is a difficult situation.' He paused and chewed his moustache. 'One could, I suppose, countenance military rule for a limited time.'

'Meanwhile,' said JJ, 'what we need is a Conservative leader who is capable of ruling in difficult times.'

'Someone who is endorsed by the Monday Club,' said the peer.

JJ nodded. 'We need to move away from Macmillan's compromises with Socialism…'

'And,' said the colonel, 'all that "winds of change" nonsense. Macmillan's decolonisation policies bordered on treason.'

'Our economy,' said the banker, 'absolutely needs white rule in Rhodesia and South Africa. British wealth and power were based on Britain's overseas colonies – any fool can see that.'

'Speaking of Heath,' said the colonel. He gave the ex-SIS officer a sly look. 'I believe, JJ, that you've got a plan.'

JJ smiled. 'He likes music – and, apparently, is an excellent organist.'

'Our choirmaster,' said the peer, 'was also an organist – and a filthy bugger. Goes with the turf.'

'When I was in SIS,' continued JJ, 'we ran a Czech agent called RADKO – the name means happy and willing in Czech, in his case always for money. The Czechs, as you know, are the paymasters for the Communists in the Labour Party – and RADKO used to be part of the distribution system. In anycase, the StB, the Czech intelligence service, decided to entrap members of the Tory Party as well. They lured our musical friend to Prague to play the world famous organ at St Vitus Cathedral. He was greeted by a very handsome young organist, who was also a sexual athlete. The seduction began in the St Wenceslas Chapel which isn't open to the public.'

'Have you got the photos?' said the colonel.

'No, but I'm sure we can get them from RADKO – except they won't be cheap.'

'At least,' said the colonel, 'we can put the frighteners on him to resign. By the way, I must tell you about my wheeze to help turn public opinion against our joining the Common Market. I believe,' the colonel looked at the general, 'that the Bundeswehr have been invited to conduct military exercises in Wales.'

'It hasn't yet been confirmed,' said the general.

'But let me know when they're coming,' said the colonel. 'We'll then find the nearest Jewish cemetery and dab black swastikas over the gravestones – and, of course, the German soldiers will get blamed for it. Can you imagine the outcry?'

'Almost as good,' said the peer, 'as popping off a few trade unionists.'

## Broadway Buildings, London: 5 April 1966

Henry Bone was sitting in an armchair with a cat curled on his lap. Both were purring.

'Isn't that Zadok?' said Catesby.

'Yes, it is. The old boy is getting on a bit, but he still likes shredding a silk curtain or sharpening his claws on a priceless piece of Chippendale marquetry. Zadok would never dream of putting a claw on something as common as late Victorian mahogany.' Bone tickled the bottom of Zadok's chin. 'Would you, boy?'

'I hope your neighbour isn't in prison again.'

'No, he's on holiday in Italy.'

'I must say, Henry, that you look more than usually pleased with yourself.'

'How little you know about me, Catesby. I am hardly ever pleased with myself.'

'But you are today?'

'Somewhat.'

Catesby nodded towards a tape recorder that was set up on Bone's desk. 'Could it be because someone has given you a nice tape? *The Goldberg Variations*, perhaps?'

'Actually, I prefer music live in concert.' Bone lifted the cat off his lap and put him on the floor. 'Sorry to disturb you old boy – go see William.'

The cat stared a few seconds at Catesby as if he were a vulgar late-Victorian sideboard, and then stalked away.

'The thing about our trade,' said Bone threading the tape, 'is how much depends upon coincidence and luck. My neighbour has a friend – in fact, they've gone to Italy together – who is a servant at a very prestigious gentlemen's club in Mayfair. For some years my neighbour's friend has silently borne a grudge, not so much against the club itself, but against some of its members. On one occasion, a drunken lord, annoyed either with lack of service or deference, hurled my neighbour's friend through a window. Fortunately, it was a ground-floor window and he wasn't badly hurt.'

Catesby smiled and shook his head.

'I know it's illegal, William, but there are no fingerprints leading back to SIS – I concocted a marvellous story involving private detectives and adultery. It's a splendid device: compact and requiring no external power supply. I pick up the conversations on a radio receiver.'

'Did your neighbour believe you?'

'Perhaps not completely, but I am sure his friend did. In any case, it gave him a chance to get back at a member that he finds particularly pompous and unpleasant. And it was also a return favour for cat-sitting. Are you ready to listen?'

Catesby nodded and Bone switched on the tape recorder. An hour later, when the tape was finished, Zadok broke cover and attacked a curtain string. 'I think,' said Bone, 'he's had enough of human beings. Cats don't talk about it, they just do it. What do you think?'

'Are you asking me?'

'Don't be facetious, Catesby.'

'I'm never surprised how vile they are, but I am surprised how stupid they are.'

'What did you find particularly stupid?'

'Their lack of evidence – their reliance on unsubstantiated rumours.'

'That's far from stupid, Catesby, that's genius. Who needs facts when you have fear and hatred? Facts are boring. Take, for example, the story about Heath and the honey-trap organist. Did you believe it?'

'It is, however, just the sort of thing the Czechs would do.'

'Except it never happened. Heath never went to Prague to play an organ at St Vitus or anywhere else. The story is totally false. We got wind of the honey-trap plan through GUSTAV and I personally warned Heath not to go. Not that it would have made any difference. Ted Heath has never had sexual relationships of any sort.'

'Just as Harold Wilson has never been a Soviet agent.'

'But the actual truth – Wilson's dull Nonconformist Northern background and his political pragmatism – isn't as interesting as a Communist cell in Downing Street. It won't sell newspapers or get people to form private armies. Why are you smiling?'

'It just occurred to me, Henry, that you might be doing a double bluff.'

'Do you really believe that?'

'No.'

'The problem, William, is that our trade is more about lying than spying.'

'Do we create more problems than we solve?'

'That's a good question.'

## Wembley Stadium: 30 July 1966

Catesby hoped that his stepchildren would never forget that he had taken them to the World Cup Final. He didn't want them to be grateful, but he did want them to realise that it was a great historic event – if, that is, there wasn't a draw necessitating a replay.

The West German equaliser in the final minute was the most painful sporting moment that Catesby had ever experienced. It began with a free kick that bounced off the England wall. It was pounced on by a German who shot across the face of goal and into the body of another German. Catesby watched breathless as the ball deflected across the England six-yard box. The England defence seemed momentarily stunned and confused.

Catesby shouted, 'Clear the ball!'

But no one seemed to hear him, for Wolfgang Weber slid in and slotted the ball into the back of the net.

Catesby turned to his twin stepchildren. 'Hey, listen you two. Don't eat your ticket stubs – and try not to chew them into a complete pulp either. We'll need them to get tickets for the replay.'

'There isn't going to be a replay,' said the stepson, 'Germany's going to score in extra-time. England are tired and playing ragged.'

Catesby shrugged. He never contradicted his stepchildren, corrected them or lectured them.

'I think anyone could win,' said the stepdaughter.

'I think you're right,' said Catesby. It was, he thought, a pretty neutral answer, but then realised that the other one might think he was taking sides. 'But I suppose,' said Catesby, 'that your brother might be right too.'

'What do you think, Will?' said the stepson.

'I'm not sure. Let's watch the game. They've come out again.'

If Catesby had learned one thing from being an intelligence officer, it was that you could never be completely certain about anything or anybody. It wasn't a life lesson that he wanted to pass on to his stepchildren, but what happened next did exactly that – and there was nothing that Catesby could have done to prevent it.

Eleven minutes later Geoff Hurst made history as he headed on to the bottom of the crossbar. What happened next? Who really knows?

At first, Catesby was one of those who really did think the ball had crossed the line. Otherwise, he thought, why hadn't the English player next to the rebound tapped it in to make sure? But then, why was the linesman shaking his head? That's when Catesby got confused. But perhaps the linesman had been shaking his head 'no' to the referee's saying the ball hadn't crossed the line. Except that the German-Swiss referee and the Azerbaijan linesman didn't share a common language. In any case, a moment later the referee gave the goal.

'It did go in,' said Catesby.

'No, it didn't,' said his stepson, 'it landed flat splat on the line. Maybe, Will, you need glasses. Most people do when they get to your age.'

'I'm only forty-three.'

'I thought you were fifty.'

'What difference does it make if the ball does land on the line?' said the stepdaugther. 'It still counts in tennis.'

Catesby decided it best not to comment. The game was back on and the Germans were desperate to score another equaliser. Unfortunately for them, Germany putting so many players forward helped Hurst get his hat trick.

At the end, Wembley was so loud with cheering that Catesby found it difficult to hear what his stepson was saying. He ended up having to shout in Catesby's ear, 'Actually, I'm glad England won – and, Will, thank you for bringing us.'

It wasn't much, but it made Catesby's eyes wet with tears.


**Kensington, London:** August 1966

RADKO started with *czernina*, duck blood soup. He didn't know whether to go on to roast goose, meat loaf or *pierogi* stuffed dumplings, but in the end he chose *pierogi* because it was the speciality of the house. It was a small restaurant near the South Kensington tube station.

JJ had been there before – and always picked up the bill. The restaurant wasn't far from the Brompton Oratory, which Sov agents, pretending to be devout Catholics, used as a giant dead letter box. The usual method was to tape the info under a pew.

RADKO had started with vodka, but shifted to wine when the meat- and mushroom-filled *pierogi* arrived. RADKO looked up at JJ. 'I tell you it going to happen. You no remember?'

'Please remind me.'

'The deal with Moscow – made year ago.'

JJ often found RADKO gnomic, but this evening was particularly difficult. 'Which deal?'

RADKO chewed a *pierogi* and closed his eyes with delight. 'Good, yeah?'

'Excellent.'

RADKO sipped the wine and made a face. It was a rough Bulgarian red. 'I no like this.'

'There's some French wine on the list.'

'No, that piss too. Let's have more vodka.'

JJ signalled the waiter and a bottle arrived.

'You find out why Heath no go Prague? Everything was all ready.'

JJ shook his head. He did know, but he wasn't going to share it with RADKO. 'Let's just say,' said JJ, 'that Heath did go to Prague and that everything went as planned. Okay?'

'You want me lie, I lie. No problem.'

'Can we get back to the Moscow deal?'

RADKO gave JJ a sly look. 'I can't believe you not remember. I tell you so many time.'

'Remind me again.'

'Khrushchev say to Wilson, "You send no British soldiers to Vietnam, I help England win World Cup." Wilson say, "Yes." Then KGB order Tofiq Bahramov help England. Everyone call him Russian linesman, but he Azerbaijan. KGB say to Bahramov, "You help England or you go Siberia."'

KK smiled. 'Yes, I do remember.'

'Hey, listen.' RADKO leaned forward and lowered his voice. 'I met Bahramov after game. We speak Russian together. I say,

"Tofiq, why you give that goal? Ball never cross line." You know what Tofiq say?'

JJ shook his head.

'Stalingrad.'

Somehow, thought JJ, that explanation sounded more likely than a deal with Moscow about Vietnam. But both were good. Verifiable factual details weren't important; they were often boring and distracting. The important thing was a wider truth; that the UK was in thrall to a Communist conspiracy. Sometimes you needed to use lies to expose the truth.

**Pimlico, London:** 18 November 1967

Catesby had inherited Frances's old television, but only used it to watch football and the news. The thing that most depressed Catesby about television news – and news in general – was the economic scaremongering. Catesby sat slumped in a chintz-covered armchair, another of Frances's castoffs, with his 9mm Browning cradled in his lap on a greasy rag. He wasn't feeling threatened, but needed to clean the pistol prior to his annual marksmanship qualification session at a shooting range in Aldershot. He stared blankly at the TV with his hand on the pistol butt.

> *Downing Street has just announced that it is lowering the exchange rate from $2.80 to $2.40. This means that the value of the pound has been cut by just over 14%…*

The voice of the presenter was momentarily blocked out by the klaxon of an ambulance rushing down Tachbrook Street. Too late, thought Catesby, to save the pound.

> *…decision followed weeks of feverish speculation about the future of sterling and frantic last-minute efforts by the Bank of England to shore up the pound from its gold and dollar reserves.*

The image on the television screen switched from the newsroom to Downing Street. Catesby thought that Wilson looked tired and fed up as he stared at the camera.

> *'It does not mean that the pound here in Britain, in your pocket or purse or in your bank, has been devalued.'*

Catesby smiled bleakly. The most interesting things about the PM's speech were the implied messages and the words unsaid.

> *'The only alternative was to borrow heavily from governments abroad – but the only loans on offer were short-term ones.'*

By 'governments abroad', Wilson meant the Americans, who were obviously trying to punish the UK for not sending troops to Vietnam.

> '…the war in the Middle East, the closure of the Suez Canal owing to hostilities and the disruption to exports caused by the dock strikes had all contributed to the pressure on the pound.'

None of what Catesby was hearing came as a complete surprise. As a Whitehall insider he had his ear to the ground, but there was one more rumour – a very important one – that still hadn't revealed itself in the Prime Minister's speech. Wilson paused and stared at the camera as if he was finished, but he began again. Catesby waited and it finally came.

> 'We're making further sharp cuts in defence spending…'

Catesby had heard that the cuts were massive, £100 million – and would also affect SIS and the Security Service. The MoD were already furious – and the Americans wouldn't like it either.

Catesby turned the television off and continued to disassemble his Browning automatic for cleaning. He remembered to make sure the safety was locked back to make sure the slide didn't fly across the room when he withdrew the retaining pin. If he damaged the pistol, it didn't look like SIS would be able to afford to buy him another one. On the other hand, they could melt it down to be part of a ploughshare.

When Catesby had finished taking the pistol apart, he stared at the wall. He suddenly felt a Kafkaesque chill of alienation run down his spine. He wanted out, but realised that he was part of a thin protecting veil. He needed to protect the Prime Minister and those like him who were prey for the dark elements of the Secret State.

**CIA HQ, Langley, Virginia:** 21 November 1967

Angleton was pleased at the news from London: the socialist British economy was foundering as chickens flocked home to roost. Although Johnson was too timid to use outright financial blackmail to force Britain to send troops to Vietnam, he certainly wasn't going out of his way to save the pound. But how long would it be, thought Angleton, before Moscow intervened to save their agents in Downing Street from the economic catastrophe for which Britain was steaming at full-speed? If the Soviet Union was propping up Castro, they would soon be propping up Wilson as well. And what favours would Moscow demand in return? Naval bases? Military and nuclear technology? The secrets that others in Washington were stupid enough to share with London? The UK was rapidly approaching a crisis scenario. But Angleton found it impossible to make his voice heard. The power players in Washington wore blinkers devised by America's own liberal left-wing press and intelligentsia. And, of course, his own agency – the CIA itself – had been penetrated by agents from Moscow. Angleton whispered the motto that had so endeared him to Allen Dulles: 'If you don't always – *always* – fear the worst, you shouldn't be a counter-intelligence officer.'

Sliding into FURIOSO mode, the Director of Counter-intelligence lit another cigarette and opened his well-thumbed copy of the collected poems of Yeats.

*Turning and turning in the widening gyre*
*The falcon cannot hear the falconer;*
*Things fall apart; the centre cannot hold;*
*Mere anarchy is loosed upon the world,*
*The blood-dimmed tide is loosed...*

He stared again at the words as the swirling haze of smoke turned Yeats's poem into an Expressionist painting shouting 'fuck you' at the world.

A letter fell out of the book. The book was bulging with yellowing letters that Angleton had exchanged with poets and writers in the 1930s. There were several about and from Yeats. He opened one and read the handwriting, which in itself was aesthetic: *It is amusing to live in a country where men will always act. Where nobody is satisfied with thought ... The chance of being shot is raising everybody's spirits enormously.* He then turned back to the poems.

> *Once when midnight smote the air*
> *Eunuchs ran through Hell and met*
> *On every crowded street to stare*
> *Upon great Juan riding by...*

James Angleton felt a sense of existential despair as he stared out the window towards Washington. He couldn't actually see the capital because the view was blocked by the trees and gently rolling countryside of northern Virginia. And that was just as well, for Washington was a shabby town. The rulers of Washington were not noblemen with the fine faces of Bronzino's Medici princes, but anonymous millionaires, fat-assed, shiny-bottomed bureaucrats and sleazy lobbyists offering cheaply scented call girls. Worse than Yeats's eunuchs, for they would be oblivious to the 'great Juan'.

He carefully opened another letter. The years had turned the paper into diaphanous parchment. He felt warmed by the dead embrace of a fellow soul. *Even violence and tyranny are not necessarily evil because the people, knowing not evil and good, would become perfectly acquiescent to tyranny. Everything must come from the top. Nothing can come from the masses.*

Angleton folded up the letters and put the book away. He opened up his daily copy of the Director's Log. Once again, he wondered if there were reports that had been deleted, censored, from the copy circulated to him. There certainly were things that Angleton, as Director of Counter-intelligence, found necessary to keep away from the eyes of the DCI. They went by the daily diplomatic bag rather than cable. It was too easy to monitor cable. But how could he be certain that someone wasn't opening and reading his handwritten communications via the supposedly secure diplomatic bag? In one of his first letters he told his man in London – who was only third in the London station hierarchy – that he would include a hair in each correspondence to verify that there had been no tampering and the London man would do the same. Later, when Angleton met his London man face to face, he told him they would *not* place hairs in their letters. Ergo, a hair would be evidence of tampering. But could he really trust the young Dep Asst OSO? Counter-intelligence was 'a wilderness of mirrors'. And how dare anyone insinuate that he was becoming paranoid?

'I am not paranoid,' whispered James Angleton as he opened the Director's Log. 'Otherwise, I would be suspicious of this log which I know – at least for now – is unaltered.'

OSO London to DCI. SM/OATSHEAF has handled the devaluation badly, but the fall of his government doesn't seem imminent. His majority in Parliament is too large. Unrest, however, among the British Security Services, military, financial establishment and press continue to bubble. Will closely monitor and assist when necessary.

SM/REVEAL, our most valuable friend in the press, appears to have been targeted by the KGB. The murder of a number of London prostitutes remains unsolved. An anonymous informer contacted the police reporting a suspicious automobile that was allegedly parked near where the body of one of the prostitutes was found. The automobile it turned out belonged to SM/REVEAL. When the police investigated, they found bloodstains in the trunk of the auto. SM/REVEAL told the police that the stains were the blood of a couple of pheasants that he had recently shot. The police forensic lab later backed up SM/REVEAL's story. There is obviously a conspiracy to smear and discredit SM/REVEAL. And whoever reported him must know he hunts pheasants. We're checking to see if anyone from the Soviet embassy has also been hunting in the same place.

SM/HOUND reports that England winning the World Soccer Championship was entirely because of the help of the

## Anti-Vietnam Protest Turns Violent

The trouble began after a rally in Trafalgar Square where an estimated 20,000 demonstrated against the American war in Vietnam. At first, the anti-war rally appeared to be good-humoured. The violence broke out when the protesters marched to the US embassy in Grosvenor Square.

The American embassy was cordoned off by hundreds of police. The police stood shoulder to shoulder to block access to the part of the square closest to the embassy. The protesters refused to back off and then pushed against the police cordon. The violence began when mounted police charged the demonstrators.

The demonstrators managed to break through the police cordon and poured onto the lawn of the embassy breaking down a fence and pulling up a hedge. A vicious and prolonged battle ensued during which stones, sticks, fireworks and smoke bombs were thrown.

Earlier, a counter-demonstration numbering a few hundred Conservatives and Monday Club supporters had taunted the first protesters to arrive in Grosvenor Square with shouts of 'Bomb, bomb the Vietcong' and 'Treason'. They were later separated by police.

The battle at the embassy continued for more than an hour before the demonstrators were finally forced to disperse by the police. Scattered groups of protesters and anarchists then headed for the Dorchester and Hilton hotels, but failed to get in.

A senior police officer accused the organisers of having exercised 'no control over their supporters' and of 'failing to abide by the agreed arrangements.' 'This,' maintained the senior police officer, 'is why the demonstration degenerated into a disorderly rabble. As soon as they entered Grosvenor Square, it was obvious that a hard core of troublemakers were determined to provoke a violent response.'

More than 300 people were arrested and over 100 were injured. Fifty people required hospital treatment including 23 police officers.

## Pimlico, London: 17 March 1968

Catesby hadn't been at the demo, but his stepchildren had and they came to his flat to tell him all about it. The stepson was full of it. He had obviously enjoyed himself and was still cruising on an adrenalin high. Catesby recognised the symptoms. He had felt the same way the first time he had been in battle. It was exhilarating – particularly if it was your first time and neither you nor your friends got badly hurt.

'The police attacked first,' said the stepson, 'and then all hell broke loose.'

'Were you,' said Catesby, 'part of the group that broke away and attacked the US embassy?'

'Yes, but don't tell Mum that. Basically, it got really exciting and I wanted to see what was happening.'

'I was there too,' said the stepdaughter, 'but I wasn't there for the excitement. I was there to make a point – to let the fucking American Ambassador know what we thought of his fucking war.'

'Right on,' said Catesby without a hint of irony.

'I wish that you had come with us,' said the stepson.

'I think in my position,' said Catesby, 'it's best that I operate from the shadows.'

'I bet,' said the stepdaughter, 'it's because you don't want to lose your OBE.'

'I wouldn't have worn it.'

'You ought to have worn it, Will. That would have been really cool.'

'I keep it in a safe place, because someday I want you to inherit it as an heirloom.' Catesby kept it in the safe at his house in Suffolk – along with important papers. There had been a spate of burglaries in London involving people in his position.

'Do you really think you should have accepted the OBE?' said the stepdaughter.

'It would have blown my cover story if I hadn't.'

'Wow, who do you really work for?' said the stepson.

'I was joking,' said Catesby.

'Back to the demo,' said the stepdaughter, 'there were some

strange people there who were not only very violent, but didn't seem to belong.'

'In what way didn't belong?' said Catesby.

'They didn't look or sound like students or protesters.'

'And one of them,' said her brother, 'had 2 Para tattooed on his forearm.'

Catesby smiled bleakly and nodded.

'What is it, Will?' said the stepdaughter.

'Thank you for being so observant – and, one more thing, I admire you for your idealism.'

'We got it from you.'

Catesby choked back the tears.

### Belgrave Square, London: 17 March 1968

The group, except for the general who was on duty, had gathered at the peer's lavish townhouse. They were in the smallest sitting room of the four-storey house where the peer kept his only television. They had just finished watching the BBC News on the anti-Vietnam demo.

'Did you hear that idiot socialist MP blaming the violence on the police?' said the banker. 'He was what? "Particularly outraged by the violent use of police horses which charged into the crowd"? That's exactly what mounted police are supposed to do.'

The retired colonel put his hands around the cut crystal glass reflecting the amber glow of twenty-five-year-old single malt whisky. The colonel winked at JJ. 'I don't believe Mungo has been fully briefed on what happened today.'

JJ looked away and said, 'Hmm.'

'You're looking more than usually enigmatic, JJ, behind those National Health specs of yours.'

'You shouldn't make fun of my spectacles.' JJ cracked a rare smile. 'I hate Socialism, but I'm not going to pass up a bargain.'

The colonel smiled. JJ was oblivious to fashion or looking smart.

'Both of you,' said the peer, 'seem to want to change the subject. Can you please tell Mungo – and myself – about what we have not been "fully briefed"?'

'One of the oldest tricks in the book,' said the colonel. 'The agent provocateur – in this case several. Did you not notice the athleticism and professionalism of a small number of the protesters attacking the police?'

The banker nodded and the peer droned a 'Yesss'.

'The lads loved it,' continued the colonel. 'All of them are ex-paras who like a good punch-up. Of course, we provided them with "get-out-of-jail-free" cards to give to the police when they got arrested.'

'Was anyone else involved,' said the peer, 'anyone more official?'

'Yes, but they don't want to be known at the time. Not leaving fingerprints is paramount. Which is why those of us who are not players on the government payroll are valuable assets.'

'You've become a big fan of privatisation,' said the banker.

'The best people,' said the colonel, 'like adventure and money – and when you put the two together you get the best results. The regiment's motto ought to be "Who pays wins".'

'The idea,' said JJ, 'is to raise the level of tension.'

'We need to create a sense of dire national crisis,' said the colonel. 'Did you see the blood? We issued the lads with plastic bags full of artificial blood. It makes for good press photos.'

'The US press,' said JJ, 'has handled the story much better. One TV station called it "a bloody riot such as Britain has never seen before." The BBC coverage is appalling Lefty rubbish.'

'The next phase is to ratchet things up to the breaking point.' The colonel gave a sly smile. 'By the way, I've managed to acquire some very nice plastic explosives.'

**London:** May, 1968

The usual suspects – the barking madmen and the gin-soaked generals – were not part of the intended coup. At least, not at first. The press tycoon, who tried to organise it, was not a right-winger. In fact, his newspaper had supported Labour in the past two elections. But once the attack dogs had picked up the scent, they were let slip and the cry was havoc. The problem, as Napoleon had once observed, is that you can do anything with bayonets except sit on them.

The meeting took place in an elegant townhouse a five-minute walk from the peer's London home in Belgrave Square. It wasn't the home of the press baron, who had convened the meeting, but of a member of the Royal Family. The press baron's plan was that the Royal would replace Wilson and lead an 'emergency government'.

Originally, it was planned as a meeting of three: the press baron, the editor of his largest paper and the member of the Royal Family. The Royal, however, had summoned the government's Chief Scientific Advisor to attend as well. He regarded the advisor, Sir Solly Zuckerman, as 'safe and sensible'.

The press baron's argument for action began with the economy. Gold had been pouring out of the Treasury in an unsuccessful attempt to prop up the pound. A second devaluation seemed inevitable. Wilson and his inner cabinet, code-named MISC 205, prepared an emergency contingency plan code-named Operation Brutus. Brutus called for import quotas; compulsory acquisition of all privately held overseas securities; the freezing of foreign sterling balances in Britain; crash cuts in defence expenditure. Essentially, Brutus meant that foreign travel would be banned and no cash allowed out of the country. Operation Brutus was a top secret emergency plan unlikely to be ever invoked, but it was too juicy to be kept secret. Inevitably, someone in the Treasury leaked it to a banker friend – and the news spread like a grassfire out of control. As far as the City of London was concerned, Brutus marked the end of civilisation.

Meanwhile, massive demonstrations and strikes were spreading across France and bringing Europe's largest capitalist economy to a virtual halt. The political leaders of France genuinely feared civil war or revolution – and there were those in Britain who feared protest and social breakdown would soon leap across the Channel.

'We must realise,' said the press baron, 'that Wilson's government is no longer in control of events. The best solution would be for him to resign and make way for a national government composed of businessmen, civil servants, all political parties – and the military.'

Sir Solly Zuckerman bristled and looked closely at the member of the Royal Family.

'But,' continued the press baron, 'Wilson isn't going to do the sensible patriotic thing and resign. He's going to cling to power like a limpet while everything disintegrates around him. We are going to see mass unemployment as factory after factory closes its doors. We're going to see a breakdown of civil order and bloodshed on the streets – and the distinct possibility of the hospitals, lacking power supplies, medicine and staff, being unable to care for the sick and wounded. In this situation,' the press baron looked at the member of the Royal Family, 'the military will have to come in to restore order – and, yes, we may see tanks and machine guns on street corners. It's better than anarchy and bloodshed.'

Sir Solly, the Chief Scientific Advisor, stirred as if he were about to speak, but the press baron cut him off. 'And may I remind you,' said the press baron, 'that there is no constitutional problem involved. The oaths of allegiance taken by the military are to the Crown, not to elected Members of Parliament.'

Sir Solly stood up. His voice was loud and firm. 'What you are suggesting is rank treachery – treason. You should be ashamed of yourself. I'm not going to listen to another word. And,' he turned to the member of the Royal Family and addressed him by the familiar name that only intimates used, 'have nothing to do with this. I know you won't.'

The Chief Scientific Advisor went to the door without looking behind him and shut it with a bang that resonated.

The press baron looked at his Royal host. 'We must act quickly and I will put it directly to you, sir – will you be the head of an emergency government?'

The member of the Royal Family first looked at the press baron and then at his editor. 'Absolutely not. Leave now and don't ask to come back. There's nothing more to be said.'

## Muckle Flugga: June, 1968

It was the best assignment the captain had ever had in his Army career. He had prepared for it by packing stout walking boots, waterproof clothing, binoculars, maps and bird guides. He wasn't supposed to be turning his recce into a bird-watching holiday, but the activities were compatible – and the bird-watching provided an excellent cover story.

The recce began on Unst where he met the most aggressive birds he had ever encountered. The great skuas dive-bombed the captain even when he was well away from their nests. The Shetlanders called them bonxies, but after several close calls the captain thought 'great skewers' would be a better name. There were also fulmars, gannets, shags, guillemots and puffins – all in large numbers. But the captain's favourite was the red-throated diver, a rare ungainly bird that only came on land to breed. He loved the diver's piercing call: 'We're a weet, we're a weet; waur wadder, waur wadder – which the locals translated as 'we're all wet, we're all wet, worse weather, worse weather.'

But the captain hadn't spotted any red-throated divers on Muckle Flugga. The island was all cliff and probably too sheer for the ungainly diver to nest – but all the other birds were there in loud number. Muckle Flugga was uninhabited except for the lighthouse keepers – the lighthouse was a listed heritage build-ing that had been built by Robert Louis Stevenson's father. The captain took several photographs of the island and made notes.

The utter inaccessible isolation of Muckle Flugga was a plus factor – escape would be well nigh impossible – the captain, however, wasn't sure it would be possible to build an internment camp on those steep cliffs. But they had managed the lighthouse in the previous century. Stevenson wouldn't have had helicopters to ferry in supplies and building equipment. The captain made a pencil sketch showing how various sites could be used for internee accommodation, interrogation centres – and, of course, quarters for the guards. Muckle Flugga would not, of course, be a camp for ordinary internees, but only for those whose status and ruthlessness posed a serious danger to national security. They would include, first of all, high-ranking government officials and members of the intelligence services who were Soviet agents. The harsh steep island was a long way from the Isles of Scilly – at the very opposite extreme of the British archipelago. But, thought the captain, we live in a time of extremes. On the other hand, the camps were just part of a 'contingency plan' and might never be used. But, as the man from MI5 had said, you always have to prepare for the worst.

The captain had fallen a bit in love with the northern wilderness of the Shetlands – and had bought a bottle of Muckle Flugga whisky to toast the austere beauty of the islands. At midnight, it was still so light that he could read his notes without switching on the lamp in his guesthouse. He wasn't looking forward to going back to Templer Barracks in Kent. It was an ugly depot full of soulless modern brick buildings with barred windows. Templer was the home of the Intelligence Corps – not a branch that was held in high esteem by the rest of the Army. They were nicknamed 'the green slime' owing, partly, to their cypress-green berets. Their corps cap badge was often referred to as a 'rampant pansy resting on its laurels'. They were said to be good at sticking pins in maps, colouring in maps and putting stickers on maps. But with things hotting up, all that might soon be changing.

The captain sipped the Muckle Flugga whisky, which tasted faintly of roasted oak and barley. His next task, when he got back to England, was making a list of 'acceptable' trade union leaders. Was it, he thought, just as hopeless a task as making a list of fulmars that don't eat fish? On the other hand, learning to be 'acceptable' might be preferable to spending a winter on Muckle Flugga.

## Explosion Damages JFK Memorial at Runnymede

Surrey police are investigating a bomb blast that seriously damaged the memorial to the American President John F. Kennedy. The seven-ton block of Portland stone was split down the middle by the explosion and may be beyond repair. A spokesman for the Surrey Constabulary has confirmed that the explosives used were 'high quality plastic explosives which are only available to the military'. An inventory is now underway to ascertain if the explosives may have been stolen from a UK military base.

Police have not ruled out the possibility that the explosion may be linked to yesterday's anti-Vietnam march in London at which demonstrators hurled staves, bottles and fireworks at police. The protest was not as violent as last May's, but the presence of a hard core of extremists was evident. US and Australian flags were burnt. At the Whitehall Cenotaph, wreathes of poppies were trampled and a Union Jack was burnt.

**Century House, Lambeth, London:** 1 November 1968

No one, except the Russians and Catesby, was happy when SIS had to relocate their HQ from Broadway Buildings to the twenty-two-storey steel and glass tower block in Lambeth. Catesby was happy because it was such a short walk from his flat in Pimlico – and also because of the river views from his office. But, for the time being, Catesby wasn't there to enjoy the views. He was on a mole chase in Southeast Asia. But the Russians were in Lambeth – and they were happy because security for SIS in their new glass home was absolutely shit. From rented rooms in the neighbouring streets, the Sovs could casually observe and photograph anyone entering or leaving Century House on foot. The rented rooms also gave the Sovs an excellent view of the entrance and exit of the underground car park. This gave them a collection of number plates – including those of cars that swapped number plates. The windows of Century House were also a security nightmare. You could draw a blind to block people looking in, but the Russians were developing technologies that could pick up conversations from window vibration. Henry Bone, however, was always ahead of the game and had his office windows hung with special curtains that absorbed sound.

Bone wished that there was someone with whom he could share his latest bugged recording from the Mayfair gentlemen's club. But Zadok was back with his owner and Catesby was abroad. Bone thought about inviting the new DG to listen in, but didn't want to embarrass him. Bugging that club was, for SIS, strictly illegal. And what a pity. Otherwise, the recording would be evidence for a prosecution. But, thought Bone, that isn't the way we do things. Criminal prosecutions are a public way of dealing with matters that are best dealt with covertly. That's why Anthony Blunt had made a full confession in exchange for full immunity from prosecution. It would have been so embarrassing – and what had he done that was so wrong? These thoughts were something that Bone could never share with Catesby.

Bone made sure the curtains were fully drawn and turned to the tape recorder. His neighbour's friend was still a steward at the club and had proved an invaluable asset. Bone switched on the recorder to listen once again to the juicy bit. The colonel's voice came first.

*…a pity there's not more indignation from across the Atlantic. The Americans ought to be boiling with rage at this insult to their martyred President.*

*Perhaps, it was too close to the American election, which seems to be occupying the media.* Bone recognised the voice as the banker's.

*Or maybe…* This one was the peer. *…the King and Robert Kennedy assassinations have made the American public a lot more difficult to shock.*

The next voice was immediately recognisable. JJ had been an SIS colleague for almost twenty years. *Our psychological operations need to be aimed at the British public. In any case, who cares – among the supporters we are targeting – about a monument to a left-wing American President being scratched.*

*Split in half.* It was the colonel again. *Credit where credit is due – and what a great lump of stone it was. Disappointing, however, that it wasn't linked more closely to the anti-Vietnam protest. We must create public fear and loathing of left-wing extremism. Pity the memorial wasn't in Ireland – I suspect Kennedy was a bit of a Sinn Féiner.*

*We need...* It was JJ again. *...to concentrate on the Communist threat to Britain. We've still got a KGB agent in Downing Street and trade unions led by Communist subversives.*

The colonel again. *I've still got some C4 plastic left. Let's try a public utility next time.*

## London to East Anglia: November, 1969

Catesby was still wearing his black tie when he got on the train at Liverpool Street, but took it off as soon as the train left London. He didn't want to carry signs of mourning back to a weekend in Suffolk. On the other hand, he had been invited to a bonfire night party postponed from the fifth, which had been the previous Wednesday – so perhaps he should put the tie back on in respect to Guy Fawkes and his own alleged ancestor, Robert Catesby. Although Catesby was a staunch atheist, his Catholic upbringing always made him feel uncomfortable in a season where Roman Catholics were gaily burned in effigy. Nonetheless, he kept the tie rolled up in his overcoat pocket in case he needed it.

The funeral had been subdued and depressing. It was the second funeral of a suicide that Catesby had attended in the past two years. Positive vetting was dangerous to your health – and carried out in an ever more vicious fashion by Ferret and his fellow inquisitionists in the Security Service. The breaking point was usually a past friendship – often as a university under-graduate – with someone who turned out at some point to have done something unwise at the behest of a charming person who worked for Moscow. And Ferret and his gang always found out, because they had broken so many others. In the end, little or no damage had usually been done. But to Ferret's way of thinking, Communism was a disease that, once contracted, was incurable. Even the slightest flirtation with the Party as a student meant you were tainted for life. The person under investigation was usually trapped by being presented with proof that they had failed to tell all – however fleeting or insignificant – at a previous vetting. And to pile on the pressure, the supposed security breach was often linked to something sexual. All this usually pertained to indiscretions that had occurred thirty or forty years before. And yet, it was enough to ruin the career of someone headed for a cabinet post or a senior position in the civil service. The person faced with 'disgrace' chose death instead.

Catesby needed a drink. He got up and made his way to the

buffet car, which was packed with the usual drunks on their way back to their weekend homes in East Anglia. Catesby tried not to be sniffy about them for, even though he was Suffolk born, he was doing the same thing. He felt a firm hand on his shoulder as he made his way to the bar.

'Hello, William.'

It was a voice that Catesby knew well. It belonged to the government's Chief Scientific Adviser.

'Let me buy you a drink,' said Catesby.

'No, William, it's my turn. What are you having?'

'A double "ring-a-ding".'

Sir Solly Zuckerman ordered the double Bell's, then turned back to Catesby. 'What do call you a Teacher's?'

'"A Sir with Love". It's a complicated family joke.'

'Many family jokes are. How are Frances and the children?'

'Fine – but we still live apart. How are Joan and your two?'

'Great, they've gone up to Norfolk ahead of me.'

Catesby noticed that Solly had also taken off his black tie. 'I'm sorry we didn't have a chance to talk afterwards.'

'I had to rush off to a meeting. How did you find it?'

'Bitter, depressing and short.'

'And none of them were there.'

'Their smiles of smug satisfaction would have been unbearable.'

'I bet you would have punched one of them.'

'That would have been playing into their hands.' Catesby smiled. 'But it would have been worth it.'

'Shall we go for a walk?'

Catesby nodded. He could see that the scientific adviser wanted to have a private chat. They moved to the gap between the carriages – a cold, draughty no-man's-land that swayed and clanked above the tracks.

Sir Solly stared out the door window into the dark. 'The problem with this train is that you can't see anything. I'm a South African-born Jew, but I love the English countryside – especially East Anglia. But you're a real East Anglian.'

Catesby shrugged. 'My background is complicated – but I can do the accent after a few pints.'

'You are a superb linguist. Your rendering of Afrikaans was absolutely perfect.'

Catesby smiled. The language he had inherited from his mother was *West-Vlaams Nederlands.* His Flemish-accented *Nederlands* was close enough to Afrikaans that, with some coaching, Catesby could pass as a native Afrikaans speaker. At one point, Catesby and Zuckerman were part of an SIS operation aimed at uncovering South Africa's role in breaking the oil embargo against the illegal regime in Rhodesia. But the op was cancelled because Catesby's cover was blown. He suspected that it was the work of JJ conspiring with dissident elements in the Security Service who were sympathetic to white rule in Rhodesia. Finding a way to act against Rhodesia had proved one of Harold Wilson's most intractable problems. And Catesby was certain that there would be more trouble from southern Africa in years to come.

Sir Solly looked at Catesby. 'They're now out to get me too.'

Catesby wasn't surprised. He knew all about the scientific adviser's role in thwarting the May 1968 coup. In fact, Catesby was the first person he had told about it. In the end, the plot had backfired and the press baron had lost his job – but conspiracy failures usually breed new conspiracies.

'How do you know they're after you?' said Catesby.

'An anonymous letter full of anti-Semitism, personal insults and threats.'

'What did you do with the letter?'

'I burned it. I wasn't going to dignify them by going to the police. You should treat these people with contempt.'

'You could have taken it to the Security Service.' Catesby smiled bleakly.

Sir Solly returned a smile that was equally bleak.

Catesby always got a lift to his house from a cowman who worked on a neighbouring farm. The cowman timed finishing his pint at The Angel with the arrival of Catesby's train. The cowman drove an ancient Commer van that needed a good bit of welding. There was, however, a loose metal plate in the foot-well that the passenger could keep in place by pressing down with both feet. The plate stopped some of the cold and some of the surface water from coming in – but it didn't work with deep puddles.

When they got to the house, Catesby, as was the custom, gave the cowman a couple of bob – hardly enough to buy a pint – but the farm worker wouldn't accept more.

The shadow of the house loomed above him as he opened the front door. It still was cold and dark – no wife or family to greet him – but it was home in a way that London or nowhere else could ever be. Catesby had been born twenty miles away and had never wanted to live anywhere else. Suffolk wasn't the only place where they said: 'The apple don't fall far from the tree.' It wasn't meant as a compliment; it meant you didn't have any ambition to get up and go. But Catesby didn't mind being that apple – he loved it.

The only post was a single letter. It wasn't unusual, probably an invitation to something local, but most of Catesby's mail was sent to his flat in London. Catesby put the letter aside. His first task was lighting the Rayburn – and getting it warm enough for cooking. Food was no more of a problem than a lift from the cowman. If you had Suffolk connections, you found things in your larder. The next task, after the Rayburn was thumping out glorious heat, was getting the inglenook roaring. Then back to the Rayburn to pop in 'le prick au plonk' – another family joke that probably wasn't that funny. While the chicken was cooking, Catesby luxuriated in front of the inglenook fire with a glass of wine. 'Ah, the letter,' he said aloud. He picked up the envelope and held it in front of the light from the fire. The address was printed by hand in block capitals. Catesby sniffed the envelope – no perfume. But that, he thought full of hope, doesn't mean it isn't a love letter. He lay back and fantasised about who it could be from. He wished above all that it was from Frances. But the printing wasn't her hand. Then, for the first time, he noticed the postmark. It was from Belfast. A chill ran down his spine.

It was, Catesby had to admit, a very well-executed line drawing. He wondered if the person who had done it had been to art school. The face of the sniper was obscured by a balaclava, but his body and hands were perfectly rendered. The posture and attitude of the shooter were also technically perfect for someone sighting in and about to pull the trigger. The rifle, Catesby noted, was an American M-14. The bottom half of the drawing was a very attractive study of the east-facing side of Catesby's house including trees and shrubbery. Each window, however, was superimposed with a bull's eye.

Catesby picked up the envelope and stared at the postmark. He wondered if it was a red herring to make Catesby wonder if he had enemies in Northern Ireland. Things were certainly hotting up there and SIS were not without enemies in the province – including members of the Security Service. On the other hand, creating suspicions and false locations of agents by deceptive postmarks, although a somewhat stale trick, was one that SIS still used.

It was a fine drawing. Catesby sipped his wine and admired it. At first, he thought he should follow the Chief Scientific Adviser's way of dealing with hate mail and destroy it. On the other hand, the artist had rendered his house and garden with skilful attention to detail. Catesby decided to have it framed and hung on his office wall as a trophy.

**Agency News:** 19 June 1970

## Surprise Victory for Tories

Edward Heath's Conservatives have defied the opinion polls to defeat Harold Wilson's heavily favoured Labour Party. The Tories, with their Ulster Unionists allies, won by a majority of 31. The victory ends six years of Labour rule.

In the run-up to the election, most opinion polls had pointed to a comfortable Labour victory. One poll had given the Labour Party a lead of 12.4% over the Conservatives.

Factors which may have contributed to Labour's defeat included a particularly bad set of balance of payments figures and England's loss to West Germany which eliminated the team from the World Cup in Mexico. Both disappointments occurred in the week before polling day and may have affected the national mood.

Other factors that may have worked against Labour included rising prices, union indiscipline, the continuing risk of devaluation and a set of unemployment figures that showed joblessness at its highest level since 1940.

It was also a bad night for the Liberal Party under their new leader Jeremy Thorpe. The Liberals lost half their seats.

**Pimlico, London:** 19 June 1970

Catesby was up watching the election results as they came in – and it was a gloomy business. His job forbade him to be a party member, but it didn't stop him from being a Labour voter. Wilson, for all his faults, at least wasn't a right-wing Gaitskellite. But how, thought Catesby, could anyone have been so reckless as to call an election in the middle of the World Cup?

The quarter-final loss to West Germany in Mexico was the most depressing sporting event that Catesby had ever witnessed, albeit by television. England had the game in the bag leading 2–0 with twenty-two minutes left. Everyone was blaming the substitute England goalkeeper for having given the game away with three howlers. Catesby was more generous: he thought the keeper had only committed one howler – or maybe one and a half. In any case, England would have won the game and Labour would have won the election if England's usual goalkeeper, Gordon Banks, hadn't come down with a serious tummy bug. If, thought Catesby, you really wanted to uncover the conspiracy to get rid of Harold Wilson, find out who slipped a poison pill into Gordon Banks's beer at the Guadalajara Country Club. In fact, he wondered if he should minute it as a serious line of inquiry. His colleagues might laugh, but rumours were still rife – particularly from rogue elements at Five – that the Soviet linesman in 1966 had been a KGB agent tasked with gifting England the cup. That was clearly nonsense, but a conspiracy aimed at eliminating the England team from the 1970 World Cup wasn't.

Catesby had already exchanged cables with the SIS man in Mexico who did, in fact, share Catesby's suspicions. The SIS man had already spotted something fishy about team captain Bobby Moore being arrested in Bogotá just before the start of the World Cup. Moore had been accused of stealing a silver bracelet from a jeweller's shop. The charges were clearly trumped-up and the case was dropped. The poisoning of Gordon Banks, England's least replaceable player, was the second stage of the conspiracy.

In Catesby's view, the finger pointed at the CIA – for two reasons. Sure, they wanted to get rid of Harold Wilson, but they also wanted to make sure that the military junta ruling Brazil stayed securely in place. And getting England out of the tournament was a big help. England was the only team in Mexico that had had the ghost of a chance of stopping Brazil. In two days' time, Brazil would face Italy in the final and would surely trounce them. And that would be great news for the junta and their CIA backers.

Catesby got up and turned off the television – then laughed and put his face in his hands. He slumped back in his armchair listening to the bumps and sounds of dark hours London. Was he going mad?

He opened his eyes and tried to focus on objective reality. With Wilson gone, what would happen to the conspiracy to get rid of him? Heath was a Tory, but not a particularly noxious one; at least not as noxious as the stuff they put in Gordon Banks's beer. Catesby knew he wasn't mad – something fishy had happened in Mexico. But what was now going to happen in England?

Heath wasn't a right-winger. The dark forces of the Secret State didn't like that. Heath wanted to take Britain into the Common Market. They liked that even less. And Heath was a bachelor – but oh, how the dark forces would love that. The innuendo and the rumours would soon be flowing.

### Harvey's Restaurant, Washington, DC: September, 1971

'You did an excellent piece of work last year, a masterpiece, and I'm putting you in for a commendation.'

The recognition had been a long time coming, but Jim Angleton was a lone and closeted manager who sometimes went years without meeting his staff. But better late than never. Angleton raised his glass of bourbon and toasted his counter-intell man from Mexico City.

'I second that,' said the counter-intelligence officer from Rio de Janeiro. 'And if Emílio Médici were here, he would cover you in kisses. *Futebol* is the religion of the masses – and they needed that win to keep them among the faithful.'

Angleton smiled. Médici was a former general and his military dictatorship was one of the strongest and most repressive in South America.

'You guys are on a roll,' said the man from Mexico nodding to his fellow counter-intell specialist. 'You nailed Marighella last year – so much for the urban guerrilla movement.'

'And we're going to splatter Lamarca this year.'

'Good luck,' said Mexico, 'but to be truthful, I don't think England would have gone on to beat Brazil even if my man didn't manage to slip their goalie a Mickey Finn.'

'Tuck into your crab cakes,' said Angleton lighting up another cigarette.

'You're a man of the arts,' said Brazil – Angleton was well known in the Agency as a man of culture and learning – 'not a gun-slinging goon like us two.'

'I'm not ashamed to admit it,' said Angleton.

'We've a problem,' said Brazil, 'with a few of our PAPERCLIP Germans – and I've heard there are similar problems with the PAPERCLIPs in other parts of the Fourth Reich.' The term was CIA slang for Latin America – even though they were told not to use it.

Angleton nodded. 'I've heard a rumour or two from Paraguay.'

'Well, you know what the Germans are like,' said Brazil. 'They love *Kulture*, they can't get enough of it. And the PAPERCLIP guys and girls like spending their ill-gotten gains on the odd masterpiece. We're not talking about a water colour that your maiden auntie's girlfriend knocked up on a trip to Venice, but the real thing. And, as you know, the PAPERCLIPs have a lot of money to splash around – not just the stuff they looted from Europe, but the cash they're making locally.'

Angleton smiled. 'Brazil's economy grew by ten per cent last year.'

'Military dictatorship is good for business.'

'Maybe,' said Mexico, 'Britain should try it – the Limeys I met during the World Cup all said their economy is shit.'

'Moaning,' said Angleton, 'is part of their culture.'

'In any case,' continued Brazil, 'we've got all these rich PAPER-CLIPs with more money than they know what to do with, so they invest their loot in works of art. They say fine art is better than shares, not just because they grow faster in value, but because you can look at them while you're eating your bratwurst or spanking your maid. Except...' Brazil paused and smiled.

'Except what?' said Mexico.

'Except when you get screwed by a crooked art dealer. The worst case I know is a PAPERCLIP farmer who owns a ranch twice the size of Belgium. He paid out the equivalent of a hundred thousand Gringo dollars for a Pussy that wasn't the real thing.'

Mexico laughed and slapped the table. 'Was this in Thailand?'

'I believe,' said Angleton, 'that the painting to which you are referring was supposed to have been a Poussin.'

'You're right,' said Brazil, 'that's the one.'

Angleton sipped his bourbon and smiled. 'This is getting very interesting. What do you know about the dealer?'

'He was half-Spanish and half-English; his name was Tommy-something. Now, the thing about selling paintings by famous artists is you can't just put one up for sale and say this here sun-flower is by van Gogh.'

'It's called attribution,' said Angleton lighting another cigarette.

'That's the word,' said Brazil snapping his fingers, 'and the attribution has to come from someone who knows the game and is trusted and respectable. Well, this Tommy guy had the best giver of attribution that money could buy. The guy was a proper English "sir" who even helps Queen Elizabeth with her pictures. Getting this guy to say a painting was genuine was as good as having the Pope sign your kid's baptismal certificate. In any case, Tommy and this "sir" ran a racket cheating PAPERCLIP Germans for more than ten years – until Tommy got killed in a car crash six years ago.'

Angleton stared sphinx-like through the haze of tobacco smoke. He knew more about Tommy and the 'sir' than he was going to let on.

'Eventually,' continued Brazil, 'one of the PAPERCLIPs showed off his priceless masterpiece to another German who had been one of those responsible for cataloguing looted art treasure from Poland. This German knew his stuff and told the PAPERCLIP that he had been sold a load of steaming *Scheisse*. As you can imagine, word spread – and soon other PAPERCLIPs realised they had been truly shafted.' Brazil paused and spread his hands. 'But what could they do, the dealer who fiddled them was dead.'

'But what,' said Mexico, 'about the "sir" guy who certified the fakes as genuine.'

'They want his blood – and I think they'll get it.'

'The problem with the British,' said Mexico, 'is…'

'You mean they've only got *one* problem,' laughed Brazil.

'Among their many problems,' continued Mexico, 'is that they never understood the importance of OPERATION PAPERCLIP. The Brits never realised the importance of the intelligence and the rocket technology that we gained. And the contribution those Germans have made to South American intelligence and security services.'

'Like your pal, Klaus Altmann,' said Brazil.

Mexico glowed with pride. He lifted his glass, 'To Klaus!'

Mexico's previous assignment had been in Bolivia. He was part of the team that tracked down and captured Che Guevara. Klaus Altmann, a.k.a. Klaus Barbie, a.k.a. the Butcher of Lyon (party membership number 4,583,085), was after Wernher von Braun (party membership number 185,068) the CIA's most famous PAPERCLIP Nazi.

'Klaus,' said Mexico, 'is the ultimate counter-insurgency expert: ruthless, thorough and cunning. He was essential in trapping Che. Klaus would never be taken in by an art dealer handling fakes.'

'I don't recall,' said Angleton, 'that Herr Altmann had much of an interest in art.'

'He's too busy. Klaus also makes a bundle in the arms trade – and the government looks the other way.'

'Out of gratitude,' said Brazil.

Angleton, now FURIOSO again, gazed through the smoke haze. Threads were twisting in the air linking up briefly – and then dissolving again. He had suspected for years that there had been a professional link between Tommy and Anthony Blunt, the spy turned art historian – and he also knew there was a close link between Blunt and Henry Bone. The FURIOSO in him knew that the British Secret Intelligence Service was even more riddled with Soviet agents than Harold Wilson's government had been. And this could be a problem for Klaus Altmann.

'How well,' said Angleton, 'does Altmann look after his own personal security?'

'He has his own bodyguards as well as Bolivian government security – and he never discusses travel plans.'

Angleton, again the obsessive paranoid bureaucrat, looked at the agent who had been transferred from Bolivia to Mexico. He was an excellent counter-intelligence officer, but sometimes too arrogant and cocky

'Getting back to Che,' said Angleton, 'why did you let the press photograph his body?'

'Because we wanted to provide proof to the world that he was dead.'

'But why were the photographers allowed so much time to take photos and from so many angles?'

The former Bolivian agent shrugged.

Angleton's eyes flashed a hint of concealed anger. 'You don't know what I'm talking about, do you?'

'Sorry, sir, I don't.'

'One of those photographers must have been an ex-art student turned Communist sympathiser. Did it never occur to you that Che, picturesquely laid out on a concrete slab in the laundry room of *Nuestra Señora de Malta*, was the very image of the martyred Christ – and this in a continent as religion crazy as South America?'

'To be honest, sir, we never considered that sort of thing. With hindsight...'

Angleton shook his head. It was like talking to a statue. At the time, an English art critic had compared one of the photos of the dead Che to Andrea Mantegna's *Lamentation over the Dead Christ*. In fact, thought FURIOSO, the resemblance was stunning. Another victory turned into defeat. Instead of killing Guevara and putting him in the trash can of history, the op had turned Che into a quasi-religious icon of revolution.

'Well then,' said Angleton pushing aside his food and lighting another cigarette from the stub of his last one. 'Well then, leaving the Che fiasco aside for the moment, I am concerned about Altmann's personal safety. The Nazi hunters are alive and on the prowl in South America. Aside from their moral self-righteousness and obsessive inability to bury the past, they are ripe for Communist infiltration. Would either of you two gentlemen care to explain how?'

Brazil answered first. 'The archives of the KGB and the East Bloc intelligence agencies would be a treasure trove for such groups. I've heard, by the way, that at least one group of Nazi hunters have already been given files by the East German Stasi.'

'Would you like to give me the name of the group?'

Brazil did so while Angleton scribbled it into his notebook.

'Ergo...' said Angleton gesturing for more.

'Ergo, it makes Nazi hunters ripe for manipulation by East Bloc intelligence agencies who could pass on the names of those they want eliminated.'

Mexico smiled. 'Even if it isn't true, tarring them with Communist connections would be excellent psy-op – and would help protect our PAPERCLIPs.'

Angleton nodded agreement and continued, 'I am sure you are aware that OPERATION PAPERCLIP was a serious post-war bone of contention between ourselves and our French and British allies. The French, in fact, have never stopped baying for Altmann's blood.' He nodded at the former Bolivian agent. 'Has Altmann ever talked about it?'

The ex-Bolivian agent looked uncomfortable. 'Klaus sometimes got kind of depressed and worried. I'd pour him a brandy and say, "Okay you're not a saint, but you're not a monster either. For Christ's sake, you were a counter-insurgency officer in an army occupying a defeated enemy country. Inevitably, there was going to be resistance and your job was to put that resistance down. You were no different from a British officer in Malaya or a French officer in Algeria or an American officer in Vietnam."'

'Did Altmann ever mention those he thinks might be on his trail?'

'Well, for a start, the Nazi hunters we just mentioned.'

'Anyone in British or French intelligence?'

The agent nodded. 'One Britisher in particular, an SIS officer named William Catesby. Klaus hates the bastard.'

'Why?'

'He says Catesby killed a good friend of his. I've checked the records and found that the victim was one of our PAPERCLIPs.'

Angleton remained in the listening mode. He didn't wish to share what he already knew.

'I've heard about Catesby.' The Brazil agent finished his crab cakes and topped up his bourbon. 'The ODESSA gang hate him too.'

Jim Angleton maintained his sphinx-like face. The CIA were supposed to have nothing to do with ODESSA, but it was a rule often broken – particularly in South America. The *Organization Der Ehemaligen SS-Angehörigen* had been secretly formed at a meeting in August, 1944 when it became obvious that Germany was going to lose the war. The important thing was to stop Germany's assets from falling into enemy hands. ODESSA became a vast money-laundering scheme, as well as an international network geared to help Nazis escape and disperse around the world.

Angleton looked at his man from Brazil. 'How do you know ODESSA hate Catesby?'

'It's complicated.' The agent wiped his lips. 'The problem with being counter-intell in Rio is that all the nutcases get shunted to you. This particular crazy was a White Russian with links to ODESSA who came to me with a totally bizarre story. One of his ODESSA pals was one of the Germans who got stung by the crooked art dealer – and so, by the way, did the White Russian. So they had this in common and were talking about ways of getting revenge. After too much vodka, the White Russian confided that he had a friend in the British intelligence service, who would be willing to carry out a hit on the art historian. When the White Russian said his name was Catesby, the ODESSA guy burst out laughing and said he'd better act quick because ODESSA were going to kill Catesby first.'

Angleton stubbed out his cigarette. 'I don't understand. Why did the White Russian come to the embassy to tell you this?'

'He wants to save Catesby's life. He likes the guy. Apparently, he had already gone to the British embassy – and the one in Asunción too – but no one would talk to him. And you could see why – he was wearing traditional Mongolian dress and not looking especially sane. So he thought we would be the next best bet.'

'He likes Catesby?' said the other agent. 'Is he that crazy or is he a Commie?'

'He's just plain stir crazy. He thinks Catesby is a descendant of Guy Fawkes, or someone like him, and that Catesby is part of a conspiracy to make England an autocratic Roman Catholic monarchy.'

'Sounds better than the England we've got now.'

'A lot of people,' said the Brazil agent, 'would pass this guy off as a cuckoo who had just escaped from the insane asylum, but I could see more to him – and I could also smell money, lots of it.'

'Which explains the ODESSA link.'

'Exactly. In any case, I wanted to know more about him. We all know a lot of guys, especially SF types, who model themselves on Attila the Hun. Well, this guy wants to be Genghis Khan. And, when you hear him argue the case for a new Mongolian empire taking over China and Siberia, he doesn't sound completely crazy. But he certainly is rabidly anti-Communist and we must never ignore such allies no matter how bizarre they sound. We need all the help we can get.'

Angleton gave a slight nod. Otherwise, he seemed lost in thought behind his veil of smoke.

'And when I got him talking about China and Russia he seemed pretty goddamn well informed. He thinks Mao started the Cultural Revolution because he's running scared of the Mongols, the Manchurians and the Tibetans. In fact, he asked me if I could arrange a meeting between him and Nixon.'

'Why does he want to meet Nixon?' said Angleton.

'Our Genghis Khan wannabe wants to persuade Nixon to visit Red China. He thinks such a visit would be a signal to the anti-Communist forces secretly at work in China and would crack the system. He thinks isolating China only gives strength to the Red Guards.'

The other agent laughed. 'The only way Dick Nixon would go to Red China would be in a B-52 with nuclear bombs.'

Angleton got up. Lunch was over. He turned to the agent from Brazil. 'If the President won't meet our White Russian admirer of Genghis Khan, I will. Arrange his transport to Washington and treat him like a VIP.'

James Jesus Angleton stayed late after he got back to his office at the Langley HQ. He was again wreathed in smoke and there was a glass of Jack Daniels close at hand. The White Russian wasn't mad – and Eliot, Pound and Yeats wouldn't have thought him mad either. Communism was a poisonous obscenity that needed to be ruthlessly crushed, but Western democracy was an insipid alternative – a plethora of committees full of fat bureaucrats and money-grubbing brokers. No wonder Pound had admired

Mussolini and that Tom had a nervous breakdown. We need strong leaders with culture, refinement and vision – Renaissance princes.

Angleton loved his FURIOSO code name. He considered himself a modern reincarnation of a Renaissance prince, a Pandolfo Malatesta tasked with defeating the Turks at any price. But as a spymaster, Angleton most admired Machiavelli and his contempt for '*la verità effettuale della cosa*' – 'the actual truth of things'. The actual truth was a weak contender against skilful psy-op and calculated disinformation – far more lethal drugs than an assassin's poison.

A vision was forming in the darkened office – and the vague outlines were becoming sharply delineated. Angleton was certain that the White Russian was a key money launderer for ODESSA. The solution to the British problem was ODESSA's money – great mounds of it. There were budget limitations as to how much money the CIA could pump into its ops in the UK – and the bookkeeper bloodhounds always wanted some form of accountability. But with ODESSA there would be neither – and, although it could never be acknowledged, ODESSA certainly owed the CIA a favour or two.

There were problems, however, and Catesby was one of them. He needed to be neutralised either by death or blackmail. There were meetings to be arranged and letters to be written.

**Century House, Lambeth, London:** December, 1971

Henry Bone had amassed an impressive collection of tapes beamed from the device hidden in the billiard room of the Mayfair gentlemen's club. One of Bone's most prized tapes confirmed that a pipeline that carried water from the Elan Valley reservoirs in Wales to Birmingham had, in fact, been damaged by an explosive charge set by what was now called 'the action committee'. It was an agent provocateur op aimed at arousing public anger against left-wing revolutionary extremists. In the end, the explosion did little damage and the sparse press coverage it did receive suggested extremist Welsh nationalists as the perpetrators. Nonetheless, the tape was a jewel that proved the group were engaged in criminal activities.

The latest tapes revealed more of what Bone had long known. JJ, his former colleague, was now a dangerous paranoid reactionary who wanted to intern 6,000 subversives – including fifty Members of Parliament, several hundred journalists and academics and religious leaders too – on a 'lesser Gaelic archipelago in the far North'. JJ was also a racist and a bigot. Once the Lefties were out of the way, he wanted to repatriate the black and Asian populations. He described it as 'a question of national survival'. Henry Bone assumed that JJ's last remark was aimed at Prime Minister Edward Heath: 'The queer will be dethroned.'

Bone turned off the tape deck and stared into the blank opaque space of his drawn curtains. Could it happen in Britain?

**Agency News:** 9 January 1972

### Threat of Lights Going Out as Miners Strike

Coal miners ceased work at midnight in their first national strike for fifty years. All 289 pits across the country have been closed by the strike.

Three months of talks with the

National Coal Board broke down as the miners rejected a pay offer of 7.9 per cent and the promise of a backdated deal for an increase in productivity.

Britain's 280,000 mineworkers are determined to break the government's eight per cent pay ceiling. The miners want an increase of up to £9 a week on an average take home wage of £25.

The miners' overtime ban, in effect since 1 November, has already cost the industry £20m in lost production.

The Trades Union Congress (TUC) has announced that it will be holding meetings at the weekend to discuss support for the strike among transport workers.

The NCB has predicted that coal stocks will quickly run down. Three-quarters of the electricity used in the United Kingdom comes from coal-burning power stations.

The miners' strike comes at a time when power stations are facing long periods of peak demand during the cold weather.

**Islington, London:** 15 January 1972

It was a dinner party where the room was full of elephants. The host was a member of the Communist Party, whereas Catesby and Frances were a part of the 'State Repressive Apparatus'. There was also a bit of awkwardness because Frances's section was actively spying on the host. But it was very friendly and all the elephants warmly acknowledged one other. Inevitably, the miners' strike was part of the conversation just as the serving of good claret was part of the dinner.

'It is ludicrous,' said the host dishing up casserole, 'don't you think so?'

'Is what ludicrous?' said Catesby.

'That Frances's colleagues think the Communist Party has anything to do with these strikes?'

'You ought,' said Frances, 'to come in to give them a talk face to face.'

'I would if they invited me – or they could simply read my articles in *Marxism Today*.'

'We do subscribe to the journal,' said Frances. Part of Five's job was keeping an eye on 'radical' groups by reading their publications. 'But I'm not sure how carefully my colleagues read it – if they read it at all.'

'I don't suppose,' said their host, 'that many of them have read Gramsci?'

Catesby laughed. 'MI5 do not live in a world of intellectual enquiry and books.'

'It's a pity they don't. If they did, they would have a better understanding of the world they are spying on.'

'The problem is that SIS snaps up all the brains,' said Frances.

Catesby laughed again. Then said, 'Let's get back to the miners' strike. Do you support it?'

'No. The strikers are pursuing their own narrow economic interests.'

Catesby smiled. Britain's leading Marxist had just condemned the miners' strike.

'Can you explain why?' said Frances.

'Capitalism has mutated. Automation and technical advances have drastically reduced the size of the industrial proletariat. What remains of the traditional working class are divided into sections based on particular trade skills or industry – mining, car manufacture, etc. Because so few of the proletariat remain, Marx's idea of a proletarian revolution is now just as obsolete as handlooms.'

'I'm not sure I agree,' said Catesby.

'Your politics, William, belong to an idealistic and romanticised past.'

Catesby was amused for two reasons. One, Britain's leading Marxist intellectual had, effectively, just criticised him for being too far to the left. Two, how totally absurd that the Security Service regarded this man as a dangerous subversive.

There was, however, a more serious issue that chilled Catesby's blood. The real threat to British democracy did not come from Communist subversives – or trade unions or kids demonstrating against the Vietnam War. It came from the Secret State itself.

## Army Kills 13 in Northern Ireland Civil Rights Protest

Troops from the Parachute Regiment opened fire on a crowd of protestors in the Bogside district of Londonderry and killed thirteen civilians.

Seventeen additional people were wounded by gunfire and another was knocked down by a speeding car.

An Army spokesman said two soldiers had been injured and sixty people arrested. Major General Robert Ford, Commander Land Forces Northern Ireland, insisted his troops had been fired on first. 'There is absolutely no doubt at all that the Parachute battalion did not open up until they had been fired at,' he said. The Bogsiders, however, maintain that the troops opened fire on unarmed civilians.

The trouble began as the civil rights demonstration approached an Army barbed wire barricade. The mostly peaceful crowd of between 7,000 and 10,000 was marching in protest at the policy of internment without trial. Some of the younger demonstrators began taunting the soldiers with chants of 'IRA, IRA'. Bottles, broken paving stones, and heavy pieces of iron pipe were thrown at the troops manning the barrier.

Although Stewards appealed for calm, more missiles were thrown. Squads from the 1st Battalion of the Parachute Regiment left the barricades and chased the demonstrators.

The Army maintains it opened fire only after being shot at by two snipers in flats overlooking the street. It claims that acid bombs were also thrown.

The gun battle lasted about twenty-five minutes.

**Pimlico, London:** 30 January 1972

Catesby turned off the radio and continued cooking his Sunday supper in silence. He had already heard about the shootings in Northern Ireland and didn't want to hear a repeat. It was as depressing as it was horrific. He knew that the Army were under terrible pressure in Northern Ireland, but something about the Army's account of what had happened did not ring completely true. Regardless of who was to blame, the thing that most worried Catesby was that armed soldiers had opened fire on civilians. Northern Ireland was part of the United Kingdom – and if it could happen there, it could happen in Britain too. But no, that's an exaggeration. It will never happen.

Catesby served up his food and stared blankly at the chicken. Violence always killed his appetite. He couldn't get what had happened in Londonderry – or Derry as most Catholics called it – out of his mind. In his gloomiest moments, Catesby wondered if elements of the Secret State were using Northern Ireland to hone and test their dark skills. But then he completely dismissed the thought. Northern Ireland was a terrible tragedy. Had not the Army been sent there originally to protect the Catholics? Generally speaking, Catesby had a lot of sympathy for the ordinary squaddie patrolling the streets and lanes of the province. But when things went wrong, other agendas took over.

Catesby hadn't finished eating his supper when the telephone rang. It was the Night Duty Officer and he had been summoned to an emergency meeting at Century House. Catesby said he'd be there and put the phone down.

It was worrying. From time to time there were rumours that he might be sent to Northern Ireland. He hated the prospect. Strictly speaking, Northern Ireland wasn't SIS turf. It was part of the United Kingdom and, as such, was the responsibility of the Security Service. But Five were, reportedly, making a hash of things. They didn't get along with the Army or RUC Special Branch.

The meeting, it seemed to Catesby, had been called as a panic measure. The DG began by announcing that all leave had been cancelled and that it was likely that a number of officers would be transferred to Northern Ireland on temporary duty.

'There is also,' said the DG, 'the likelihood of IRA retaliation on the British mainland in response to what happened today. For this reason, our colleagues in the Security Service are stretched to breaking point. It may be necessary to give them temporary support in terms of personnel and resources.

DIR P/A, who controlled Personnel and Central Registry among other departments, came in hard. 'I would like to point out, sir, that we are also fully stretched – and there are also statutory requirements limiting our ability to operate within the UK.'

'Those requirements would be waived in such a situation because SIS officers would be operating under the auspices of the Security Service.'

Catesby remained silent. He knew that, despite DIR P/A's reservations, many of his colleagues were aching to be let loose on the UK mainland. As much as they enjoyed spying on Communists in Germany, Eastern Europe and the rest of the world, they were longing to have a crack at home-grown Reds – or anyone they could smear as a Red. It was, thought Catesby, a depressing and dangerous development. The Secret State was a beast best left to prowl in foreign places.

**Agency News:** 9 February 1972

## State of Emergency Declared

The Government has just issued the following statement. It was made in the House of Commons by the Secretary of State for the Home Department (Mr Reginald Maudling).

'Faced with the disruption of coal and electricity supplies caused by industrial action in the coal industry, the Government must take steps to discharge their responsibility to maintain essential services and to minimise the threat to the life of the community. They have therefore thought it right to advise the proclamation of an emergency under Section 1 of the Emergency Powers Act, 1920, as amended, followed by the making of regulations under Section 2.

'The regulations will come into operation at midnight tonight. Copies will be available this afternoon. My right hon. friend will be making an announcement tomorrow about the arrangements for debating these regulations next week. They are based on those made in 1970, with some modifications, and confer on Ministers enabling powers which they will use only to the extent that necessity requires.'

Mr Maudling was questioned by Labour Shadow Home Secretary, Shirley Williams, on 'whether the Government have any intention of using the Armed Forces in a situation which might involve them in moving through picket lines, and whether he is aware of the considerable crisis this would bring, granted the history of the coal mining industry?'

Mr Maudling replied: 'The Government would contemplate the use of the Armed Forces only if that were absolutely essential to maintain vital services to the nation.'

## Century House, Lambeth. London: 15 February 1972

The first thing Catesby found in his inbox was an envelope addressed to him with Chinese ideograms. He guessed that was the meaning of the Chinese, for his name and title were written in English below – the sender had correctly assumed that the mailroom staff were not fluent in Mandarin. Catesby knew it wasn't from Mao, because there wasn't a stamp or street address on the envelope – it was internal circulation.

Catesby opened the envelope and found a greeting card featuring a multi-coloured animal with a long tail and more Chinese writing. The inside of the card had HAPPY NEW YEAR written in a largely friendly hand and was signed, *Best wishes, Paul* – in Chinese and English. Paul was head of China T Section and someone Catesby liked and trusted.

The next item in the inbox was from the SIS legal team and concerned the 'State of Emergency' that had been declared by the government. The legal team advised that, 'under Section 1 of the Emergency Powers Act, 1920', it would be 'right and proper' for SIS officers 'to render all assistance possible to the Armed Forces in order to maintain vital services to the nation.' In other words, thought Catesby, we are entitled to spy on trade unions and political activists in order to assist the Army.

Catesby put down the memo and picked up the greeting card

celebrating the Chinese lunar new year. He looked again at the stylised animal on the front of the card. It was the beginning of 'The Year of the Rat'.

## London: 15 February 1972

The letter had JJ's name typed on it, but there was no address, stamp or postmark. It had been delivered when no one was at home. The first thing that JJ noticed when he opened the envelope was the size of the stationery. It was 8x10 rather than A4. It wasn't definite proof, yet a strong indication that it had been written in the USA. But the fact that it had been hand-delivered in London indicated local connections. The letter itself was typewritten and bore no date, salutation or signature.

I can't identify myself for reasons you can well appreciate. I am, however, certain that you will have a good idea of who I am. Needless to say, I am sympathetic to the causes you represent and to your concern about the present situation in the UK. My sympathy must, however, remain top secret.

There are still traitors in the service in which you were once a distinguished officer, but I am sure this will come to you as no surprise.

The most insidious traitor is Henry Bone. He was a long-term friend and protector of Kim Philby and aided and abetted his escape to the Soviet Union, but he was not the only one to do in the Secret Intelligence Service. Bone has also had a close relationship with the 'Fourth Man' and has been involved in art fraud, as well as spying for the Soviet Union. As you know, there was a Communist cell in 10 Downing Street during Harold Wilson's premiership. Bone was instrumental in destroying SIS files that would have revealed Wilson as a long-term Soviet agent. Bone also destroyed and suppressed intelligence material relating to the Communist backgrounds of members of Wilson's cabinet and the Labour Party.

Another dangerous Communist agent is William Catesby. He became a Communist while a student at Trinity College, Cambridge. When he was called up for military service, a Soviet agent in military intelligence arranged for Catesby to be assigned to the Special Operations Executive.

He was later parachuted into central France where he aided and abetted the Maquis Rouge – the Communist section of the French Resistance movement. While in France, Catesby devoted much of his time helping the Maquis Rouge set up Communist cells that would remain stay in place after the German defeat. These Communist cells have remained active ever since and many of Catesby's former Maquis Rouge comrades played an important role in organising strikes and disruption during the events of May, 1968.

In May of 1951, Catesby murdered a former German Army officer in Bremen. If Catesby is ever brought to account for this murder, he will argue that he did so because the ex-German officer was a war criminal who was about to escape justice. This is a lie. Catesby murdered the German because he was a former intelligence officer who had detailed knowledge of Catesby's Communist activities during the war and afterwards as well. Catesby is a long-serving Communist agent. He has spent much of his career advising Communist members of the Labour Party and Communist trade union leaders on how to avoid detection by the Security Service.

As you well know, the Secret Intelligence Service has been totally penetrated by the KGB. This is why Communist spies like Catesby and Bone are allowed to prosper and how others – on the brink of exposure – have been helped to slip away.

I can also confirm that the former head of the Security Service, Roger Hollis, is a Communist spy. He was recruited by left-wing American journalist, Agnes Smedley, to whom he was very close, when he was working for British America Tobacco in Shanghai. During his time in China, Hollis also had connections with the Soviet spy, Richard Sorge.

I hope that in the near future the organisations that you represent will be in receipt of considerable financial assets in order to help in your struggle against Communism and social decay in the United Kingdom. I am sure that you will be able to use your newly acquired skills as a merchant banker to facilitate receipt of these funds and to disguise their origins.

JJ had always suspected that he had powerful allies and this letter proved it. Most of the information in the letter confirmed what JJ had long suspected. But the possibility of large financial support would be an enormous help to plans still in embryo. ROC and

POC were already set up. ROC, the Resistance Operations Committee, was an anti-Communist guerrilla force largely formed from reserve and retired officers. At the core of POC, the Psychological Operations Committee, were former members of IRD, the Information Research Department. The IRD was a secret organisation founded in 1948as a response to the 'developing Communist threat to the whole fabric of Western civilisation'. The aim of IRD was to spread anti-Soviet propaganda through the news media, which included working with the CIA in supporting *Encounter* and other Mockingbird op magazines. Eventually, the IRD exceeded its original brief by using covert means to attack the British Left and the Trade Union movement through lies and distortion. JJ entirely agreed. The fight against Communism, decadence and immigration was a no-holds-barred fight to the finish.

**10 Downing Street:** 18 February 1972

Catesby's rise through the ranks of SIS hadn't been meteoric, but it had been steady. He wasn't yet a director, like Bone and the other mandarins, but he was head of his own department, the Sov Bloc T Section – a slight promotion from his former post heading up the E. Europe P Section. Catesby wasn't a permanent member of JIC, but he was often co-opted to Joint Intelligence Committee meetings.

JIC usually met just around the corner at the Cabinet Office at 70 Whitehall, which actually was a much more stately building. Catesby didn't know why the meeting had been changed to 10 Downing Street, for it didn't look like the Prime Minister would be attending after all – the PM had, apparently, been summoned to a crisis meeting elsewhere. But the change pleased Catesby. He much preferred the intimacy and status of the Cabinet Room. It was, however, a bit dingy even at midday. There was so little natural light that the three brass chandeliers had been switched on. And it was eerily quiet too. The heavy doors were sound-proofed and the curtains were thick velvet. All the better, thought Catesby, for bugging devices. There was a rumour that a microphone was hidden behind Gladstone's portrait, which loomed down over Catesby. He was tempted to say, 'Testing one, two.' But it wouldn't be a very tasteful joke for someone in his position.

The atmosphere was febrile and furtive owing to the ongoing crises in Britain and Northern Ireland. The JIC members formed little conspiratorial knots as they moved around the room drinking coffee or tea from bone china cups. The tones were hushed, but all the snatched conversations that Catesby picked up were about the State of Emergency – which, however, was conspicuous by its absence from the agenda. As soon as the JIC chairman entered the room, the knots began to disperse and sit down.

None of the late Victorian chairs – that Bone decried as 'ghastly' – had armrests except for one. The general, deputising for the Chief of Defence Staff, was about to plop himself into the chair with armrests and Catesby had to stop him. 'I'm sorry,' said

Catesby, 'that chair is reserved for the Prime Minister. He's probably not coming, but it's best…'

'Certainly,' said the general moving to an armless chair, 'one mustn't breach etiquette.'

Catesby smiled smugly. He had never bossed around a general before. How he wished his stepson had been there to see it.

Most of the Cabinet Room was taken up by a forty-foot-long table shaped like a boat. Another Downing Street newcomer leaned over to Catesby and said, 'Did the Prime Minister bring in this table because it reminds him of sailing *Morning Cloud*?'

'No,' said Catesby beginning to relish his status as a Number 10 insider, 'it was actually Harold Macmillan who commissioned this table. He wanted one shaped so that he could make eye-contact with his entire cabinet.'

Just as the meeting was about to begin the clock on the mantelpiece began to chime – and five seconds later, a clock on a table opposite the PM's vacant chair began to chime. Harold Wilson had brought in the second clock so he could time his meetings without awkwardly looking at his watch or twisting around.

'I suppose,' said the general, 'that one is Washington time and the other is Moscow time.'

The only smiles were bleak ones. Catesby felt vaguely sorry for the general and hoped that he would never have to shoot him to prevent a military coup.

The first part of the JIC meeting was taken up by Northern Ireland where the situation continued to deteriorate rapidly. Last month's shooting in Londonderry was already known as Bloody Sunday. The Army officer gave an update on the situation and the state of the casualties. Many were still in a critical condition. Catesby listened with horror and fear. If it could happen in Londonderry, why could it not happen in London or Yorkshire? In Ipswich or Norwich? Once again, Catesby realised that he didn't have much of a stomach for violence. He wished that he could weave a magic protecting veil that he could spread over the island nation that he loved.

The second agenda item was 'SIS and SALT'. Although the UK was not directly involved in the Strategic Arms Limitation Talks that now alternated between Helsinki and Vienna, it was important that HM's government had some idea what was going on behind the scenes. The DG began with a summary and then passed over to Bone and Catesby who provided details and helped answer questions.

The next item belonged to Catesby alone. It was about a discussion document entitled, 'An Intelligence Assessment: Defectors and Double Agents', Catesby had written and that had been circulated to JIC members.

'I don't want to bore you,' began Catesby.

Bone gave an ironic smile.

'Thank you, Henry. I will be as quick as possible. Most of you know that I am not a big fan of defectors as intelligence assets, particularly walk-ins. Most defectors fall into two categories. The worst, but only arguably the worst, are fake defectors who have been planted by foreign intelligence services to spread disinformation and cause chaos in our intelligence services. The other type of defector is what the Americans call "bona fide"; I prefer calling them "genuine" or "not planted".'

'As opposed to "unplanted",' said a JIC member from the Lords who had had a good lunch, 'such as seed potatoes chitting in one's greenhouse.'

'Quite,' said Catesby smiling at the peer and reminding himself that he still hadn't bought his seed potatoes. 'The so-called genuine defector,' continued Catesby, 'can cause just as much damage as a planted one. They are usually motivated by ego rather than ideology. Their reasons for defecting are often shallow: they're bored with their job; they're unhappy in their marriage – or they want a lot more money than they could ever make as a KGB colonel. The intelligence provided by such defectors is always contaminated by embellishment and the need to impress their handlers with their own importance.'

The head of the Security Service was nodding approval – which made his odd-shaped ears jiggle. Catesby trusted him because of his suburban ordinariness. He played tennis, went bird-watching and loved amateur dramatics. In fact, the head of the Security Service lived in the same garden suburb as Harold Wilson – and they both loved Gilbert and Sullivan.

'I think,' said the head of Five in his most portentous am-dram voice, 'that we know to whom you are referring.'

Catesby looked at the JIC chairman. The chairman turned to the stenographer, 'Don't copy or minute this.'

'We're obviously talking about EMPUSA,' said Catesby, 'who in my view, is a confidence trickster who has split the CIA into two camps. The problem is that EMPUSA has an enormous influence on ADDOCI.'

'In plain English,' said DG SIS, 'ADDOCI translates as CIA Head of Counter-intelligence. Our code name for him is FURIOSO, but his actual name is James Angleton.'

'I'm not sure,' said the JIC chairman, 'that we should continue this discussion. I hope that all of us present realise that we have strayed on to a very sensitive area.'

'I appreciate that, Sir Stewart, therefore I will now proceed to discuss my paper,' Catesby paused, '...in theoretical terms without reference to specific individuals.' Catesby continued, 'It is possible that certain defectors will try to impress their handlers with far-fetched conspiracy theories involving impossible assassinations...'

'Mr Catesby,' said the chairman.

'I apologise, Sir Stewart.'

'The truth of the matter,' said Catesby, 'is that it is almost impossible to tell the difference between a planted and a genuine defector. One test that agent handlers should apply is to tell would-be defectors that they would be much more useful by staying in place and passing on intelligence by spy-craft methods such as dead letter drops.'

The well-whiskyed JIC member from the Lords intervened. 'Not an option for a spineless coward.'

'Quite,' said Catesby, 'which is why the stay-in-place option is a useful test of commitment. Which brings us to another assessment problem, "the dangled double". Once again, any Sov Bloc intelligence officer who freely offers his or her services should be regarded as highly suspect.'

'Can you think of a single instance,' interrupted the Chairman, 'when a defector or double agent has been a woman?'

Catesby smiled. 'I can think of several women spies – particularly the *Rote Kapelle*, who spied against Hitler's Germany – and women spies have been excellent, brave and ideologically motivated.'

'I believe that the *Rote Kapelle*, or Red Orchestra, were spying for the Soviet Union.' The person who intervened was the Permanent Secretary of the Civil Service Department. He was a stout walrus of a man who some referred to as the 'Deputy Prime Minister'. Catesby, and others, had concerns about him. He was normally a solid type, but had lately turned nervous and volatile.

'At the time,' said Catesby, 'there were no Western agents in Berlin to whom the *Rote Kapelle* could have passed their information.' Catesby realised that he had dropped himself in it by praising the Red Orchestra. It was rumoured that the Permanent Secretary had joined the ranks of those who believed Red monsters were lurking under every bed – and he was getting worse.

The Permanent Secretary stared at Catesby over arched fingers.

'If an agent,' said Catesby trying to return to the original subject, 'is a dangled double, the intelligence provided will at first be highly accurate, but harmless to Moscow. The disinformation will begin once the agent is trusted by his handlers.' Catesby glanced at the Permanent Secretary. 'A standard tactic used by planted defectors or false doubles is to suggest that those who don't believe them are, in fact, moles who are trying to protect themselves.'

The representative from GCHQ took off her reading glasses and looked at Catesby. She had known Catesby's sister before she was forced to resign and her look was a mixture of sympathy and suspicion.

Catesby understood and smiled back.

'Is it ever possible to be absolutely certain – 100 per cent certain – that a defector or double agent is genuine?'

'Yes,' said Catesby, 'but not until they have been assassinated or executed by the service they betrayed.'

**Manassas, Virginia:** April, 1972

It was the CIA's best safe house: totally isolated in hilly woodland, but only a forty-minute drive from Langley. The house had a swimming pool, lake frontage and an outdoor bar and barbecue. But what Angleton liked most about it were the spectacular azaleas, which were bursting into full bloom. The house had been built in the 1950s using local stone and wood. There was nothing vulgar about it – except a water feature with Koi carp and a statue of Pan – but the overriding aesthetic style was unashamed American assertive.

It hadn't been easy to lure the new Genghis Khan, code-named MH/KHAN to Northern Virginia, but Nixon's recent visit to China persuaded him that it was time to talk to the CIA.

'As you know,' said KHAN sitting cross-legged at a low table that the Tibetan caterers had supplied especially, 'I petitioned your President to make the visit. But whether or not he paid any attention to my petition, I have no way of knowing.'

'What,' said Angleton, 'do you think Nixon's visit will accomplish?'

'It may be many generations before we know, but I think it will mean the end of Communism in China.'

'What would you like to see after that?'

'A new world order based on religion and monarchy. The Great Khan, by the way, was tolerant of most religions. Like myself, he was a Tengrist, a follower of a religion that combines shamanism with animism and ancestor cults. Tengrist shamans have the power of prophecy – and so do I.'

'What can you prophesy?'

'I prophesy that I am going to have some of that *lunggoi katsa*.' KHAN smiled and spooned a large portion of stewed sheep's head into his bowl. 'Thank you for arranging Tibetan food. I am a great admirer of all things Tibetan and a practitioner of Tibetan Buddhism as well as Tengrism.'

Angleton smiled. They hadn't been able to find any Mongolian caterers who were security cleared for the safe house, but CIA regularly used the Tibetan cooks when the Dalai Lama or his brothers, Tak-teer and Gayalo, were guests at the house. Tibet had been part of a strategy to roll back Red China.

'But,' said KHAN, 'I will give you another prophesy – and one that may well happen within our own present incarnations.'

Jim Angleton poured himself another bourbon. The safe house drinks cupboard was well stocked with beverages other than the yak butter tea that KHAN was happy with.

'Tengri,' said KHAN, 'is the force which determines everything from rain or snow to the fate of nations and empires.'

Angleton knew it was best not to press him about the prophecy that he had promised. He could see that KHAN was difficult to predict. The Tengrist admirer of Tibet hadn't turned up in a Mongol caftan, but in a perfectly cut Savile Row suit. On the other hand, KHAN wore a Genghis-style beard and had his hair tied back into a bun.

'Tengrism,' continued KHAN, 'was once the predominant religion of Central Asia. Its spread followed the Great Khan's conquests. One must not forget that the Mongols invaded and lay waste to much of Bulgaria, Hungary and Poland – and annihilated all of the major cities of Russia.' KAHN paused and stared at his host with a look that seemed oddly sane and reasoned. 'I prophesy that the Soviet Union will fall by the end of this century and that the new millennium will see Communism and other forms of godless materialism replaced by religion.'

'You speak of materialism with contempt,' said Angleton, 'and yet Genghis Khan needed currency, gold and other financial assets to carry out his great conquests.'

'Money is a means to an end,' smiled KHAN, 'not an end in itself.'

'And you have access to huge quantities of it.'

KHAN wiped his lips and sipped his yak butter tea.

Angleton could see that he was a person of refinement and breeding – and far from mad. Later they would talk about poetry.

'Yes,' said KHAN, 'I am rich, but my personal fortune is of no importance.'

'You manage the money and assets of others.'

'Of course,' said KHAN, 'it is part of our plan to bring down Communism. Communists are hopeless with wealth. They destroy it rather than create it. Look what Stalin did to the kulaks.

It is fine to rid a country of useless mouths, but not of those who produce.'

'And what of artists – and works of art?' Angleton fixed KHAN with a knowing stare.

'We love art, but something in your look suggests you know about the scandal.'

Angleton nodded.

'The people I represent were very upset. In fact, I was cheated myself. But I believe the dealer responsible is no longer with us.'

'The art dealer was killed in a car crash in Spain.' Angleton smiled. 'I knew him. The circumstances were suspicious – and there are those who say it was an act of revenge carried out by ODESSA.'

KHAN remained silent.

'The enemy of your enemy is your friend,' said Angleton. 'And ODESSA have no greater enemy than Communism. It was Communism that destroyed their land and raped their women.'

'What are you offering?'

'Britain, once the world's greatest empire, is falling apart. The Labour Party and the trade unions are controlled directly from Moscow. Britain will be the next domino to fall to Communism.'

'I once met…'

'William Catesby?'

KHAN nodded.

'Catesby deceived you. He is a long-serving Soviet double agent.'

'I am disappointed.'

'But we have true friends in Britain; friends who can reverse the rot.' Angleton paused. 'Can you help them?'

'My friends might be interested – tell me how.'

Angleton told him.

## Salvador Allende, President of Chile, Overthrown in Military Coup

Salvador Allende, the world's first democratically elected Marxist head of state, has died in a revolt led by Army generals.

It is still not clear how the Chilean President met his death. One report says that he committed suicide rather than surrender to the Army commanders who were bombing and besieging the presidential palace. The siege began when tanks opened fire after President Allende had rejected an ultimatum to resign.

Martial law has been declared throughout Chile and a curfew has been imposed. Tanks continued to blast buildings in the city centre until early evening in an attempt to root out pro-Allende supporters who were still holding out. Helicopters repeatedly machine-gunned the top floors of buildings near the British embassy. Bullets ripped through the windows of the embassy – but no casualties were reported.

**Century House, Lambeth, London:** 12 September 1973

Catesby was depressed. He had just read the cables from Santiago – and they were grim. In a way, thought Catesby slipping on his Machiavellian mask, it was a pity that no one had been hurt at the embassy – not seriously, of course. It would have given HM Government an excuse to make a diplomatic protest against the junta.

It was still too soon to know how the Foreign Office was going to react to the coup, but Catesby suspected that, after some wriggling, the FCO would give their blessing to the junta. When the smoke cleared, it was all about business and exports.

The Western Hemisphere wasn't really any of Catesby's business, but that didn't stop him from poking his nose around and getting top secret docs from Registry. Occasionally, he got a memo from Dir/Americas telling him to 'get off the grass', but

Catesby had enough weight of his own to ignore it. In fact, he impressed Dir/Americas by mentioning that he had actually met the woman who had originally said, 'Get your tank *orf* my lawn.' She was an upper-class Englishwoman married to a wealthy and elderly Bremen merchant. They lived in the staid Schwachhausen district of Bremen. In the aftermath of the Battle of Bremen, the Englishwoman twitched her curtains and was shocked to see a tank from the Scots Greys parked on her lawn. The corporal in charge of the tank apologised and quickly moved his tank back on to the street. If Catesby had been there, he would have ordered him to move it back again. The woman wasn't a Nazi supporter, but she was oblivious.

One of the files on Catesby's desk was from the SIS man in Santiago, who had been Catesby's protégé in Bonn. Gerald had moved up from a clerical grade to become a fully fledged intelligence officer. Gerald, who still ruffled feathers by flaunting his proletarian origins, had been a good choice to send to Allende's Chile. Gerald's cables from Santiago, dating back to the beginning of Allende's presidency, were now heartbreaking.

Allende government initiatives are bringing the arts to the mass of the Chilean population for the first time. Cheap editions of great literary works are produced on a weekly basis, and in most cases are sold out within a day. The government is also transforming Chilean popular culture through changes to school curriculum, state-sponsored music festivals and tours of Chilean folklorists.

The Women's Secretariat, established in 1971, has been a great success. It has improved social and economic conditions for women through public laundry facilities, public food programs, day-care centres, and women's health care (especially prenatal care). The duration of maternity leave has been extended from 6 to 12 weeks.

The Allende government is making education available for poorer Chileans by expanding enrolments through government subsidies. University education has been 'democratised' by making the system tuition-free. This led to an 89 per cent rise in university enrolments between 1970 and 1973.

Since 1970 there has been a dramatic increase in social spending particularly for housing, education, and health. A major effort has been made to redistribute wealth to poorer Chileans. The redistribution of income has seen wage and salary earners increase their share of national income from 51.6 per cent to 65 per cent. Family consumption increased by 12.9 per cent in the first year of the Allende government.

Catesby pushed the file aside and stared out the window. No wonder they killed him. And what would they do to a British Allende? Ten years ago talk of a British coup would have been unthinkable, but times were changing. Why? Was it because America was more aggressive? Because big money was becoming more ruthless? Catesby didn't know the answer, but once again he wanted to weave a protecting veil and spread it over his country.

**Mayfair, London:** 13 September 1973

'Good news from South America, eh?'

'Cheers,' said the general toasting with his gin and tonic.

The mood in the billiard room of the exclusive gentlemen's club was better than of late. The retired colonel and JJ were also members and contributors to a think tank called the Forum for Conflict Studies, usually known as the FCS. Also present in the room was the founder of FCS, an Australian-born journalist named Brian. The FCS had been formed three years before as a limited company. It had struggled at times, but recently funding had become more lavish.

'Chile,' said Brian, 'was a domino that couldn't be allowed to topple. Allende was a virus that could have infected all of Latin America. I think that we will see what happened in Chile marks a turning point in US foreign policy. Neither Johnson nor Nixon was tough enough in Vietnam.'

'I hope so,' said JJ. 'There's already a lot of claptrap flying around in the left-wing press about Allende having been democratically elected. The people of Chile don't deserve democracy if they are duped into voting for a Communist.'

'And what about the people of Britain?' said the colonel. 'It has happened in the past – and seems likely to happen again in the future.'

The banker shook his head. 'It will be Heath's fault. He turned out to be a useless twat.'

'Grocer's son,' said the peer.

'And he's queer,' added JJ.

'By the way,' said the general pointing at JJ, 'can't you use your connections and wiles to get copies of those photos the Czechs took of him in bed with that ballet dancer?'

'Organist,' said JJ.

'Are you sure those photos even exist?' said the colonel.

Brian laughed. 'What difference does that make?'

'Heath,' said the banker, 'has been absolutely feeble – doesn't have the balls to stand up to the miners or any other union.'

'The Conservative Party will get rid of him as leader,' said JJ. 'I know that for certain.'

'But not before the next election,' said the colonel.

JJ shrugged.

'We must,' said the general, 'make completely certain that Wilson doesn't get back in.'

'The problem,' said JJ, 'is that a Tory election victory will make it more difficult to get rid of Heath. In a way, Wilson getting back in power may be a good thing.' JJ smiled slyly. 'It opens up … possibilities.'

'In any case,' said the colonel, 'I am pleased to see that our various, uh, policy institutes, are well and thriving.'

'I believe,' said the banker, 'that the Americans call them "think tanks".'

'Steel tanks,' said the general, 'are much more effective.'

'Don't underestimate the power of propaganda,' said Brian.

'Is FCS,' said the colonel with a mischievous smile, 'still getting dosh from the CIA?'

There was an embarrassed hush.

'Oh, come on,' said the colonel, 'everyone knows that FCS is part of the Congress for Cultural Freedom – and everyone knows where their cash flow comes from.'

'The answer,' said JJ, 'is obviously yes, but I hope that soon the bulk of funding will come from elsewhere.'

'Totally agree,' said the colonel. 'In fact, I would one day like to see privately funded organisations – or even actual limited companies – replace the likes of MI5 and MI6.'

'And the Army?' said the general.

'Absolutely,' said the colonel, 'and as I've said many times, "Who pays wins".' He looked at the former MI6 man and gave him a conspiratorial wink. 'Come on, JJ, tell us more about our new and mysterious benefactor.'

'It's complicated,' said JJ. 'The source of our funding doesn't wish to make his identity known – and that requires a complicated process of...'

'Money laundering,' said the banker.

'Oh dear,' said the peer, 'I hope this room isn't bugged.'

Catesby knew that he was being followed and it wasn't the first time. Until now, he hadn't been taking counter-surveillance measures. There was no reason to. He wasn't slinking off to a rendezvous with a secret agent; he was merely going back to the flat after a day at the office. His usual route was down Westminster Bridge Road to the river, then left along Lambeth Palace Road to Lambeth Bridge, across the Thames and then left down Millbank. Sometimes, he didn't cross over the river until Vauxhall Bridge: he liked the view of the Tate in the setting sun. But today, being a Friday, he suddenly veered up York Road and into Waterloo Station. The place was heaving with City types off for a weekend to the West Country and Catesby quickly lost his tail. But he didn't lose sight of her. Catesby circled back around a news kiosk and found the woman staring into the mass of commuters and weekenders trying to ascertain which bowler hat was his. She was tall, East Asian and fortyish – and looked vaguely familiar.

Catesby came up behind her and said, 'Can I help you? You look as if you're lost.'

She looked directly at him. There was no apology. 'I think it's time that we had a talk.'

'Then why didn't you stop me sooner.'

'First of all, I wanted to make sure it was you.'

'We've met before,' said Catesby.

'Yes – can you verify where?'

Catesby could see she wasn't taking any chances. 'At a castle overlooking the Rhine in 1951.' Catesby smiled. 'I must look a lot older.'

'And so do I.'

Catesby was too polite to agree. But she was no longer the winsome eighteen- or nineteen-year-old she had been at the time. Her face was lined and worried-looking.

'Just before I left,' said Catesby, 'you said, "The East is Red. Long live Chairman Mao." Did you mean that?'

'Of course I did – and I still do.'

'You must have political differences with your uncle.'

'We argued bitterly and he finally disowned me. Which was a good thing, because it liberated me.'

'Why are you in London?'

'I live and work here. I'm a lecturer at SOAS. I've also worked with Ralph Miliband at LSE. He knows you and says you're a diplomat, but I suspect he knows the truth.'

Catesby smiled. 'Sticking a bunch of spies in a glass tower block wasn't a brilliant idea. How is Ralph?'

'Not very well. They've moved to Leeds and he's finding the admin of being a head of department a strain.'

Catesby personally knew Ralph Miliband, Eric Hobsbawm and a number of other London academics and intellectuals. They knew he was an intelligence officer, but gave him information and points of view that they hoped would make HM's government a more thoughtful and rational place. Other spies cultivated industrialists and bankers, which was also useful, provided you didn't get used by them. Catesby made a mental note to remember to send a present to the youngest Miliband boy. Born on Christmas Eve, it was important not to let the holiday overshadow Edward's birthday.

'Shall we go someplace for tea or coffee?' said Catesby.

'The station caff will be fine.'

'Grab a table.'

As Catesby queued for a pot of tea he gave the woman a furtive glance. She was quickly brushing her hair and checking her face in a compact mirror. Maoist revolutionary academics were just as insecure and concerned with their appearance as everyone else. Catesby smoothed his own forelock with a bit of saliva.

The first part of the conversation was about mutual acquaintances and life in London. The polite pleasantries of British life were a gentle web that had bound together, however temporarily, an anti-imperialist revolutionary and an officer of Her Majesty's Secret Intelligence Service. The polite dreariness of Britain, along with weak tea and warm beer, were something worth keeping – even dying for.

'You must be wondering,' she said, 'why I contacted you.'

Catesby remained silent.

'My uncle is not just mad and eccentric; he is dangerous and associates with dangerous reactionaries.'

'There are a lot of them about.'

'I hardly ever see my uncle, but he is getting very old and he is my nearest living relative. I recently combined a research trip to South America with a visit to where he lives most of the year in Paraguay.'

'Did you argue?'

'I endured several rants about Allende being a Communist disease that could infect the whole continent if it wasn't eradicated. Little did I know at the time that a coup was about to take place.'

'It must have been difficult for you.'

The woman smiled. 'I didn't argue back – it would have been pointless. Instead, I humoured him and cooked his favourite meals.' She looked at Catesby. 'I bet you're wondering why I didn't poison him.'

'I wasn't.'

'But, if you were wondering, I do have some family sentiment – and, besides, I wouldn't have got out of Paraguay alive.' She smiled. 'Also, my uncle wouldn't eat anything unless I tasted first. He made a joke of it, calling me "the Great Khan's food-taster-in-chief". In any case, after a couple of days he began to trust me and gave vague hints about what he was up to. He was bragging, trying to impress. He even began to leave his study door unlocked, but not the safe or filing cabinet.' She reached inside a large leather satchel and handed over a fat envelope. 'The only documents I could copy were ones left on his desk.'

'Thanks. But why are you handing these to me?'

'Ideologically or personally?'

'Both.'

'From an ideological point of view, it is a good strategy to have the imperialists fight among themselves. It weakens the forces of oppression.'

'Personally?'

'I like living in Britain – and so did Karl Marx. I don't want to see this country torn apart by mad reactionaries as now seems likely.'

We are an odd lot, thought Catesby. What other country could have produced Magna Carta, the Industrial Revolution, *Das Kapital* and The Beatles?

Catesby took the documents the woman had given him to his house in Suffolk. He knew they would be much safer there in the previous owner's ingeniously hidden safe than anywhere in London – including the SIS registry, which gave access to officers with secret agendas. You could trust no one.

Catesby loved the unearthly quiet of rural Suffolk on a calm autumn night. The quiet and darkness – no street lamps for miles – soothed the body and calmed the nerves. But he decided to have one more look at the documents before he put them away. Catesby was impressed. The woman's uncle may have been a mad follower of Genghis Khan, but he was also a brilliant and thorough accountant. Everything was dated, invoiced and numbered. The ODESSA bureaucracy was as meticulous as it was chilling. As soon as Catesby was finished, he put the papers back in their envelope and carried them to the secret place. He removed the loose block of fifteenth-century oak and opened a panel that was disguised as rough rendering over wattle and daub. The safe was now exposed. Catesby twirled the dial to the combination and the safe door popped open with a welcome hiss. The safe was empty – except for a single piece of paper that read: FUCK YOU CATESBY.

Catesby's first concern wasn't for himself, but for the elderly retired colonel from whom he had bought the house. It was only through him that the safecrackers could have found out where to find the safe. Catesby rang the colonel's number at the house they had bought in Surrey to be nearer their daughter.

'Hello.' It was a woman's voice.

'Hello, I'm William Catesby – the person who bought Colonel…'

'I'm his daughter and I'm very pleased that you rang. Have the police been in contact with you?'

'No, what's happened?'

'Two masked men broke into my parents' house at 4 a.m. this morning.'

'How are they?'

'Shaken but unhurt.'

'Please give them my warmest regards.'

'They are concerned about you – and wish they had been able to get in contact. But it was difficult when they were tied up.'

'What did they want – the masked men?'

'They wanted to know where you live and all about the house. My father refused to tell them until they put a knife to my mother's throat.'

'They're very brave.'

'I know. They were tied up until I popped in to see them this afternoon – desperate for the loo of course, but also to let you know what happened.'

'Please thank them.'

There was no quiet for Catesby the rest of the evening. The Suffolk Constabulary turned up and tried to take fingerprints, but there were none. 'Very professional job, sir.'

Catesby spent a restless night with the woman's documents under his pillow and his Browning 9mm close at hand.

**London:** October, 1973

JJ was very proud of the labyrinthine web of trusts, bank accounts and shell companies that he had created. Basically, money laundering is making money that comes from Source A look as if it comes from Sources B, C, D, E, F, G and so on. There are three stages: placement, layering and integration.

Placement is the most difficult stage, particularly if you are dealing with paper currency. A million dollars in US banknotes weighs more than a rugby prop forward, just over eighteen stone. But most of the money that JJ was dealing with was wire-transferred across multiple borders to end up in various shell companies in offshore money havens or European mini-states.

The next stage is layering. This involves converting the shell company deposits into monetary instruments – money orders and bankers' drafts – that can be used to buy assets that are then resold for totally clean clash.

The final stage is integration. This is re-introducing the cleansed money back into the economy. JJ was doing so through foreign banking systems, like Switzerland's, with strict privacy laws. The money from various numbered bank accounts then found its way back into the UK via front companies, personal 'loans' and donations from both named and anonymous benefactors. The organisations that enjoyed windfalls included right-wing think tanks and magazines, but also anti-Communist guerrilla units.

JJ's favourite brainchild was CAF, the Combined Action Force. CAF had only been recently formed, but already had more than five thousand members and was rapidly growing. A typical CAF unit leader was a right-wing polo-playing athlete and yachtsman with a private pilot's licence. CAF units were not just secretly training to fight a guerrilla campaign against what they perceived to be a Communist government, but also how to deal with the effects of major industrial action. CAF envisioned a growing chaos of national strikes that would cripple essential services. CAF volunteers were being trained to run power stations and sewage plants. They were also learning how to drive trains and heavy vehicles. Much of the training took place on country estates – and was 'great fun'.

It was time for JJ to have fun. Fun for JJ didn't happen very often, but he was now in the mood. He telephoned the number to make an appointment. It wasn't a busy night and she was there an hour later with the usual gear. The woman had a lot of strange clients, but JJ was the only one who asked her to dress up in a Soviet Army uniform.

**Agency News:** 13 December 1973

## Heath Announces Stringent Measures
## to Conserve Electricity

Industrial and commercial users of electricity will be limited to a total of five days' consumption over the fortnight beginning 17 December and ending 30 December.

### Three-Day Week for New Year

From midnight on 31 December, industrial and commercial consumers of power will be limited to three specified consecutive days per week. They also will be prohibited from working longer hours on those three days.

Only services deemed essential – such as hospitals, supermarkets and newspapers – will be exempt. Television companies, however, will be required to cease broadcasting at 10.30 p.m. to conserve electricity.

The government's immediate objective is to avoid a total shutdown. It is hoped that the reduction in working hours will prolong the life of available fuel stocks and allow business continuity and survival. It is also hoped that the measures will prevent further inflation and a currency crisis.

The restrictions are the result of industrial action by coal miners combined with the effects of the OAPEC oil embargo that began in October. The embargo was imposed as a response to American support for Israel during the Yom Kippur War.

**Agency News:** 5 January 1974

## London Rocked by Bomb Explosions

Two bombs exploded within minutes of each other in central London. The first blast occurred at Madame Tussauds. Over a thousand visitors and staff were inside the building when an anonymous telephone call was received. All were safely evacuated and no one was injured.

A few moments later, a second bomb exploded during the annual Boat Show at Earls Court. The bomb was hidden inside a £20,000 luxury motor cruiser. Debris was scattered across the exhibition centre damaging other boats. A telephone warning had been given and more than 25,000 Boat Show visitors were evacuated before the blast. There were no injuries.

London has been subjected to a large number of bomb attacks in recent months. During December alone, 73 people were injured in 24 separate attacks involving explosive devices.

**Agency News:** 9 January 1974

### Heathrow Surrounded by Ring of Steel as Army Move to Prevent Terrorist Attack

Troops and tanks have been deployed in and around Heathrow Airport in response to an unspecified terrorist threat. Terrorists are thought to be in possession of Soviet SAM-7 anti-aircraft missiles. The SAM-7 is a compact shoulder-held heat-seeking missile with a range of three miles that can reach a maximum height of 3,000 feet. Troops are sealing off areas around the airport where aircraft pass low as they take off and land.

There are also reports that a number of American-made Redeye missiles have been stolen from a Belgian Army base at Düren near Cologne. The Redeye has similar characteristics and range to the SAM-7. It is thought that the Redeye missiles may now be in the possession of extremist left-wing groups with links to similar groups in the UK.

**A Regimental Officers' Mess:** London, 23 January 1974

'Craggs?'

'Yes, sir.'

'Is the room fully rationed?'

'Port, brandy, whisky, Madeira, ice and soda siphons, sir.'

'So you won't have any reason to be summoned for anything lacking?'

'No, sir.'

'And you've put it all on my mess bill?'

'As you requested, sir.'

'We are not to be disturbed, Craggs.'

'Understood, sir.'

'Key?'

Craggs handed the general a large brass key.

The general smiled. 'I am sure, Craggs, that if anyone tries to come into this room who has not been invited by myself that, if necessary, you will sacrifice your life in denying them access.'

'Of course, sir.'

'That was a joke, Craggs. I am grateful for your loyalty, but a loud shout would be sufficient.'

'Thank you, sir.'

A number of officers were already lounging about the room, which was oak-lined and furnished with leather sofas and armchairs. The general handed a map file to the most junior officer who pinned it to one of two display boards covered in green felt that were mounted on trestles. The general nodded at another junior officer, 'I would appreciate some Jock juice, Hugo.' The officer went to the drinks table to fetch the general a whisky. Four more officers entered the room. As the door closed behind them, there was a sudden and awkward hush.

'I think that's all of us,' said the general. 'Please help yourselves to drinks before we begin.'

The officers milled around the room: some talking in hushed tones; others laughing nervously.

A colonel from a line infantry regiment came up to the general. 'Another Heathrow?'

'Maybe more.'

'I'm telling my chaps to follow the chain of command and do it by the book.'

'Very good advice,' said the general with a glint.

'I don't want to end up with pineapple chunk all over my best frock.'

'You should take lessons from the duchess. She swallows it all.' The general glanced at his watch. 'I think it's time to begin.'

The general walked over to the two display boards and stood between them. An uneasy quiet fell on the room.

'Thank you for coming,' said the general, 'I don't think that I need to tell you that Britain is facing a crisis of national survival – greater than that of 1940. In 1940, our cities were darkened to thwart enemy bombers. Today, our cities have fallen dark because of industrial action. We have been forced to close factories and schools to conserve fuel stocks. People, wrapped in blankets, work by candle and torchlight. In our homes, mothers boil water to wash. On the days when schools are open, children are sent to school with luminous yellow bands so they can be seen in the gloom. In 1940, we were a united country facing an external enemy. Today, we are a divided nation facing internal enemies that are insidious and who work undercover. We are going to see a lot more terrorism and sabotage – and we must make contingency plans on how to respond to these threats.'

There was a nervous shuffle and a few coughs.

'I apologise for telling you what you already know.'

A colonel in the front row with a moustache that was a perfect triangle nodded.

'Let's get down to practical issues – and one of those issues is the number of troops available. The recent deployment at Heathrow involved a single elite unit of 400 troops mounted on Scorpion tanks and Saracen, Saladin and Ferret armoured cars. In an emergency, we could easily and rapidly muster five additional units of similar size for deployment in and around London.'

The general flicked back the cover of the map file to reveal central London. He pointed to Buckingham Palace. 'Our first priority is protecting Her Majesty. That is the job of the Foot Guards across the road at Wellington Barracks, who are always in a position to do so – and have light armour backup if necessary. The next priority is protecting the seats of government in and around Whitehall. We are lucky that our key levers of state are concentrated in such a small geographical area. The troops securing Downing Street will also be in position to support those at the Foreign Office, Admiralty and Houses of Parliament.'

The general flipped to another large-scale London map. 'Our other objective of overriding importance is to secure the BBC. A single battalion of foot supported by a squadron of light armour should be sufficient to deal with Broadcasting House and the World Service at Bush House. In the case of the BBC, it is not just a question of physical security, but also of broadcasting security. The troops deployed at the BBC will need considerable support from technical and media specialists from the Royal Corps of Signals.' The general paused. 'I would like to emphasise that what we are discussing are worst-case contingency plans.'

There was an uneasy murmur of approval with solemn nodding.

'Any questions?' said the general.

'Yes.' The questioner was a sharp-faced commander of an armoured reconnaissance squadron. 'Napoleon occupied Moscow, but still lost the war – and most of the *Grande Armée*.'

'Exactly,' said the general with a smile. 'And thank you for pointing that out.' The general flicked back to the map of Westminster and Whitehall. 'Having control of central London, regardless of the circumstances, would not solve the problem.' The general paused. 'And it doesn't solve the critical problem we are faced with now.'

'And it won't,' said the line infantry colonel, 'turn the lights on again.'

'Precisely.' The general flipped aside the London map to reveal one that covered the whole of Britain. 'Those red blotches represent coal-fired power stations. How many do you think there are?'

A captain from the Royal Corps of Engineers answered first, 'One hundred and seventeen.'

The general smiled and nodded. 'Pleased to see that someone has done their homework. No prize for guessing that the black blobs represent coalmines – and how many of them do you suppose there are?'

'Two hundred and fifty.' The officer who got that question right was a captain in the Intelligence Corps.

'Righto. What a clever lot you are,' said the general. 'As you can see, securing fuel and power for Britain is an enormous problem that cannot be solved by a few London-based battalions who are capable of deploying quickly and secretly. We need to work with county regiments and the local police. Ideally, the Army will provide security to help local constabularies arrest union leaders. In some cases, however, the Army itself will have to intern union leaders without help. That will require local intelligence and informants.' The general paused. 'And we cannot, unfortunately, rule out the use of violence and deadly force. It is better than letting Britain freeze to death.'

An infantry major with a kind face said, 'What about deploying soldiers in power stations and mines to do the work themselves? Surely, the Spanner Wankers,' the captain was referring to the Corps of Engineers by their nickname, 'would love a bash at running power stations.'

The general shook his head and pointed at the map. 'There are too many sites. We haven't got the manpower or sufficient expertise to do it. The only alternative to strike-breaking is recruiting volunteers to take over the power stations and work the mines. There are, I believe, many such action groups springing up over the country. There are tens of thousands of people who will not let this country be held to ransom – and we must work with them. But strike-breaking is still the best option.' The general nodded at the Intelligence Corps captain. 'And I believe you have acquired some expertise in this area?'

'I have,' said the captain, 'compiled a list of what we can call, "acceptable union leaders". This doesn't mean that they are ideal at this moment, but faced with a winter interment in the Shetlands or a size-ten boot planted firmly on their testicles, they may become more than acceptable.'

'How are the camps progressing?' said the general.

'The larger one at Unst should be ready soon. The one on Muckle Flugga, for the more important internees, is proving something of a challenge.'

'I believe there are contingency plans to requisition the *QE2* as a floating and temporary internment facility,' said the general.

'Too good for them,' growled the triangle-moustached colonel. Like many fighting men, the colonel had an engaging simplicity of mind.

'It is important,' said the general, 'that we use code names when referring to actual military units.' He revealed a chart on the display board divided into two columns. 'We've opted for champagne brands to identify certain regiments. Mine is the Bollingers; Jumbo's is the Chandons and Tim's, the Perignons. We have been probably less kind to our fellow warriors in the provinces. In any case, I'm sure that most of you will know who the Sheep Shaggers refer to as well as the Turnip Tossers. And the Mangelwurzels and the Swede Bashers are also regiments with a proud history.'

'The sooner we act the better,' said the colonel.

'May I remind all of you,' said the general, 'that the purpose of this meeting is only to discuss contingency plans.' The general smiled. 'For events that will probably never happen. The last thing we want is rumours about a military coup. If you hear such rumours, dismiss them as nonsense and utter drivel. But may I also remind you that your oath of loyalty is to the Crown, not to the prime minister of the day.'

The formal part of the meeting went on for another hour. Afterwards, the assembled officers availed themselves of the general's hospitality. As the drink flowed, tongues loosened. The captain from the Intelligence Corps wasn't particularly happy with the tone of what he heard.

### Pimlico, London: 25 January 1974

It was an odd letter. Anonymous letters are usually odd – if not totally mad or just plain weird. Every few months Catesby got one from a nun urging him to discover love and forgiveness. Perhaps he was being too harsh on the nun and should have taken her advice. This most recent letter was a bit weird, but also oddly well informed and rational too – and had a postmark suspiciously near the Intelligence Corps depot at Templer Barracks in Kent. In addition to the postmark, the sender further botched his attempt at anonymity by writing in longhand. Or was it, thought Catesby, a double bluff? It was a difficult time and no one trusted anyone. Madness was in the air.

Dear Mr Catesby,

We've never met, but I know who you are through my job and via my access to JIC minutes.

.I recently attended a meeting where last month's troop deployments at Heathrow were discussed. No mention was made of the terrorist threat or the SAM missiles that were cited in the press as the reason for the deployment. Normally, someone in my job would have been informed of the intelligence sources behind such a threat. But I have seen or heard nothing. In fact, the mood at the meeting suggested that whether the terrorist threat was true or false was totally irrelevant. I am also concerned about several senior military officers who seem to have political agendas. My next assignment is Northern Ireland. The squaddies call it 'the Emerald Toilet' – not an attitude that will gain the support of the local people. I'll let you know what's happening.

Stay cool, Mr Catesby, OBE. Who knows what you really think and who you really are?

Give peace a chance.

Best wishes,
Captain Zero

PS: Have you heard about the internment camps on the Scottish islands?

Catesby put the letter aside. He was sure it was genuine – and that Captain Zero was a lot more sane than many of his colleagues. Zero was also totally correct about the fact that there was no intelligence about terrorists equipped with anti-aircraft missiles. Catesby had already checked out the press report that Redeye missiles had gone missing from the Belgian Army base at Düren. The base was home to the Belgian Army's 13th Missile Wing, but most of the security was provided by the Americans. The US Army had a much larger base, the Fifth Artillery Group, next to the Belgians, which was equipped with nuclear weapons.

Part of the intelligence op was open, routine and straightforward. Using a NATO secure voice scrambler, Catesby telephoned the Belgian base commander who was a French speaking Walloon. They chatted amicably in French as the Belgian officer assured

Catesby that no Redeyes were missing – and Catesby reassured him that it was just a routine call. Catesby then made a similar secure voice call to the American officer in charge of security at Duren. The American assured Catesby that the press reports were 'undiluted bullshit' and that, otherwise, he, the American, would be 'hanging upside down by his balls in Fort Leavenworth Prison'. But, realised Catesby, they would say that, wouldn't they.

The verification part of the op was a Catesby special. He sent in a team of spivs, pimps and lonely people looking for sex with young men. The soldiers at Düren were bored out of their minds and looking for diversion. The drink and the sex provided it. The booze and the loneliness certainly loosened tongues, but there wasn't the faintest squeak of a rumour about missing Redeye missiles. The press reports were not just the attempts of a journalist trying to juice up his copy with rumour. No, the press reports were calculated disinfo – deliberate lies fed to the media. But by whom?

**Century House, Lambeth, London:** 4 February 1974

The news left Catesby stunned and angry. A meeting had been convened in Henry Bone's office to discuss what had happened the previous midnight and in what ways it might affect SIS. Strictly speaking, it was a criminal act that had occurred on the British mainland and as such was a matter for the police and the Security Service.

Catesby picked up the newspaper and stared again at the head-line: **Soldiers and Children Killed by Coach Bomb**. He then looked again at the hastily written confidential report, which differed little from the news coverage. A bomb had exploded on a coach that was carrying fifty people. The passengers were off-duty soldiers and their families returning from weekend leave. The most sickening fact was that an entire family had been wiped out: a soldier and wife of twenty-three and their two boys aged five and three. Seven other soldiers had died and bodies and body parts had been scattered along 250 yards of the M62.

'How, William,' said Bone, 'does this event tie in with your theories of disinformation and *agents provocateur*?'

**261**

'It doesn't tie in at all. It is clearly an IRA atrocity.'

'Anything else?'

'I fear the military and the Security Service will use it to justify their own actions – a perfect marriage of tragedy and cynicism.'

The only other person at the meeting was the SIS officer in charge of liaising with the Security Service.

'It will,' said the liaison officer, 'undermine the role of SIS in Northern Ireland. The Security Service will blame us for an intelligence failure and for not being sufficiently ruthless.'

Whether or not, thought Catesby, SIS should be operating in Northern Ireland at all was a good question. As part of the UK, the province should be out of bounds for an intelligence service limited by statute to operating outside the UK. But boundaries were being fudged.

'And,' said Catesby, 'they'll use this to bash the trade unions as well. They'll say the soldiers had to travel by coach because the railway workers were on strike. Any excuse for it, any excuse.'

'Any excuse for what?' said Bone.

Catesby was reluctant to say it in the presence of another SIS officer, but the whispers and rumours had been rife for some time. 'Any excuse for a military coup.'

## Cabinet Office, 70 Whitehall, London: 6 February 1974

There had been a family argument the previous evening that had left Catesby unsettled and not in the mood for what was going to be a very tense JIC. He and Frances were still living apart, but from time to time they met for supper with one or both of the stepchildren. On this occasion, there was only the daughter. She teased Catesby about his bowler hat and suit – and suggested that he buy a pair of flares. Catesby hated flares – and replied that he would rather 'eat his lower colon raw than wear flares'. For some reason this got Frances going. She told him not to use such language in front of the children. Catesby replied by saying: 'They are no longer children. They are twenty-eight years old.' Then added, 'And lower colon is not a swear word. If you want me to use a fucking swear word I'll use a fucking swear word.'

The daughter found it all amusing, but Frances rounded on him.

'Why,' she said, 'do you always need to shock and show off? You're fifty years old, nearly fifty-one, and still haven't grown up.'

'Shall we compare payslips? My immaturity doesn't seem to have affected my career.' Catesby's grade in SIS was three civil service levels higher than Frances's in the Security Service and he didn't mind rubbing it in.

Frances smiled with a steely glint. 'It hasn't affected your career *yet*. I hope you get a haircut before the JIC meeting.'

'I think,' said the daughter, 'you should grow your hair even longer – and do get a pair of flares.'

'I'm really hungry,' said Catesby with a benign smile. 'I love you both. Let's give peace a chance.'

Frances had left a lot unsaid. Her job at Five and the vicious infighting swirling around her was taking its toll. Her marriage to Catesby, even though they didn't live together, put her under constant scrutiny – as did the radicalism of her children. Her daughter was an acclaimed architect, but one who lived in a squat and was a member of the Socialist Workers Party. Her son was a barrister who specialised in controversial human rights cases. He hadn't joined the CP, but often bought the *Morning Star*. It flustered judges when they saw the newspaper scattered among his legal briefs. Although Frances never made the accusation directly, she suspected that Catesby's influence might have helped radicalise her children. Catesby would always reply that young people should be taught to stand up to bullies – and the JIC meeting was going to be a case in point.

The M62 coach bombing was too recent to be included as an agenda item. Instead, the first item on the agenda was 'Heathrow Deployment and Evaluation', but the most contentious was 'FLUENCY: Report and Evaluation'.

Catesby hated FLUENCY with a passion. It was an interagency working party that had been set up to investigate allegations that the UK's intelligence and security services had been penetrated by the KGB. FLUENCY had quickly turned into a paranoid witch-hunt. Catesby knew two FLUENCY victims who had been hounded to suicide. Another, who had since retired and died, was the very head of MI5 himself. The allegations were pure venom intended to destroy, and were largely based on the director having signed a chit to look at a file. According to EMPUSA, a copy of the file ended up in Moscow. Anyone, thought Catesby, who was going to copy a file to send to Moscow Central would never be so stupid as to sign a chit for the file.

Catesby had decided to keep quiet on the Heathrow item unless he was asked questions. He had already prompted the number cruncher from Treasury with some useful lines of enquiry that he might pursue. As the meeting began, Catesby noticed that the Chief of Defence Intelligence had sent his apologies and was represented instead by his deputy. Discretion is indeed the better part of valour. Catesby thought the colonel standing in for his boss would be out of his depth. The soldier began by reading a report justifying the Heathrow deployment. 'The decision was made with the highest possible level of certainty following an exhaustive review of intelligence reports plus diplomatic and open sources.'

Catesby smiled. How easy it would be to chop the colonel's report to shreds. 'Diplomatic sources' were a euphemism for chitchat that you half-heard at a drunken embassy party. And 'open source intelligence' is what you get from reading newspapers. And it's easy to find what you want. Planting false stories and then harvesting them as truth is one of the best ploys in the trade. Basically, intelligence officers give off-the-record anonymous briefings to tame journalists. The briefings are often full of disinfo and smears. When the information, secretly provided by the intelligence officers, is turned into printed news or broadcasts, the intelligence agencies than glean the news reports as 'open source intelligence' which support the suspicions that the intelligence officers fed to the press in the first place. Another gambit is to covertly feed disinfo to double agents and defectors and have them playback the disinfo in 'official' debriefs to yourself and to other intelligence agencies.

The colonel concluded, '…a clear pattern of terrorist threat and activity has therefore been established.'

The Treasury member looked at Sir Maurice, the head of SIS. Maurice, bespectacled and plump, looked more inoffensive than he was. Underneath the round layers, he was hard and sharp.

'What intelligence,' said the Treasury member, 'did SIS have about the likelihood of terrorist anti-aircraft missile attacks at Heathrow Airport?'

'No more than normal,' said Sir Maurice, 'which is to say nothing specific. There is a possibility that SAM-7 missiles may have fallen into terrorist hands, but we have no firm intelligence anything like that has happened.'

'Did not Defence Intelligence share their information about a threat of terrorist attacks with SIS?'

Sir Maurice's eyes crinkled behind his glasses. 'Yes, we received their intelligence reports – just after midnight on the day of the Army deployment to Heathrow.'

'How would you describe those reports?'

'There's nothing I have to add to the statement, which was just relayed to us, from the Chief of the Intelligence Staff.'

There were sighs and a shuffle of feet. The Permanent Secretary to the Civil Service, the one they nicknamed 'Deputy Prime Minister', cleared his throat and shifted his bulk.

The colonel came in first. 'The armoured units that went to Heathrow are a rapid reaction force – and the essence of rapid reaction is just that. With all respect to our colleagues from SIS, military intelligence is a different animal. Military intelligence serves the rapidly shifting contingencies of the battlefield. A commander in the field does not have the luxury of waiting for raw intelligence to be processed, analysed and evaluated before acting.'

The colonel nodded at Sir Maurice. 'Nor can we wait for feedback, however considered and valuable, from our intelligence colleagues in other agencies. We perceive a suspicious shape in the fog, metaphorically of course, and react to deter a possible threat. We will never know for sure, but our presence at Heathrow may have saved lives.'

Catesby realised that he had been wrong about the colonel. He wasn't out of his depth – and was probably doing a better job than his boss would have. But there was also something sinister and too cocky in his manner. Catesby could imagine him on a BBC bulletin after normal broadcasting had been suspended.

Sir Maurice smiled bleakly. 'SIS face the same dilemma that stifled religious sceptics through the centuries. We cannot prove a negative. Just as a Renaissance sceptic, walking a tightrope between rationality and death by burning at the stake, could not offer definitive proof that the supernatural did not exist, we cannot prove that a terrorist armed with an anti-aircraft missile – or an atom bomb – does not exist. But we do have to operate within the limitations of budget and staffing – and, therefore, have to evaluate levels of risk with the detached professionalism of a triage doctor at a motorway pile-up.'

The man from Treasury nodded approval.

The Permanent Secretary didn't seem pleased. 'Terrorists are not imaginary demons dancing on the head of a pin. Monday's coach bombing was bloody and real. And last month's bomb attacks at Madame Tussauds and the Boat Show were just as real. We are a country facing a serious crisis. I fully endorse the measures taken by the Army – and hope they go much further.'

The recent bomb attacks, as Catesby and everyone else around the table well knew, were the works of the IRA. But as he feared, the Troubles were being used as an excuse for security measures and spying that had nothing to do with Northern Ireland.

The discussion of the Heathrow deployment droned on. Catesby closed his eyes and pretended to be listening intently, but was actually fantasising about a woman he desired and how nice it would be to disappear with her to a hotel with clean sheets. The Heathrow discussion ended with an agreement – largely cosmetic – on improved methods of intelligence sharing.

As soon as the meeting passed on to the FLUENCY agenda item, Catesby was again fully alert and the adrenalin was flowing. There were three things to remember: no one believed anyone else; no one knew what the other one knew, and the war between Five and SIS was approaching fever pitch.

There were two representatives from Five at the meeting: the DG and Ferret. The latter, like Catesby, was co-opted to JIC. The interesting thing was that the DG didn't know all the secrets of Ferret and FLUENCY. But Sir Maurice and Catesby did know – and had decided to dance a carefully choreographed ballet around their rival service.

The discussion began with the DG reminding JIC that FLUENCY was a top secret committee set up ten years previously to investigate Soviet penetration of Britain's security and intelligence services. The problem with FLUENCY, and the reason it was on the agenda, was its failure to catch a single mole. But, as Ferret would maintain, it depended on how you defined 'catch'. He would claim that Soviet moles – including a former DG – had been caught and identified, but not prosecuted. And why not? Obviously, a cover-up instigated by other Soviet moles to protect their comrades. Madness beckoned. In Catesby's view, FLUENCY was a dangerous and deadly American import concocted by FURIOSO – who was completely insane. And the person exploiting FURIOSO's madness and orchestrating FLUENCY was the defector EMPUSA. But he couldn't quite say that at JIC.

After the Security Service DG had finished, Ferret began. He glanced hard at the JIC members from SIS and bowled the first ball. 'FLUENCY will not succeed without the full and enthusiastic cooperation of other intelligence agencies – and that cooperation hasn't always been forthcoming.'

Catesby glanced at his own boss, 'Should I answer that, Sir Maurice?'

'Please.'

'One recurring complaint against us,' said Catesby, 'is our failure to publish and circulate FLUENCY conclusions in my section and others. May I remind JIC, that FLUENCY has no formal or statutory status. It is an informal working party that does not have the power to issue instructions, but only to make recommendations.' Catesby paused. He could see that Ferret was boiling.

'And you've consistently ignored those recommendations.'

'We certainly have ignored those recommendations which, if followed, would be a breach of security. On one hand, you recommend that certain officers be denied access to secrets until further positive vetting. But, on the other hand, you criticise us for not widely circulating FLUENCY conclusions which contain sensitive secret information that should only be shared on a need-to-know basis.' What Catesby really wanted to say was that FLUENCY created an atmosphere of fear that destroyed morale. Ferret and his ilk wanted to bring the McCarthy-ite witch-hunt to Britain.

Ferret tried to come back in, but Catesby caught the eye of the chairman. 'May I continue, Sir Stewart?'

'What point do you wish to make, Mr Catesby?'

'I want to put FLUENCY investigations into the wider context of intelligence gathering and espionage – and explain what effect FLUENCY is having on those operations.'

'Go on, but be brief.'

'FLUENCY is counter-espionage – and counter-espionage is a defensive operation. The more time and resources you spend on counter-espionage, the less you have for offensive operations.' Catesby paused and looked around the room. 'An excellent strategy for an enemy intelligence service is to trick the services opposing them to spend more on counter-intelligence – hunting moles and threats that don't exist. In fact, by creating an atmosphere of fear and paranoia, you can destroy an intelligence service.' Catesby paused again. 'I am not saying that this has happened here, but it is something of which we should be aware.'

The Permanent Secretary stirred. 'Are you suggesting that dedicated counter-intelligence officers, our brave spy-catchers, may, in fact, be undercover Soviet agents?'

'No, but they may be unwitting dupes of those who are.' Catesby made an effort not to look directly at Ferret, but could see from the corner of his eye that the Security Service DG was restraining him. The committee room had descended into an embarrassed hush.

'As Head of Sov Bloc T Section,' said Catesby, 'the essence of my job is keeping an eye on Soviet weapons and their deployment. One recent initiative – and please don't minute this – is investigating the drinking habits of Soviet officers and personnel who have control of nuclear weapons. I'm not being facetious; this is a serious issue. At the moment, a nuclear war that destroys

Britain is more likely to begin by accident than intention. Such intelligence could prove a useful bargaining point for the Foreign Office and the Americans in their ongoing SALT discussions – an agreement about monitoring the alcohol use of personnel dealing with nuclear weapons could save all our lives. Vodka in the control room is more likely to cause a nuclear war than ideology. In any case, such intelligence gathering is seriously hindered when the officer leading the op is summoned to FLUENCY for his umpteenth positive vetting. Meanwhile, the Strategic Rocket Force boozers and the KGB are delighted, because we – too busy gazing into our own navels – are off their backs.'

The peer, even though he seemed a little more whiskyed than at the last JIC, gave a firm nod of assent.

The Permanent Secretary, on the other hand, wasn't giving any sign of approval. As Catesby finished and sat back, he noticed that the Permanent Secretary was staring at him in a strange way. Catesby wondered if he should have had his hair cut before the JIC.

Before they could move on to the next agenda item, the Permanent Secretary intervened. 'Your argument, Mr Catesby, against wasting money on FLUENCY and counter-intelligence in general is a very convincing one.' He paused, but continuing staring. 'In fact, just the sort of argument an undercover Soviet agent would make.'

The embarrassment was tangible. People didn't know where to look.

'Not,' said the Permanent Secretary, 'that I'm accusing you of being a KGB spy.' He paused and looked around the table. 'Which isn't to say that there are no Soviet spies in this room. I am sure there are.'

Catesby noticed others exchanging glances and surreptitious nods. He obviously wasn't the only one who had noticed that the Permanent Secretary had been strange of late.

The Permanent Secretary looked at his watch. 'I must leave now. I have a meeting with the Prime Minister about something of urgent state importance. Utterly urgent. Please don't stop on my account. Carry on the meeting and send me the minutes by courier.'

There was complete silence as the Permanent Secretary made his way to the door and down the stairs. The mandarin from Treasury got up and looked out the window, obviously checking on the Permanent Secretary's exit and progress.

'Is he all right?' said the Chairman.

'I think so,' said the man from Treasury. 'But I'd better check just in case.'

'By all means.'

Treasury collected his papers and left.

The rest of the meeting went smoothly and quickly and ended twenty minutes later.

As Catesby emerged from the Cabinet Office building, Whitehall was bathed in a rare burst of winter sun. He was looking forward to a brisk walk back to Century House across Westminster Bridge, but with umbrella at the ready. It had been a wet winter, although a mild one. God only knows what would have happened if the current fuel shortage had been exacerbated by a winter like '47 or '63.

Catesby had got no further than Downing Street when he sensed someone at this elbow. It was the Treasury mandarin who had left the meeting early.

'Mr Catesby, could I trouble you for a second?'

'Of course, how can I help?'

'We're having a spot of bother at Number 10.'

'Only a spot?'

'Well, it is a rather large spot.'

Catesby smiled. 'How can I help?'

'I believe that you were in SOE during the war?'

Catesby nodded.

'So you know all about hand-to-hand combat and first-aid.'

'I'm sure the duty cop on the entrance would be better at both.'

'But I think a member of the Secret Intelligence Service would be more appropriate.'

'This sounds intriguing.'

The man from the Treasury gave a weary smile. 'It is rather bizarre.'

\*

The Permanent Secretary was lying on the floor in the Prime Minister's study. He was totally naked and smoking a cigarette. At first, Catesby thought he looked like a Rubens' nude. Although on reflection, Lucien Freud's recent work would be a better comparison. The Permanent Secretary's body was fleshy, but not sensuous. In fact, neither artist would have given the subject the human compassion he deserved. The Permanent Secretary was in a terrible state and Catesby felt sorry for him.

It was the first time that Catesby had met the Prime Minister and he seemed to be taking it very calmly. Heath looked at Catesby and said, 'We've telephoned his wife and the hospital, but he won't move – and he is a big man. He started behaving strangely this morning before the JIC meeting. He said he had something vitally important to tell me, but that we had to go some place that wasn't bugged.'

Maybe, thought Catesby, the Permanent Secretary wasn't as mad as he seemed.

'When he came back from JIC,' said the Treasury man, 'he told all his staff to go home and prepare for the Battle of Armageddon.'

'That,' said Catesby nodding at an assortment of inkwells, teacups, fag packets and matches meticulously arranged in opposing battle formations, 'explains the armies.'

The Permanent Secretary stirred and pointed across the carpet. 'That is the Red Army. They landed in East Anglia last night and are wheeling south to capture London in a pincer movement with other Red forces who landed on the South Coast at midnight.' He pointed to a line of bone china nearer him. 'The Blue Army is here. I fear they've deployed too late. Frankly,' the Permanent Secretary for once sounded oddly sane and articulate, 'our system is collapsing and our world is coming to an end. And I'm sorry to report, Prime Minister, that there is very little we can do to prevent it. Calling a snap general election won't help.'

The Prime Minister looked around at those present. 'Even if you are not a member of the Privy Council, please treat that piece of information as if you are.' The Prime Minister leaned over and spoke to the Permanent Secretary in a kind voice. 'Thank you for your advice. You need a bit of rest. Why don't you go home and come back tomorrow which is going to be very busy.'

'No, Prime Minister, I am not going to leave my post at such a crucial moment in our country's history.'

Catesby remembered the tour Henry Bone had given him so long ago of the secret tunnel system known as Q-Whitehall. He turned to the Treasury mandarin and whispered, 'I believe that 20 Downing Street is part of your patch.'

'Yes, it is. Used to be the Tithe Commission, but we took it over.'

'Have you got a discreet parking place for your vans full of gold bullion?'

'There is a parking place on the Whitehall side.'

'Can you get an ambulance there?'

'Shouldn't be a problem.'

Catesby turned to the PM and shouted, 'Prime Minister, we can longer guarantee your safety in this location. We must evacuate you and your essential staff to Q-Whitehall.'

'I agree,' shouted Heath.

Catesby leaned over the Permanent Secretary. 'The Prime Minister would like to have a word.'

The PM leaned over and said, 'We need, Permanent Secretary, to evacuate to the war room in Q-Whitehall.'

'Q-Whitehall,' echoed the Permanent Secretary. 'For god's sake, I've been urging relocation there ever since we declared a State of Emergency. Thank god someone's finally listened.'

A few minutes later they had descended through the basements of Downing Street and into the tunnel system. The Permanent Secretary was led back up into the Treasury building at number 20 and into the waiting ambulance. As a result, the nervous breakdown of one of the UK's most senior civil servants had been kept from public view and treated with dignity.

It was raining again when Catesby walked back over Westminster Bridge. The surprising thing wasn't that one Permanent Secretary had broken down under the pressures of 1974, but that others had not. The senior civil servant had caught a bad dose of Red virus. Its victims were not just the targets of the witch-hunts; the Red virus destroyed the hunters too. Madness was in the air.

**Agency News:** 7 February 1974

## Heath Calls Snap Election

The Prime Minister has called a snap general election in response to the coal miners' threat of industrial action. Edward Heath has appealed to the miners to suspend their planned strike action during the three-week election campaign.

After a week with no sign of a breakthrough in talks with the National Union of Mineworkers, the Prime Minister has decided to call an election to 'let the voters decide who governs the country'. Mr Heath said the country was 'fed up with industrial action' and has called on people to use their vote to show the miners how they feel.

**State of Emergency to Continue**
The crisis began in the autumn when war in the Middle East sent oil prices soaring. The miners introduced an overtime ban in November – and the electricity workers followed suit.

Mr Heath responded by introducing petrol rationing and declaring a State of Emergency and a three-day working week

The miners, however, have stood firm and support for them appears to be strong despite widespread power cuts.

It now seems almost certain that the miners will go ahead with their industrial action, which is due to start in three days' time.

Conservative MP Enoch Powell shocked colleagues at Westminster by announcing he would not be standing in what he called 'an essentially fraudulent election'. In a letter to his constituency chairman he wrote: 'I consider it an act of gross irresponsibility that this general election has been called in the face of the current and impending industrial situation.'

Today has also seen the second in a series of one-day strikes call by ASLEF, the rail drivers union, which has caused more disruption to services.

## CIA HQ, Langley, Virginia: 16 February 1974

It was a Saturday, but Angleton was still at his desk. He gazed through a haze of cigarette smoke and tried to catch a fleeting glimpse of the deceptions hidden in the mist, but they remained in hiding. He was lost in a wilderness of mirrors. The Watergate nonsense was also dragging him and everyone else into the mire. For the first time he began to wonder if his position was secure. But, he thought with a smile, Britain was in even more of a mess than the USA. It was a country that he knew well. He had been educated there at a leading public school before going to Yale. Some said that he still spoke with a slight English accent. Despite the betrayals of Philby and the others, he remained fond of Britain. Perhaps he could do something to help the Brits, to put them back on the right path while he still had the power to do so.

The latest cable from London had come directly to him bypassing the Director's Log. Angleton knew that the DCI wouldn't be pleased. On the other hand, the Director would never find out.

From OSO London Station to ADOCCI:

Despite the best efforts of SM/DOGGED, who remains our most important asset within the British Security Service, MI5 are still restricted and squeamish about doing the things that need to be done to counteract Communist subversion in the UK.

The upcoming UK general election poses a dilemma for US interests. In some ways, it's a pity there has to be a winner – and maybe there won't be. Edward Heath has proved a weak and ineffectual Conservative Premier. On the other hand, the return of Labor under Harold Wilson could be dangerous. The following are very serious points of concern:
- A new Labor government would impose severe reductions in UK defense spending.
- Wilson would also bring in budget and personnel reductions in the Security Service and the Secret Intelligence Service, further hampering their already

limited effectiveness in tracking down subversives.

- An incoming Wilson government would increase trade with the Soviet Union providing greater opportunities for KGB activity in Britain.

At the moment, our best successes in the UK have been with the press and media. We have discussed with SM/ REVEAL the possibility of a no-holds-barred anti-Wilson media campaign involving personal as well as political innuendo. Meanwhile, the FORUM FOR CONFLICT STUDIES is going from strength to strength. It has recently received a considerable financial boost from an anonymous millionaire benefactor. FCS has recently succeeded in placing front-page stories about 'Sources of Conflict in Industry' which suggest Communist influence in the Trade Union movement. Another brilliant FCS coup was getting a television documentary about the KGB sandwiched between two Labor Party political broadcasts. Perfect!

Angleton lit another cigarette. It was far from 'perfect', but it was better than nothing. Perhaps the answer to the British problem weren't the security agencies – which were totally corrupted and penetrated by Soviet moles – but private armies and media propaganda supported by big money.

**Mayfair, London:** 19 February 1974

The banker eyed down his cue stick. He had finally agreed to give the colonel a game.

'Difficult shot,' said the colonel trying to put him off.

'Shh,' said the banker. He then gently and perfectly potted the black to win the frame. The banker smiled, 'Who pays wins.'

Meanwhile, the general topped up his whisky. 'What about you, JJ?'

The ex-SIS officer held out his glass. 'Thank you.'

'What a mess, eh?' said the general.

'Heath doesn't deserve to win,' said JJ. 'We tried to give him some ammunition and he turned it down.'

'Which particular ammunition?' said the colonel.

'The CIA docs about Soviet involvement in the miners' strike for one.'

'What was Heath's excuse?' said the peer.

'He said the CIA investigation wasn't definitive and he didn't want to alienate the trade unions.'

'Feeble,' said the banker.

'And Heath also said,' continued JJ, 'that he doesn't want the Conservative Party to get its hands dirty with personal smear stories.'

'We all know why that is,' said the peer.

'In some ways,' said JJ, 'it would be a good thing if Heath loses this election. It means we can replace him with a strong leader with a backbone – someone who will take on the unions and the Reds.'

'Who do you have in mind?' said the colonel.

JJ told them.

'Nice pair of ankles,' said the peer.


**Pimlico, London:** 22 February 1974

As soon as Catesby saw the Lisburn postmark on the letter he knew who it was from. But before opening it, he checked the letter for wires. It wasn't heavy enough for a big device, but he didn't want to lose a finger or an eye. He decided it was safe and slid out the latest from Captain Zero.

Beware, Mr Catesby. The Powers of Darkness are in the ascendant. This place is not so much a military headquarters as Dante's Ninth Circle of Hell. Our job is supposed to be public relations work and psychological warfare operation against the IRA, but there are other aspects that have nothing to do with Northern Ireland. Beware of something called Operation Clockwork Orange. It will be very interesting to see who wins the coming election and what happens next.

More anon. Meanwhile, stay cool.

CZ

Catesby put the letter in his suitcase. Since his safe had been cracked, he had found another way of hiding secret documents in the wilds of Suffolk. He wanted to protect Captain Zero. No one should ever leave anything lying around in a London flat. Ferret's gang at the Security Service were the capital's best burglars.

**Agency News:** 4 March 1974

### Wilson Returns to Downing Street

Four days after an election that saw the first hung Parliament since 1929, Harold Wilson has entered Downing Street as leader of a minority government.

Following the failure of coalition talks between the Conservatives and the Liberals, Edward Heath announced his resignation paving the way for Wilson to become prime minister for the second time.

Labour remain 17 seats short of a majority and a new election looms.

**Lord North Street, London:** Midnight, 4 March 1974

Harold Wilson may have returned to Downing Street as prime minister, but they weren't going to live there. Mary didn't like the flat at 10 Downing Street. Her favourite house had been the one in Hampstead Garden Suburb, but Lord North Street was infinitely preferable to the Downing Street goldfish bowl. They had both decided to remain in their Lord North Street house.

Wilson poured himself another whisky and stared into the darkness. It wasn't an election that he had particularly wanted to win – and in a way he hadn't won it. Labour had, in fact, won fewer votes than the Tories, but they had taken more seats, 301 against 297. After the votes had been counted, there were four days of tense uncertainty as Heath wooed the Liberals to form a coalition. In the end, the coalition attempt collapsed and, at four o'clock that afternoon, the Prime Minister's Principal Private Secretary had telephoned to say that Heath was on his way to the

Palace. Three hours later, Wilson kissed Her Majesty's hands and once again became prime minister.

Wilson was feeling very tired. He would now have to deal with the almost impossible challenge of heading a minority government that could fall at any time – and the spark and energy was no longer there. He knew he wasn't a charismatic figure like Kennedy or Churchill, but he also knew that he was a decent human being with considerable political and technocratic skills. He was a realist, but one with a vision. But some parts of that vision he couldn't express in public, because he would have been derided. He hated war and violence. His refusal to send British troops to Vietnam was personal as well as political. Likewise, and somewhat shamefully, he demurred from sending British troops to oust Ian Smith's racist regime from Rhodesia. But, and this was a worrying question, would the generals have obeyed his orders if he had sent them to Rhodesia?

There were other things too that Wilson couldn't admit, but these views would have opened him to attack from the left of his party. He aligned himself with the socialist wing of the Labour Party, but he was a pragmatist rather than a socialist. Just as part of him was a pacifist, another part of him – and a very Northern part of him – believed in trade, enterprise and hard work. And that coincided with his pacifist instincts. Trading partners don't go to war with each other. The trade links he tried to forge with the Soviet Union were not just to secure valuable materials for the UK from the vastness of Russia, but also to turn Soviet missiles into consumer goods – and bring peace. How silly and ludicrous were the lies smearing him as an undercover Communist agent.

But Wilson was well aware that his most dangerous enemies were on the Right. A book that he had written in 1953, *The War on World Poverty: An Appeal to the Conscience of Mankind*, had raised a lot of hackles on the British Right and also in Washington. The book was a radical anti-imperialist manifesto and blueprint for first-world aid to developing countries. World poverty was never going to be solved unless the Soviet Union became part of the international financial community. Washington hated that

– and also his plea that 'peaceful co-existence had to be turned into peace.' That wasn't on the Pentagon's agenda. But Washington's agendas had to be ignored. It was no secret that Wilson wanted Britain to break away from the USA's political and economic stranglehold. And unfreezing the Cold War and creating economic relationships with the East Bloc was the best way to do so. No wonder the Americans had wooed the slavishly pro-US Gaitskell and tried to split the Labour Party.

For a fleeting moment Wilson felt his old energy come back. He remembered one of his finest hours, his 'White Hot Heat of Technology' speech in 1963. His vision of Britain was that of a scientifically and technologically advanced society earning her living through trade, but with a strong welfare safety net that would protect the vulnerable, the elderly and the ill. People are happiest and work hardest when they don't have to worry. And education – it must be available to all. If you don't educate your people, 'the white hot heat' will fizzle out.

Wilson poured another whisky and gave himself the luxury of reading the sports pages of yesterday's Sunday papers. He knew that his beloved Huddersfield Town had drawn with Halifax Town – as if they were copying Labour's election result – and seemed to be heading for a mid-table finish.

The Prime Minister peered into the darkness of his dim midnight study. He tried to discern the future, but there was only uncertainty and confusion. Price rises looked out of control, the balance of trade deficit was massive and inflation continued to rise. He knew that he would soon have to call another election – if possible, in the autumn. And then what?

He tried to soothe his jabbing worries by imagining a summer's day in the Isles of Scilly. They had both fallen in love with the damp gentle warmth of the islands. So far and so different from his native Yorkshire. But the islands, the remotest southwestern traces of Britain's archipelago, had become part of him. And one day he would be buried there.

Back to harsh reality. The smears and lies were taking their toll. One thought from the past came back to haunt him. So long ago. It had been a beautiful early spring day when they lived in

Southway in the Hampstead Garden Suburb. A young SIS officer named Catesby,pretending to be an FO diplomat, had turned up out of the blue and warned him:

*There's one thing that you should never forget. The Americans will never forgive you for selling those Rolls-Royce jet engines to the Soviet Union.*

They were out to get him – and it wasn't just the Americans.


## A Regimental Officers' Mess, London: June, 1974

Once again, it was an informal meeting of a select group of officers. But this time, the general had asked officers to contribute to the drinks bill.

'As most of you know,' said the general, 'we will soon be deploying once again to Heathrow.'

'Another threat from terrorists wielding SAM-7s?' said a cheeky major.

'No, this time our terrorist chums have been absolutely no help at all.'

'Maybe we frightened them off with our deployment in January,' said a colonel of infantry.

The general looked at the colonel and tried to discern whether he was being ironic or just stupid.

'Perhaps,' said the general, 'but since then the Secret Intelligence Service has cast doubts upon our own intelligence gathering methods.'

The colonel with the perfect triangle of a moustache spoke out. 'Why don't you call SIS by their proper name: the London Office of the KGB?'

The general smiled. 'I think their bosses in Moscow must be concerned about the thinness of their cover story – I am joking, of course. May we get back to Heathrow?'

The colonel nodded.

'In the future, our deployments to Heathrow – and other facilities – will be referred to as "exercises". We need no longer justify our presence as a response to a specific threat. One can truthfully say that the threat is constant, both from abroad – and from within. We will be carrying out such *exercises* on a fairly regular basis – perhaps once every two months.'

'As a press officer,' said the cheeky major, 'how should I respond to questions?'

'You will be issued a briefing paper – and asked to make your own contributions and alterations. Crisp professionalism is the key.' The general paused and looked at the others. All the officers were fine soldiers, but not all of them were the brightest pebbles on the beach. 'Listen carefully. This is our official Heathrow line. In normal times, the policing of Heathrow and other airports is the responsibility of the British Airports Authority Constabulary – the BAAC. Please do not confuse them with the airline with similar initials. The BAAC was not set up to deal with the sort of threat that we are now facing and it has, therefore, to receive assistance from elsewhere. For a number of years, armed members of the Metropolitan Police have assisted the BAAC. There is now an ongoing contingency plan for the Metropolitan Police to obtain the assistance of the military.'

A colonel from an elite reconnaissance unit weighed in. 'What if the police decide that they don't need our help and refuse to request it?'

The general frowned. 'We'll deal with that problem when it arises.'


## 10 Downing Street: June, 1974

The Prime Minister and his closest advisors were gathered in his study overlooking Horse Guards Parade. His political secretary seemed particularly troubled and annoyed. She looked around at those present.

'Was,' she said, 'no one informed in advance that the exercise at Heathrow was going to take place?'

Her question was met by silence and shaking heads.

'Do you suppose,' said the Prime Minister, 'that the troops at Heathrow could be used in a different way? Could that lot be turned against the government?'

The Political Secretary stared out the window and pointed. 'There. I reckon they'll put the guns in Horse Guards.'

The Prime Minister wanted to say more, but didn't want to sound paranoid. He had recently asked MI5 to show him his own secret file. They had replied that no such file existed. There were, however, rumours that Conservative ministers had been allowed to see secret files on Labour shadow ministers. But now, having been returned in power, Labour ministers were not allowed to see their own files.

There was another reason why Wilson was reluctant to say more. He feared that Number 10 had been bugged. But if he complained or even expressed suspicions of bugging, the Tory right wing and others would accuse him of undermining confidence in the Security Service. They got you both ways.

## Suffolk: July, 1974

Over much of Britain it was an unsettled month with Atlantic frontal systems bringing in rain and strong winds, but in Suffolk it was drier than normal for July. Catesby had a week's leave and was trying to leave London and his job as far behind as possible. Each day began with a cycle ride to Walberswick and a long swim in the sea. In the afternoons he worked in the garden – and then cycled to the Waveney for a fresh water swim. In the evenings, he either cooked for himself or friends or went to the pub.

At the end of Catesby's blissful week, his stepson turned up with his Malawian girlfriend for the weekend. As a favour, the stepson had gone to the Pimlico flat and picked up Catesby's post. Catesby wished that he hadn't.

'There were,' said the stepson, 'several letters with Moscow postmarks, but I thought they might be urgent, so I dropped them off at MI5 instead.'

'I don't work for MI5; your mum does. I work for the Foreign Office.'

'Sure, Will.'

'In any case, the KGB never send me letters. They pay my salary directly into a numbered Swiss bank account.'

The banter was a private family joke that had been going on ever since the twins twigged their parents did something in the spook world. Outside the home, the children were totally discreet and never talked about their parents or their jobs. The Malawian girlfriend, who was in the garden gathering vegetables for a meal that she and his stepson were going to cook, really did think that Catesby was a middle-ranking civil servant crunching numbers at the Foreign and Commonwealth Office.

Catesby looked at the post. It was all ordinary stuff: two post-cards from friends on holiday, a building society statement and some insurance stuff. But there was one personal letter. Perhaps it was best that the stepson had picked up the post. He recognised the handwriting and the Northern Ireland postmark. It wasn't a letter that Catesby would have liked lying about for a week on his doormat in London while the Security Service were merrily burgling and bugging across the capital. Catesby surreptitiously slipped the letter into his pocket.

'Something interesting?' said the stepson.

'It's something you didn't see.'

'Sorry, Will. Maybe I shouldn't have gone around, but Mum also wanted to check the locks and the burglar alarm. She says there are a lot of problems with break-ins when people are away.'

'She went with you?'

'Yes.'

'Did she look at the letter?'

'No, I just gathered up the post as we were leaving.'

'I don't have any secrets from your mother – personal or professional. I just don't want to give her more worries than she already has.'

'You're both giving through hell, aren't you?'

Catesby nodded and gave his stepson a hug. It wasn't a usual gesture for Catesby's generation – but Catesby wasn't a usual product of his generation.

He waited until his stepson and his girlfriend had gone to bed before he looked at the letter. The thing that bothered Catesby most about Captain Zero was the risks he was taking.

Clockwork Orange is a work of Evil Genius! Being in this place is like doing a post-grad degree in dirty tricks psy-op. The mood music of the moment is how to do an effective smear campaign. One ingredient, but by no means an essential one, is a kernel of truth. If you can be bothered to find a kernel of truth, your next job is to attach as many lies to that kernel as you can. One does not simply have a friend from Eastern Europe; one has a 'mysterious Eastern European benefactor bankrolling your political agenda'. Likewise, no one simply goes to a party. One goes to a drug-fuelled orgy involving unspeakable vices in a mysterious block of luxury flats. And there are no Russians who are not KGB colonels. And, of course, they are no homosexuals who have not been blackmailed or honey-trapped by KGB colonels into turning over state secrets.

Speaking of which, this leads us to 'the double bubble'. This is a technique not intended to spread lies, but to bury uncomfortable truths. Say, for example, that a journalist has uncovered a lead linking BOSS, the South African secret service, to a British service – and that both services are trying to smear a British politician. And the story about BOSS interfering in Britain is painfully true and needs to be quashed. What you do is get a handsome young man or woman to go to that journalist and tell him that he or she was hired by someone with a South African accent to take part in an orgy with a certain politician that involved 'unspeakable vices' and filming. Once the story has been published, the pretty young thing goes to another newspaper and admits that he or she made up the whole thing because the investigative journalist paid for the story. Hey presto, the journalist's reputation is wrecked and the true part of the story is also rubbished. You get rid of the truth by contaminating it with lies. Show me a hero and I'll show you a secret vice.

Catesby folded up the letter for filing – under 'Zero, Captain'. It was midnight on a summer Friday, too late to hear the nightingales and he was already back at work.

## Labour Win Slim Majority

The Labour Party led by Harold Wilson has won a small majority of three seats. The result was far from the decisive landslide that Wilson pulled off in 1966, but it ends the uncertainty of a hung parliament.

Wilson acknowledges that high inflation remains a problem, but ending the miners' strike has returned some stability.

Wilson's narrow victory means that Edward Heath's days as Conservative Party leader may be numbered. After suffering three defeats in four elections, the Tories will be looking for a change at the top.

In addition to inflation, the key challenges for Wilson's incoming government will be industrial relations and dealing with the cycle of violence in Northern Ireland.

**Mayfair, London:** 11 October 1974

'Tactically,' said the colonel staring at the amber liquor in his Waterford cut-crystal glass, 'this is a good result.'

'It means the end of useless Heath,' said the peer.

'And his replacement by a strong leader,' said Brian the journalist, 'who will put the unions in their place and get rid of the Reds in parliament and Whitehall.'

'What do you think, JJ?' said the colonel. 'Did FCS do a good job?'

'As you know, we didn't let FCS off the lead. In fact, there's a lot of CIA info and disinfo on Wilson that we didn't use – but we have kept it in reserve for a better time. The last thing we wanted was a successful press and media psy-op campaign that put Heath back in power. As it is, we've got a weakened and worried Wilson back in Downing Street with a slim hold on power.'

'But the Army aren't happy,' said the general.

'Good,' said the colonel.

'Another four or five years of Wilson,' said the banker, 'will totally wreck the economy.'

'Don't worry,' said the peer, 'he won't last half that long. 'My astrologer says he's doomed to fall in the Year of the Dragon.'

'You mean,' laughed the banker, 'the Chinese guy who gives you acupuncture for your sciatica.'

'Yes, he's excellent. You ought to try him.'

'You don't,' said the colonel, 'need an astrologer to tell you that Wilson and his Communist cell are doomed.' The colonel's eyes twinkled. 'I give him one year.'

JJ gave the colonel a knowing glance. 'It might coincide with events in Australia.'

Brian nodded approval. 'Whitlam is another Red who ought to bite the dust.'

'Who knows,' said the colonel, 'it could be a practice run. We tested our nuclear weapons in Australia. We can now use Oz as testing ground to see how to explode Wilson.'

'I understand,' said the peer, 'that the Heathrow exercises are going to become a regular occurrence.'

'I think,' said the general, 'that we have to get the public used to seeing military deployments.'

'Our soldiers,' said JJ, 'are a much finer example of British manhood than the sort of scum we see in our universities. It's utterly ridiculous that the taxpayer pays their tuition fees and contributes towards their living expenses. We're subsidising universities to indoctrinate our youth into becoming Marxist revolutionaries.'

'It is utterly bizarre,' said the peer. 'How did our ancient universities end up controlled by those who propagate ideologies hostile to the historical values of Britain. The Pied Pipers of revolution, masquerading as lecturers in sociology, economics and politics, are as dangerous as they are ridiculous.'

'I think,' said the colonel, 'that our action committees need to start planning now. We can't let this state of affairs continue.'

**Century House, Lambeth:** 16 October 1974

*...planning now. We can't let this state of affairs continue.*

Henry Bone turned off the tape recorder and stared hard at Catesby.

'They are vile,' said Catesby.

'I don't care about their being vile. I care about their being dangerous. They're becoming a serious threat. I need a drink.' Bone got up and walked over to an eighteenth-century sideboard. It was a privately owned piece of furniture that Bone had brought to Century House to try to bring a hint of culture and humanity to the building's Kafkaesque alienation. In fact, the sideboard made the alienation even worse by emphasising it. Catesby thought it made Bone's office look like the Louis XVI-style bedroom that somehow found itself in the spaceship in *2001: A Space Odyssey*.

'Is twenty-five-year-old VSOP brandy all right with you, Catesby – or would you prefer a cup of tea? It will have to be Typhoo from a bag.'

'Brandy, please.'

Bone poured and served the brandy. Catesby noticed that his hands were shaking. He suddenly realised how much Bone had aged in the past few years. He must be approaching retirement age.

'I would,' said Bone, 'appreciate it if you transcribed Captain Zero's letters into a typed document. Please don't photocopy them. It would be tempting fate to have examples of his handwriting lying around. I will, of course, closely guard the typed copies.' Bone sighed and sipped his brandy. 'That young captain is taking an awful risk.'

'How do you know he's young?'

'All captains are young nowadays – and an older man wouldn't be so foolish.'

'I wouldn't be so sure.'

'Well, I suppose, Catesby, that you are an argument to the contrary.'

'Touché,' said Catesby raising his glass. 'I never thought we would be in this position. I always thought Britain was destined for decades of reassuring dullness alternating between One

Nation Tory fossils and Labour government pragmatists bent on betraying their socialist principles. It wasn't ideal, but it was safe.'

'Remember, Catesby, what I said to you all those years ago when I gave you that somewhat drunken tour of the Q-Whitehall tunnel system?'

'Spain.'

'Well remembered – and I bet you thought at the time that I was mad?'

Catesby smiled and nodded.

'There's no reason,' said Bone, 'why 1930s Spain can't happen here.'

Catesby raised his fist in salute: '*¡No pasarán!*'

## Pimlico, London: 1 November 1974

The latest letter from Captain Zero was disturbing for a number of reasons. Not just for the information it contained about Operation Clockwork Orange, but because of what it revealed about the captain's precarious position. Catesby picked it up and read it again.

Greetings Mr Catesby,

Things are increasingly strange here at Operation Clockwork Orange. I've been bollocked a few times for being too nosey and asking 'too many fucking questions' – especially about mysterious meetings with the press. Part of our job is briefing foreign and British journalists who come to Northern Ireland to experience the thrills and spills of a war zone, but on most days there is very little happening. The sleight-of-hand skill required is to turn a briefing about the situation in Northern Ireland into a briefing against Harold Wilson and members of his government. One standard technique is to feign a weary sigh before whispering, 'This is off the record and strictly confidential'. The briefing officer then complains that the security services in Northern Ireland are underfunded – and things are going to get worse because Wilson's Labour government are cutting spending on defence and the intelligence services. Another covert briefing line is that Wilson has alienated the CIA on whom the UK relies for much Cold War intelligence and expertise in SIGINT and other expensive technical matters. From there on, provided the journalist is a sympathetic right-winger, it's easy to move on to rumours of Communists, orgies, unspeakable sexual practices and mysterious Eastern Europeans with deep pockets.

One of the most worrying things is proliferation of forged documents – and I think I know the identity of a few of the forgers. The motto seems to be: 'If you can't find it; make it up.' One line, which is difficult to conceive even with the most twisted leaps of illogic, is a link between Moscow, Wilson and the IRA. It's like saying the Pope is a Soviet agent. These people have leapt into another dimension.

I want out and hope to be leaving the Army in the near future. Meanwhile, I feel that I am under suspicion and being spied on – so I must be careful. But I will stay in touch.

I've just found out that I'm Night Duty Officer this weekend. Being alone in the office means that I will have a chance to check out a few secret files. I know that there is at least one bombshell I should be able to get my hands on. I will tell you about it when I write again early next week.

Best wishes,
Captain Zero

PS: I would describe what is going on as a black propaganda in preparation for a coup d'état.

At first, Catesby had an ominous feeling about the letter, but then thought that Captain Zero was indulging a taste for self-dramatising. It wasn't an unusual trait for members of the intelligence community. He continued to stare at the letter and hoped that he was right.

**Suffolk:** 16 November 1974

Catesby had waited in London until the Saturday post was delivered, but still no letter from Captain Zero. Nor had the letter arrived the previous week as promised. Catesby now knew that there weren't going to be any more letters. Ever. He looked again at the newspaper story which was brief and relegated to the inside pages.

### Body of British Army Officer Found in Carlingford Loch

The body of a British Army captain, missing for a week, has been found in Carlingford Loch. He is thought to have been abducted and executed by the IRA. It has not been confirmed, but the missing captain is thought to have been an intelligence officer who was kidnapped while operating undercover...

Catesby continued staring at the newspaper. No one would ever know the truth. The article didn't give the officer's name, but indicated that he originally came from Wales.

It was nearly midnight when Catesby found the tape and put it in the recorder. When the twins were young, before the stepson's voice broke, they had been in a choir. One of Catesby's favourite pieces had been the choir's rendition of the Welsh lullaby, *Suo Gân*.

> *Huna blentyn ar fy mynwes*
> *Clyd a chynnes ydyw hon;*
> *Breichiau mam sy'n dynn amdanat...*
> *Sleep child on my bosom*
> *Cozy and warm is this;*
> *Mother's arms are tight around you,*
> *Mother's love is under my breast;*
> *Nothing may affect your napping,*
> *No man will cross you;*
> *Sleep quietly, dear child...*

The words were still ringing in Catesby's ears when he went to the village war memorial in the churchyard. There were nine names on the memorial – a lot for so small a village – and there were nine poppies from Remembrance Day. Catesby added a tenth poppy – even though he knew it was so far from the captain's native Wales. 'Rest in peace … whoever you were.'

Angleton knew his days as Head of Counter-intelligence were numbered. He knew that he had lots of enemies – and several of those enemies were KGB moles who had penetrated Western intelligence agencies. But his more numerous and powerful enemies – if power is defined as bureaucratic weight – were those who were the dupes of the Soviet agents. These latter were the ones who were going to get rid of him.

Nixon's resignation hadn't helped either. Angleton was no great admirer of Nixon, but it had been the President himself who had encouraged him to continue HT/LINGUAL and MH/CHAOS

HT/LINGUAL was the sort of operation that any intelligence agency worth its salt would have undertaken. It involved opening mail addressed to and received from the Soviet Union, Red China and other Communist countries. The letters were opened and recorded at CIA facilities in New York and LA. HT/LINGUAL certainly provided an impressive list of fellow travellers, pinkos and Soviet agents. Peace groups and civil rights organisations in particular were ridden with covert and overt Communist sympathisers.

MH/CHAOS had been set up on the urging of Lyndon Johnson. Its purpose was to uncover foreign influences on the anti-Vietnam war protests. And there was certainly a lot of anti-war stuff coming from Britain. In fact, a lot of the culture of anti-establishment protest came from Britain – not just the Beatles and the Rolling Stones, but from art-house films and Communist intellectuals like Eric Hobsbawm. And the influence of Bertrand Russell, although he was now dead, had done a lot of damage too. Russell's lordly manner and breeding had made cowardly pacifism smart and fashionable. He was largely responsible for CND, which still threatened the future of US nuclear bases in Britain. Angleton lit a cigarette and smiled. Russell had also been screwing T.S. Eliot's first wife. Sexual betrayal and national betrayal often went hand in hand. All of Britain's Soviet spies had either been homosexual or serial adulterers.

Angleton stared through the haze of smoke. And now LINGUAL and CHAOS had been turned against him. Someone within the CIA, perhaps one of the Soviet moles, had leaked information about the two operations to the press. You weren't supposed to spy on American citizens. It was a violation of the CIA charter. So what? The charter was only a piece of paper – but the CIA was a secret intelligence organisation tasked with protecting America's security. And now they were using the bureaucratic nicety of the charter to get rid of him.

But, for the time being, he had still had a job to do. Angleton opened his latest cable from London.

From OSO London Station to ADOCCI:
The Wilson regime is quickly proving to be the nightmare predicted. The Labor government have already declared an arms embargo against South Africa and Chile. Détente with Russia is already back on the table. And, most outrageously, Wilson has ordered the British secret services to stop trying to suborn and recruit Soviet diplomats stationed in the UK. His rationale is that it could affect trade relations. It's almost as if Wilson's foreign policy is being dictated directly from the Kremlin.

But there's a bright side. Wilson won't last long. There are rumblings on the ground and we're doing everything to help.

By the way, we've just received news that a former Wilson cabinet minister has been reported missing in Florida. A pile of his clothes was discovered on a Miami beach this morning. The ex-minister in question was almost certainly a spy in the pay of the Czechoslovakian intelligence service. The London-based defector, RADKO, confirms this.

More information from your sources in Miami about the 'drowning' would be much appreciated.

We need, thought Angleton staring at the cable, to keep our side in London well supplied with ammunition. As Yeats said of Dublin in 1916:

> *All changed, changed utterly:*
> *A terrible beauty is born.*

It is now London's turn.

## Century House, Lambeth: 23 November 1974

Catesby and Bone had just spent an exhausting weekend going through files at the behest of Sir Maurice. John Stonehouse, the missing ex-minister now presumed a suicide drowning, was a big headache – and Sir Maurice had correctly predicted that he would be summoned to Downing Street to give the PM an intelligence briefing on Stonehouse.

'What do you think?' said Bone.

'Once again, it all boils down to Wilson's penchant for trade with the East Bloc. Stonehouse was a junior minister in the Ministry of Technology in Wilson's last government. Stonehouse, following Wilson's "white heat of technology" line, was particularly enthusiastic in supporting the export of technologically advanced products to the Soviet Bloc. It reminded the Cousins of the hated Rolls-Royce jet engines deal; they were furious and out to get Stonehouse.'

'I think,' said Bone, 'he could have been more sensitive to the Washington perspective. But how did Five feel about letting you nose around in their Registry?'

'Superficially friendly and cooperative, but I'm certain that the most interesting files had been pulled or were never there in the first place.'

'What did you find?'

'Stonehouse was very fastidious about reporting to Five all his contacts and conversations with anyone from the East Bloc. He obviously knew that he was under surveillance and suspicion.'

'With good reason?'

Catesby smiled. 'I wouldn't have given Stonehouse a top secret security clearance, but I wouldn't have put him in handcuffs either.'

'Is there definitive concrete evidence that he accepted money from the Czechs?'

'Absolutely none – and certainly not enough evidence to merit a prosecution.'

'But you have your suspicions?'

'I think Stonehouse was dodgy with money. If he did spy, it wasn't ideological; it was for cash. At least Wilson had the good sense not to bring him back into the government.'

'You think he was guilty?'

Catesby nodded. 'But thinking it and proving it are two different things.'

Bone nodded. 'Apparently, he was in deep financial trouble – which was why he went for a swim.'

'Or didn't go for a swim.'

'Exactly.'

Catesby smiled. 'If he turns up again, I bet it's more likely to be in Melbourne than Moscow.'

'You see where this is heading?'

'They're going to plant stories about Stonehouse and use them to smear Wilson.'

'Go on.'

'They're going to say that Wilson had full knowledge that Stonehouse was a Czech spy and covered up for him – and the cover-up proves there is a Communist cell at the heart of Downing Street.'

'I hope, William, you realise how serious this is.'

'You think we're heading for a *coup d'état*?'

Bone nodded.


**Mayfair, London:** 27 November 1974

'I wonder,' said the general, 'how long it will be before the blighter turns up in Moscow?'

'Or Prague,' said JJ.

The colonel turned to a newcomer in the club. 'Would I be correct in assuming that there is proof that Stonehouse accepted money from the Czechs when he was junior minister for aviation?'

'You realise that I am in a very difficult position in terms of diplomatic protocol.' The newcomer spoke with an American accent. 'May I remind you that you have never seen me and don't know who I am?'

The others nodded.

'You could say,' said the American, 'that I'm the man who never was – but don't dump me in the sea.'

There was an awkward silence.

'The key source of our information on Stonehouse,' continued the American, 'is the Czech intelligence service defector codenamed RADKO. We have sent a transcript of the sections of his debriefings pertaining to Stonehouse to your Security Service.'

'Why hasn't our own Security Service debriefed him?' said the colonel.

'I believe they have,' said the American, 'but you may find our debriefings more … more detailed and convincing. RADKO's memory seems to be improving. And you could also say that we are a neutral third party without any domestic axes to grind.'

JJ nodded. Getting intelligence from other agencies or sources that confirmed and supported your own conclusions was always a good idea when presenting the information to politicians or journalists.

'And by the way,' said the American, 'I am leaving you a copy of the RADKO-Stonehouse transcript. The only things deleted are those which could link the document back to us.'

'Can we pass it around?' said the banker.

'With a little bit of care,' said the American. 'But choose your journalists carefully.'

'"Communist Cell in Downing Street" is a great headline,' said the peer.

'The trick,' said JJ, 'of successful psy-op is not overegging, but giving a steady drip-feed.'

'And timing,' said the colonel. 'We want the balloon to go up next November in the week after Remembrance Sunday.'

'The public,' said the general, 'are always well disposed to the military at that time of year.'

**Century House, Lambeth, London:** 2 December 1974

*...are always well disposed to the military at that time of year.*

Bone turned off the tape recorder and looked at Catesby, 'We've got to do something.'

'We could leak these tapes to the press or go to the police.'

'That would be the kamikaze option. It would destroy me, which is fine, but it could also destroy SIS. A revelation that we bugged UK citizens within the UK would be the most serious violation of our legal remit ever made public. There would be a public outcry – and prosecutions. In fact, it might even backfire in favour of the coup plotters. But having said that, we might have to go public – when the time is right.'

'Or,' said Catesby, 'we can take covert action.'

Bone stared hard at Catesby. 'What do you mean by covert action?'

'Removing them as a problem – and making it look as if someone else did it.'

'How ruthless are you, William?'

'Not as ruthless as I should be.'

'It was so long ago,' said Bone, 'I bet you don't even remember.'

'How long ago?'

'The mid-fifties. In fact, it was 1956 – a year we all remember well.'

Catesby smiled. 'What a year indeed. Kit Fournier got appointed CIA Head of London Station, Buster Crabb disappeared, probably with Fournier's help – and Eden made a complete mess of Suez.'

'Actually, I was thinking of something more low-key, but perhaps not less important.'

'You've lost me.'

'You and Frances went to a party at the Gaitskell's house in Frognal Gardens to check out the US labour attaché who was hobnobbing with the Gaitskell crowd.' Bone lifted a file on his desk. 'And you wrote a report on the evening for me – for which I am very grateful.'

'I'm starting to remember. Please go on.'

'You met a man who spoke French with, as you so astutely

noted with your excellent ear for nuances of language, "an Eastern European accent".'

Catesby nodded. 'And he looked a very tough customer – not someone you would want to meet in a dark alleyway.'

'But what disturbed you at the time, William, was that the man knew about the Nazi that you had killed in Bremen.'

'And he thanked me for it.'

'And said that he would help if you ever wanted to take part in other retribution killings.'

'I don't think,' said Catesby, 'it takes much imagination to work out who he represents.'

'And we don't want to know who he represents.'

'Absolutely.'

Bone looked at Catesby's yellowing notes from so long ago. 'I hope they haven't forgotten you.'

'They never forget.'

'In any case,' continued Bone, 'I was impressed by the dramatic flair of the contact details you so accurately reported: *Go to the grave of Charles Baudelaire in the Montparnasse Cemetery. You will see a likeness of the poet recumbent on his grave. Put a tiny chalk mark on his left big toe – then return to the cemetery at noon on the first Friday of the month. Someone will be there to meet you and will say, "Venge-moi".' You will identify yourself by replying, "Demain, aprés-demain et toujours!" Then tell them what you want.*

Catesby frowned. 'And now you want me to go to Paris and take up their offer?'

'No, I don't.'

'Then why have you brought this up?'

'I've always been fond of Baudelaire,' said Bone smiling. 'I've booked a brief leave in March when I will be visiting his grave in Paris.'

'Don't forget the chalk.'

'I won't,' said Bone. 'Meanwhile we must compile a present for them – a present so useful to their cause that they will do us a big favour in return.'

'What sort of present?'

'A package of files on ODESSA and their networks – and as many details and addresses of PAPERCLIP émigrés as we can find.'

## Suffolk: Christmas, 1974

Catesby was cooking a goose for Frances, his stepchildren, his sister and his eighty-seven-year-old mother. *Moeder* was in a grump and refusing to speak English or French. It meant that the only people she could communicate with were Catesby and his sister, no one else being fluent in *West-Vlaams Nederlands*.

Catesby had tried to humour his mother by taking her to Midnight Mass in Southwold. She brightened up when she noticed that the Italian priest was another foreigner. She whispered to Catesby that the priest looked 'very aristocratic' and the 'very image' of the late Pope Pius XII. Catesby said, 'Shh, he's his son.' Either his mother didn't get the joke or really did believe that the priest was the Pope's son. Catesby had slowly come to realise that his mother was more sophisticated about what Popes and other people got up to than she let on.

Even though he had taken her to Mass, *Moeder* knew that Catesby and his sister were non-believers. One of the things Catesby most admired about his mother was the way she gave up on lost causes. When they were children, she had tried to bring them up as good Roman Catholics. But as puberty beckoned, she realised that neither her son nor her daughter had any interest whatsoever in religion and stopped trying. Or maybe, thought Catesby, she herself had just got bored of catechism and rosary reciting. In any case, what fascinated Catesby was the languages his mother used when discussing religion. When she talked about God – all Three of Them – she spoke *Nederlands*. When she talked about the Blessed Virgin, she shifted into French. But when she talked about Satan, she always spoke English.

Sometimes, thought Catesby, dealing with his mother was like dealing with a foreign agent. And Catesby never forgot her Jesuit friend from Ireland who, after a few sherries one Christmas, had pronounced Protestantism as 'the religion of the cash register'. The remark reminded Catesby of other issues too. No Roman Catholic could ever be King or Queen – and merely marrying a Catholic disqualified a person from succeeding to the Crown. Would, Catesby thought, British Catholics ever be completely trusted? It was a more subtle issue than the hysteria about undercover Communists. But maybe, in a historical context, not completely unrelated.

The Queen's Christmas broadcast broke the ice – and Catesby's mother deigned to speak English again. She admired the Queen – and was proud that they were both the same diminutive height. She had briefly met the Queen when Catesby got his OBE.

It hadn't been a bad Christmas in many ways. The goose in Catesby's oven wasn't the only one cooked. The mad and paranoid FURIOSO had finally been forced to resign and John Stonehouse had been arrested in Melbourne. But in neither case was the news completely good. No longer distracted by FURIOSO's mad mole-hunts, the CIA could now be more aggressive abroad. And Stonehouse turning up alive in Australia would add fuel to the rumours of Communists in Downing Street.

## Margaret Thatcher is New Tory Leader

Margaret Thatcher's sudden rise to become leader of the Conservative Party has sent shock waves across the political landscape. When Ted Heath called a leadership election just one week ago, many expected the contest to be a walkover. There appeared to be no alternative to Heath from the right of the party. The standard-bearer of the Tory right, Keith Joseph, had effectively ruled himself out after his controversial comments calling on poor people to have fewer children.

In a surprise move, however, Margaret Thatcher opted to stand and rallied the right-wing behind her with. At first, Thatcher's support seemed minimal with the Conservative daily newspapers backing Heath. As the election ground on, however, it became clear that the race was going to be much closer as Thatcher gained the support of discontented backbenchers. Thatcher forced Heath to resign when she trounced him in the first round of the leadership race with 130 votes to his 119.

Key to Thatcher's victory was the support of the influential right-wing 1922 Backbench Committee whose 276 members have become important power brokers. Edward du Cann, Chairman of the 1922 Committee, described Margaret Thatcher as 'a new and rather exciting leader' who will 'make the Tory Party distinctive'.

Mrs Thatcher, who served as Edward Heath's Secretary of State for Science and Education, exclaimed, 'It's like a dream.'

But the new leader rejected suggestions of a victory celebration: 'Good heavens, no. There's far too much work to be done.'

**Courtauld Institute, London:** 13 February 1975

There were several reasons why Henry Bone had visited the famous art historian. One of the reasons being that Anthony Blunt was in a terrible gloom and needed cheering up – not that there was much cheer that Bone could convey. At one time, the two had been close friends – and Bone still felt a brotherly compassion for him. They began by talking about the MI5 officer that Catesby called Ferret.

'I know that Catesby despises Peter, but after half a bottle of gin, he becomes almost bearable. He begins to show his insecurities and vulnerabilities.

Very touching in some ways. Little outward hostility, we even exchange Christmas cards.'

'How often,' said Henry Bone, 'do you have these interviews?'

'At present, hardly at all. Almost a mere formality – perhaps twice a year, just to keep in touch. But after my so-called confession in 1964, he would interview me every month – often until the early hours of the morning.'

Henry Bone found Blunt's private rooms at the Courtauld extremely austere. The floors were covered in curling grey linoleum with a few worn rugs, but on the walls above the lino were a Rubens nude and a Picasso Blue Period etching. The Picasso was of a lean couple in threadbare clothing sitting at a table with empty bowls and an empty wine bottle. The man is wearing a homburg hat. The only clue that the woman is female is her meagre hanging breasts. Blunt noticed Bone staring at the etching.

'That one's called *A Frugal Meal*. I've hung it here,' said Blunt with a bleak smile, 'because it suits the room – a counterpoint to the lush Rubens.'

'The couple in the Picasso remind me of Beckett's characters.'

'One of my lovers,' said Blunt, 'thought the man, with his gaunt drawn look, resembled me. Too true. I've been very tired and my eyes are going – I find it difficult to read. I rely on others and I'm starting to crave company.'

'Would you like another series of interrogations?'

'In some ways I miss them. There is a symbiotic relationship between the interrogator and his victim. We often ended up talking about love, friendship and betrayal rather than espionage and spies.' Blunt looked at Bone. 'I assume, by the way, they have passed on copies of my interrogation transcripts to SIS?'

'They have.'

'Is there any chance that I could see them? I can't remember much of what I said. I'm always afraid they will try to catch me contradicting something I'd forgotten I said.'

'I'll see what I can do.'

'I'm also very depressed and worried about Thatcher becoming Tory leader. Have they lost their senses? Would you like more whisky?'

Bone nodded and Blunt topped up their glasses – literally, to the top.'

'I rather liked Heath,' said Blunt. 'He may have had very little personal charm, but he had an appreciation of the arts – and was a very fine amateur musician.'

'And a superb yachtsman.'

'And so, Henry, were you.'

Bone had represented Britain as a yachtsman at the 1936 Olympics. It was part of his complex and mysterious hinterland – as was his decades long friendship with the art historian.

'I'm afraid, Henry, I'm afraid.'

'Of what?'

'If she ever becomes prime minister, she won't respect the immunity agreement and she won't keep my confession an official secret – which was also agreed. Until now, the confession hasn't affected my life.'

Bone nodded and took a pad and pencil out of his pocket. He began to scribble quickly, but then remembered that the art historian had difficult seeing. He wrote in large block capitals: THIS ROOM IS BUGGED. LET'S GO FOR A WALK.

Anthony Blunt nodded. 'I need some fresh air. Fancy a stroll to the off-licence?'

It was a mild evening for February with only a hint of dampness. Bone and the art historian walked up Baker Street – to where there really was an off-license that was still open.

'Officially,' said Blunt, 'I'm no longer Director of the Courtauld.'

'Nothing to do with…?'

'No, I need more time to write. Victor and Tess Rothschild have offered me lodgings. They've looked after me before when I've been ill.'

Bone nodded. The couple had also taken care of Heath's

Permanent Secretary when he had a nervous breakdown in Downing Street the previous year. Their wealth and generosity provided warm embraces for those in need of protection – and kept them hidden from prying eyes.

'I want,' said Bone, 'to talk about you and Tommy – and that little business you ran.'

Blunt coughed and stumbled.

'Are you all right?'

'Oh dear, Henry, now I am in trouble. No wonder you wanted to get me away from the hidden microphones. In a way, it was great fun. Isn't it odd?'

'Isn't what odd?' said Bone.

'That my MI5 interrogators never asked me about my most important betrayals – my betrayal of art? Giving false attributions and creating bogus masterpieces was far more insidious than anything I ever did for the Russians.'

'We've had this conversation before.'

'And, Henry, I want to have it again. Nothing I ever passed on to Moscow ever damaged Britain, but it did help Russia defeat Nazi Germany.'

Bone stared blankly into the traffic headlights heading down Baker Street. There were many ways to define 'damage'.

'But,' continued Blunt, 'damaging the reputation of great artists with a false attribution is like hurling acid at a real Poussin.'

'But it was lucrative,' Bone paused, 'and I helped too. What a pity that Tommy didn't live to enjoy the proceeds.'

'A lot of it went to good causes. But there's one thing that has always bothered me and never been resolved.'

'What?'

'Do you suppose they found out that Tommy had swindled them and then killed him in return? The car crash was very suspicious.'

'If they did kill Tommy, now is your chance to get back at them.'

'I'm not a vengeful person.'

'But some people are – and have every right to be.'

'What do you want, Henry?'

'I want you to give me all the files and all the information you have on your former customers in South America – especially the ODESSA ones.'

'Why haven't you asked before?'

'Because we had no means of bringing them to justice – not to mention the fact that many of them are protected by the Americans and their host countries.'

'How soon do you want this information?'

'By the end of the month.'

'You will have it – and I hope by so doing I can restore a few reputations too.'

'There are things more important than art.'

'Do you actually think, Henry, that I have not considered that many times lying awake in the dark watches of the night?'

'And what's the answer?'

'Ask me when I'm on my death bed.'

**Paris:** 7 March 1975

It was a cold bleak day in the Cimetière du Montparnasse. Henry Bone was wearing a black roll-neck jumper and his black leather jacket. His Fitzrovia gear doubled as cover for blending into the Left Bank. Bone wondered whether he should stroll into Les Deux Magots on St Germain-des-Prés to test his cover and practice his French on Jean-Paul Sartre and Simone de Beauvoir. Actually, there was a philosophical issue that Bone would have liked to discuss with them. Sartre had recently said that terrorism was a 'terrible weapon, but the oppressed poor have no others'. And it was a question not unrelated to the reason Henry Bone had come to Paris.

Bone huddled inside his leather jacket; the wind was biting cold as only a March wind in a Parisian cemetery can be. He checked his watch. His contact – if there was going to be a contact – was already ten minutes late. Bone had done everything required, including the chalk mark on Baudelaire's 'left big toe'. But perhaps the network that contacted Catesby nineteen years ago was no longer active. In fact, it was unlikely. But Bone continued waiting. If necessary, he would freeze for another hour or try another month.

Bone looked across the graves. The cemetery wasn't empty of the living, but few were about. The person nearest was a woman in black jeans wearing a scarf and heavy coat. She had a bouquet of hyacinths and seemed to be dawdling among the graves. She didn't appear to be aware of Bone's existence, but was getting closer. She finally approached. Her eyes were fixed on Baudelaire's sarcophagus and completely ignoring Bone. In a gesture that was more violent than respectful she threw the hyacinths on to Baudelaire's tomb and whispered a hoarse, *'Venge-moi!'*

Bone answered with the agreed words, *'Demain, aprés-demain et toujours!'*

The woman replied in English, 'You speak French like a very English "milord" who has come to Paris for a bit of fun – and, my god, don't you look like one.'

Bone wasn't often nonplussed, but when it happened it was usually a woman doing the nonplussing. He struggled to regain some semblance of dignity. 'I am sure that your English is much better than my French.'

'I was told that the person I was meeting spoke absolutely fluent French – and you look nothing at all like the description I was given. So who are you?'

'I work closely with the person your representative met. The meeting occurred quite a long time ago – in 1956.'

'Our records are very fastidious. Each contact is assigned a different dead poet and a different line of poetry. I was briefed to meet a certain William Catesby. Why hasn't he come?'

'He was more than willing, but I wanted to take personal responsibility for what I am giving you – and what I would like to get in return.'

'I won't ask your name, nor am I going to tell you mine, but I am sure we will both make accurate assumptions about our jobs.'

Bone nodded and looked closely at the woman. She was older than she appeared at first, probably more than fifty. Her face was thinly lined and her looks were Mediterranean or Middle Eastern. Her black hair was probably dyed.

'Where,' she said, 'are the things you wish to give me?'

'In a locked briefcase – with an incendiary device to destroy the contents if it is forced open – in a safe at my hotel.'

'You take no chances. Were you followed?'

'One can never be sure, but I follow standard counter-surveillance procedures.'

'Are you alone?'

'Utterly,' smiled Bone.

'Are you flirting?'

Bone was nonplussed once more. He tried French again: *Je suis un vieil homme dans une saison sèche.*

'That was much better, milord.' She offered her arm. 'Shall we go, sir, to your hotel?'

The woman had spread the documents over the bed and many had spilled on to the floor. There was a wealth of information:

it included all of Catesby's files, including those from the SOAS lecturer; all of the art historian's files and recollections and much else that Bone had personally garnered and guessed. Bone was helping her tie various leads together. Much of the information expanded intelligence that the woman's organisation already had in part, but which led to cul-de-sacs.

'I hope you will find these documents useful,' said Bone.

'They fill in many missing spaces in the jigsaw – and will bring people to justice. That is certain.' The woman paused and stared hard at Bone. 'But your gifts have come wrapped in a mystery. And you are a mystery too. Aren't you warm in that jumper?'

Bone smiled. Women were often very interested in his art historian friend too. Was it because of Blunt's refinement and good looks? Or was it the challenge of the unattainable? Except that, on occasion, Anthony had, not so much given in or succumbed, but complied.

'I would,' said Bone, 'like to ask for your help.'

The woman smiled. 'With your jumper? I'd love to buy you a new one.'

'Thank you, but with something else too.'

'Go on.'

'I need a very special type of listening device. Most bugs, as you know, are activated by voice or a radio signal. They are small and very difficult to detect.' Bone was thinking of the very excellent one that had been installed in the billiard room of the Mayfair gentlemen's club. 'But I would like a large, lumpy listening device that can be easily discovered – by emitting, say, a tell-tale sound that appears to be accidental. Something such as a cassette-tape recorder with an internal microphone.'

'But surely you could easily buy one in any shop.'

'Ah, I left out an important detail. I should have said, something that *appears* to be a large listening device.' Bone paused. 'What I am really looking for is a bomb disguised as a bug.'

The woman looked perplexed. 'Why have you come to us? I know who you are and I am sure your own technical support teams could provide exactly what you want.'

'The operation I want to carry out is not one sanctioned by the

UK Government or by British law. It is, in fact, an illegal operation, but one intended to save my country. I am sure that your organisation has faced similar dilemmas.'

'How do you know that you can trust us with this information?'

'Because I am ruthless enough to expose your operations if you expose mine.'

The woman stared at Bone. 'That sounds fair. Tell me more about this explosive device.'

'I want a bomb that will appear to have been a typical IRA device. Therefore, please don't use anything that the Provos would not have access to. I will provide you the technical details.'

'That would be useful.'

When Bone had finished his briefing on the bomb, the woman put down her pencil – and then picked it up again. 'Do you mind if I sketch you?'

'If it pleases you.'

'Sit over there by the window. I'm not, however, going to do it in this notebook.' She took a sketch pad out of her bag. 'I like drawing. It also teaches you to notice things and people.'

'What have noticed about me?'

'You would be surprised, milord.'

After an hour the woman handed the completed sketch to Bone. He looked old, troubled and conflicted. She hadn't signed it, but she had given it a title: *Un vieil homme dans une saison sèche*.

The woman leaned close to Bone and whispered, '*Maintenant, regardez-moi.*' Her voice was worn and hoarse.

## Green Park, London: 20 March 1975

Catesby and Bone had just been to a meeting at the FCO about the effects the fall of Saigon, which now seemed inevitable, would have on UK foreign policy and intelligence needs. The most immediate problem would be the evacuation of British passport holders. The next issue would be refugees and asylum seekers. These problems mostly concerned Dir/FarEast, but there were wider implications that concerned all of SIS. The most important was how the Americans were going to react to the humiliation of losing in Vietnam. There were already signs that Washington was going to lash out and pursue even tougher and more aggressive policies to prove that America was still the world's most powerful country. This could lead to tenser confrontations with the Soviet Union and a greater risk of war. There was also a possibility that Washington would want to 'punish' the allies who 'didn't do enough' to support the US in Vietnam. These would include Britain, Canada and the Gough Whitlam government in Australia.

It was the first time that Catesby and Bone had a chance to talk since Bone had gone to Paris. When the FCO meeting was finished, they made their way to a bench in Green Park for a private chat amid the daffodils and primroses.

'How was Paris?' said Catesby.

'I accomplished what I set out to do.'

'You're not going to tell me more?'

'No.'

'I had,' said Catesby, 'an interesting chat with Sir Maurice while you were gone. He's not as mild and cuddly as he seems.'

'You've just noticed that?'

'I had my suspicions before, but I came away feeling that I had just been to a meeting with a Borgia prince plotting murder and torture. But he's holding off until the summer. He wants to give his victim more time to incriminate himself.'

'Who is the intended victim?'

Catesby told him.

**10 Downing Street:** August, 1975

The Prime Minister's visitor had arrived via Q-Whitehall, the secret tunnel system that linked the seats of government. The visitor's purpose was largely bureaucratic infighting – and also an attempt to protect himself and his agency when the simmering volcano erupted. The visitor was hoping for a peaceful transition that would still leave him in a position of power and influence. He didn't want a military coup, which would leave him vulnerable. The visitor had personal secrets of his own.

The visitor declined tea, coffee or something stronger and launched straight in. 'Your secret personal file, Prime Minister, bears the pseudonym Norman John Worthington. Such a person, of course, has never existed.'

'And only those who know I am Mr Worthington have access to my file?'

'That is correct, Prime Minister. If, on the other hand, you were to go to Registry and try to find Harold Wilson in the central index, your search would come back "No Trace".' The visitor paused and frowned. 'And in the past year, the DG has taken further measures to conceal the existence of your secret file.'

The Prime Minister lit his pipe with shaking hands. 'When,' he said, 'did all this begin?'

'It began in 1947 just after you were appointed President of the Board of Trade.'

Wilson looked out the window across Horse Guards. A squadron of cavalry in red plumes were practising a drill. He remembered what Sir Stafford Cripps had said to him as he handed over his Board of Trade post: 'I hope, Harold, that the jet-engines-to-Moscow deal doesn't prove to be a poison chalice.' It had.

'What in essence,' said Wilson, 'does the file contain?'

'Quite a lot. But what seems to concern the Security Service most are your past and present contacts with suspected or real KGB officers, Communists, Russians and Eastern Europeans in general.'

'It sounds like the file is also a recipe book for how to smear me and my government.'

'That's a point of view that one could understand.'

'Have they,' said Wilson, 'ever kept files on any other British prime minister?'

'No, they haven't – and, I must say, not all of the information that they have compiled is accurate.' The visitor reached into his briefcase and handed over a photograph. 'This particular one is blatant – and I've attached a note explaining why.'

When Sir Maurice Oldfield left 10 Downing, via the same Q-Whitehall tunnel by which he had arrived, he was feeling very pleased with himself.

### 10 Downing Street: August, 1975

The Prime Minister was on the warpath and had fortified himself for the confrontation with a whisky or two. The head of the Security Service hadn't been invited to Downing Street at a time that would be mutually convenient, he had been instructed to cancel all other appointments and come immediately.

'You and your service have been waging a smear campaign against me and my government that has been going on for years. You have conducted illegal activities, including burglary and bugging, which you have succeeded in covering up.'

The Security Service DG was a large man with a red face, nicknamed Jumbo. He wasn't used to being carpeted – and wasn't completed prepared to refute the Prime Minister's accusations. He was aware, however, that someone had stabbed him in the back – and he had a good idea who it was. Whitehall was a bear pit and things were getting worse. The best thing to do in his current situation was the tried and tested one: shit over your subordinates.

'There may, Prime Minister, be a small number of disaffected officers who have been plotting against you. They do not represent the Security Service as a whole – and their activities have been completely unauthorised. I am currently engaged in a root and branch review to put an end to it.'

'And you have never been personally involved in a campaign to smear me or my ministers?'

'No.'

'That's a lie – an outright lie.' The Prime Minister was seething.

'You have repeatedly tried to smear Judith Hart, until recently my Minister of Overseas Development. You have made her life and the lives of her family a misery with false accusations and innuendo.'

Jumbo turned even redder. 'I am not sure, Prime Minister, that I know what you are talking about.'

'This is what I'm talking about.' Wilson pushed an old photograph from the *Daily Worker* across his desk. The photograph showed a 'Mrs Tudor-Hart' at a Communist-sponsored meeting in Warsaw. 'Your smear describes the woman in this photo as Mrs J. Tudor-Hart, my former minister. The woman in this photo is Edith Tudor-Hart, an Austrian-born British photographer, who died two years ago. She was a Communist sympathiser, married to a GP called Alex Tudor-Hart. It is possible that she spied for the Soviet Union in the 1930s, I'm not denying that.' The Prime Minister raised his voice. 'But Edith Tudor-Hart, as you well know, was no relation to Judith Hart – who was never a *Tudor*-Hart – and they never met. The only *J.* Tudor-Hart in the equation is not even a woman, but Edith's son, Julian, who, like his father, is a GP in Wales.' Wilson picked up the photo and pointed it at Jumbo. 'This is not just a vile smear, but a feeble one too. And yet you have been passing this photo around – and the lies that go with it – to the press in unattributable briefings.' Wilson paused. 'How do you explain it?'

Jumbo twisted in his chair. 'It is unfortunate.'

'And you have tapped her telephone as well. You have targeted her because she is a fierce opponent of apartheid and Pinochet's coup in Chile. You hate her because she stands up for fairness, peace and human decency – everything you despise.' Wilson stared hard at the head of the Security Service. 'You are a shit – and a fucking disgrace to your office. Get out.'


**London:** August, 1975

Ferret was playing complex office politics. Neither his job nor his pension was secure. And FURIOSO's sacking had deprived Ferret of his most important American ally. His vindictiveness was only tempered by his financial need. Aligning himself with JJ's plots was an option, but there were other possibilities. Ferret was one who could run with the hares and the hounds at the same time. JJ had already heard the rumours – Whitehall was abuzz with them – and was pleased that Ferret had suggested a visit to his house. JJ's home was spartan, except for a few artefacts received as presents from his time in the Middle East, but he did serve good whisky.

'The leader of the Communist cell in Number 10 just threw his toys out of his pram?'

'So, I've heard,' said JJ, 'pouring a top-up.'

'Shouting, swearing; a force 10 tantrum.'

'It sounds like Wilson is losing what little grip he ever had.' JJ looked hard at Ferret. 'I don't suppose this incident had anything to do with you?'

'In what way?'

'There's a rumour that someone, perhaps from your own department, might have leaked info – and disinfo – to SIS which made its way to Downing Street and prompted Wilson's rage against Jumbo.'

Ferret gave a sly smile. 'Nothing to do with me personally. But it might have been a good idea for two reasons. One, it will help push Wilson over the edge. Two, it will keep Jumbo in his place.'

'Why does he need keeping in his place?'

'He's a bit too ready to dump on other people to save himself.'

'That's not the way we play the game. You have to be true to the cause and to your friends even if it means taking a bullet or two.'

'What's next?'

'The current situation,' said JJ with what some would have called a demented stare, 'cannot go on. The unions have got the country by the throat and are choking us to death. Every time you turn on the television you see factory car parks full of Communist-led trade unionists raising their fists to call for more strike action. Car parks, can you imagine? In the Russia, that our union leaders so much admire, the enslaved workers don't have cars.' JJ sipped his whisky. 'And speaking of cars, why has no one done anything about Red Robbo?' Red Robbo was the press's nickname for Derek Robinson, a shop steward at Leyland.

'The trade union movement is controlled by the Communist junta in Downing Street. They're all protected.'

'We can't wait. We need to take action.'

**Century House, Lambeth:** 11 November 1975

It was 9 a.m. and Catesby was in his office staring at a bare blank wall. The last two months had been miserable and tense. The atmosphere in Whitehall was now so full of hate and malice that Catesby, still a firm non-believer, wouldn't have objected if every Whitehall department was assigned a resident C of E exorcist. SIS and the Security Service would require several.

Catesby was waiting for news from Australia, as were many of his colleagues, and couldn't concentrate on anything else. The situation in Canberra was still on edge. Australia had nothing to do with Catesby's job as Head of Sov Bloc T Section, but everything to do with his position as a worried British citizen who was privy to insider information. If it could happen in Canberra, it could happen in London.

There was a firm knock on his door. Catesby got up and opened the door and took the cable from a cipher room clerk. It was from SIS Head of Station Canberra and was marked UNCLASSIFIED.

### Australian Prime Minister Dismissed by Governor-General

Prime Minister Gough Whitlam of the Australian Labor Party has been sacked. Governor-General Sir John Kerr has appointed the leader of the opposition, Malcolm Fraser, as caretaker prime minister.

FYI: The Australian Constitution firmly places the prerogative powers of the Crown in the hands of the Governor-General as the representative of the Queen of Australia. The only person with the authority to appoint an Australian prime minister is the Governor-General. The Queen has no part in the decisions that the Governor-General takes in his interpretation of the Constitution.

Gough's dismissal has received mixed coverage in the press ranging from approval to condemnation as a 'constitutional coup'.

An hour later, Catesby was in Bone's office discussing the implications of the Australia situation.

'It is ominous,' said Bone. 'The role of Governor-General is supposed to be ceremonial. What he's done is like Black Rod arresting the Prime Minister.'

'You know,' said Catesby, 'that the US Ambassador in Canberra is a total shit.'

'So I've heard.'

'His American colleagues call him "the coup maestro". He helped bring a general to power in South Korea. He got rid of Sihanouk in Cambodia – which was an open sesame for the Khmer Rouge. He had a role in the Suharto coup against Sukarno in Indonesia – which resulted in more than 500,000 dead. And now he's done the deed in Australia.' Catesby paused. 'I wonder when they're going to send him to London.'

### CIA HQ, Langley, Virginia: 11 November 1975

The DCI was extremely pleased. After the partial institutional paralysis brought on by Angleton's paranoia, the CIA was back on its front foot again – however cloven a foot – and waging offensive operations again. The CIA's relationship with the State Department had also much improved since Angleton's dismissal. The appointment of Marshall Green as US Ambassador to Australia had been carried out in consultation with the CIA – and proved a marvellous move.

The fact that America's two most important English-speaking allies – Great Britain and Australia – both had governments and prime ministers who were hostile to the United States was an intolerable situation. One prime minister had refused point-blank to send troops to Vietnam and the other had not only pulled out troops sent by previous Australian administrations, but had insulted America by condemning the US bombing of Vietnam as 'corrupt and barbaric' – a step further than Wilson went. The British PM, of course, lived in constant fear of the US Treasury pulling the plug on the pound.

The DCI picked up the cable from Canberra. It was going to be sweet reading.

**TOP SECRET/DO NOT FILE/DESTROY AFTER READING**
DISSEMINATION CONTROL:
NOFORN
NOCON
ORCON
PROPIN

DISTRIBUTION LIST:
<u>EYES ONLY</u>
POTUS
DCI
NSA
SECSTATE

FROM: OSO CANBERRA
DATE: 11 NOVEMBER 1975

<u>REPORT ON THE DISMISSAL OF PRIME
MINISTER GOUGH WHITLAM</u>

Gough Whitlam was Australia's Salvador Allende, but
compared to Allende he will get off lightly – even though
he doesn't deserve a soft landing. In addition to pulling
Australian troops out of Vietnam, Whitlam ended
conscription and released draft resistors from jail. But
more worryingly, Whitlam was moving Australia towards
membership in the Non-Aligned Movement – following India,
Ghana and Egypt out of the Western camp. This would, of
course, have meant Australia leaving SEATO and reneging
on Australia's responsibilities for regional security. Whitlam
also supported so-called 'zones of peace' and was fiercely
opposed to nuclear weapons. In effect, Australia would have
become the Cuba of the South Pacific. The Head of CIA/EAST
was completely justified in describing Whitlam as a 'serious
threat to Australia's national security.'

The most pressing and immediate issue facing US
interests in Australia was Whitlam's threat to close the

CIA listening station at Pine Gap. Whitlam's first words to Marshall Green after Green arrived as US Ambassador were: 'Try to screw us or bounce us and you can kiss Pine Gap goodbye.' As you know, when Ambassador Green reported this conversation, the NSA nearly had a heart attack en masse. In those words, Whitlam wrote his own obituary.

What more can you say? There's a lot more to say. The socialist Whitlam said that he would 'reclaim' ownership of Australia's oil refineries and mining industries. In response, we covertly cultivated the news empires that control the Australian media.

The hero in this affair has been the Governor-General Sir John Kerr. Kerr is, not just 'the Queen's man', but our man too. He is a longstanding member of the Australian branch of the Congress for Cultural Freedom. In return, we have paid Kerr's travel expenses and built up his prestige. We shall also underwrite his probable relocation to London as it is likely that his recent intervention may make him a target of left-wing factions in Australia.

Throughout this affair we have had the cooperation of Australia's Defence Signals Directorate, their equivalent of our NSA. The day before Whitlam's dismissal, Kerr was briefed by them on Australia's 'security crisis' which had become a matter of 'extreme urgency'. Basically, Kerr did what he was told to do – and none too soon. Whitlam was reportedly about to address parliament about CIA activities in Australia. Any such speeches now would be regarded as sour grapes.

The Whitlam problem has been solved. One down, one to go. Best wishes to our colleagues in Britain.

The DCI sat back and reflected. The previous April had seen the fall of Saigon. America had been humiliated in Vietnam and it was never going to happen again. A wounded beast of prey is a dangerous animal. The USA was rising from the ashes of Vietnam and would never back down again.

The DCI began to dictate a cable for his London Head of Station.

**A Regimental Officers' Mess, London:** 14 November 1975

There were only a handful of officers present – and none below the rank of major.

'I know,' said the general, 'that all of you are familiar with *The Manual of Military Law*. You probably refer to it most often when sending some hapless squaddie to Glasshouse for the usual drunken offences. So you might have forgotten that *The Manual of Military Law* goes beyond sentences for pub fights or cacking on the parade ground. The manual also defines the situations in which the military, not only *can* – but is *required* – to intervene by long-established standards of military law and usage.' The general paused. 'In certain circumstances, it is our *duty* to take action, *whether or not* we have been ordered to do so by the government. These circumstances include: riot, insurrection and unlawful assembly.'

The general looked at his watch. 'We'll rendezvous here again tomorrow. 'I'm now off to another meeting.'

The mood in the exclusive gentlemen's club was nervous, but expectant. It reminded the colonel of the sense of excitement before battle; in many ways, a very pleasant sensation. It made you feel so intensely alive – even if you were on the brink of being intensely dead

The general pinged his whisky glass for attention and silence.

'Shhh,' said the colonel. 'He has an announcement to make.'

The general cleared his throat. 'It's set for next Friday, the twenty-first. The following weekend will be useful for calming things down. It would be a mistake to do it before a normal working day because of likely disruptions in public transport and other utilities.' The general looked at the banker. 'How are your friends in the city?'

'A large mining company will be providing emergency generators and staff to keep electricity going in the event of strike action. Likewise, a number of newspaper owners have taken emergency precautions to make sure papers are still printed and distributed.'

'What about the *QE2*?' said JJ.

'The *QE2* will be available for charter – that was, in fact, provisionally agreed last July.'

'Continuing,' said the peer, 'a long proud tradition of British prison ships.'

'And we mustn't rule out deportations,' said the colonel. 'Ships are useful for that.'

'I don't want to sound like I'm having cold feet,' said the banker.

'Then shut up,' said the colonel.

'That's a bit rude,' said the peer, 'so unlike you.'

The colonel nodded at the banker. 'Apologies, Mungo, my nerves are a bit raw. It hasn't been that long, you know? Just over fifty years ago when our homes were burnt down and members of my family were assassinated. We were British subjects living in an Ireland that was still British – and the government in London abandoned us to the mob. It must not happen here.'

'It won't happen here,' said the general. 'But can we hear what Mungo has to say.'

'These things,' said the banker, 'can often have a bad effect on the markets. Markets don't like uncertainty. Are there any alternatives?'

'None,' said the colonel.

'Only Wilson's resignation,' said the general.

'Can we get back to planning?' said JJ.

'A couple of my retired REME friends,' said the colonel, 'have a smashing plan to flood the House of Commons with sewage from the Thames.'

'Who would notice?' said the peer.

'Quite,' said the colonel.

The general cleared his throat. 'Basically, we are going to put in place a plan that is called Transition to War. It's a set of contingency plans for a nuclear conflict with the Soviet Union – and will, in fact, be much easier to implement without nukes going off. Another tactical operation is called Protective Control Zones. This effectively means sealing off harbours and airports.'

'What are the Americans going to do?' said the peer.

'They're going,' said JJ, 'to stay under the radar and operate covertly as they did in Australia and Chile. They will provide valuable intelligence and psy-op.'

'Most of the American news media,' said the banker, 'will welcome this. We will see carefully screened American "tourists" taking photos of smiling British soldiers.'

'The psy-op theme,' said JJ, 'is that the coup will be a return to British normality, not a departure from it.'

The general looked at his watch. 'I've got to paddle off.'

'But you will be here next Thursday?' said the colonel.

The general nodded. 'Our final meeting before the balloon goes up.'

The retired colonel toasted the general. 'We will be behind you every step of the way.'

### Century House, Lambeth, London: 17 November 1975

'You look awful, Henry.'

'Thanks for your concern, Catesby.'

'Lack of sleep, too much drink?'

'I haven't been sleeping well.'

'Would you like to hear the latest from our friends in the billiard room?'

Catesby nodded and Bone turned on the recorder.

*...final meeting before the balloon goes up.*

It hadn't been easy listening. Catesby's face had turned ashen.

'Any comments?'

Catesby shook his head.

'I've never told you,' said Bone, 'exactly why I went to Paris.'

'You seemed very cagey about it and brushed me off whenever I mentioned it. Why?'

'Our listening device in the billiard room needs replacing.'

Catesby stared blankly.

Bone got up and went over to the eighteenth-century sideboard which tottered on its thin tapering legs. He opened a cupboard door, took out a cardboard box and put it on a coffee table between himself and Catesby.

'I received this from a Dutch-registered yacht that arrived in

Orford last August. Customs and Excise are always late checking yachts there – and sometimes never arrive. I made sure they
didn't on this occasion.'

'Are you okay, Henry? Your hands are shaking.'

'Maybe I have been drinking too much.'

Catesby smiled. 'It's an SIS tradition.' He then noticed that
Bone really did look upset. 'Sorry, Henry, I shouldn't have been
flippant.'

Bone folded back the cardboard and took a cassette recorder
out of the box.

Catesby knew the recorder wasn't what it seemed.

Bone opened the lid on the back of the recorder and revealed a
pattern of wires and explosives.

'What next?' said Catesby.

'We'll have to use my neighbour's friend who still works at the
club. By the way, they now live together, thanks to Harold Wilson's decriminalisation act which got rid of those barbaric laws.'

'More ammunition for the bigots.'

Bone nodded. 'In any case, I'll have to make up a story as to
why we want to replace the original listening device – which is
compact and easy to conceal – with this lumpy thing. I'm going
to tell him that the radio signal is being blocked.'

'And when the thing blows up, your neighbour's friend will
know that you duped him into placing it there.'

'I'm going to have to silence him. You can't fight a war, even a
just war, without civilian casualties. In any case, the bombing will
be blamed on the IRA – all the components point to their bomb-
making techniques. And they have bombed a gentlemen's club
in the past.' Bone paused, but continued looking at the device.
'What do you think, William?'

When Bone looked up Catesby's back was turned and he was
already heading for the door.


**South Kensington, London:** 20 November 1975

It was 2 a.m. and Henry Bone was unable to sleep. He was in his
sitting room wearing slippers and a silk Chinese dressing gown

that he had inherited from a naval officer uncle who had served on China station in the nineteenth century. He had Vaughan Williams on the phonograph and was hoping that a combination of 'The Lark Ascending' and brandy would lull him to sleep.

The next day was going to be difficult, critical and heartrending. The neighbour's friend, who was actually now a neighbour, didn't leave for work at the club until 11 a.m., but then worked until midnight. Serving staff worked awful hours for pitiful wages. Bone was taking the morning off and was, in a gesture worthy of Judas, going to cook breakfast for his neighbour while explaining how to install the new 'listening device'.

The awful part would come later. Bone insisted that the neighbour accept money for what he was doing and the risks he was taking. 'If they find out what you've been up to,' said Bone, 'you'll lose your job. We're going to pay you a thousand pounds, but I have to draw the money in used notes from a special fund.' It was agreed that they would meet in an underground car park near the club at 2 p.m. – two hours before the bomb would be discovered and detonated by an anti-disturbance device that became activated once the buzzer went off. Bone had to admit that the bomb was a brilliantly engineered piece of death. Bone hoped that at 2 p.m. the underground car park would be dark and deserted. But instead of receiving a thousand pounds in used banknotes, the neighbour – who was a very pleasant person with a beautiful smile and a great sense of humour – would receive three bullets in the back of the head from a .22 pistol fitted with a silencer. The extra bullets were necessary because of the low calibre of the pistol. A larger gun would be impossible to effectively silence in the echoing space of a car park.

The Vaughan Williams had finished. Bone replaced the record with a William Byrd Marian Mass. How, he thought, had Byrd, so obviously an undercover Roman Catholic, got away with it? Was it because Elizabeth was an undercover Catholic too? The fear of Communists in Downing Street was part of a long British tradition of suspecting treachery in high places.

Bone had finally begun to doze off when there was an urgent knocking at the door. He looked at his watch: it was nearly 3 a.m.

The knocking continued and became even more urgent. Bone looked at the desk drawer where he kept the pistol.

'I'll be there in a second,' he shouted at the door.

Bone walked over to the desk, slid the drawer open and concealed the pistol in the folds of his dressing gown.

'Who is it?' said Bone when he got to the front door. He hadn't turned on the hall light and was flat against the wall.

'It's me.' The voice sounded slightly drunk.

'Oh, it's you,' said Bone opening the door. 'Come in quick.'

Bone's visitor was an old friend and sometimes lover. He didn't work for the intelligence service, but he was the ultimate Whitehall insider. The visitor glanced down and saw the barrel of the pistol bulging in the pocket of Bone's dressing gown. 'I wish that you were pleased to see me instead.'

'I am sure that isn't the reason you are here.'

'It isn't – and I can't stay long.' He gestured over his shoulder to the sound of an idling car engine. 'The meter's running, but I've got something very important to tell you.'

'What is it?'

'Something that changes everything – but it's not really surprising. How much pressure can you put someone under?'

'What's happened?'

The visitor told him.

'Are you sure this is true?' said Bone.

'Absolutely, a hundred per cent.' The visitor then gave a list of names with whom Bone could check to confirm the story.

'Thank you.'

'I'm off now, duty done.'

Bone shut the door and went back to the sitting room. He was in a much lighter mood, but the news was still disturbing. It meant the plotters were going to win by other means. Bone returned the pistol to his desk and took an ancient Underwood typewriter out of a cupboard. It was American-made and had a US typeface. Bone used the typewriter when he wanted to sow confusion – which was his intention now. But he would have to do something about the Underwood afterwards. There had been a rash of burglaries – and it would be awkward if

Special Branch ever got a search warrant and confiscated the typewriter. You could easily trace an anonymous letter back to the typewriter. Sadly, the Underwood was destined for a trip to the bottom of the Thames. Cautious of fingerprints too, Bone slipped on a pair of surgical gloves to handle the stationery. He began typing.

COMRADELY GREETINGS TO MY FELLOW BILLIARD ROOM PLOTTERS…

When Bone got back to his flat, it was six o'clock in the morning, but still dark. The Underwood had been rechristened an Underwater – and a letter addressed BILLIARD ROOM: PLEASE DELIVER AT 4 P.M., had been dropped through the letter box of the Mayfair gentlemen's club.

Bone was tired, but it wasn't his first sleepless night of late. His next problem was how to explain to his neighbour that there had been a change of plan. Perhaps he ought to give him a thousand pounds after all. What does one say? *Sorry, I was going to give you three bullets in the back of the head, but perhaps you would be so kind to accept this money instead.*

## Pimlico, London: 20 November 1975

'You haven't slept at all, William.'

Catesby got up on his elbow and looked at the alarm clock. It was twenty past five. 'Shit, I'd better get up.'

'What's wrong?'

'I did sleep a little, but I had an awful dream.'

'Can you remember it?'

'Everyone was telling me why they don't like me. It started with family. I was a bad son, a bad brother, a bad husband, a bad stepfather – and then it moved outwards. I was an incompetent officer, a disloyal colleague, not a team player, a lying subordinate, a bullying boss.' Catesby smiled. 'And then the Queen even got involved. She grabbed the OBE she had just pinned on my lapel. "Give that back," she said, "you don't deserve it." Then I woke up.'

'It sounds like a guilt dream.'

'Thanks.' Catesby gently rested his hand on Frances's arm.

'And thank you for coming. I didn't want to be alone last night – I needed comfort.'

'Please tell me what's wrong.'

'Just a small problem at the office.'

'I don't believe you, but I'm glad you're smiling.'

'I've decided to do something about it.'

The important thing, thought Catesby, was to find a telephone kiosk where no one who knew him would spot him. Instead of walking directly to Century House, he took a detour into a residential area of Kennington near where Charlie Chaplin was born. He dialled the number of the gentlemen's club in Mayfair and hoped they would believe him.

**Mayfair, London:** 20 November 1975

The general was late. As he walked in, the colonel said, 'You missed all the excitement.'

'There was a bomb scare,' said the banker.

'And a very feeble one,' said the peer. 'The man on reception is from Waterford…'

'We shouldn't worry,' said the banker, 'he was thoroughly security-checked as soon as the Troubles began.'

'Please let me finish, Mungo,' said the peer. 'In any case, our safe security-checked mick from Waterford told the cops that the caller's Irish accent was totally bogus.'

The general shifted nervously. It was obvious that he wasn't at all interested in the bomb scare and had something more important to deal with. The words came out quick and decisive. 'I've come to tell you that it's not happening.'

The room descended into an embarrassed hush and everyone looked at the general, who unusually, was in uniform. The retired colonel stared at him with utter contempt.

'Why?' said JJ with his characteristic simplicity.

'Because I don't take orders from the likes of you.'

The general put his hat back on, turned on his heel and marched towards the door.

'What a fucking performance,' shouted the colonel after him. 'If you wanted to save the honour of the British Army you should have thought of that fifty years ago.'

'Calm down,' said the banker.

'Fuck you too.' The colonel grabbed the banker by the lapels. 'When's the last time you were spattered with body tissue and blood from a soldier exploding in front of you?' The colonel paused and looked down into his palms. 'I am sorry. I shouldn't get emotional – very ashamed in fact.' He extended his hand to the banker. 'Apologies, Mungo.'

The banker took his hand and said, 'I understand.' But he neither understood nor respected the colonel's outburst. The world of 'battlefield glory' and the trauma that went with it were not good for the markets.

Although the colonel seemed calmer, he still seemed ready to pounce. 'JJ and I were here when the cops and the bomb squad were searching the building. They were, of course, bored and fed up because they knew the call was obviously from a time-wasting bomb hoaxer with a grudge against posh clubs.'

'Not only the bogus Irish accent,' said JJ, 'but there were no code words.'

'The Sinn Féin terrorists,' said the colonel, 'don't want anyone else to claim responsibility for their atrocities so they use code words and pseudonyms which frequently change. It helps them, but it also helps the police cut out hoaxers. As the caller to the club was so obviously a hoaxer, the police let us back into the building towards the end of the search.' The colonel smiled. 'They didn't find a bomb, but they found something even more interesting.'

'It was what we call in the trade,' said JJ, 'a passive cavity reso-nator. A very simple and effective listening device.'

'They found it,' said the colonel pointing, 'in the base of that sideboard.'

'An excellent place to hide it,' said JJ. 'The resonator picked up the sound waves from our voices as they vibrated against the thin veneers of the sideboard.'

'Do you suppose,' said the banker, 'our conversations were recorded?'

'Almost certainly, but not here. A resonator of that type is activated by a radio signal sent on a set frequency. I would assume,
therefore, that the person on the receiving end knows the times
that we meet here. The device had a monopole antenna about
eighteen inches in length, which was hidden along the base of
the sideboard, and transmitted our voices to a radio receiver –
which could have been anywhere in central London. I could tell
you more, but unfortunately the police confiscated the device.'

'Thank you,' said the peer, 'for sharing your considerable technical expertise.'

'We've seen listening devices like that before,' said JJ. 'The Sovs
used a similar one to bug the US embassy in Moscow.'

'Can we assume then,' said the banker, 'that the Russians were
bugging us?'

JJ shook his head. 'Absolutely not. But whoever planted that
device might want us to think so. It's called "a false flag ploy". We
use them ourselves.'

'So,' said the peer refreshing his G&T, 'it could have been our
military friend who just stomped off in a huff.'

There was another embarrassed silence that was broken by
someone knocking on the door.

'Come in,' shouted the colonel.

A servant entered with a letter on a silver tray.

'Thank you,' said the colonel taking the letter. The servant left.
The colonel looked taken aback.

'Who's it for?' said the peer.

'It's addressed to the billiard room. Should I assume that identity and open it?'

The others grunted approval.

As the colonel read the letter his face first turned pale and then
crimson.

'What is it?' said the banker.

'Here.' The colonel passed it over to the others.

COMRADELY GREETINGS TO MY FELLOW BILLIARD ROOM PLOTTERS.
NOW IT IS TIME FOR ME TO COME CLEAN. I AM NOT THE PERSON YOU
THINK I AM. I AM A SPY IN YOUR MIDST. IF YOU TAKE THE TROUBLE TO

EXAMINE THE BOTTOM DRAWER OF THE MAHOGONY VENEERED SIDE-
BOARD, YOU WILL FIND A LISTENING DEVICE. I PERSONALLY PLANTED
THAT DEVICE IN 1966 AND, WITH THE HELP OF A COMRADE, HAVE BEEN
RECORDING OUR CONVERSATIONS EVER SINCE. I NOW HAVE A MOST
INTERESTING COLLECTION OF TAPES. THINK OF ALL THE THINGS YOU
SAID DURING ALMOST TEN YEARS OF PLOTTING. YOU ARE ALL TRAITORS
AND THE TAPES ARE PROOF OF YOUR TREASON.

NOW LOOK CLOSELY AT THE OTHER FACES IN THE ROOM. WHICH ONE
OF YOU IS ME?

The banker gave a nervous smile and broke the uneasy silence,
'Well, it can't be our gallant friend the general, because he's not
here.'

'It must be him,' said the peer, 'he's doing what JJ calls a "false
flag". He's betrayed us. Didn't realise the Communists had infiltrated the Army – that's why he's called off the coup.'

'He may be shirking his duty,' said the colonel, 'but he is certainly not a Communist. In any case, I don't think the person
who wrote that letter and planted the bug is one of us. I think
it's someone from outside trying to stir up trouble – probably
someone in SIS.'

The banker gave the colonel a sly smile. 'You would say that,
wouldn't you?'

'Don't make accusations that you can't prove,' said the colonel.

'Don't bully me,' said the banker.

'What I can't understand,' said the peer, 'is how the bomb scare
and this letter happened the same day. It can't be a coincidence.'

'He's trying to create confusion,' said the banker, 'what JJ calls
"disinfo". And, JJ, why have you gone so quiet?'

'Because it's him,' laughed the peer.

'It isn't me,' said JJ, 'but I know who it is.'

'Tell us then,' said the peer.

JJ told them, but they weren't all convinced.

**Century House, Lambeth, London:** 21 November 1975

It was late afternoon and Catesby was pleased there were still no tanks on the streets of London. But he knew that he was about to receive a royal bollocking from Henry Bone. Although Bone had no way of proving that the phone call warning of a bomb had come from him, Bone would assume it had.

Catesby wound his way down the Kafkaesque corridor. The ubiquitous white of Century House made him nauseous after a sleepless night. He arrived at the featureless door that, aside from a white plastic plate lettered DIR W. EUR & SOV. BLOC, was identical to a thousand others. A joker could cause chaos at Century House by removing those plates, which were, in fact, easily detachable. Catesby knocked.

'Come in.'

The first thing that Catesby noticed was the cassette recorder on Bone's desk. It looked identical to the one that had been turned into a bomb. Surely, the police hadn't returned it.

'You look confused, Catesby.'

'I haven't been sleeping well. I didn't know you had a spare bomb.'

'No,' said Bone nodding at the recorder, 'it's the same one.'

'You changed your mind?'

Bone nodded.

'Was it a matter of conscience?'

Bone pursed his lips and squinted. 'It was largely a decision based on new information – which isn't to say that I didn't have moral reservations.'

'I thought moral reservations were irrelevant to our trade.'

'They are, but it doesn't mean they don't exist.'

'We shouldn't lower ourselves to their level – and, besides, blowing the bastards up might have caused an authoritarian backlash.'

'That too was a factor.'

'What was your new information?'

'I can't tell you – and I shouldn't have been told either. The information was delivered via our most effective listening device – alcohol-fuelled indiscretion.' Bone was referring to his late-night visitor.

'Was it good news?'

'Not particularly, maybe not at all. It merely signals a change in tactics.'

'Can you elaborate?'

Bone stared at a blank wall. 'I hate this place.'

'You said, Henry, a change of tactics.'

'Oh, that. We're moving into an even more modern age. You don't need an Army to stage a coup.'

'What do you need?'

'Do you know, William, what was the most chilling thing we heard from the bugged billiard room?'

'No.'

'It came from the colonel. In many ways, he was the shrewdest and brightest of the group.'

'What did he say?'

'*Who pays wins.* So simple, so obvious and so devastatingly true.'

'Where does that leave us?'

'In the past with the dinosaurs. In a few decades, spies paid from public funds are going to be an extinct species. It's not just nationalised industries such as car factories and steel that are doomed, but the whole state-funded machinery of government too.'

Catesby got up to leave.

'And by the way, William, although I respect your reasons for doing it, your bomb-scare phone call to the club wasn't a good idea. The plotters would never have turned over the bug to the authorities – it would have cast suspicion on themselves. But the police now have our listening device – and I fear it will come back to haunt us.'

**Downing Street:** March, 1976

The past few weeks had been quiet, but the calm had been deceptive. Catesby now knew he was facing the end. He knew they weren't going to offer him immunity in exchange for a confession. Such gentlemanly conventions belonged to a different era. Nor would they let him keep his pension. He would lose his much-loved house in Suffolk in exchange for a cell in Wormwood Scrubs.

Catesby looked at the Cabinet Secretary, for all intents and purposes the most powerful person in Britain. The only other person in the room was a woman who sat poised to take notes with a lethal-looking fountain pen. Catesby remembered her from the war and SOE. She was a few years older than him. He knew that she hadn't traded being a spook for shorthand typing, but was now a senior officer in the Security Service. She was a rarity in MI5 – cool, competent and shrewd – the sort of interrogator that Catesby liked to avoid. She knew that he knew where the bodies were buried – or had been deep-sixed. She also knew that Catesby was a professional spy and spies were professional liars.

Catesby avoided her eyes and looked at the Cabinet Secretary. If he was dealing with him alone he could have handled the situation. Catesby knew that he could have lightened the mood with a smile that was both warm and supercilious. The Cabinet Secretary's opening question – *What do you know and when did you know it?* – was ludicrous. In a normal situation, the Cabinet Secretary would have found it difficult to ask with a straight face. But this wasn't a normal situation. Catesby was being asked to make a full and frank confession.

The Cabinet Secretary repeated his question and it rankled even more. 'What do you know and when did you know it?'

Catesby realised it was pointless to pretend that he didn't know what the Cabinet Secretary was talking about, but he wasn't going to go down without a fight. He was sure that Henry Bone was receiving a similar grilling. Catesby looked at the woman from Five. She hadn't been one of the anti-Wilson plotters. In fact, most of the service had behaved professionally, but Five's reputation had been damaged. The woman's eyes had turned flinty and cold. She was out for blood – particularly the blood of SIS officers who didn't play by the rules themselves and then castigated the Security Service for doing likewise.

'I do know,' said Catesby, 'that there is a plot against the Prime Minister.' He returned the cold stare of the senior MI5 officer. He was going to give it both barrels even if he went down in flames. 'And the plot involved past and serving officers of the Security Service.'

'Can you name them?' said the Cabinet Secretary.

Catesby did – and then smiled at the woman. 'And I am sure that none of these names come to you as a surprise.'

'And what activities,' said the Cabinet Secretary, 'were these MI5 officers involved in?'

'They were engaged in unauthorised burglaries, phone tapping…'

The Cabinet Secretary interrupted, 'Have you evidence of that?'

Catesby smiled. 'If you pass me a chisel and a screwdriver I'm sure that I could produce some – and not very far from where we are sitting.'

'That's an outrageous insinuation,' said the woman from Five.

'I suggest, ma'am, that you tell that to the Prime Minister.'

The woman stared hard at Catesby. 'Is he the source of that story?'

'Why don't you ask him?'

'Because I am asking you, Mr Catesby.'

'I think it is fair,' said the Cabinet Secretary, 'that you answer the question.'

'Yes, the Prime Minister believes that 10 Downing Street is bugged – and also his home in Lord North Street.'

'Did he tell you that directly?' said the woman.

'No.'

'This is getting tedious. Can you tell us how you know?'

'The Prime Minister expressed his fears to the DG last summer.'

'Can you be certain that your DG didn't seed those suspicions in the Prime Minister's mind?'

'I am sorry, ma'am, but in this case, you really will have to ask Sir Maurice.'

'That,' said the Cabinet Secretary, 'is a fair reply.'

Catesby realised that he was no longer a young man. A thirty-year-old Catesby would have weaved and dodged with skill and cutting arrogance. Part of him no longer wanted to play the game. But there was still a fire inside him. You didn't claw your way out of the shit poverty of the Lowestoft docks, where babies died because their parents couldn't afford a doctor or prescriptions, if that fire didn't exist. Catesby may have had an OBE and was only two levels from the top rank of Britain's intelligence agency, but he remembered himself as a tattered ten-year-old begging herring from the drifters to feed his family. And the driftermen, because they had known the same poverty, were generous with their catch as they tossed them to the ragamuffins waiting by the dockside – even when the owners were looking. The kids scrabbled on the wet cobblestones for the fish, but there was no competition – only a hurry to bring the fish to their homes. Catesby saw the better Britain he had loved and fought for slipping away, but he wasn't going to let her go without a fight. The words unfurled in his mind like a banner of rage:

*Bring me my chariots of fire!*
*I will not cease from mental fight;*
*Nor shall my sword sleep in my hand.*

'There is a conspiracy to wreck the democratic process in this country and replace it with rule by a small ideological cabal – who also serve the interests of a foreign power.' Catesby could see that the Cabinet Secretary was confused. 'I am not, Sir John, talking about the Soviet Union; I'm talking about the USA. And there has been collaboration – and conspiracy – with the Central Intelligence Agency.'

'Could you be more specific?' said the Cabinet Secretary.

'James Jesus Angleton for one – as well as several CIA officers who have been stationed in London over the past thirty years.'

The other two stared at Catesby in stony silence.

'Those who shout loudest about Moscow gold,' continued

Catesby, 'have been stuffing their own pockets with Washington dollars.' He looked at the woman from Five. 'As you well know, the Security Service has spent years sniffing around for covert East Bloc funding of trade union leaders and Labour politicians – and hardly found a rouble. But that hasn't stopped elements of the Security Service from giving unattributable press briefings smearing Labour politicians and trade unionists with what they couldn't find. The smears have involved lies, forgeries and illegally obtained information.' Catesby could see that the woman was poised to pounce. 'And while I admit that these elements are a rogue minority, you have failed to control them. They even accused your former director general of being a Soviet spy – wrecking his health and driving him into early retirement.'

The woman from Five put down her pen so hard it shook the table. 'Sir John, Mr Catesby has turned what should be a serious interview into a rant against the Security Service.'

'Mr Catesby,' said the Cabinet Secretary, 'your language is immoderate and provocative. Can you please stick to facts?'

'Fine, let's start with CIA-funded front organisations such as the Congress for Cultural Freedom which have been active in the UK since the early 1950s.' Catesby then spent twenty minutes coolly giving a list of magazines, groups, journalists and politicians in receipt either directly or indirectly of money or support from the CIA. He also revealed how officers both from MI5 and SIS had been complicit. He was pleased that the Cabinet Secretary seemed concerned and surprised. The woman from Five seemed bored and fed up.

'Is there anything that you would like to add, Mr Catesby?'

'Quite a bit actually.' Catesby began by condemning the abuse of positive vetting, which was used to 'intimidate and break loyal and honourable civil servants and politicians'.

The woman from Five retaliated by accusing Catesby of 'comparing the Security Service to the Spanish Inquisition'.

Catesby listed the suicides that had followed in the wake of extended positive vetting sessions.

The Cabinet Secretary intervened to lower the temperature and calm tempers.

The next part of the interview shifted to matters involving the military. Catesby began by mentioning the anonymous letters he had received from the Intelligence Corps captain spilling the beans on Operation Clockwork Orange and its attempts to smear the Prime Minister and other politicians.

The woman from Five, to her credit thought Catesby, seemed genuinely concerned. 'Do you know the name of this captain?' she said.

'No, but his body was found in Carlingford Loch in November, 1974. It might be an idea to re-investigate the circumstances of his death.'

The woman made a note on her pad.

'Another set of events that concerned us were the military deployments at Heathrow Airport. I've already discussed this at JIC – so this is nothing new. Neither SIS nor the Prime Minister were informed in advance of these terrorist alerts and exercises.'

'What are you implying, Mr Catesby?' said the Cabinet Secretary.

Catesby paused and considered 'I don't,' he said in a quiet voice, 'want to sound alarmist – or provocative.'

'We will indulge you, Mr Catesby,' said the woman from Five.

'May I remind you what happened in May, 1968? A very powerful newspaper proprietor, with a large number of rich and powerful backers waiting in the shadows, tried to persuade a member of the Royal Family to become head of the UK government following a military coup. I suggest you interview Sir Solly Zuckerman, who was the government's Chief Scientific Adviser at the time. He was present at the event. Fortunately, the Royal showed the plotters the door.'

The two others remained stony-faced. Knowing about it wasn't something they could admit in front of Catesby.

'Since that time,' continued Catesby, 'a far more radical clique has been pressing for direct action.'

'What do you mean by direct action?' said the Cabinet Secretary.

'I mean a *coup d'état* – and they have had contact with senior military officers.'

'And what, Mr Catesby,' said the woman from Five, 'was the reaction of the military to these promptings?'

'The Army, to their credit, seem to have rejected them.'

'So that,' said the woman, 'is the end of the conspiracy?'

'No, it isn't. They still want to force Wilson out of office either by blackmail or simply wearing him down mentally and emotionally with smears and innuendo. The worst part of this scandal is the way journalists and rogue officers have collaborated.'

The woman from Five narrowed her eyes. 'You mentioned earlier, "a far more radical clique". Can you tell us who they are?'

Beginning with JJ, Catesby named them all.

'And how, Mr Catesby, did you find out about them?'

It was a killer question, but one that Catesby had been anticipating. 'The group – and their private armies and emergency committees – are fairly well known.'

'But you are accusing them of contacting the Army and trying to stage a coup. How do you know these details?'

'I would have to check my files and have discussions with my colleagues.'

'Perhaps, Mr Catesby,' said the woman from Five rising like a matador for the kill, 'we can help you. You discovered this information via a listening device that was hidden in the billiard room of a gentlemen's club in Mayfair.'

'I don't know anything about it.'

'Don't you find it odd that the clique you named are all members of that club?'

'I'm sure,' said Catesby, 'it's just a coincidence.'

'And is it also a coincidence that the listening device was similar to those often used by the Secret Intelligence Service?'

Catesby was annoyed at the woman's deliberate lie. Bone, trying the false flag ploy, had constructed the type of device the KGB used. Catesby didn't know why he said it, but the words just spurted out. 'And even more similar to ones the Russians use?'

'How do you know the one found in the club is similar to the listening devices the Russians use? Have the police shown it you? I am sure they would have made a record of your visit if they had.'

Catesby winced, but remained silent. To call it a gaffe was an understatement. The American version, which he often heard used by US soldiers in Germany, seemed more apt: *Hey man, you just stepped on your fucking dick.*

The woman from Five looked at Catesby with something that could be described as pity – but it was the pity of a hangwoman fitting the noose.

The Cabinet Secretary intervened. 'I must inform you, Mr Catesby, that the principal reason that you have been summoned here today is to discuss some very serious allegations against yourself. We have not yet made a decision whether or not to pass on these allegations – and accompanying evidence – to the Crown Prosecution Service, but it cannot be ruled out – and seems increasingly likely.' The Cabinet Secretary took off his reading glasses and stared out across Horse Guards. 'At one time, a frequent formula was, "it is not in the national interest to prosecute" – but that is an option we can no longer use as often as we did in the past, if at all.'

Catesby looked down at the table and saw his reflection twisted and distorted by the ancient oak grain beneath the polish. It was the end.

'Unauthorised listening and wire-tapping is, Mr Catesby...' the Cabinet Secretary was still speaking, 'a very serious offence, but murder is a capital offence. We have received information, two files from separate sources, alleging that you killed a former German Army officer in Bremen in May, 1951.' The Cabinet Secretary looked over his reading glasses at Catesby. 'You obviously do not have to respond to this accusation at this time and without legal counsel.'

The telephone rang.

'Excuse me,' said the Cabinet Secretary as he picked up the phone. The person on the other end was doing most of the talking. Catesby watched the Cabinet Secretary nodding and saying 'yes'. Finally, the Cabinet Secretary put his hand over the mouthpiece and looked at Catesby, 'Would you mind waiting outside?'

Catesby got up and went into the anteroom. There was only one chair: an ugly Victorian antique upholstered in green velvet – with what looked like a poo stain in the middle of the velvet seat.

Perhaps, thought Catesby, the last person grilled in the Cabinet Secretary's office had been even more frightened. He decided to remain standing. He stared across Horse Guards to the old Admiralty building. The Empire hadn't been built by being soft and kind – and what was left of it wasn't going to be kind to him. Catesby had long expected it – and why should he complain? Like Cromwell and More before him, he wasn't an innocent civilian caught in the crossfire. Catesby looked at his watch; the Cabinet Secretary was having an awfully long telephone conversation.

Catesby was kept waiting another twenty minutes. Finally, the door opened and Catesby was summoned back in. An officious-looking young man had joined the other two and was staring at Catesby as if he were a tramp that had crashed the Queen's Garden Party. Catesby almost wanted to shout, 'Oi, mate, I've got an OBE.' But decided to keep quiet.

The Cabinet Secretary spoke first. 'This meeting is suspended. If and when it is reconvened, we will let you know. You are free to go. My assistant will show you to the door.'

Catesby nodded a goodbye to the woman from Five. She looked at him with an expression that gave nothing away. The young assistant touched Catesby's elbow and said, 'I'll show you out.'

They walked down the stairs, along the corridors and through various rooms. Everywhere were knots of people speaking in hushed tones, as if a death had just been announced. When people saw Catesby – clearly a Downing Street outsider – they averted their eyes and stopped talking.

Catesby was relieved when the door of Number 10 closed firmly behind him. He was glad to be outside – in the cool damp air and away from the funereal tones. In contrast to the gloom inside Downing Street, the street outside was party time: packed and pulsating with people. There were television vans all over the place and what seemed a hundred people snapping pictures or talking into microphones. A reporter lurched up to Catesby and put a microphone in his face, 'Can you tell us the latest, please?'

Catesby waved the reporter away and turned to the policeman guarding the front door, 'What's happened?'

'The Prime Minister, sir, has just resigned.'

Catesby understood why the meeting had been suspended. Compared to a prime minister, he was too small a prize to pluck and gut. They had got what they wanted – at least, for the moment.

In the years that followed, Catesby developed a grim admiration for the merciless genius of the Secret State. The suspension of the meeting with the Cabinet Secretary had not granted him freedom, but the opposite. The Secret State had given Catesby notice that a sword hung over his head – and the hanging sword would remain there for the rest of his life. The state's other technique was the honeyed carrot. When Henry Bone retired, Catesby was promoted to Bone's former post as Dir W Eur & Sov Bloc. Afterwards, they remained friends and confidantes. Catesby was not surprised to learn that Bone had several swords hanging over his own head. But the swords did not entirely shut them up. A lifetime in espionage meant that Catesby and Bone knew how to pass on information without leaving fingerprints.

The best spies are the ones who know they are sometimes going to get it wrong. The worst spies are the ones who, like Angleton, can never admit they're wrong. When Catesby lectured SIS trainees at Fort Monckton, he always told them that the trade closest to that of intelligence officer was being a bookie. Even though you keep a close eye on the teams and the horses, you can't offer your punters a dead cert, you can only offer odds. The job of an intelligence service is to provide assessments and probabilities. Politicians, however, twist an intelligence officer's guess about a threat into a certainty to justify their own actions. Although Catesby was resigned to inaccuracies of the spy's crystal ball, he did become increasingly frustrated by not knowing what actually had happened afterwards. Catesby never found out who had burgled his safe, who had sent him threatening letters – and why Harold Wilson resigned. Life wasn't a tightly knit detective novel where there are no loose ends.

Catesby would never know how close Britain had come to a military *coup d'état*. Perhaps not very close at all. Sending in the tanks and bombing the presidential palace was a very old-fashioned way of changing governments – but it did make good television footage. The British way, like so much of British life, wasn't the stuff of action films. Ruthless viciousness certainly existed in Britain, but it wasn't the openly displayed malice of a moustachioed generalissimo waving a pistol at elected legislators. The British way was hidden and subtle.

In retrospect, Catesby agreed with Bone that the most astute of the coup plotters had been the retired colonel. Money always wins. If you owned or controlled most of the press and the news media, the soldiers could stay in their barracks. You didn't need to control *all* the press, just the big ones that account for eighty per cent of circulation. The small prints, intended for political fringe groups or the intelligentsia, don't matter. The long-term plan, as Bone had predicted, was to privatise the civil service and the rest of the public sector. *Who pays wins.*

Margaret Thatcher becoming prime minister was the beginning of the end for Catesby. He reluctantly continued in post for three years, but finally resigned in complete frustration. The third person Catesby told, after his wife and the DG, was Henry Bone. Bone was living in nervous and edgy retirement – owing partly to Thatcher outing Anthony Blunt as a Soviet Spy.

'I told you that she was evil.' Bone spoke from the shadows of a wide-brimmed straw hat. They were drinking gin and tonic in the garden of Bone's South Kensington home.

'That's one explanation,' said Catesby.

'What finally made you jump ship?'

'She sabotaged the Peruvian Peace Plan – but will never admit it.'

'I can assure you, William, that the cables, documents and logs have either been destroyed or will never see the light of day.'

'I was, by the way, a hawk when the Argentines invaded. I fully supported sending the Task Force south, but I thought Galtieri would withdraw after a show of face-saving bravado.'

'So did we all. How were you involved?'

'I was only on the fringes – a bit of backdoor diplomacy, but mostly liaising with other intelligence agencies.'

'How did the plan play out? I'm no longer in the loop, you know.'

'The first version called for Peruvian and US troops to replace the Argentines. But Buenos Aires rejected American troops and London wouldn't have Peruvians. So back to the drawing board.

Version Two had Mexican, West German and Canadian troops as peacekeepers. My job was largely reassuring the Germans.'

'Was it really signed, sealed and delivered?'

'Who knows? As you suggested, the docs are either deep-sixed or in the burn bag.'

'I've heard,' said Bone, 'that Galtieri sobered up enough to sign the agreement fourteen hours before she sank the *Belgrano*.'

'I thought you weren't in the loop.'

Bone smiled.

'I was,' said Catesby, 'in the West German embassy in DC when I first heard there had been an agreement. I'll never forget it. It was three o'clock in the morning and we were tired and bleary-eyed. I was looking at maps with the West German military attaché and a Canadian when the Night Duty Officer came into the room. He said there had been a telephone call from the White House saying that Argentina had accepted the Peace Plan and that the Peruvians were relaying the news to the British Foreign Secretary. The military attaché sent for a bottle of *Sekt* and we toasted the peace.' Catesby sipped his gin and tonic and stared at a climbing rose. 'And twelve hours later it all descended into irrecoverable chaos.'

'As I said, she's evil.'

There was nothing more to say. The rest, thought Catesby, was history. The first torpedo blew off the ship's bow. The second torpedo exploded in a stern engine room and knocked out the cruiser's electrical system. There were agonising screams and cries for help from the sailors who were trapped in the dark below decks – and the first to die. Of the 323 who perished, 200 were under the age of twenty.

Afterwards, Thatcher claimed that news of the Peruvian Peace Plan did not reach Downing Street until three hours after the *Belgrano* was sunk. Catesby knew this was a lie, a total nonsense. He was sure Thatcher had sunk the cruiser to sabotage the Peace Plan. In addition, the *Belgrano* had been carefully staying outside the 200-nautical-mile exclusion zone that Britain had declared around the Falklands. It was, thought Catesby, like saying to someone: 'If you step over that line, I'm going to punch you.' And then you punch them even though they didn't step over the line.

\*

A year later, Catesby was watching a BBC TV phone-in when the teacher, Diana Gould, questioned Thatcher about the *Belgrano* sinking. The mood quickly turned bitter and emotional. Once again, Thatcher denied having heard about the Peace Plan and insisted the *Belgrano* was a threat despite being outside the exclusion zone and heading away from the Falklands. Catesby later heard that Denis Thatcher had thrown a wobbly after the interview. He shouted at the programme's producer that his wife had been stitched up by 'bloody BBC poofs and Trots'. Catesby was depressed by the story, but not surprised. Britain had become a different place. The genteel veneer was gone. Power had been passed on to a coterie of spivs and saloon bar bores.

Catesby had always enjoyed quiet pleasures. There was now a lot more time to garden, to read and to do up his house. One repair required stripping away the rendering of an exterior wall. The uncovered wattle and daub had last seen the light of day 450 years before. The newly bared wall was patterned by the fingerprints of those who had pressed the daub into the wattle all those centuries before. He tried to put his own fingertips into the shallow depressions – he wanted to connect somehow with that past generation. But Catesby's fingers wouldn't fit. The indelible marks in the daub had been made by the fingers of children. Catesby flashed back to an image of himself as a tattered ten-year-old begging herring from the Lowestoft drifters to feed his family. He placed his palm over the finger marks on the wattle and daub.

**St James's Park, London:** June, 1993

It was one of the saddest sights that Catesby had ever seen. The ex-Prime Minister was sitting between two winos on a park bench. The dementia must have really kicked in. He was clueless and babbling. Catesby bribed the winos to leave them alone with a fiver each. He sat down next to ex-Prime Minister.

'Would you like to go home?' he said.

'What, to Huddersfield? No, I'm in the House of Lords today.'

'Would you like to go back to the Lords?'

'Yes, there's an important debate on the Open University. I'm very proud of that, you know?'

'You have a lot to be proud of, Lord Wilson – you made Britain a more civilised place.'

'Are we going back to the Lords?'

'Yes, let me help you up.'

Catesby could see that Wilson was in no fit state to go back to the House of Lords.

'I think,' said Catesby, 'that we should go home first.'

'Huddersfield?'

'No, Lord North Street. I think Mary is making you lunch.'

'Good idea.'

It wasn't far to walk. Lady Wilson was surprised to see her husband, but pleased that Catesby had bought him there. Apparently, he had slipped his minders in the Lords and they were very worried too.

It wasn't much of an act kindness. But, Catesby later thought, it's probably why he got invited to the funeral.

## Saint Mary's Old Church, Isles of Scilly: 7 June 1995

The morning after the funeral, Catesby got up early. As he got older, he found it difficult to sleep – particularly in the summer light of a June early morning. He found himself wandering back to the grave site and stood for a few seconds paying his personal respects. The churchyard was a riot of green and birdsong and he could hear the gentle sough of the sea. Catesby reached for a tissue and found something else stuffed in his pocket. It was the funeral programme.

**The Right Honourable
Lord Wilson of Rievaulx
K.G.O.B.EF.R.S.**

**James Harold Wilson
1916–1995**

It began with the order of service and protocol for the funeral. There was then a list of hymns. The final page was Mary's poem to her husband. Catesby read it in silence – and hoped no one could see his tears.

> *My love you have stumbled slowly*
> *On the quiet way to death*
> *And you lie where the wind blows strongly*
> *With a salty spray on its breath*
> *For this men of the island bore you*
> *Down paths where the branches meet*
> *And the only sounds were the crunching grind*
> *Of the gravel beneath their feet*
> *And the sighing slide of the ebbing tide*
> *On the beach where the breakers meet.*

It was a very British ending.

## Acknowledgements

First of all, most grateful thanks to Lady Mary Wilson of Rievaulx for giving me permission to use her poem which concludes my novel. It is a perfectly balanced poem and one of the most moving elegies of recent times. I would like to point out that Lady Wilson's poem was not part of the Order of Service at Lord Wilson's funeral, but was written a number of years later. This book is a work of fiction.

As always, thanks to Julia for her encouragement, understanding and patience.

My agent Maggie Hanbury is the best agent a writer could have. Once again, she has proved a valuable source of guidance and good sense. I would also like to Harriet Poland at the agency for being cheerful, helpful and efficient.

I am very grateful to my publisher, Piers Russell-Cobb, for valuing and trusting me as an author. Our conversations are always enjoyable and extremely useful. And thanks also to Joe Harper at Arcadia Books for his help and enthusiasm.

My editing team, Martin Fletcher and Angeline Rothermundt, are absolutely fantastic. Martin has the intuition of an artist. This is the second time he has breathed life and fluency into my rough draft. Angeline has now polished five of my books into shape. I cannot thank her enough for turning me into a much better author than I was eight years ago.

This was an extremely difficult book to write. The Secret State and the machinations of power are almost impossible to research. Perhaps there are times when a novelist can make better sense of things than a historian. In any case, the following bibliography is from where I started.

## Bibliography

Aldrich, Richard J. *The Hidden Hand: Britain, America and Cold War Secret Intelligence.* The Overlook Press, Woodstock and New York, 2002.

belgranoinquiry.com/article-archive/the-peruvian-peace-plan

Bristow, Bill. *My Father the Spy: Deceptions of an MI6 Officer.* WBML ePublishing & Media Company Ltd., Ross-on-Wye, 2012.

Bristow, Desmond with Bill Bristow. *A Game of Moles: The Deceptions of an MI6 Officer.* Little, Brown and Company, London, 1993.

Carter, Miranda. *Anthony Blunt: His Lives.* Macmillan, London, 2001.

Corera, Gordon. *MI6: Life and Death in the British Secret Service.* Orion Books Ltd, London, 2012.

Davenport-Hines, Richard. *An English Affair: Sex, Class and Power in the Age of Profumo.* William Collins, London, 2013.

Director's Log – CIA FOIA

Dorrill, Stephen and Ramsay, Robin. *Smear! Wilson and the Secret State.* Grafton, London, 1992.

Kotkin, Stephen. *Stalin: Paradoxes of Power 1878–1928.* Allen Lane, London, 2014.

Leigh, David. *The Wilson Plot: The Intelligence Services and the Discrediting of a Prime Minister.* William Heinemann Ltd, London, 1988.

Macintyre, Ben. *A Spy Among Friends: Kim Philby and the Great Betrayal.* Bloomsbury, London, 2014.

Peruvian Peace Plan – RNA 10 Area www.rna-10-area.net/files/peru.pdf

Pimlott, Ben. *Harold Wilson.* Harper Collins, London, 1993.

Watson, Ian. *Riverbank City: A Bremen Canvas.* Blaupause Books, Hamburg, 2013.

Wright, Peter. *Spycatcher.* Viking Penguin, New York, 1987.